PROTECTING WREN

SEAL OF PROTECTION: ALLIANCE
BOOK 2

SUSAN STOKER

Edited by Kelli Collins

Cover Design by AURA Design Group

Manufactured in the United States

CHAPTER ONE

Wren Defranco woke suddenly. One second she was sound asleep, the next she was awake. She'd always been like that. Her childhood had made it a necessity. And just like when she was a child, she didn't immediately open her eyes and sit up. No, she assessed her current situation with her other senses.

Nothing about what she heard sounded right.

Her apartment was quiet. She'd purposely picked it because it was away from any busy streets in a fairly safe part of the city. She needed a place that was secure. A place where she could let down her guard. For so much of her life, she'd felt unsafe, on edge. She'd wanted somewhere she could completely relax when she went home at the end of the day.

The things she heard now were definitely not the usual noises when she woke up. Laughter outside from...children? A rhythmic clanking. Music.

When she took a deep breath, still without opening her

eyes, she smelled...coffee. Really good coffee. Not the crap she usually grabbed at the corner mart on her way to work.

Squinting, Wren opened her eyes a fraction. Not wanting to advertise the fact that she was awake to anyone who might be watching. Again, something she'd learned as a child.

The room was lit up by sunlight streaming through the pale shade covering a window on the opposite wall. It wasn't early morning, which was surprising, because she usually got up before the sun rose. Not only that, but the space was completely unfamiliar.

Sitting up slowly, Wren looked around and saw she was alone. She was lying in a queen-size bed with what looked like a homemade quilt covering her. It had leaf patterns sewn all over it and was made of bright, cheerful colors. There were two nightstands, one on either side of the bed; a blue throw rug on the floor; a small dresser on the wall facing her; and a picture of a mountain landscape on the wall to her left. It looked...homey.

But Wren didn't relax. Not at all. Looks could be deceiving. She knew that better than most.

There was only one door to the room, so no attached bathroom. There was nowhere to hide. The only escape was the window. She had no idea how far off the ground she might be, but if she needed to get away from a kidnapper, she'd go out the window, no matter what floor she was on.

Swallowing hard, Wren did her best to work out what had happened and how she'd ended up in what looked like a grandma's bedroom. Like a light switch flicking on, memories flooded back into her brain.

Aces Bar and Grill. Being annoyed with her date. The guy bringing her a drink. Feeling woozy. And then...

Nothing.

Son of a bitch—he'd drugged her!

Alarmed, Wren threw the covers back and swayed with relief when she saw she still wore her slacks and the pretty scoop-neck T-shirt she'd found to wear on her date. Bending her legs to her chest to hug her knees, she was even more relieved not to feel any pain between her thighs.

Confusion set in. If her date had drugged her and brought her back to his apartment, why had he simply put her to bed? Was he waiting for her to wake up to attack her? Some men were turned on by a victim's pain and fear. Maybe he was one of them?

Then something else caught her eye. On the nightstand closest to her was a bottle of water. An unopened bottle. There was also a note.

Looking around, wondering if she was being watched, Wren slowly reached for the piece of paper.

Any moment, she expected the door to fly open and someone to charge in and start hurting her. Memories threatened to overwhelm her, but Wren pushed them down. She wasn't a kid anymore. She wasn't helpless.

Taking a breath, she read the note.

You're safe. You asked me to help you, so I brought you to my home. If you want to leave, go out the door, turn left. The door at the end of the hallway leads to the garage. There's a bus stop down the street. I've left money under your phone.

. . .

Wren's gaze flew to the table next to the bed once more. Behind the water bottle was her phone and, as promised, a twenty-dollar bill beneath it. She'd missed it earlier. Looking back to the note in her hand, she continued reading.

Alternatively, if you turn right in the hall, there's a bathroom next to your room. And I'd like to make you breakfast, make sure you're okay. I can take you back to Aces or to your home, or anywhere else you might like to go. I'm sorry you had to experience what you did last night, but I give you my word that you're safe here. -Bo

Wren's head felt as if it was filled with cotton. She hadn't experienced that post-drugged feeling in years, and yet she remembered it as if the last time was yesterday.

But never, not once in all those times, had she ever woken up and felt...safe.

The man who'd written the note had used that word twice. *Safe*.

For a woman who'd spent her childhood never feeling safe, distrusting everyone, wondering what everyone's motives were, she was feeling awfully unconcerned right now.

Reaching for the water on the table next to her, Wren cracked the seal and brought it to her lips. She chugged at least half of it without stopping to take a breath. It could still be drugged, there were ways to sneakily drug water without breaking the seal on the cap, but if whoever had helped her last night had wanted to hurt her, he'd had more than enough time to do so.

A vague memory of Aces being full of good-looking Navy SEALs flashed in Wren's mind. Had one of them seen her date drugging her drink and decide to step in? She had no idea what happened after Matt—the man she'd severely underestimated and thought was a geek—spiked her lemonade. But for some reason, she wasn't panicking.

She should do exactly what her savior said. Walk out the door and go to the bus stop. But even as Wren swung her legs off the mattress and reached for her phone and put it in her pocket, she knew that wasn't what she was going to do.

Leaving the money on the table, she headed for the door. She was a little unsteady on her feet, but she was determined to find out what had happened the night before. After opening the door, Wren looked left. The hallway wasn't anything special. Wood floors, a few more landscape pictures on the walls. There was a doorway to the left, at the end of the hall, as the note writer had claimed.

Taking a deep breath, Wren stepped into the hallway...and went right.

She might regret this, but she couldn't leave without, one, knowing what happened the night before, and two, finding out who this Bo person was, and why he'd helped her.

CHAPTER TWO

Bo "Safe" Cyders leaned against the kitchen counter, staring into space. It was ten in the morning, and he felt just as anxious and worked up as he did before a mission. He hadn't slept more than an hour or two combined, but he didn't feel tired in the least. Last night had been...intense. And he'd second-guessed himself every minute since he'd left Aces Bar and Grill with the pretty young woman who'd asked him for assistance.

Intellectually, he was aware that the only reason she asked *him* for help was because he happened to be in that hallway at the same time she was. But the desperation and fear in her eyes still ate at him. What if he *hadn't* been there? What if someone with fewer scruples had crossed her path? What if her asshole date had followed her and whisked her out the back door?

The what-ifs were horrifying to imagine. Especially after seeing how vulnerable the woman had been.

Safe had brought her home, put her in his guest bed, used his medical training to quickly check her out...and she hadn't moved an inch.

He'd also checked on her throughout the night. Every thirty minutes or so, he'd gone into her room and made sure she was still breathing. She hadn't stirred. The thought of someone hurting that woman while she was unconscious made his skin crawl.

The last time Safe had checked on her, his anxiety ebbed a fraction. He'd been about to call for an ambulance—since she *literally* hadn't moved for ten hours—when finally he'd seen signs of her rousing. He'd left the room quickly, not wanting her to wake up with a man she didn't know hovering over her, and went into the kitchen to wait to see what she'd do.

He wanted to talk to her. Make sure she was all right. But if she wanted to leave, he wouldn't get in her way. She had to be confused. Scared. And Safe had no idea what, if anything, she remembered about the night before. All he could do was make sure she had some water, her phone, a bit of money, and let her make her own decisions.

Taking a sip of the gourmet coffee he was addicted to, Safe continued to wait.

He heard the creak of the guest room door, and he held his breath as he stared at the hallway, willing her to appear. To not slink off like a thief in the night...er, morning. The neighborhood his house was in wasn't the best, but his neighbors were all good people. Struggling in this economy, but they wouldn't hurt the woman if they saw her walking down the sidewalk.

His next-door neighbor, Abigail, had left a few hours ago

to head to her job at the grocery store down the road. Her mom, Carleigh, was there babysitting. Abigail was a struggling single mother with three kids—Albert, who was four; Adam, three; and Adley, the baby, was two. Thankfully, her mom could watch them while Abigail was at work. The kids weren't the silent types. They were currently outside in their yard, playing on the swing set Safe had helped set up, screeching and laughing.

The sound made him smile. Hearing happy kids was much better than the terrified screams of children he often came across overseas while on missions.

He could hear music playing from the house across the street, as well. The sounds of an active neighborhood were all around him, had become second nature to Safe. But at the moment, all he could concentrate on were the footsteps of the woman who'd taken up much of his brain space in the last twelve hours or so.

To his immense relief, they were heading toward him, rather than away.

Forcing himself to look as relaxed as possible, Safe stared at the hallway. When the woman appeared, it took every ounce of discipline he possessed not to step toward her. To stay where he was, slouched against the counter as if he didn't have a worry in the world.

She was pale, her short black hair mussed around her head, and she had dark circles under her brown eyes. Her clothes were wrinkled and her hands fidgeted nervously where she stood, at the entrance to the living room.

"Morning," Safe said softly.

"Where am I?" she asked, not beating around the bush.

Safe approved. "About three miles from Aces. My house. I brought you here after you asked for my help at the bar. You passed out right after you asked for assistance."

"He drugged me," the woman said. She hadn't moved from the hall entry, but his home wasn't huge. He had no problem hearing her across two rooms.

So Safe stayed where he was too. She was skittish, rightfully so. He didn't want to do anything to make her feel any more unsure than she already was. "Yes," he confirmed.

"Then what?"

"I brought you here. Put you in my guest room, checked on you periodically during the night to make sure you were still breathing...and here we are."

She tilted her head as she stared at him, as if assessing him from afar.

"I'm Bo. Bo Cyders. My friends call me Safe."

"Safe?" she questioned, her brow furrowed.

His lips twitched. "Yeah. Hazard of being a military guy. Everyone gets a nickname."

"What's it mean?"

Her questions were short and to the point. Something Safe found...adorable. No, that wasn't right. She was scared and worried about her security. She wasn't trying to flirt or be cute. She was simply trying to get information.

No. He found it brave and admirable.

"I was actually dubbed Cyborg in boot camp, because of my last name. One of my drill instructors thought he was funny by calling me that. But when I first joined a SEAL team, we were playing softball for PT one day, and I stole home. The catcher called out, 'Safe! He's safe!' when I slid into home base. A huge argument broke out, with my team insisting I was safe and the other insisting I was out. The umpire whistled loudly with his fingers and shouted, 'He's safe! Hear me? *Safe*!' And from then on...I was known as Safe."

When a small smile crossed the woman's lips, Safe felt as if he'd crossed some major hurdle.

"I'm Wren. Wren Defranco."

"It's nice to meet you, Wren Defranco," Safe told her.

"It's nice to meet you too, Bo Cyders."

For a moment, neither moved. Then Safe straightened and motioned to his coffee machine with his head. "Coffee?"

For the first time, Wren's gaze moved away from him. As Safe expected, her eyes widened in surprise.

"I know, I know," he said before she could ask. "It's a little over the top. But I like my coffee. When I'm on missions, we often have to drink the most vile sludge that tries to pass itself off as coffee. It's disgusting, but if I want my caffeine, I don't have a choice. So when I'm home, I spoil myself by making the best stuff I can."

"Wow," she said, sounding properly awed.

Safe chuckled. "There was a coffee place that went out of business. I bought this baby from them. It makes espresso, cappuccino, and any other kind of frou-frou drink you can think of. But I do switch it up. Sometimes I drink the plain stuff. Okay, that's a lie. It's not plain. This morning, it's double chocolate. Tomorrow, I might go with Michigan cherry. I like to mix it up."

As he was talking, Safe had reached for a coffee cup. And not just any cup. He liked the giant-size mugs. Figuring if anyone needed a large-size coffee this morning, it was Wren, he filled it almost to the rim and slipped it across the counter toward her. Then he stepped back, giving her space.

She slowly walked across the living room toward the kitchen as if she were a feral dog, wary of the rescuer who was throwing treats just out of reach. Wren closed her hand around the mug handle—it looked tiny next to the large cup—then took a few steps back as she brought the beverage to her lips.

She hesitated for a moment, her gaze coming up to meet his. The wariness was back in her eyes, which Safe hated.

"It's clean," he told her softly. "You're safe here. I'm drinking the same coffee you are."

"I'm safe?" she asked.

"Yes."

"I thought *you* were safe."

It took him a moment to realize she was teasing him. His admiration of her rose another notch.

He didn't know this woman. Hadn't really had any kind of conversation with her until this morning...and yet at her gentle teasing, her direct stare, he felt an unfamiliar stirring deep within him. A yearning for something that had always felt out of his reach.

A longing for a connection with another human being that went bone deep.

Shaking off the sudden feeling, Safe forced himself to slouch against the counter again.

Wren finally took a sip of the coffee, and Safe watched with satisfaction when her eyes closed and she let out a little moan. "Holy crap," she breathed as she opened her eyes to look at him.

"Good?" he asked.

"No," she said with a small shake of her head. "It's amazing. You've ruined me forever. I can never see poor Pablo at the corner mart again because his coffee is crap, even if he's a good guy who tries so hard to make it palatable."

Safe chuckled low and easy. "I'm a coffee snob. I admit it," he said without a shred of remorse.

Wren smiled at him for a moment, then the grin faded. "Can I ask you something?"

"You can ask me anything," Safe told her, his own voice turning serious.

"Did you call the police? Why did you bring me here? Did you confront my date? Do you have my purse?"

Of course she had questions. "I'll tell you everything...over breakfast. You need some nutrients, and getting food in your belly will help chase away the cobwebs from whatever that asshole gave you. I've got omelet fixins or I can make pancakes. I might have some bread around here that isn't moldy. Maybe."

"Do you have any cereal?" she asked.

Safe was surprised. "Cereal?"

"Yeah. I know it's stupid. But it's what I usually eat in the mornings."

"It's not stupid," Safe countered. "You just surprised me. And yes, I have cereal, but I'm not sure I'll have what you like."

"Probably not," she mumbled under her breath. Then louder, said, "Whatever you have is fine."

Feeling his cheeks heat, Safe turned toward his pantry to hide his embarrassment. He wasn't ashamed of his vices, like his coffee machine, but he was fairly certain his choices in cereal didn't exactly match his image of being a hard-ass Navy SEAL. "I've got Apple Jacks, Fruit Loops, Frosted Flakes, and Frosted Krispies," he told Wren, wishing he had at least one box of something semi-nutritious. If a box of Wheat Chex or Bran Flakes magically manifested into his pantry, he'd be appreciative right about now.

"Seriously?"

Reluctantly, Safe turned to face his unexpected houseguest and shrugged. "Yeah. I didn't expect company, otherwise I would've gotten something more appropriate. I usually make something more adult when I have someone stay over, which isn't often. I wish I could blame my cereal choices on my neighbor's kids, who I sometimes invite over to give their mom a break when their gigi can't babysit, but what can I say? I like the sugary, crappy stuff."

He was babbling, but Safe couldn't seem to stop himself. He was embarrassed as all get out that all he had to offer this woman, who'd been through something horrific, was kids' cereal.

"My favorite is Lucky Charms, but Fruit Loops come in a close second. The best part is drinking the milk when the cereal is gone. It's pure sugar, but so good."

Safe stared at Wren for a moment, thinking she was fucking with him, but when she gave him a small shrug and a little smile, he realized she was serious.

That funny feeling in his belly returned. What were the odds that the woman he saved from a possibly horrible fate not only liked his flavored coffee, but was a fan of super-sugary cereal?

Ignoring the little voice in his head that was telling him to grab hold of this woman and never let her go, Safe reached for the boxes of Fruit Loops and Apple Jacks. He placed them on the table in the small dining area off the kitchen, then headed toward the fridge to get the milk. Once he had the table set with two bowls—oversized, of course—and spoons, he pulled out a chair for Wren, then sat across from her.

She slowly walked to the table and lowered herself into the chair. Giving him another small smile, she put her coffee cup down and reached for the Fruit Loops. They ate their cereal in silence, the only sound their crunching.

When they'd both slurped up the milk left in the bowls after they'd eaten, Safe stood.

He didn't miss the way Wren flinched at his abrupt movement. Cursing himself for scaring her, Safe froze. "I'm going to put our dishes in the sink. If you want to go sit on the couch and get comfortable, I'll be there in a moment and I'll tell you about last night."

"Okay," she said, pushing away from the table and quickly standing and taking a step backward.

Safe grabbed the bowls and spoons and went into the kitchen. Out of the corner of his eye, he saw Wren step into the living room. She chose to sit in his recliner, and Safe couldn't help but think she looked tiny in the oversized chair. He wasn't a giant at six-one, but he wasn't a small man either. Wren looked to be average height for a woman, around five-five or five-six, but she was slender and looked almost frail.

When she tucked her legs under her in the chair, Safe smiled. She hadn't hesitated to make herself comfortable, and the fact that she wasn't perched at the edge of the seat, ready to bolt, told him that on some level, she had to trust him. At least a little.

And it was that small act of trust that had him mentally vowing to do whatever it took to make sure this woman felt safe. With him *and* after what happened the night before. He didn't know who her date was, but he'd find the man and, with the help of his team, teach him what happened when you preyed on innocent women.

The thought was a little bloodthirsty, especially given he'd just met Wren, but Safe couldn't help it. After watching over her all night, after she'd asked him for help at the bar, he felt protective of her.

Finished cleaning up their breakfast dishes, he took the pot of coffee over to where she was sitting. "Refill?" he asked quietly.

"Yes, please," she said, holding out her mug.

Safe filled it—feeling ridiculously happy that she liked his coffee—refilled his own mug, then sat on the couch on the other side of the room from his recliner. He didn't hesitate to tell her what she wanted to know.

"I saw you in Aces with that guy you were with. Didn't like the look of him. No, that's not true—I didn't like the way he was looking at *you* when your head was turned."

"How was he looking at me?" Wren asked.

"Like a lion watches his prey," Safe told her.

She winced. "He seemed harmless. I met him online. We talked via chat several times. He told me he was an accountant. That he likes to play chess in his spare time. I'm such an idiot," she said with a sigh.

"You aren't," Safe insisted.

"What happened next?"

He hated she thought that way about herself. Meeting people to date was hard. And the Internet made it easier in some ways, but much more difficult in others. People could hide their true nature until it was too late.

"Bo?"

His name on her lips made that funny feeling deep inside rise yet again, but once more, Safe pushed it down. "Sorry. So, I saw you at the table with that asshole, but since two strangers having a drink weren't any of my business, I kind of pushed you guys to the back of my mind. A while later, I had just used the restroom and was heading back to the bar when you appeared in the hallway. You didn't look good. You were stumbling and slurring your words. You asked for my help, then you passed out.

"My first thought was to get you out of there. I probably should've brought you to Jessyka's office—she owns the bar—but instead, I followed my gut. I went out the back door and straight to my car. I drove us here, made sure you were all right medically—I have some training, since I'm a SEAL—then called Jessyka."

"Not the cops?" Wren asked.

Safe winced. "Yeah, I should've called them," he admitted.

"No! I mean, maybe," she hedged. "But I'm not a fan of the police."

Safe instantly wanted to ask why. Wanted to know everything about this woman. But when she didn't volunteer the information, he continued, "Like I said, I called Aces and spoke with Jessyka. Told her what happened. That you were safe here with me, but I wanted to make sure she knew your date was bad news and to ask some of the guys to detain him."

Wren sat up. "Did they?"

"Unfortunately, no. He was gone. But I thought you might want to see what happened for yourself after Jessyka learned what you went through," Safe told her. He pulled out his phone and brought up the video Jessyka had sent him a couple hours ago. He stood up and took the few steps over to the chair and handed Wren his phone. "Just click play when you're ready. I've already turned the volume up."

Nothing about what happened to Wren was funny...but Safe freaking loved what happened after they left.

He listened along to the video as she watched, knowing what Wren was seeing. Jessyka had turned up all the lights in the dimly lit bar to full strength and turned off the music. She climbed onto the bar to make an announcement. He could hear Jessyka's speech through the speakers on his phone as Wren watched.

"Attention everyone! I've gotten a report that someone who was here earlier tonight drugged a woman's drink. Please, every woman, put down whatever you're drinking immediately. Don't take another sip! I'll replace your drinks for free. The young lady who was drugged has been taken to a safe place—literally—but if you feel sick or weak, please let me or one of my staff know."

Wren paused the video and looked up at Safe. "But if the

guy I was with was gone, why'd she do that? It had to have cost her a lot of money."

"Jessyka takes her role as bar owner seriously. There's no way she'd sit back and do nothing after hearing what happened to you. She takes the safety of her patrons even *more* seriously. And she was pissed that you were drugged right under her nose, in *her* bar. From what I understand, the lights stayed on for over an hour, the music stayed off. No one complained."

"Wow."

"But she's really upset that they didn't catch the guy. She's got a ton of cameras all over the bar and the parking lot. She's been studying them, and she actually found the clip that showed your date putting the drug in your drink at the bar, right after the bartender turned his back. She has the clip of you going down the bathroom hallway, talking to me, and me taking you out the back door. Another camera captured me carrying you to my car. And when you didn't return to the table, she also has your date on film, getting up and leaving. But he didn't park in the Aces parking lot. He walked away as nonchalantly as if he was taking a leisurely nighttime stroll."

"So no license plate to report," Wren concluded.

"Exactly."

"He told me his name was Matt. Matt Smith."

Safe's lip curled in a grimace.

Wren nodded. "Yeah. Probably made up. But we should be able to trace him through the app, right?" she asked as she leaned forward and pulled her phone out of her pocket.

"Maybe," Safe said. "I know a guy who used to be a SEAL, and he can do just about anything with electronics."

"Oh no!" Wren exclaimed as she frowned down at her phone.

"What? What's wrong?" Safe asked.

"He deleted them."

"Deleted what?"

"Our messages! We communicated through the app, because I didn't want to give him my phone number. We had a couple hundred messages back and forth as we got to know each other, and they're gone."

"Is his profile still up?" Safe asked.

Wren sighed and let the hand with her phone drop into her lap. "No. He's gonna get away with it. There's no telling how many other women he's done this to...*will* do it to."

"Don't count my friend out yet. He's pretty...thorough." Safe was going to say sneaky, but decided that might not be the best word to use to reassure Wren right now.

"It doesn't matter. I got away, thanks to you." She looked at her watch. "And I've taken up enough of your time. I'm sure you have better things to do this morning than babysit me. I appreciate your help. If you'll give me my purse, I can give you some money to reimburse you for your trouble. Then I'll get out of your hair and go home."

Safe frowned at her. "Your purse?"

Wren frowned back. "Oh. Yeah. I guess I didn't have it with me when I saw you in the hall? It's probably still at the bar then."

Safe didn't have a good feeling in his gut. And as a Navy SEAL, he never ignored his feelings. He stood and said, "May I have my phone back?"

"Oh! Yes, sorry," she said with a slight grin as she held it out.

Without a word, Safe took it and dialed Jessyka's number. She'd had a long night, as had he, but he was fairly sure she'd be up. He put the phone on speaker so Wren could hear his conversation.

"Safe. Is she okay?"

"Wren is fine," he reassured her.

"Wren! That's a pretty name."

Safe thought so too, but he had more important things on his mind. "Did you find Wren's purse at the bar last night? At the table where she was sitting?"

"Her purse? No, I don't think there was anything left at the table in the corner. Oh, shit—did that asshole take it?"

Safe met Wren's gaze, and he could see she was just as concerned as he was about this new twist. "Apparently," he told Jessyka with a sigh.

"What a dick!" Jessyka spat. "I'll go to the bar right now to see if it was turned in. I'll call as soon as I know one way or another. But, Safe, if he has her purse, he knows where she lives...and probably even has the keys to her place, unless she had them on her?"

Jessyka wasn't saying anything Safe hadn't already thought. But by the look on Wren's face, she was just now realizing how messed up this situation truly was.

"I know. Let me know if the purse turns up," he told Jessyka. "I need to go."

"Okay. But please tell Wren we're all glad she's okay. And that shit doesn't usually happen at my bar. We're all going to do a better job of trying to keep an eye on women there. I realize it's not all on me, but I need to do something. I've been thinking about making a special section for first dates, so women can feel safer. A few tables that're closer to the bar, and make it mandatory that drinks be brought directly to those tables by a bartender. And we'll add more cameras. Of course, that doesn't mean someone has to sit there if they don't want to, but at least the option will be there. We'll market it and make sure everyone knows that if they want to meet someone for the first time at Aces, they'll be as safe as possible."

"I'm sure that'll be appreciated. I'll talk to you later."

"Okay. Safe?"

"Yeah, Jess?"

"She really did luck out when you were there at exactly the right moment."

Safe knew what she was talking about. Lots of bad things had happened to Jessyka and her friends, but they'd all been lucky enough to have a Navy SEAL available to help when the shit hit the fan.

"Right," he said after a moment.

"Benny has already contacted Tex to see if he can find out where that asshole went after leaving Aces. Track him on street cameras to see where he parked, and to see if we can find his license plate number. If anyone can find him, Tex can."

"Not going to argue with you there. I really need to go now, Jess. Tell Benny I said hello, and I'll talk to you soon."

"Okay. Later, Safe."

Safe clicked off the phone and opened his mouth to say

something reassuring to Wren, but the second he hung up, she was up and out of the chair, pacing his living room.

"Shit! He has the keys to my car, my apartment. My IDs, my address. He knows where I live!"

Safe couldn't stand seeing this woman so freaked out. He intercepted her and put his hands on her shoulders, stopping her in her tracks. "Take a breath, Wren."

"I can't!" she said, but she did as he ordered anyway. "I remember leaving my purse at the table now. I just needed to get away from him! I knew he'd drugged me, and I didn't want to pass out at the table."

"I know."

Wren closed her eyes and took another deep breath. Then she straightened her shoulders and looked up at him. "I appreciate you doing everything that you did. A lot of people wouldn't have. Thank you for breakfast. I'll call for a ride from my phone."

"Wait—what?" Safe asked with a frown.

"You probably have stuff to do. You're a SEAL, right? Like, you probably need to go to work. Save the world, things like that."

"I saved the world last week. I have this week off," Safe quipped, only half kidding. They'd just gotten back from a mission, and he had a few days off, which was why they were all at the bar last night.

Wren huffed out a small laugh. "Of course you did. Well, anyway, thanks again."

"Wren, *wait*," Safe said, tightening his grip on her shoulders. He didn't want to scare her, but the last thing he wanted was for her to walk out. He didn't know nearly enough about this woman. And while he wouldn't hold her hostage, he honestly didn't think it was all that smart for her to go back to her place. Not with Matt, or whatever his name was, out there with all her info.

"It's not safe for you to go home. He has your address and your *keys*, Wren. Let Tex work his magic. Do what he can to find this asshole so you can press charges. Jessyka has the video of him spiking your drink. In the meantime, we just need to make sure you're in the clear to go home. Also, we can change your locks so he can't get in, set up escorts so you can get in and out without being harassed by him."

Wren was staring at him with an odd look on her face.

"What?" he asked, afraid she was simply going to thank him again and try to walk out.

He had the strangest feeling that if she did, he'd lose the best thing that ever happened to him. It was cheesy as hell and totally crazy...but that's what his gut told him, and he'd never backed down from a gut feeling before. He wasn't about to start now.

"I don't have anywhere to stay while this random amount of time goes by," she told him with wide eyes.

"You can stay here," Safe blurted. He hadn't planned on inviting her to move in, but now that he had, he couldn't say he was upset about the idea.

"Um, *what?*"

"You can trust me. You can stay in the same room you slept in last night. You have my word I'm not going to try anything hinky. I'll even get some Lucky Charms so you can have what you like for breakfast."

"I don't have any of my clothes or anything," she said incredulously.

Thrilled she wasn't saying no, or screaming that he was a psycho, or backing away from him, Safe pushed a little harder. "We can go to your place and get what you need for a few days."

"I thought you said it wasn't a good idea for me to go home."

"Well, I'm thinking I can use some of my SEAL skills to get in and out of your place without being detected," he teased.

"You aren't going through my stuff and packing for me," she told him with a small frown. "Wait, what am I saying?" she asked, more to herself than to him. "Am I really considering this?"

"Yes," Safe answered for her. "You'll be safe here. From me *and* from assholes who might want to hurt you. I can give you the numbers of my friends, who will vouch for me."

"Of *course* your friends will say good things about you," Wren said with a roll of her eyes.

"Right. Then I'll give you the numbers of *Jessyka's* friends. Her Navy wife friends. They're all with retired SEALs, and I promise you they won't beat around the bush about me. They'll give it to you straight. Wait...on the other hand, maybe I don't want you gossiping with them about me."

To his amazement, Wren smiled at that. Then she quickly sobered. "I really don't want to be a bother."

"You won't be. You aren't."

"Bo, I spent too many years couch surfing, feeling as if I

was taking advantage of people. I vowed never to do that again."

Safe didn't like that. At all. The thought of this woman not having a home of her own and relying on the generosity of others to have a place to sleep at night made him feel... unsettled. And he itched to know her story. All of it.

"You aren't taking advantage of me if I'm offering," he said after a small pause. "And for the record, I don't expect you to do a damn thing. No cooking, no cleaning. Nothing. You're here as a guest. You don't have to pay me back by thinking you need to be my maid or something."

"It's a good thing, because I'm a crap housekeeper," Wren told him. "I just got a new job, and I won't be around a lot anyway."

It sounded like she was leaning toward staying with him. It was crazy that he'd just met her, and yet he wanted her to stay more than he'd wanted anything in a very long time. "So you'll stay?"

"Just for a few days. Until my locks are changed and we know Matt isn't going to be hanging around."

Safe would take that. "Okay."

"Okay," she echoed.

They stood there staring at each other for a beat before she sighed. "So...are we gonna plan this get-my-stuff mission or what?"

If there was one thing Safe was good at, it was planning missions. "Yes, ma'am," he said with a smile.

CHAPTER THREE

Wren wondered what she was doing for the hundredth time. She was staying? At a stranger's home? It was crazy. Ridiculous. Stupid.

And yet, she couldn't deny that being here in Bo's little house made her feel...safe.

She nearly snorted at that. Figured that the guy's nickname was Safe and he made her feel exactly that way. But it was true. After the initial panic when she'd woken up and realized she didn't know where she was, she'd calmed after seeing the note he'd left. He'd given her a choice, and that was one thing she hadn't had much in her life while growing up.

And then the cereal thing had further relaxed her. Any man who had a pantry stuffed with sugary cereal, and actually enjoyed eating it, was a man she wanted to get to know.

The physical appeal was obvious. He was tall, over six feet. Had thick light brown hair that stuck up all over his head when he ran his fingers through it, a closely cropped beard and mustache, light brown eyes that were intense when focused on her. And a tattoo. She wasn't a tattoo kind of girl, but she couldn't deny the snake image on his right arm was hot.

Yes, it was safe to say—Wren tried not to snort at herself for the pun—she was drawn to Bo. But looks could be deceiving. She'd learned that the hard way. Her own mom was very well put together, tall, slender, beautiful...and a deceitful, lying, depraved bitch. And the men she'd brought into their house were just as bad.

So she knew better than to trust someone based on their looks. She wanted to learn all she could about Bo Cyders. What his childhood was like. What he did in his free time. How he interacted with his friends. Those were the things that would tell her a lot about him as a person.

She thought she'd vetted Matt Smith, but she'd been wrong—*very* wrong. So maybe the things she'd thought she needed to know about someone weren't actually very good metrics on what kind of person they were after all.

"What are you frowning about?" Bo asked.

They'd moved back to the dining table to plan the "mission" to her apartment. Wren had thought Bo was kind of cute when he'd pulled out some paper and began to draw the roads around her complex and explain how they would approach the building.

"Nothing."

"Don't do that," he said, putting down his pen and turning his golden-brown eyes on her. "If you don't think something I'm suggesting will work, speak up."

"It's not that. I just...I was thinking about how I thought I was a good judge of character, but apparently I'm not."

At that, Bo picked up his phone and dialed a number. He once again put it on speaker and placed the phone on the table. Wren was about to ask what he was doing when someone answered.

"Yo. Safe. What's up? You good?"

"Hey, Preacher. I need some help."

"Anything."

That single word made Wren's eyes tear up. It was so silly, but hearing such simple and immediately proof of the friendship between Bo and the man on the other end of the line, someone who would clearly do *anything*, without even knowing what might be asked of him, wasn't something she'd ever had. And it hurt.

"First, I need you to talk to Wren. Tell her all the bad shit about me that you know."

"Wren?"

"The woman from the bar last night."

"Ah. She okay?"

"She's fine. But she's not sure she can trust me."

"That's not—" Wren tried to interject, to tell Bo that wasn't what she meant by her earlier statement, but the man on the phone talked over her.

"Something happen?"

"No. I told her she could stay here at my house as long as she needed, because we're pretty sure the asshole who spiked her drink last night has her purse. But after what happened, she doesn't think she has a good asshole-radar anymore."

"Ah, I get it. And *shit*. He knows where she lives and can get into her place."

"Exactly."

"All right. I'm happy to tell her all the dirt I have on you."

"Relevant shit, Preacher," Bo warned.

The man on the phone chuckled.

Bo turned to Wren and said, "Ask Preacher your questions, Wren. I'll be outside." And with that, he stood and walked toward the sliding door that led into the backyard without another word.

"Wait, Bo..." But he was already closing the door behind him.

"Wren?" Preacher asked.

She turned back to the phone lying on the table. "Um... yeah. Hi."

"Are you really all right? No side effects from whatever that asshole put in your drink?"

"No. I'm okay. A little headache, but that'll go away in a few hours, I'm sure."

"I'm sorry we didn't catch the guy," Preacher said.

This was such a surreal moment. Talking to someone she didn't know about something horrible that had happened. Wren was much more used to sweeping this kind of thing under the rug and never mentioning it again. "It's okay."

"It's absolutely not. Safe was pissed last night. After he talked to Jessyka and told her what happened, he called Kevlar to ask for advice."

"Who?"

"Kevlar. He's our team leader, our go-to guy."

"Oh. Advice about what?" Wren asked.

"You. He was second-guessing his decision to take you to his house. He wanted Kevlar's opinion, since he's got Remi and all."

"Remi?"

"Shit. Hasn't Safe told you *anything*?"

Wren didn't like Preacher's scolding tone. "I just woke up about an hour ago. We ate breakfast, talked about what happened after I passed out last night, and then started making plans to infiltrate my apartment using super-secret SEAL techniques, so sorry that Bo hasn't had time to give me the 4-1-1 about his entire life history."

She immediately regretted her snarky tone, but to Wren's surprise, Preacher chuckled.

"Right. Sorry. So...you know Safe is a Navy SEAL."

"Yes. He just got back from saving the world on a mission and has a few days off."

"Yup. I'm one of his teammates. There are six of us...no, sorry, seven. I told you about Kevlar. There's also MacGyver, Flash, Smiley, and Blink. He's our newest teammate. Anyway, Kevlar was on vacation in Hawaii and got left out in the ocean while on a diving trip. He and the woman he was left with, Remi Stephenson, were rescued, came back to California, got together, and then shit *really* hit the fan."

Wren leaned forward in her chair. "What happened?"

"We used to have this man on our team, Howler. He went to boot camp with Kevlar. They were best friends. Had been on the same team for years. Turns out he was jealous as fuck of Kevlar, and he was the one who arranged for him to get left in the ocean."

Wren gasped. "Seriously?"

"Yeah. And that's not the worst part. He kidnapped Remi. Took her into the hills, where he had a grave already dug. Planned on burying her alive, then 'helping' the search parties find her dead body."

"Why? Why would he do that to his best friend's girlfriend?" Wren asked, completely enthralled with the story.

"Jealousy. He wanted the team leader spot. Instead of being a man about it and going to our commander to talk to him about the possibility of leading another team, he tried to kill Remi, knowing it would destroy Kevlar emotionally. He figured he could take over our mission to Chad once Kevlar was out of the picture."

"Holy crap," Wren breathed.

"Yeah."

"I'm assuming since you're telling me this story, his plan failed?"

"Yup. Blink, who's now the newest member of our team, was able to convince Howler he was on his side and when the opportunity arose, took him out and rescued Remi."

Wren figured she knew what "took him out" meant, but it still shocked her.

"So, you thinking you're not a good judge of character? Believe me when I say, *anyone* can hide their true selves from the world. From the people who know them best. You think Kevlar hasn't been beating himself up for not seeing that his *best friend* was green with envy for years? That all of us aren't pissed that we didn't see the crazy in Howler, a man we spent thousands of hours with? For not realizing he was the one who'd arranged for Kevlar to die in the ocean? That he was capable of kidnapping Kevlar's girlfriend and murdering her?

"You were on a *first date*. Not seeing through that asshole's smokescreen and realizing he intended to drug you doesn't say anything about you. It says everything about *him* being a deceitful predator."

Wren's mind was spinning. "That's a good point," she blurted.

The man on the other end of the phone chuckled. "Glad you think so."

"How's Remi?" Wren asked. "That couldn't have been a fun experience."

Preacher didn't say anything for a long moment, and Wren got nervous. "Sorry, was I not supposed to ask that?"

"No. I was just thinking how perfect you are. Most people would be freaking out over the attempted murder thing and the fact that a member of our team tried to kill people—twice. But instead, you're worried about Remi."

"I'm not perfect. Far from it," Wren told him. "And I'm pretty hard to freak out."

"I'm guessing there's a reason for that."

"There is." She didn't elaborate.

Preacher didn't sound like he expected her to as he continued. "Right, so...Safe. He told you about how he got his nickname?"

"Yeah."

"Well, he wasn't kidding about that story, but his nick fits him in every way. He's the guy who worries over all of us when we're on a mission. Not to say we all don't watch out for each other, but Safe is always trying to keep *everyone* protected. Even the civilians we run across. He wants us to complete our mission, but he wants everyone to stay safe as we do it. So you asking him for help last night? You picked the exact right person."

"I didn't really pick him. He just happened to be in that hallway."

"You telling me you didn't pass anyone else on your way to the hall?" Preacher asked.

"I don't remember," Wren told him honestly.

"You did," Bo's teammate said. "I saw the tape. You passed three other men who would've helped you. But you waited until you were with Safe."

Wren wanted to keep arguing. Say something about how she probably wanted to be out of sight of Matt before asking for help, but she didn't get a chance because Preacher went on.

"Safe asked me to tell you all the bad shit about him, so you'd know what you were getting into. Let's see—"

"No," Wren interrupted. "I don't want to hear it."

"But you're worried about being a bad judge of character..." Preacher said, letting his words hang.

Wren chuckled. "You guys totally planned this, didn't you?" she asked.

Preacher sounded more serious than ever when he said, "No. Absolutely not. Look, Safe isn't a saint, none of us are, even me, with a nickname like Preacher. But you seriously couldn't have picked a better man to be your champion. Let him help you, Wren. Let all of us help you. There's nothing that pisses us off more than a guy hurting a woman. And that asshole from last night? He's on the top of our shit list right now. We're gonna find him and make sure he gets what's coming to him."

"You aren't going to kill him, are you?" Wren whispered.

Preacher laughed. Hard. When he had himself under control, he said, "No. Now—what's this about plans to infiltrate your apartment using super-secret SEAL techniques?"

Wren realized that he recalled word-for-word what she'd said earlier. She briefly explained Bo's plans to go to her apartment to get her things.

"Tell him I'm in. As are the rest of the guys. This'll be fun."

"Fun?"

"Oh yeah. None of us do downtime very well."

"Well, um...okay."

"Sorry. I get a little too gung-ho sometimes. But seriously, tell him if he needs help, any of us are more than willing to have your backs while you go inside."

"I'll let him know."

"Good. Wren?"

"Yeah?"

"Glad you're okay. No woman should have to worry about that shit when they meet someone for the first time."

"Thanks. I agree."

"I know Jessyka probably wants to make things right with you. Please don't let this incident keep you from going back to Aces."

"She told Bo she wanted to create special tables for people on first dates...where they can be reassured they'll be safe."

"That sounds like something Jessyka would do. Let Safe take care of you for a few days. You won't regret it."

Wren wanted to tell Preacher that she wasn't the kind of woman who needed taking care of. That she'd been taking care of herself since she was around six years old. But she didn't get the chance because he'd ended the connection.

She sat at the table for a minute or two, going over in her head everything she'd just learned, before pushing back her chair and heading over to the sliding-glass door.

Looking out, she saw Bo standing over by the backyard fence, staring at a couple of squirrels eating nuts off the ground, his hands in his pockets.

As she pushed open the door, he turned but didn't walk toward her. "You okay?" he asked.

Wren nodded. She felt awkward all of a sudden.

Bo strode toward her. So quickly she took a step backward. He stopped immediately.

"If you want to leave, I understand. I can take you wherever you want to go, but I still don't recommend you go back to your apartment until my friends and I can get your locks changed."

"If I want to leave, you're still going to change my locks?"

"Yes."

"You should know, Preacher didn't tell me anything. I mean, he did, but not about you."

Bo looked kind of irritated. "He was supposed to tell you all the bad shit about me so you could trust me."

Wren couldn't help it. She laughed. "How is telling me negative things about you supposed to make me trust you?"

Bo frowned. "Uh...I don't know. It just seemed like a good idea at the time."

"Well, he didn't, and I still trust you. I was unconscious, you could've done anything you wanted with me...and you didn't. I could've been just another sad story about a murdered body washing ashore, but instead I woke up warm and safe, had a perfect breakfast, and I feel better about the upcoming days than I did when I woke up a couple hours ago, despite knowing Matt probably has keys to my apartment. Oh, and Preacher told me to tell you that if you need help with your super-secret SEAL mission to get into my apartment, he's available."

"You told him about that?"

"Yeah."

"All right. You want to go back inside and continue with our plans?"

Wren stared at him. "This is weird."

"Yup," he agreed.

Wren made a spontaneous decision. Something she'd never done in her life. She was a planner. Didn't like making decisions without thinking about everything that could go wrong. "If the offer is still on the table, I'd like to stay. Here. With you. At least until we can figure out who Matt is and if he's going to be a problem."

"Good."

"I have today off, since it's Sunday, but I do need to go to work tomorrow."

"Can I ask where you work?"

It hit Wren then that as much as she didn't know this man, he also didn't know her. But she felt more comfortable with him than she had anyone else in a very long time.

"You can. After we've planned our get-into-my-apartment mission."

Bo smiled. "Deal." He gestured toward the door. "After you."

As Wren led the way back to the table, her mind spun with everything that had happened in the last sixteen hours. She'd been on a first date, drugged, passed out, woken up in a stranger's house, found out she and the man who'd saved her from what could've been a horrific experience shared a love of sugary cereal, had talked to a friend of his who'd spilled some pretty intimate details about Bo—and the rest of his team—and now they were figuring out how to get into her apartment without anyone knowing.

When she'd taken the new job here in Riverton, California, she never would've guessed in a million years her life would be so eventful. But the funny thing was...she wasn't upset about it. Her adult life had been one long rut. Alive but not *living*.

Meeting Bo was exciting. She didn't like the circumstances under which she'd met him, but she had to admit, spending time with him was one of the better things that had happened in her life thus far.

CHAPTER FOUR

"I'm not so sure about this plan," Wren told Safe with a small furrow in her brow.

It was around three in the afternoon, and Safe was sitting on the couch, with Wren back in his recliner. They'd heard back from Jessyka a few hours ago, who confirmed her purse *had* been found in the bar, but her keys were missing. And her driver's license. Which was super creepy. Safe could picture the guy rifling through a purse specifically for those two items. It put a menacing spin on his actions that gave him the chills.

Wren had given Safe as many details as she could about her apartment complex, and then he'd pulled it up on a satellite map program he used for the Navy. He'd scoped out the surrounding streets and figured out the best way to approach her apartment without having to drive up to the complex on the main street. He had no idea if Matt was watching for her to return, but he wasn't going to take any chances.

Yes, drawing him out might make it easier to figure out who he really was, but he would never use Wren as bait. He had confidence that Tex would find out his real name and give the info to the police so Wren could press charges. The last thing he wanted was for Wren to have to face the asshole today, when everything that happened was still so fresh.

Now they were relaxing—or trying to—and waiting for night to fall before heading over to her place. Kevlar had apparently talked to Preacher, because he'd called Safe and informed him that *he* was going to come with him and Wren to her place. Safe was happy for the backup. He didn't need the entire team, that would make them more conspicuous, but he could use Kevlar's assistance.

"What aren't you sure about?" he asked Wren.

"Um...everything? Bo, you're acting as if there are gonna be bad-guy Matts hanging out on every corner and under every bush. You seriously want to *climb up* to my second-story balcony and break in through my patio door? That's...crazy!"

"If this Matt guy is hanging around, the last thing I want is him seeing you," Safe said calmly.

"But if you're with me, there's no way he'd do anything."

"Seeing me with you could actually set him off. His big plan didn't go the way he wanted it to last night. I just don't want him doing anything rash."

"Like climbing onto my balcony and breaking in?" Wren muttered.

Safe thought she was kidding, but now he could see she was honestly concerned. He leaned forward. "I can be a lot," he told her seriously. "I get a little too excited about things sometimes. You should see me around the holidays with my sister's kids. I go overboard every year. Buy too many presents, go over to their place at midnight and tromp around the yard in my boots...hell, I've even bought reindeer poop on the Internet and sprinkled it in various places in their yard and on their roof."

A smile formed on Wren's lips. "Let me guess, your SEAL training has helped you never get caught."

"Of course," Safe told her. "And while this might seem a little overboard..."

One brow raised, and Safe shrugged.

"Right, it probably *is* overboard. This Matt guy could have stolen stuff out of your purse solely to terrify you. To make you uproot your life and move out of your apartment, or even out of town, all while he's actually long gone. But...what if he's not?"

Wren's expression wiped clear of any kind of amusement.

"I just want you to be safe. I can't stand the thought of you walking into your apartment and this asshole getting his hands on you."

"Why? You don't know me," Wren said quietly.

"Honestly?"

"Always."

"You're right, I don't know you. But there's just something about you. And I know that sounds like a line, but it's not. A part of it is because you came to *me* for help, because *I* was the one in that hallway when you needed assistance. But it's more than that. I've dated my share of women. And you know how many of them thought my choice of breakfast cereal was appropriate?" Safe didn't give her a chance to answer. "Zero."

"I'm not sure sharing a love of sugary cereal is a reason to be going as out of your way for me as you are," Wren said with a shake of her head.

"It's not just that. It's you talking with my teammate for a full twenty minutes and not thinking it was weird. It's me going overboard with this infiltration of your apartment thing, and you not immediately walking out the door. It's you not freaking out after you woke up in a stranger's house this morning and giving me the benefit of the doubt. It's simply talking to you, Wren. Your blunt honesty and the way you cut straight to the point. You're...interesting. That's a lame word, but it'll have to do for the moment.

"There hasn't been one second today when I've second-guessed what the hell I'm doing. Wishing I could take back my invitation to have you stay here for a while. I feel as if I've known you for years, and yet I get little butterflies in my belly every time you smile at me. I sound like I'm a schoolkid with my first crush, but...well...I *like* you, Wren."

Safe wanted to kick himself. Too much, too soon. He sounded like a psycho. But he wouldn't lie to this woman. There was something about her that had caught his attention from the get-go. And being around her today hadn't dampened his interest in the least. It had only grown.

And he still didn't know a damn thing about her.

Was this normal? No.

Did he care? Also no.

"I'm not normal," Wren told him with a completely straight face.

Safe couldn't help it—he laughed. Using that particular word only made him realize they were on the same wavelength.

At the look of hurt she quickly tried to hide, Safe said, "I'm not laughing at you. Honestly. It's just...I'm definitely not normal either. I spent hours today planning an infiltration of your apartment as if it was a life-or-death situation deep in the heart of enemy territory...and I had fun doing it. I don't *want* normal, Wren. I want...companionship. Fun. Someone who lets me be my weird self, but who still knows when to tell me to tone it down. I want loyalty, support, and someone who's just proud to have me as her man. As proud as I am to have her."

Okay, this conversation had gotten way too deep, and now Safe felt like an idiot. It was too soon. Way too damn soon.

"It's just...I didn't have a good childhood," Wren admitted. "My teen years weren't much better. I'm almost thirty, and I haven't found even one person I can trust implicitly. Because of that, I constantly look for the bad in people before the good, and yet I'm stupid enough to not learn my lesson and come back for more even when I get screwed. I'm not a good bet, Bo. And you seem like the kind of good guy who deserves a woman who isn't...broken."

Safe wanted to take this woman in his arms more than anything. But he also didn't want to freak her out. "My sister, Susie, was roofied in college and gang-raped by three men."

Safe closed his eyes and took a deep breath. Jesus. So much for not freaking her out.

He opened his eyes and met her gaze, not surprised by the shock and concern he saw there.

"She was devastated. I was pissed. Beyond pissed. It took her a long time to get over what happened. She pressed charges, and the men were found guilty...thanks to the video one of them took of the entire incident. It was on his phone. He'd deleted it, but it was still in the cloud. Watching that video in court was the hardest thing I've ever done in my life. And that includes every single mission I've ever been on. Seeing those assholes violate my sister while she was unconscious made me want to kill *all* of them. Seriously. I almost attacked them in court. But I didn't...because it would have hurt Susie even more if her big brother went to prison.

"Now, my sister is married, and they have two of the most adorable kids on the planet. My point is, it wasn't easy for her. She couldn't trust either. She always looked for the bad in men after that. And yet...today, she's happily married with a family. It's still not easy sometimes. She doesn't like to be out after dark. She can't and won't do the Halloween thing with her kids, because it requires being out after dark, and because adults wearing masks give her the creeps. Meeting new people is still difficult for her, especially men. And she doesn't ever go to bars anymore. She simply can't be around so many men while they're drinking. And yet she's one of the strongest people I know.

"Our experiences shape us. They make us into the people we are today. You, Wren, wouldn't be the woman I want to get to know better, if you hadn't gone through whatever you've gone through. I don't know what happened to you, but I hope I earn enough of your trust for you to tell me one day. Whether I do or not, I have no doubt it's made you into the strong woman I see before me right now. Despite your difficulty trusting others, you weren't sitting at home, feeling sorry for yourself. You were attempting to meet people, to find someone to be your partner in life, like all of us do. And when that date went wrong, you didn't just sit at that table in Aces and accept your fate. You fought to get help.

"I'm not asking you to marry me here, Wren. I'm just asking for you to let me help you. To get to know you better. It's much more likely you'll want to kick *my* ass to the curb long before I want to do that to you. For now, we can just be friends if you'd like. That's it. If you can put up with my quirks, I'll give you a safe place to stay while my people find this Matt asshole. Then you'll go back to your apartment and hopefully we can stay in touch, and we'll go from there. Okay?"

Safe knew he'd said too much. Had gone on and on and on. But this was important. He felt that down to his toes.

"What are their names? Your sister's kids?"

Safe blinked. After all he'd word vomited, *that* was her question? "Anders, who is five, and Inez, who's three."

"Oh, those are unique names," Wren said.

"Weird, you mean," Safe said with a small smile. "And don't worry, she'd agree with me. But she wanted her children to have unique names that would stand out. They're great kids. Happy, healthy, and curious as all get out."

"They live here in Southern California?"

"In Ohio, actually. I wish they were closer, but I make the most of the time I get to spend with them when I can."

Wren licked her lips, then nodded. "Okay."

"Okay?" Safe asked.

"I'd like to be friends. Stay here for a while and...then see what happens."

Safe beamed. "Awesome."

"And, Bo?"

"Yeah?"

"I might have given you crap about going overboard in planning a mission to my apartment, but I have to admit...it all sounds kind of fun. Do we get to wear black clothes and put black goo on our faces to blend into the darkness?"

Safe laughed. "Dark clothes, yes. The other stuff, no. It's so damn hard to get off."

"That's what she said," Wren muttered under her breath.

For a moment, Safe wondered if he'd heard her right, and when she blushed and looked up at him, he realized he had. He couldn't hold back the belly laugh.

This woman...He had no idea what she'd been through in her life, he didn't doubt that it wasn't good, but she wasn't broken. She was resilient, just like his sister. And nothing she might've said or done in that moment could've drawn him to her any more. He wanted a strong woman. Someone who wouldn't break at the slightest bit of adversity thrown her way.

"Sorry, that wasn't appropriate," she said.

"It was hilarious," Safe countered. "You'll hear a lot worse from my friends. They try to be good, but we're military guys who hang out with other military guys and deal with some pretty bad shit. We tend to say whatever comes to mind, which isn't always appropriate. Come on, I need to find you something to wear other than your pretty outfit."

Wren gave him a small smile, and her cheeks pinkened again. Safe had the thought that she hadn't been complimented enough, if his words were enough to embarrass her. He made a mental note to rectify that.

He stood and stepped toward his recliner and held out a

hand. She smiled wider and took it, and he helped her up. Holding her hand in his felt...right. But since he didn't want to make her uncomfortable, he let go as soon as she was upright.

They stood there for a beat, staring at each other. It took every ounce of discipline Safe had not to lean down and kiss her, but they'd just agreed to be friends. He couldn't screw that up right out of the gate.

Turning, he said, "Come on, follow me and I'll find you one of my T-shirts. It'll be too big, but we can tie it at your waist or something. Pants might be more of an issue, but maybe Susie left something here that'll work. She's constantly forgetting clothes in the guest room when she comes to visit."

"Bo?"

"Yeah?"

"If I forget to tell you later, thank you. For everything."

"You don't have to thank me for doing the right thing."

"Actually, I do. Because most people wouldn't go this far out of their way to help a stranger."

"We aren't strangers anymore, remember?" Safe said.

"Right. Friends."

"That's right," he agreed. Even though he wanted more, he'd settle for being this woman's friend...for now.

CHAPTER FIVE

Wren couldn't keep the smile off her face. Bo was...cute. He was completely into this. She still wasn't sure why they couldn't just go up to her front door, but seeing Bo and his friend, Kevlar, in SEAL mode was worth the over-the-top stealth.

Kevlar was a tad shorter than Bo, but no less intimidating...or good-looking. Though she found she preferred Bo's leaner look to Kevlar's muscles. They'd driven to the strip mall not too far from her apartment complex and pulled up next to a Crosstrek. When a man got out of the vehicle, Wren stiffened, but then Bo greeted him warmly and she realized it was his friend.

After being greeted with a chin lift, which made her kind of smile at the masculine and serious gesture, Kevlar and Bo discussed the plan.

She and Bo were going to go through the trees and shrubs

on the back side of her apartment, while Kevlar would go around the front and scope out the parking lot to make sure Matt wasn't there. Of course, none of them knew what kind of car he drove, so that part of the plan was tricky.

While Bo's teammate watched the front, Bo would climb up onto her balcony, help her up—she still wasn't clear on exactly how that would happen, but she was going with the flow—then Bo would pick her lock and they'd go inside and get what she needed to survive at his house for a few days. It sounded easy enough, but Bo had warned her that many times, best-laid plans had a way of going bad.

She wondered how many times that had happened to him while on a mission, but she didn't get a chance to ask. The longer she was around the man, the more she wanted to know about him. Which was a change for her. Usually the better she got to know someone, the more disappointed she became. She'd find out they didn't like animals, or old people freaked them out, or they smacked their lips when they ate. It was ridiculous, how judgmental she'd become, but she knew it was a way to keep people at arm's length. She was working on that, which was why she'd decided to go on the date with Matt in the first place.

She snorted. Look how that turned out.

"You okay? You can stay here if you want," Bo told her, obviously hearing her little snort.

"No, I'm good. You wouldn't know what to pack anyway. You'd probably come back with all shirts and no pants or something," she teased.

"You got your ears in?" Kevlar asked Bo.

He nodded and tapped his ear. Wren had seen them test the little radios in their ears earlier.

"Okay, I'll let you know if I see anything hinky," Kevlar said.

"Roger. Ten minutes. That's the goal. No more," Bo told his friend.

"We'll meet back at the car in fifteen. Give me five to scope out the front, then I'll give you the signal to make your move."

Bo nodded again, and then Kevlar was gone. He disappeared as if into thin air. Wren was impressed. For the first time, she got a little nervous. This was all over the top and kind of fun before, but now that they were about to go slinking around in the dark and breaking into her place, it was more real.

"Breathe, Wren," Bo told her. He was standing right next to her. Not touching, but close enough that she could feel the heat coming from his body. Looking up at him, she swallowed hard. He was wearing a black T-shirt, a pair of black cargo pants, and black boots. The only thing not black on him was his hair.

She felt a stirring of attraction deep in her belly. He was *hot*. She'd never been the kind of woman to be attracted to a man in uniform, but now she understood the draw.

"Wren?" he said softly, the concern easy to hear.

"I'm good," she said quickly.

"You sure?"

"Yeah. I just...I think it's the dark making me nervous."

"I won't leave your side. Well, except when I climb up to

your balcony, but I'll have eyes on you at all times. You're good."

Wren nodded. She wiped her suddenly sweaty palms on her thighs. The black T-shirt Bo found for her had been huge on her slender frame. She'd tied a knot in the material at her side, so now it was tight against her body. Bo had also found a pair of leggings in the dresser in the guest room that belonged to his sister. She was obviously taller than Wren, and while they were baggy at the ankles, they fit well enough. Shoes were more problematic, as she couldn't wear Bo's, so she had to wear the black sandals she'd worn on her date with Matt. As soon as they got inside her apartment, she'd switch into sneakers.

They walked toward the edge of the parking lot and before they stepped into the trees, Bo turned to her. "Ready?"

Wren nodded, her mouth too dry to speak. Was she really doing this? Acting as if she was some kind of commando? What if her nosey neighbor saw them and called the police? What if she messed up somehow? What if Bo fell as he was climbing to her balcony? What if he couldn't pick her lock? All the what-ifs they'd already discussed came roaring back into her head. All the things that could go wrong.

"Stop thinking so hard," Bo scolded. "We've got this." Then he reached out and took her hand in his. "We've got this," he repeated, squeezing her fingers.

Amazingly, his touch calmed her. Enabled Wren to take a long, slow breath, and offer a nod.

Bo nodded back, then stepped into the trees. Thankfully, he didn't let go of her hand. Having that connection with him and seeing his confidence made her feel a lot better.

A minute later they were standing under her balcony, looking up.

"Kevlar gave the all clear," Bo told her. "Let's do this. You know the plan. I'll shimmy up, then help you."

Wren nodded. This was the part of the plan she wasn't looking forward to. She wasn't exactly the athletic type.

Bo squeezed her hand again before dropping it and reaching for the rope he had coiled at his side. He wrapped his arms around her, and Wren took a deep breath. He smelled amazing. Musky, earthy, manly. He tied the rope around her waist, then gave her a small, apologetic smile before weaving the ropes between her legs and around her thighs.

Wren steadied herself with a hand on his shoulder as he knelt and tied the makeshift harness around her. The feel of his hands on her body made her shiver...in a good way. It had been years since she'd been touched with such gentleness.

Before she was ready, Bo stood. He had the end of the rope in one hand, the other end tied around her in an expert type of harness. "Give me two minutes and I'll start helping you up." Then he reached for the support beam and shimmied up as if he climbed poles for a living...which she supposed he probably did.

After he boosted himself over her railing, he looked back down. "Ready?" he whispered.

Wren nodded and stepped closer to the support pole he'd just climbed. She tried to wrap her hands around it as she felt the rope around her waist tighten.

The truth was, Wren was no help whatsoever in getting herself up the twelve feet or so to her balcony. It was all Bo.

She tried, she really did, but after a few awkward attempts to maneuver her arms and legs around the pole, she simply let Bo pull her up.

Before she knew it, she was over the railing and Bo was hugging her against him.

She held on tightly, returning the hug. It wasn't that she was scared, exactly, but it wasn't the most comfortable feeling to be hanging in midair.

"We'll leave the rope harness on, so I can lower you down when we're done." He was coiling the rope as he spoke, attaching it to one side of the harness at her waist.

"You sure we can't just go out the front door?" Wren asked softly.

"It's probably better to go back the way we came. Just in case. But if you really don't want to, I'll check with Kevlar and see what he thinks."

"No, it's fine. I just...It's fine," Wren told him.

Bo studied her for a beat, then nodded before stepping back and reaching into one of the pockets of his cargo pants. He pulled out what he'd called his lock picking tools and bent over her door.

It shouldn't have surprised Wren when he broke in so quickly, but it still did.

"After you," Bo told her with a satisfied smirk on his face.

Wren stepped into her apartment and without thought, reached for a light switch.

But Bo grabbed her hand, stopping her. "No lights," he warned.

"Right, sorry. I forgot."

To Wren's surprise, he didn't let go of her hand. Nor did he move. He simply stood still by her sliding glass door.

"Bo?"

"I'm assuming you didn't leave your place looking like this."

"I can't see anything," she admitted. "What's wrong?"

He didn't speak, but instead clicked on a flashlight he'd brought that had a red light instead of white and shone it around the room.

Wren gasped.

The room was trashed. Her sofa had huge slashes in the cushions, the stuffing all over the place. The few knickknacks she had were broken and crushed on the floor. The food in her fridge had been removed and thrown all over every surface. Glasses and plates from her cabinets were lying in pieces on the floor and ground into the carpet. Even her TV had been tipped over.

For a second, Wren couldn't breathe. "Who...when..." Her voice trailed off in shock.

"I think we know who, and the when was probably last night," Bo said.

Thankful he hadn't let go of her hand, Wren held onto it as if it was the only thing holding her together. Which it probably was.

"I don't even know him...why would he do this?"

"Because he's an asshole. Because he was pissed he didn't get what he wanted."

Wren closed her eyes, despair swamping her. She'd just gotten her apartment all set up after moving here. She'd spent the little extra money she had to try to make it feel homey and comfortable. And now...it was all ruined. She didn't have enough in her savings to replace all her things. Stupidly, she also didn't have insurance.

Without a word, Bo pulled her back into his embrace. Wren went willingly. She buried her nose in his chest and dug her nails into his back as she held on, trying not to break into a million pieces. This was just one more shitty thing to happen to her in her shitty life.

"Shhhh, I've got you," Bo murmured.

Her breath hitched and it took every ounce of strength Wren had not to burst out crying. It took a few minutes, but eventually she was able to get control over her emotions. She went to pull away from Bo, but he didn't let go.

"Look at me," he ordered.

She didn't want to, but she tilted her chin up to meet his gaze. She could barely make out his features in the dark room, but she could still see the emotion swirling in his eyes. Feel the tenseness of his arms around her. It felt as if, without Bo holding her, she'd simply sink into a heap on the floor and never be able to get up again.

"You're safe. You can stay with me for as long as you need to. Got it?"

She didn't deserve this man. But she wasn't strong enough to disagree. To tell him she could go to a hotel. That she'd be all right. Right now, she didn't feel as if she'd ever be all right again. So she did the only thing she could. She nodded.

He studied her for a moment, then nodded. "Right, let's get your stuff and get the hell out of here. We'll call the police and make a report tomorrow. Okay?"

"Okay," she said softly.

Bo turned her but kept an arm around her waist as he led them carefully toward her bedroom. He knew the layout of her apartment because she'd drawn him a picture when they were planning this little mission. Of course, she'd thought he was overreacting, but now...it seemed as if he knew exactly what he was doing.

They stepped into her bedroom, and it seemed as if it was in worse shape than the main living area. Her closet doors were open and as far as she could tell, every piece of clothing that had been hanging up had been removed. Slashed and destroyed. The clothes from her dresser too.

Except for her underwear. She saw a pile of it sitting in the middle of her bed. The mattress had been slashed, but the pile of undies were obviously carefully placed.

Wren would've been embarrassed that she didn't have any sexy lingerie—she was a cotton comfort girl—but she was too worried about what she saw all over the small stack. "Is that what I think it is?" she whispered uneasily.

"Hopefully."

Wren's head whipped up at that. She stared at Bo. "What? You *want* it to be semen?" she asked, horrified.

"DNA," he said succinctly.

Wren sighed. He was right. Matt jacking off on her underwear would be gross, sick, but it would be excellent as far as pressing charges went.

"Stay here," Bo ordered.

"No, I—"

"Please," he interrupted.

Wren thought about his request for a split second. Did she want to get closer to what was probably the grossest thing she'd ever seen in her life? No. She definitely did not. She nodded.

"Thank you. Don't move."

Wren had no intention of moving from the doorway. She watched as Bo stepped toward her bed. He leaned forward, studied the pile of underwear, then stood. He looked around the room and stepped toward her small, attached bathroom. The red light from the flashlight disappeared for a moment, and for some reason, Wren suddenly felt extremely alone.

But Bo returned just seconds later. He strode toward her at an unnaturally fast pace.

"What's—"

"Under the bed. Now," Bo ordered.

He took her arm and steered her toward the destroyed bed. He got down on his knees and pulled on her hand, encouraging her to do the same.

"Bo?"

"Heard from Kevlar. He saw someone matching Matt's description heading up the stairs. We know he's got a key, so I need you to get out of sight while I go intercept him when he opens the front door."

His words made Wren freeze in terror. "I can't," she whispered.

"You have to," he returned, pulling harder on her hand, his other on her back now, trying to get her down to the floor.

"No, you don't understand! I can't!" Wren repeated. "When I was little I had to hide under my bed from the men Mom brought home who didn't think anything was wrong with having sex with an eight-year-old! I was terrified they'd find me and hurt me. I can't get under there! The memories..."

Even as her words trailed off, Bo was moving. He stood and wrapped his arm around her waist as he scanned the room, obviously looking for somewhere else to hide.

Wren's breathing was way too fast. She felt lightheaded. This was supposed to be *fun*. She'd humored Bo. Despite knowing her date had taken her ID and keys, she didn't think in a million years he'd *really* come to her apartment. But nothing about this was fun anymore. She was terrified.

Wren gripped Bo's shirt and looked up at him, not caring that her terror was overriding her good sense. "Please! Don't leave me here alone!"

Bo paused for just a moment—and they heard the sound of a key in the lock at her front door.

He spun, taking her with him, and quickly stepped behind her bedroom door. He clicked off the flashlight in his hand and pulled her against his body, wrapping an arm around her, holding her so tightly she could barely breathe.

But she didn't care. Wren did her best to burrow even further into him. Their hiding place sucked. If whoever was coming into her apartment—almost certainly Matt—turned on the light, he'd see them immediately. Though Wren had no doubt that the man holding her wouldn't let anyone hurt her. It was both a scary thought and a relief at the same time.

In her twenty-nine years, she'd never had anyone put themselves between her and danger. Certainly not her mom, not the father she'd never met, not teachers, not the many foster parents and siblings she'd lived with.

But this man, someone she'd met not even twenty-four hours ago, was doing just that.

She finally understood why people did crazy things in the name of love. She didn't love Bo, but she could see herself falling for him.

They heard the front door creak open, and every one of Bo's muscles tightened. As if he was readying himself to confront whoever entered.

But before he could move, they heard voices. Then shouting. Then footsteps pounding down the stairs away from the apartment.

"Shit! Fuck! Damn it!"

Wren lifted her head off Bo's chest. That was Kevlar's voice. "Something's wrong!" she exclaimed. "Go check on him!" she urged, pushing Bo. Now that her date had obviously run off, she found the strength she'd lacked a few seconds ago.

"Settle, Wren. It's okay."

"It doesn't sound okay," she insisted as Kevlar continued to swear.

"Asshole maced him. It hurts, but he'll be all right. Just stay here a little bit longer until he makes sure it's safe."

Confused for a moment, Wren finally realized Bo must have heard whatever happened through the little receiver in his ear.

After what was probably only about thirty seconds, but seemed like an eternity, Bo moved. To Wren's surprise, instead of insisting she stay put, he grabbed her hand and pulled her behind him as he left her bedroom and headed down the short hallway.

Kevlar was standing in her kitchen, his head bent over her

sink, the dim under-counter lights on as he used the extension thing to spray water on his face.

"Fucker got away," Kevlar said as he did his best to get the mace off his face. "Was gonna go after him but didn't want to risk him having a buddy or something who might come in after Wren."

Wren stilled. Two. That was two men in the last five minutes who had gone above and beyond to protect her. And *this* man she'd only met ten minutes ago. It was confusing as hell. Experience had told her that she wasn't worth anyone stepping up for, but these men were blowing what she thought about herself to smithereens.

"Guess we're moving to plan B," Bo said with an unamused huff of laughter.

"With the sound of those sirens, I'd say so."

For the first time, Wren heard the sirens. "Should we leave? What're we going to do? What do we tell them?"

"Stop panicking," Bo ordered. "We were going to call the police tomorrow anyway. This is just speeding up the process. We haven't done anything wrong."

"Bo! We broke in! Climbed up the balcony."

"It's not breaking and entering if it's your own apartment. Breathe, Wren. It's going to be okay."

"If you guys get in trouble, I'll never forgive myself."

"We aren't going to get in trouble," Kevlar said.

"Should I take this rope thingy off?"

"Wren, look at me," Bo said, instead of answering her question.

She looked at him.

"It's fine. You're the victim here. *Breathe*."

"I don't like the police. Things don't turn out well for me when I talk to them."

Bo framed her face with his hands and tilted her head up so she had no choice but to look at him. Her hands rested on his chest as she did her best to keep from freaking out.

"Things are different now," he said firmly. "Kevlar and I are here. You're okay."

Wren tried to calm down. She really did. But he didn't understand. Didn't know how many times she'd trusted authority figures to have her back, only to be let down.

"Come here," Bo whispered, then pulled her against him once again. Wren went eagerly. She felt safe with his arms around her, his scent in her nostrils. She trembled as she held onto him.

"The situation in her bedroom the same as in here?" Kevlar asked.

"Yeah. Fucker piled her underwear on her bed after he trashed the place. Then dumped conditioner on it to look like...you know."

"Conditioner? Are you sure? Why would he do that?" Wren asked against his chest, not lifting her head.

"Because he's a fuckerhead," Kevlar responded.

Amazingly, that made Wren smile. She picked her head up and turned to look at the other man. He'd turned off the water, but he was drenched from his chest down to his toes. His eyes were bloodshot, and he looked extremely pissed off. But Wren wasn't scared. Not of him. It was obvious where his ire was aimed, and it wasn't at her.

"I'm gonna turn on more lights," Kevlar warned.

Wren felt Bo's hand at the back of her head, encouraging

her to place it against his chest. She did so willingly and closed her eyes. She heard Kevlar's indrawn breath at whatever he saw once the bright overhead lights were on. Felt the way Bo's body once more tightened against her.

She didn't want to look. But she had to. It was her life. Her things.

The sirens were louder now, as if the police officers had turned into her parking lot. It was just a matter of time before they arrived at her door. She bet her nosey neighbor had called them when Kevlar had gotten maced. For the first time, she wasn't upset at the older woman. She supposed it wasn't a bad thing to have someone so...invested in the lives of the people who lived around her.

She looked around the kitchen and flinched. In the dark, the destruction had looked bad, but in the light it was so much worse. There wasn't one dish or cup that wasn't broken. Wasn't one inch of carpet that hadn't been covered in food or debris. There wasn't anything that Wren could see that would be salvageable.

She'd have to start over. Again.

She felt Bo's arms squeeze her reassuringly.

But the difference was, this time she wasn't alone. She had no doubt that this man and his friends would be there to help her.

Her spine straightened. If Matt, or whatever his name was, thought she would be destroyed by what he'd done, he was wrong. All her life, she'd had bad shit happen to her. She'd survive this, just as she had everything else. *Fuck him*. Seriously.

She took a deep breath and pulled out of Bo's embrace. As

nice as it felt, she had to face the police on her own two feet. Matt wasn't going to get away with this. Destroying her things, hurting Kevlar. She'd make the report and hope that he'd be found, and that he'd pay for being a fuckerhead. She liked that term. Vowed to use it more often.

"Wren?" Bo asked.

"I'm good," she told him, surprisingly feeling as if she was.

"We'll get this cleaned up. Replace your things," he told her.

"It's okay. It was just stuff. Thrift stores always have cute things. It's fine, Bo. *I'm* fine. Promise. I'm actually just mad. I thought this whole thing tonight was a little much. Didn't really think Matt would do anything. But I was wrong. This... him doing all this. He needs to be stopped."

"Yeah, he does," Bo agreed.

"Doesn't Commander Hurt's wife, Julie, have a second-hand shop?" Kevlar asked Bo.

"Yeah. My Sister's Closet, I think it's called. Caroline and the other women love to shop there. I bet they have lots of things that would be affordable," Bo said.

"I'm sure Remi would be happy to go shopping with you."

"Not to mention Caroline, Alabama, Fiona, and the others. Especially after Jessyka tells them about what happened at Aces," Bo agreed.

"First things first," Wren protested. "We need to figure out what we're going to tell the cops who will be here in a minute or less. Not worry about shopping."

"You tell them the truth," Kevlar told her calmly.

"That we snuck in through my balcony door?" Wren asked incredulously, still not sure that was the best idea.

"Yup. Because when you tell them why you felt it was necessary, that you were afraid the man who drugged you and had your address and keys might be here, they aren't going to have a problem with it," Bo told her.

"If you say so."

"I do. Remember, we're here. No one is going to fuck with you, Wren. *No one.*"

With Bo's words ringing in her ears, Wren turned to her front door when she heard a very hard, loud voice yell, "Put your hands up where we can see them!"

CHAPTER SIX

Safe was exhausted. He hadn't slept much the night before, and tonight wasn't looking much better. But he was also keyed up. Tonight hadn't gone the way he'd expected. Yes, he'd planned the trip to Wren's apartment as if it was a SEAL mission, but he'd learned the hard way that people couldn't be trusted to do the right thing. And, unfortunately, tonight he was proven right.

The man Wren knew as Matt had not only already been to her apartment, and had apparently trashed it, he'd returned to lie in wait for her to return home.

The police had taken her statement, advising her to stay away from her apartment until they could figure out who Matt was and hopefully find him. Neither Safe nor Kevlar had mentioned they already had someone looking who had a much better shot at figuring out the mystery before the cops did. Tex could find this Matt guy, then notify the police.

And Safe had no doubt when Tex found the guy, he'd use

his computer skills to make sure the man's life went to shit. It was amazing how much everyone's lives were connected to computers these days, even when they actively tried to stay off the radar. And Matt would find out the hard way. He'd be ruined after Tex got his hands on his electronic footprint.

As pissed as Safe was at this Matt person, at the moment, he was more worried about the woman on his couch. He couldn't keep some of the things she'd said tonight out of his head. When he'd asked her to get under the bed to hide, she'd been truly terrified. It was the kind of terror that went bone deep. Her breathing had spiked, her pupils had dilated, and her limbs were frozen.

Her words echoed in his head...

When I was little I had to hide under my bed from the men Mom brought home who didn't think anything was wrong with having sex with an eight-year-old. I was terrified they'd find me and hurt me.

The thought of any child having to hide under their bed from real-life monsters rather than make-believe ones was infuriating. He wasn't naïve. He knew the kinds of evil that existed in the world better than most. But the thought of Wren suffering...it hurt him in a way he couldn't explain.

Then there was her obvious unease with the police. Yes, things had been tense when the cops first arrived. When they didn't know whether he, Kevlar, and Wren were good guys or bad guys. But even after that had been straightened out, Wren remained uneasy.

She'd been the same way with him when she'd woken up in his home. Skittish and not very trusting, which was totally normal considering the circumstances. But she'd relaxed fairly quickly. Not the case with the police. He was surprised to find she didn't relax even a little with the officers. He was well aware there were shitty cops out there, men and women who gave the badge a bad name, but most people were relieved to see the police after a break-in.

Not Wren.

He remembered her comment about how things didn't turn out well for her when she spoke to the police. That comment, along with other things she'd said, made him think not a single person had stepped up to help her escape her obviously shitty home life. Which sucked.

Safe was sitting in his recliner, his mind racing, while Wren slept on the couch. She didn't want to be alone when they returned to his house, so he'd suggested she sleep out here. She hadn't agreed until he'd reassured her that he'd be right here as well, in the chair.

As she slept, Safe studied her. Her short black hair was sticking up all over her head, which made him want to run his hand through it to smooth it down. She didn't have any makeup on, but her lashes were long and her lips seemed naturally plump. Curled into a small ball on her side, she looked vulnerable, more so than usual.

What was it about this woman? Why was she getting under his skin so fast? Was it that she'd needed him to play the knight in shining armor? Safe didn't think so. Yes, Wren might've needed help in Aces, but he had a feeling she wasn't the kind of woman who relied on others much. She'd even been practical about all her possessions being trashed.

No, it wasn't that. It was...simply *her*.

Wren intrigued him. He wanted to know everything about the woman with the apparently horrific childhood, who was still brave enough to try to meet new people. Wanted to know how she'd survived growing up in a household where hiding under her bed was a regular occurrence.

Hell, he still didn't even know where she'd moved here from or what she did for a living. All he knew was that she had to go to work in the morning. Not knowing even the simplest things about her made Safe want to wake her up to talk. But that was the last thing she needed.

So he settled back in his recliner and kept his gaze locked on the woman who'd intrigued him without even trying.

Eventually, he fell asleep, but not before vowing to do right by Wren. He wanted to show her that not everyone was out to do her wrong.

* * *

Wren woke up and for a split second, she tensed, wondering where she was. Then she remembered. The date at Aces with Matt, being drugged, breakfast with Bo, going to her apartment last night, the police...

It was a lot. Even for her.

She was used to life giving her shit sandwiches, but the last couple of days were a bit much. Turning her head, she saw Bo asleep in the recliner. One leg was peeking out from the blanket over him, and his chest was also uncovered. He had on a pair of sweats and a T-shirt, and Wren had the sudden thought that she wished he wasn't wearing anything so she could get a better look at his muscular body.

The thought shocked her. She wasn't a prude, wasn't a virgin, but this was the first time in her life she was as drawn to anyone as she was to Bo. It wasn't just his body, although that wasn't a turn-off for sure. He was just so...*good.*

It was kind of sad that she was attracted to a man just because of his goodness, but it was true. She'd learned, because of the way she grew up, how to distinguish fake niceness from genuine concern and goodness in others. And Bo was a good man from the top of his head down to the tips of his toes. Kevlar was the same way. She assumed the rest of the men on their SEAL team probably were, as well.

Sadly, Wren knew how rare that was. She'd learned the hard way that people were generally selfish. They'd do things to look good to others, not because it was the right thing to do. And if money was involved in any way, they'd do whatever it took to either get their hands on that money, or do as little as possible so they didn't have to *spend* money.

It was a horrible way to look at life, but it was what Wren knew.

As she stared at Bo, he stirred. His eyes opened, and the first thing he did was swing his gaze toward her.

"Morning," he croaked huskily.

The hair on her arms stood up at the sound. His voice was deeper than usual, and the immediate thought that sprang into her mind was how intimate it was to see him seconds after he woke.

"Hi," she said, feeling shy all of a sudden.

"What time is it?" he asked.

"No clue."

"What time do you need to be at work?"

Work. Shit! Wren had forgotten all about it! If she hadn't just started a new job, she would totally call in sick. But she couldn't. They were currently planning an important overseas trip that she was a large part of, so she couldn't miss a day. "Eight."

Bo sat up, reached over to a small table next to his chair, and grabbed his phone. "Six forty-five. What time do you need to leave to get there on time?"

"Um...probably seven-thirty," Wren told him.

"Shit. You probably need to start getting ready then. You want cereal this morning? Or do you want me to make you something different?"

Wren blinked. "I have plenty of time to get ready," she told him.

Bo's gaze focused on her. "Yeah?"

"I'm sure you didn't miss it but my hair is short. It doesn't take long for me to shower and run a brush through it. I don't need hours to get ready. Fifteen minutes, tops."

She couldn't interpret the look on Bo's face. Then it hit her—and she grinned. "You were stereotyping me, weren't you? Figured since I'm a woman, it would take at least an hour for me to shower and get ready for my day."

He looked a little sheepish. "Yeah, I guess I was. Sorry."

That was new. A man apologizing when he was wrong.

Internally, Wren sighed and shook her head. That wasn't fair. And now *she* was the one stereotyping. She knew it, but it was difficult to change her thinking when she'd been let down so many times by men. Well...and women, actually. "It's okay. We all do it sometimes. And cereal is fine. It's what I usually eat every morning."

"Can I ask you something?"

This was kind of nice. Lying under warm blankets, not

having to leap out of bed and rush around. She and Bo waking up together, quietly talking. "Sure."

"It's okay if you don't want to say, but I was wondering where you work. What you do."

"Oh! It's weird. I feel as if we've known each other for a long time, but I guess we don't know even the most basic things about each other, huh?" Wren asked.

"Pretty much."

"It's not a secret. I moved here from New York last month. I work at BT Energy. It's a part of the pipeline sector. Their specialty is gas pipelines. I'm their PR person. Have you seen *Criminal Minds*? I'm kind of like JJ, the girl who was the liaison between the BAU and the media."

Bo sat up, lowering the footrest on his recliner and leaning forward. "Really?"

"Yeah."

"That's...cool. I mean, that's an important position. I know we rely on people like you when we have high visibility missions and have to get information out to the general public, and yet still have to keep certain things classified."

"Yeah. I'm still learning the ropes of the company, but so far I like it. We're actually in the middle of installing a new gas pipeline in Africa, and believe me, there's been a lot of interest and information we have to get out."

"Africa?" Bo asked with a frown.

"Yeah. It's going to be a great boost to the local economy and it should bring a lot of jobs too, which they need."

"Where in Africa?"

Wren's brows furrowed. The sleepy tone in Bo's voice was gone. Replaced by a stern, bossy Bo. "South Sudan."

"Sudan," he repeated.

"South Sudan. It's different from Sudan. They got their independence in two-thousand eleven."

"I know," Bo bit out.

Wren hurried to continue. "I know the country has had some issues lately, but the people I've been interacting with to plan the trip have been lovely," Wren said a little defensively.

"Wait, *what*? What trip?" Bo asked.

"The media blitz trip, when we announce the pipeline and talk about the logistics of installing it," she told him a little warily. She wasn't sure she liked this side of Bo. The feeling reminded her that she really didn't know him. Just because he'd helped her...twice...didn't mean he might not be hiding a temper and wouldn't hurt her if she said or did something he didn't like.

"Are you fucking kidding me?" Bo asked. The question was all the more scary because of the low, controlled way he asked.

"Um...no?"

"You can't go to fucking South Sudan!" he exclaimed, louder now. Then he stood up, making Wren flinch with his quick movement. But he didn't come near her, simply began to pace back and forth across the small room. "There's a level-four 'do not travel' advisory for the country! That means the US Embassy has suspended its operations! The State Department has ordered all US direct-hire employees and family members to get the hell out. Our government can't offer routine or emergency consular services to any US citizens in the country because of what's happening there. And you're going? Voluntarily? For a *job*?"

Wren sat up and wrapped her arms around her knees protectively. Bo wasn't telling her anything she didn't already know. She'd been concerned when she'd heard she would be traveling to the country with her new boss and a few of his top executives. She'd researched the country online and hadn't liked what she'd read. But when she'd brought up security concerns to her employer, he'd blown them off. Saying that it wasn't as bad as the media was portraying.

"We'll be in the southern part of the country, down in Juba, the capital. That's where the pipeline is going to start. In the mountains south of there. It'll eventually go through the country, through Sudan, and end up at the coast, but we're starting with a press conference in Juba to introduce what's happening. They need the money, there are a lot of famine and food and water issues there. This will *help*."

But Bo was shaking his head. "I can't believe this."

Wren swallowed hard.

"Sudan. Fuck!" he exclaimed. He turned to her. "We just finished a mission in Chad. It's to the west of Sudan and South Sudan. It was horrific. The people over there...they're suffering. They're desperate. And desperate people do things they normally wouldn't otherwise. Fuck, I'm not supposed to be telling you any of this—but, Wren, trust me when I say you *cannot* go to Sudan."

"South Sudan," Wren corrected without thought.

"You aren't listening to me!" Bo yelled.

And just like that, the fear and unease Wren had been feeling disappeared. Anger welled within her. Bo was treating her as if she was an idiot. As if she didn't know the dangers of traveling to a country the State Department had issued warnings against entering. She did. She was already scared, and she didn't need his judgment on top of all the other stress she was under at the moment.

Standing, she stalked over to Bo, who was glaring at her. She poked him in the chest with her finger. "I know," she said between clenched teeth. Then repeated herself as she poked him again. "I *know* it's bad over there. But this is what I was specifically hired to do, travel with the team when they go to different countries to be a liaison between the execs and the media. I didn't know South Sudan was on the agenda when I got the job, but honestly, it doesn't really matter. I don't have a choice, Bo. Can you go to your boss, commander, whatever, and tell him that you don't want to go to Chad? No. You can't. You do what you're told because it's your *job*!"

"My job and yours aren't the same," Bo protested, reaching up and grabbing hold of her finger so she couldn't poke him anymore. But he didn't squeeze it. Didn't shove her away. Simply held onto her finger gently.

"No, they aren't. But I just got this job. I actually like it. Enjoy talking to locals, encouraging them to see the good side of what my company does. I realize that some will think we're exploiting natural resources, but I truly believe the jobs it'll create, and the money it'll bring into the area, will help. I literally don't have a choice other than to go, Bo. Housing isn't cheap, and now I have to replace every single possession I own—as you well know! Money isn't going to rain down from the sky and fill my pockets. I have to work. I need this job more than ever. And right about now, I could use your support. Even your expertise, to tell me what I should and shouldn't do if anything goes wrong. Not your lectures and judgment and anger."

Wren was panting by the time she finished. She was also shaking. With frustration, fear, and worry.

Bo let go of her finger, then wrapped his arm around her waist and pulled her into him.

She was getting used to being surrounded by him like this. Plastered against his front, her nose buried in his chest.

"I'm sorry," he said quietly. "I just...*fuck*, Wren. I've been there. South Sudan. It's...not a place for someone like you."

"Someone like me?" she mumbled into his chest.

"Yeah."

He didn't elaborate. Wren wasn't sure she really wanted him to.

"Is there any chance this trip won't go as planned?"

She shrugged against him.

"When are you supposed to leave?"

"Just over two weeks."

"*Shit*. Look at me," he ordered.

Wren didn't want to. Wanted to close her eyes and avoid reality for a little longer. But life always seemed to have a way of kicking her in the ass. She lifted her head.

"Talk to your boss. I know you're new, but tell him that you know people, a team of SEALs, who are willing to come in and talk to the group that will be traveling to South Sudan. We can give you all tips on what to do if shit hits the fan. Violence, threats, kidnapping."

Wren froze. "What?"

"We can come to your offices. Meet with the group. Answer questions. Give advice."

"You'd do that? When you think it's a horrible idea that we're going in the first place?"

"It's definitely a horrible idea," Bo said. "But I understand not having a choice. I want you safe. As safe as you *can* be under the circumstances. If you have to go, I want you to have as much information as you can about what to do if things go south. Information is power, and I'm in the unique position to have information about the region you're going into."

Wren's eyes filled with tears.

"Don't cry. Please don't," Bo begged.

"I can't help it," Wren said as she lowered her forehead to his chest. She felt his hand push through her hair and cup the back of her head. His other hand pressed to her lower back, holding her against him.

"This isn't the way I envisioned this going," he muttered above her.

"Envisioned what going?" she asked softly.

"Courting."

Wren tilted her head back, but he didn't take his hand out of her hair. "Courting?" she asked with a small frown.

"Yeah. Usually when someone meets a person they're interested in, they take them out for coffee. Then maybe a dinner or two. Goodbye kisses at the door. Maybe a movie date where there's a little making out on a couch. Then another dinner, more romantic this time, some fancy restaurant with flowers and candles, and if he's lucky, he brings her back to his place and she lets him make love to her all night long. Then more dates, more loving...eventually they move in together, he proposes and they get married. Maybe have a kid or two and live happily ever after."

Wren's heart felt as if it was in her throat at his words. She'd never seen *any* of that for herself. She'd always felt too... broken. A happily ever after wasn't ever in her visions for her future. Maybe snatching some good times here and there, but she didn't think anyone would be able to put up with her quirks long term.

She wasn't sure what to say to him, but Bo didn't seem to expect a response. He went on.

"Instead, I whisk you to my house while you're unconscious, where you wake up in a strange location with a man you've never met. Haul you up to your balcony with a rope, break into your apartment, discover it's been trashed by a psycho, take you back to my house instead of to a hotel. You sleep on my sofa instead of a bed, and the next morning, I proceed to yell at you for something you have no control over."

"Honestly, this feels more appropriate for my life," Wren told him.

Instead of smiling at her joke, Bo frowned. "I don't know much about you, Wren Defranco, but what I *do* know is that you're strong as hell. The last couple of days has shown me that crystal clear. And if you forgive me, and let me start over, I want to court you properly. As properly as I can, considering we skipped a few steps and we're already living together."

Wren couldn't help but giggle at that. "Just until they get this Matt guy."

"Right."

Given his wry tone, she didn't know if he was agreeing

with her or arguing with her. But she supposed it didn't matter. "I probably really do need to start getting ready for work now. Even though it doesn't take me all day to shower and change, I'm guessing I'm going to be cutting it close in getting to work on time."

"I washed your clothes from yesterday, they're in the bathroom already. I'll get a bowl of cereal ready for you for when you get out. I'll take you to work and pick you up when you're done. If you give me your sizes, I can stop by My Sister's Closet and see if Julie can help pick out a few things for you until you have time to shop for yourself."

Wren was floored. "You want to get clothes for me?"

"Well, yeah. We can continue washing what you've got every night, but I'm guessing you don't want to wear the same thing every day for the next however many days."

That wasn't quite what Wren meant, but he wasn't wrong. "I can stop by a big box store and get some things," she told him.

"Or I could stop by my friend's store and get you some good stuff. It's not new, but it's still nice."

"Okay," Wren said softly. She was almost overcome with emotion. It wasn't the fact that Bo was going to get her clothes, it was more how he made what he was doing for her not seem like it was a big deal. For her, it was a *huge* deal. Her own mother didn't go out of her way to do anything for her daughter. She certainly didn't bother herself with what Wren was wearing.

"Talk to your boss," Bo told her, making it clear her pending trip to South Sudan was still very much on his mind.

"I will."

He pulled back slightly and moved his hand from her hair to her nape. He stared down at her for a long moment.

"What?" Wren asked.

"I want to kiss you."

Her heart skipped a beat and she licked her lips. His gaze tracked the movement before meeting hers once more.

"Yes," she said with a small nod.

Bo smiled a little before lowering his head. His lips brushed against hers in a chaste, sweet kiss. Then he looked her in the eyes before lowering his head once more. This time the kiss *wasn't* sweet. It was electrifying.

He licked her lips, asking for permission to enter, which Wren gave right away by opening to him.

He dominated the kiss, but not in an overbearing, macho kind of way. He groaned low in his throat, letting Wren know he was as overwhelmed by their instant chemistry as she was. She grabbed his shirt in her hand, wrinkling the material but needing something to hold onto as he took possession of her mouth.

His fingers tightened on the back of her neck as he held her and they kissed for what felt like forever. She felt surrounded by him. Safe.

She felt safe with Safe. There was nowhere she'd rather be than right here. In his arms. His tongue swirling with hers. His taste on her lips.

This time when he pulled back, they were both breathing hard.

He licked his lips and smiled gently at her. He ran his thumb over her bottom lip. "We might not be conventional, but I'm still definitely courting you. In case you didn't know."

"I'm okay with that."

"Good."

His hands dropped from her and he took a step backward. "Go shower, Wren. I'll have breakfast and coffee waiting."

Wren swallowed hard and nodded. Then she backed away, not wanting to lose eye contact with him. At the last minute, she turned and headed down the hallway toward the bathroom.

It was crazy how much her life had changed in the last couple of days. She'd gone on a first date, and ended up basically moving in with a different man that same night. But she couldn't help but think that she hit the jackpot.

Bo Cyders was a good man. Things might not work out between them long term, but she was going to enjoy the ride for as long as it lasted.

CHAPTER SEVEN

Wren felt as if she were eight years old again and called into the principal's office. Of course, back then, no one believed her when she told them what was going on in her house, but she wasn't that scared kid anymore. She was a grown-ass woman who was perfectly able to hold her own.

Maybe.

Okay, maybe not.

Colby Johnson intimidated her. Her boss was tall. And broad. And muscular. She was pretty sure he enjoyed using his size to loom over other people. As if simply because he was a large man, that somehow translated into him being better than others.

He had brown hair, brown eyes, and what seemed to be a perpetual frown on his face. She hadn't seen him in anything other than designer suits and ties. Colby was also a "loud-talker." Pretty much everyone in the office could hear him when he forgot to close his door.

It wasn't as if Colby was a bad boss. He wasn't. He had a way of getting his employees to go that extra mile. To voluntarily work overtime when there was an important project in the works. He was bold, brash, and had single-handedly started BT Energy.

He was also generous. Which was ultimately why Wren had taken the job. It was expensive to live in California, but her salary reflected that. She was making more here than she ever had at any other job. Of course, money wasn't everything, but in her interviews, Wren had also liked what she'd seen and heard. And her research had shown the company was very successful.

Even though she'd been there for a month, meeting with her boss was still intimidating for Wren. Especially when she had a feeling she knew what the outcome of this meeting would be. But Bo was generous enough to offer to meet with the group that was going to South Sudan, and since canceling the trip wouldn't happen, she figured maybe, just maybe, Colby would jump at the chance to get some intel from Navy SEALs.

"Good morning, Wren. What can I do for you?" Colby boomed from his seat behind his desk. It was a large piece of furniture. Taking up almost half the space in the room. There was a computer with three screens on one side, and papers strewn all over the rest of the surface. It was only ten in the morning, but he looked harried and stressed, which made Wren think this wasn't the best time to talk. But since they were supposed to leave for the African continent in a little over two weeks, she didn't have a choice but to talk to him sooner rather than later.

"Morning, Colby. I wanted to talk to you about our upcoming trip."

"You aren't going to try to talk me out of it again, are you?" he asked. His voice was calm enough, but she could hear the irritation under the words. He hadn't been happy when she'd brought up safety concerns previously.

"No, sir. I was talking to a friend, he's a Navy SEAL, and he offered to have his team come in and talk to those of us going to South Sudan about safety. About things we should and shouldn't do, and what to do if something happened." Wren said the words quickly and as unemotionally as she could, knowing the businessman in front of her would appreciate that, since he was always very busy.

"That won't be necessary. My security team is putting together a flyer for us and they'll be there in case anything happens. Is there anything else?"

Wren wanted to protest. Wanted to say that a stupid flyer wasn't going to make *her* feel any safer, but hearing from a group of SEALs who'd been in countless dangerous countries *would*. But she recognized a blowoff when she heard one. "No, that was it."

"Wren, we're all glad you're here. You're good with the media. You have a softer edge than the rest of us. But you were hired to be the face of BT Energy, not to make the heavy decisions that have to be made. I'm not saying that to be a jerk. Trust me, I'm not going to do anything that will jeopardize this deal or hurt my company. Things are going to be fine. We'll go to Africa, have a press conference, meet with a couple of bigwigs, participate in a few photo ops, then we'll leave millions of dollars richer. This pipeline is going to put us on the world's stage. You just have to trust me."

Yeah, that wasn't going to happen. Wren didn't trust easily.

But dutifully, she said, "Yes, sir."

"I sent you notes on some of the men we'll be meeting with. I've also emailed you some stats on South Sudan and their customs. Make sure you read everything carefully, the last thing we need is our PR person breaking some taboo on camera."

She nodded and turned for the door. At the last minute, she turned back. "Can I ask the others if they want to talk to my friend and his teammates with me?" She wasn't sure where she'd found the courage to ask, but if *she* heard after the fact that one of the people going to Africa had the kind of connections she did, and she wasn't asked if she wanted in on a safety meeting, she would be upset.

"I don't think it's necessary, but if you want to, feel free. Just not during work time and not here in the office. The last thing I want is word getting out that we hired the Navy as consultants. Would make it seem as if we don't trust our South Sudanese hosts."

She nodded and stepped out of Colby's office. She breathed a sigh of relief, but also of frustration. Being safety conscious didn't have anything to do with distrust of the people they were going to be meeting in Africa. It was simply a smart thing to do when you were going into a country that wasn't exactly stable.

Wren went back to her cubicle and brought up the information Colby had sent her. It took a while to read through it all. The South Sudanese people were generally stoic and private about their emotions. The cultural norm was to hide pain and struggles. Resilience, self-restraint, and physical courage were admired.

None of that came as a surprise to Wren. After years of violence in the country, those traits would be normal so families could try to stay under the radar of those who might wish to do them harm.

The material her boss had provided was interesting, but it wasn't really anything that would help her in her job while she was there. One thing she'd already been warned about was that media freedom was lacking. She'd have to be very careful about everything she said at the press conference. She wasn't to say anything negative; everything had to be framed in a positive light.

Sighing, Wren sat back and arched slightly, trying to work out the kinks she had from being hunched over her computer for so long. She jerked in surprise when her cell phone vibrated on the desk next to her notepad, then laughed at herself. Wren didn't get a lot of calls. She simply didn't know that many people, especially here in California, where she'd only been living for just over a month.

Thinking it had to be Bo—he'd insisted on getting her number when he dropped her off that morning—Wren looked at the screen. To her disappointment, it said "Unknown" instead of Bo's name. She wasn't in the mood to talk to a scammer or telemarketer, so she didn't answer. If it was someone important, she figured they'd leave a message.

"Hey, Wren."

She jumped what felt like two feet and spun around to see

Luke standing behind her cubicle. He had a smirk on his face, as if he enjoyed how badly he'd startled her. He was the youngest of the guys she was traveling with to South Sudan. At twenty-five, he seemed to think he was still in college. He frequently went out and got drunk during the workweek, and Wren had heard him bragging about the various women he'd picked up at bars more than once.

But he was also funny. And good-looking. And had been genuine in welcoming her to the company.

"How many times have I told you not to do that?" she scolded. "I'm totally getting you a bell to wear around your neck so I know you're coming up behind me."

He laughed, then said, "Moooooo."

Wren couldn't help but laugh.

"You get the forty-page document on culture we're supposed to memorize too?" he asked.

Wren grimaced. "Yeah. It's a lot for sure."

"I'm sure it'll be cool. We just have to be polite, don't make eye contact for too long, and I have to make sure not to touch any woman's shoulder, otherwise I'll find myself being hustled off to a hut to be married."

Wren rolled her eyes. "That's not true."

"All right, it's not, but all the rules still make me a little nervous."

She figured this was the perfect time to bring up Bo's offer. "Hey, I know a guy, he's a Navy SEAL. And when I told him about the trip, he was worried since there's a lot of stuff going on over there. He offered to meet with me and anyone else who wants to go over safety protocols. You know, what to do if something happens and how to stay safe. You want to meet his team with me?"

For a second, Wren thought Luke was going to agree. Then he stiffened right before someone stopped next to him.

"You scared, Wren?" It was Archie. He was the oldest of the group taking the trip. At fifty-two, he thought he knew everything about anything. And for some reason, Luke looked up to him.

He slapped Luke on the shoulder and chuckled. "The little woman is frightened of the bogeyman."

Wren frowned. "I'm not—"

But she didn't get a chance to finish her sentence as Archie said, "Luke, I could use a second set of eyes on the specs of the pipeline south of Juba. I'm thinking we'll need to move it a mile or so west because of flooding in the area and how swampy the ground gets."

"Sure. No problem, Arch."

The men turned to leave, but Luke turned back. He shrugged. "It's going to be fine, Wren. Nothing's going to happen. Colby's bringing a security detail. Besides, you'll be surrounded by all of us men at all times. It's all good. But sometime I want to hear the story about how you hooked up with a Navy SEAL." He wiggled his eyebrows suggestively.

Wren couldn't help but roll her eyes at the ridiculousness of her coworker. He was constantly on the prowl.

When she was alone in her cubicle once more, she sighed. If Archie got to the other guys going on the trip before she could talk to them, they'd probably turn down her offer as well.

Maybe she was being paranoid, but she didn't think so.

Especially when she remembered Bo's reaction to hearing where her company was taking her. If a Navy SEAL was uneasy and freaked out that she was traveling to a certain country, who was she to blow off his concerns?

Turning back to her computer, Wren decided to send an email to Aaron, Dallas, and Oliver. She'd extend the invitation to meet with Bo and his team. If they declined, that was fine. Regardless, she was eager to hear what the SEALs had to say.

She was halfway through sending the email when her phone vibrated again. Looking down, Wren saw it once more said the caller was Unknown. For the first time, a little niggling of worry hit her.

Surely Matt wouldn't be calling her...would he?

She hadn't given him her number. But that didn't mean he couldn't have found it. He'd been inside her apartment, it probably wouldn't have been hard for him to find something that had her phone number on it.

Biting her lip, Wren stared at her phone. It stopped ringing, but whoever was on the other end didn't leave a message.

It was probably a telemarketer. It wasn't Matt. Why would he call her?

Her mind made up that the next time she got an unknown call, she'd answer it, Wren turned back to the computer and the email she was writing to her coworkers.

* * *

"Yo!"

"It's about time you got here."

"What's up?"

Safe smiled as he walked toward his friends and teammates. Even though they had a few days off, they'd planned to meet at the beach to work out. He was a little late, since he'd taken Wren to work.

"Hey," he said as he approached the others. Blink was doing sit-ups in the sand with Flash. Smiley and MacGyver were doing burpees. Kevlar was standing next to Preacher, watching him as he approached.

"How are you feeling?" Safe asked Kevlar.

"Eyes are still bloodshot, but I'm good."

Everyone stopped what they were doing and stood, brushing off sand as they did so.

"So? What the fuck's going on?" Flash asked. "I get a call from Smiley this morning and he tells me that Kevlar got maced while at some chick's apartment with you?" He gestured to their team leader. "But Kevlar didn't want to tell us about it until you got here."

"Yeah. Some stuff has happened since I last saw you at Aces," Safe said.

"No shit, Sherlock," MacGyver said. "Start talking."

"We can talk and run," Kevlar informed them, gesturing to the beach.

Safe nodded, and the seven men started down the beach at a fast jog.

"Right, so, Wren, the woman who was drugged at Aces, spent the night at my place. We found out the asshat she was with stole her ID and keys out of her purse."

"Shit. So he knows where she lives," Smiley said.

"Exactly. I offered my place to her for a few nights while we get her locks changed and stuff, but she needed clothes and some of her things. I didn't think it was a good idea to just walk up to her apartment, so we went in through the back door," Safe said.

"The second-floor balcony door," Kevlar added.

"Aw, man, and you didn't call us to have some fun?" Smiley bitched.

"I figured seven men lurking in the bushes might draw a bit too much attention," Safe said with a small chuckle.

"You're probably right. Okay, go on," MacGyver said.

"So we got inside, but the place was already trashed. Fucker moved fast. Probably went over there right after he left the bar. And when I say trashed, I mean *trashed*. All her clothes were slashed, dishes were all broken, he knifed her furniture. It was a mess."

"Tell them about the panties and the conditioner," Kevlar said.

"I'm getting to that. Jeez," Safe complained. "Asshole had also taken all her underwear out of her drawer, piled it on her bed, and squirted a bunch of her conditioner on top. Her *white* conditioner."

"Gross."

"Ewwwww."

"That's some sick shit."

Safe agreed with his friends. "Yeah. Obviously was smart enough not to actually jack off on them, because DNA, but still. The fact that he wanted *Wren* to think that's what it was indicates this guy isn't your average weirdo."

"Please tell me Tex is on this," Flash asked.

"He is." It was Kevlar who answered. "But there's little to go on. This guy's smart. Didn't park in Aces' lot. Walked to the bar. And Tex tried to track where he went with traffic cameras, but he lost him a few blocks from the bar when he walked back into a neighborhood. And he walked to Wren's apartment too. No car on any cameras he appeared on that Tex could see. So that's a no-go."

"He already did his tracker thing from last night too?" Safe asked Kevlar.

"Yeah. When he heard what happened to Wren's place, he was pissed. Said he was making this a priority."

"Is she all right?" Blink asked.

Safe glanced at the newest member of their team. The man had been through hell on a mission where some of his previous teammates had been killed, the rest injured so badly they were medically retired from the Navy. He'd been on convalescent leave when Remi, Kevlar's girlfriend, had been kidnapped. If it wasn't for him being in the right place at the right time, and acting so convincingly, Remi wouldn't be with them today.

Kevlar had asked that Blink be assigned to their team, and he'd accepted. They all owed the man a huge debt of gratitude. If Remi had been hurt or killed, Kevlar would never have been the same. It was likely they would've lost him as a teammate.

Blink would never be the most talkative, but when he did speak, it was usually for a good reason.

"She's okay," Safe told him and the others. "Hanging in there. I was late because I dropped her off at work."

"Damn, she's tough if she insisted on going to work after everything that happened," Smiley said.

"She is," Safe agreed.

"So how'd Kevlar get maced?" Flash asked.

"While we were in her apartment, trying to figure out if we could salvage anything, her date returned. Probably to hide out in her place and wait for her. Or to see what other shit he could do to terrorize her. I tried to get her to hide under the bed while I went to help Kevlar subdue the guy, but she froze. And when I say froze, I mean she *froze*. Went into immediate panic mode." Safe didn't hesitate to tell his friends what happened. He trusted them with his life. Which meant he trusted them with *Wren's* life, and that was a huge deal.

"Why?" Blink asked.

"I'm not sure. It's too soon for her to open up to me...but she's let a couple things slip. About her childhood. It wasn't good. I think her mom was abusive, and she's been let down by a lot of authority figures in her life. Something about hiding under the bed brought back memories of doing that as a child...hiding from her mother's boyfriends."

"*Fuck*."

The vehement word from MacGyver summed up the situation pretty nicely.

"Yeah. Anyway, I slipped behind her bedroom door, and couldn't leave her because of how panicked she was, and Kevlar confronted the guy. Asshole had the mace ready and surprised him. Instead of chasing him as he ran off, Kevlar stayed to guard the door."

"See? You should've called us too," Smiley said.

Safe nodded. "In hindsight, I should've."

"So what's going on now?" Flash asked.

"A nosey neighbor heard the ruckus at the door and called the cops. They came, made a report, suggested Wren not go back to her apartment for a while until they could investigate and figure out who trashed the place."

"If Tex can't find him, they won't either," Blink said firmly.

Safe agreed with him. "So she's staying with me for now. I called Julie before getting here, and she agreed to pull together some things for Wren to tide her over."

"Remi would love to meet her. Help her get whatever else she needs," Kevlar volunteered.

"I appreciate it. I mean, we can probably get a lot of stuff online, but eventually she's going to need to replace literally everything. Dishes, pillows, bedding, every piece of furniture." Safe sighed. "Fucking asshole."

"So what now? She moves in and you play happy couple for a while? Then...?" Smiley asked.

Safe looked at his friend. Smiley had dark hair and overall looks...and kind of a dark vibe to go along with them. It wasn't surprising he sounded a bit cynical. "I don't know. We're taking things a day at a time. But I'll tell you this...I like her. A lot."

"Oh shit," Flash said with a grin. "First Kevlar, now you."

Instead of being offended, Safe merely shrugged. "If you think I'm going to get defensive and tell you there's no way anything serious will come out of this, you're wrong. Wren is...she's different. Vulnerable, yet tough as nails. I think whatever happened in her past, she's learned that she has no choice but to stand on her own. She has no idea what it's like to have someone at her back."

"And you want to show her," Smiley said.

"Yeah. I want to show her," Safe agreed.

"She's definitely different," Kevlar told the group. "I don't know what it is about her, exactly. But like Safe said, I felt a need to protect her, but at the same time wanted to stand back and watch her kick ass on her own. It's an interesting dichotomy."

"Well, shit. Now I want to meet her," MacGyver said.

"Me too," Flash agreed.

"I have an idea," Kevlar said.

Safe braced himself, not sure what his friend was about to suggest. He was a great team leader, but sometimes he also had some pretty wild ideas.

"Here we go," Preacher said under his breath.

Safe chuckled.

"I think we should show Wren what it's like to have people who will be there for her without strings. I know Remi will have no problem helping her out, but what if we got Caroline and the others involved too? You've already talked to Julie, so what if we bring in Alabama, Fiona, and Summer? And we know Jessyka will be in. She's so pissed that Wren was drugged at her bar, she's already gotten out the pitchforks."

"And Tex is already involved," MacGyver said with a nod. "I like it. We can talk to Wolf and the others as well. When we aren't around, they can act as escorts if needed."

Safe swallowed hard, suddenly overcome with emotion. These men didn't know Wren. Other than knowing he liked her and was impressed by her, she was a complete stranger. And yet, they were still willing to go above and beyond to try to show her that she wasn't alone.

He remembered something else he wanted to talk to his friends about.

"Thank you. I think that's a great idea. There's something else you can help me with."

"Anything, you know that," Kevlar told him.

"She just moved here to California and started a new job. She's the PR liaison for BT Energy."

Preacher whistled long and low. "Impressive," he said.

"Right? Well, they have a big trip coming up that she's going on. I guess a new gas pipeline is being installed—in South Sudan."

"Are you kidding me?"

"What the *fuck?*"

"You can't be serious."

"Wait—what?" Kevlar asked, stopping in his tracks. Everyone else stopped running and stood in the sand, staring at Safe.

He pressed his lips together and nodded. "Believe me, she knows exactly how I feel about her going over there. I was kind of a dick about it, but she doesn't have a choice. She just moved here, just got the job. Probably partly *because* of this trip. She can't say no."

"It's insane that anyone thinks it's a good idea to go over there. And putting workers in the country to set up a pipeline? That's a recipe for disaster with the way things are right now. Not saying they won't get better in the future, but the country is extremely volatile at the moment," Flash argued.

"I know. And she knows too. I think she's terrified, but trying to put on a brave face about it. I told her I'd be happy to go in and talk about safety with her boss and anyone else who's going. What to watch out for, what to do in case the worst happens."

"Her boss knows that foreigners are more likely to be kidnapped and held for ransom than the locals, right?" Smiley asked.

Safe shrugged. "I'm assuming so, yes."

"And that violence against women is common?" Flash added.

Safe nodded grimly.

"Fuck. This has disaster written all over it," Kevlar muttered.

Safe couldn't disagree. "I can only hope something happens in the next couple weeks that makes the trip impossible. I feel like a dick saying that, but it's true."

His friends all nodded.

"What do you need from us?" Blink asked.

"Will you come with me to talk to the group, if her boss agrees?"

"Of course."

"You don't even have to ask."

This was why he loved and respected these men so much.

"Speaking of Africa..." Kevlar said.

Everyone groaned.

"We already had a feeling this was coming, and I got official word this morning...even though we completed our objective in Chad, things haven't settled. They've gotten worse with the new guy taking over, actually. Or...the *not* new guy. Whatever. We're being sent back in."

"Fuck," MacGyver sighed. "When?"

"Most of the research we did for the last trip is the same. I don't have details yet, but we'll probably be wheels up in ten to twelve days."

Anxiety churned in Safe's belly. It was looking like he'd be gone when Wren went on her trip. It was somewhat ironic that they'd be on the same continent and in countries right next to each other. But it wasn't as if he'd be able to keep in contact with her.

"We'll talk to her, tell her everything she needs to know to stay safe," Kevlar told him, as if he could read the riotous emotions whirling through his brain.

"Yeah," Safe said.

But inside, he had a bad feeling. And no SEAL worth his Trident ignored those feelings.

"Not only that, but I bet some of Wolf's team would be happy to come too," Preacher said.

Safe nodded. He was grateful for his friends and the other SEALs, but nothing could quell the uneasy feeling in his gut.

"Safe," Kevlar said, approaching to put a hand on his shoulder. "Talk to us."

"I just...I'm thinking so many things. I just met this woman. I'm not sure why I'm so...invested."

"I know how you feel. I felt the same way about Remi. There was just something about her that made me *know* she was different. Special. And I was right. Don't discount your feelings. Is there any way at all that you can talk her out of this trip?"

Safe pressed his lips together and shook his head as he remembered the conversation from that morning.

"In that case, we'll make sure she has all the tools—figuratively and literally—that she needs to get through any situation. Tools that can escape the average person's scrutiny."

"Oh. This is gonna be fun," Smiley enthused. Then he

sobered. "I mean, it stinks that Wren will be in a potentially dangerous situation, but coming up with ways to hide survival tools on her will be an interesting challenge."

For the first time, Safe began to feel a little better about Wren's upcoming trip. He still didn't want her to go, but he understood better than most that she really didn't have a choice. And if she had to go, at least he and his friends could make sure she, and the people traveling with her, had the necessary means to get out of any kind of shit-hits-the-fan situation. Because the truth was, there was a higher-than-average chance of things going south.

South Sudan. *Shit*. Her boss must be insane.

"Right, so how about we think of ways to outfit Safe's woman while we're working out?" Kevlar said in his I'm-the-boss voice.

Everyone laughed, but immediately resumed their run.

Safe's mind worked as his friends bantered back and forth while they ran. If he was shipping out in less than two weeks, he had a lot of work to do. Help figure out who this Matt guy was and make Wren's apartment safe, help her replace her belongings, get to know her better, show her that she wasn't alone anymore, that she had him and his friends at her back, teach her how to be safe in a volatile country, and help Kevlar and the others plan their own mission back to Chad.

There wasn't nearly enough time to do everything that needed to be done. Especially with both him and Wren working full time.

But he'd do it. He had to. Safe had a feeling if he didn't figure out how to fit everything in, it would haunt him for the rest of his life.

CHAPTER EIGHT

Wren waited inside her office building for Bo. He'd sent her a text asking her to please not wait outside, to stay in the lobby until he pulled up. Of course, that had Wren worrying all over again. Her phone had rung once more earlier this afternoon with an unknown number, but she'd chickened out in answering it. She didn't want to deal with neither Matt nor a scammer. She had to hope that Matt, if it was him calling, would eventually get tired of messing with her and simply disappear.

But since the man had been in her apartment—where he'd snapped her work ID in half, while breaking everything else—he obviously knew where her office was located. And the last thing she wanted was to have a confrontation with him on the sidewalk. So she had no problem waiting inside until Bo arrived.

Eventually, after she replaced her car keys, she'd have to

start driving herself to and from work, but for now she was perfectly all right with Bo chauffeuring her around.

Their plans for the evening included going to that shop that he and his friend had mentioned, My Sister's Closet, to see if she could find anything appropriate to wear to work. She had to look polished and professional, and the thought of all the clothes she'd painstakingly picked out being shredded on her closet floor made her heart hurt.

Not only that, but she needed everyday clothes as well. Jeans. T-shirts. Fat pants. Underwear. The thought of picking out panties and bras with Bo nearby made her blush. It shouldn't. She was a grown-up. But she couldn't help but be embarrassed. She wasn't well endowed and had always struggled to keep weight on. Most women would love to be in her shoes, but after a lifetime of hearing comments about her being flat as a board, too skinny, not curvy like a real woman, it was hard to think of herself as sexy.

Wait...why was she even thinking about *that*? She should be thinking about nothing other than the giant mess her life was right now. She had a potential stalker who wanted to do who-knew-what to her, who'd broken into her apartment and destroyed all her stuff; she was still getting to know the ins and outs of a new job; and she was traveling to a country the State Department had deemed too dangerous to visit. She shouldn't be thinking about the man who'd selflessly taken her under his wing and given her a sanctuary when her life had gone to shit.

But she couldn't help it. Bo was...different. Different from the men she'd known in her past. He was honorable. It was kind of an old-fashioned word, but it was true. Feeling safe around men wasn't something Wren was used to. But with Bo? That's exactly how she'd felt pretty much from the moment they'd met.

The text tone on her phone dinged at the same time she saw Bo's Jeep Wrangler pull up at the curb. She waved at the security guard on duty before heading for the doors. Bo jumped out and ran around his Jeep, opening the passenger door.

Wren smiled at him and climbed in. He held out the seat belt for her before closing the door and running back around to the driver's side.

"How was your day?" he asked.

Wren shrugged. "Fine."

Bo touched her arm briefly, making her look at him. "I wasn't asking to be polite," he told her. "I really want to know. It had to be difficult. Going back right after our conversation and what happened at Aces and your apartment. And I didn't mean to put more worries in your head than you probably already had about your upcoming trip. So...how was your day?"

This man.

Wren swallowed hard, trying to compose herself. In the past, she'd always assumed people really weren't interested in hearing the truth when they asked questions like that. If they asked how she was, she always simply said fine. But it seemed as if Bo truly wanted to know about her day.

"It was...kinda hard. I couldn't stop thinking about all the things I needed to do. All the stuff I need to replace. I also talked to Colby, my boss. He wasn't interested in having you and your friends talk to us about the trip. I'm sorry."

Bo pressed his lips together before pulling away from the curb. "What else?"

"Well, I did ask him if he would be okay with me and the other guys who will be on the trip meeting with you and talking safety, and he said that would be fine, as long as we didn't do it during work hours."

"Magnanimous of him," Bo muttered.

"I know he sounds like a jerk, but he's actually a good boss," Wren said, eager to defend Colby. "This contract is going to put BT Energy in the big leagues, and it's really important."

"Important enough to cost the lives of possibly himself and his employees?" Bo asked.

Wren looked down at her lap. He was right. While this was an important contract, it wasn't worth anyone getting hurt.

"Sorry. I'm sorry," Bo said, shaking his head. "I'm still trying to come to terms with you going to freaking South Sudan. So when are we meeting with you and the others?"

"Um...we aren't," Wren told him.

"What? Why?"

"They aren't interested. I think I probably could've talked some of them into it, but Archie got to them first. Made it sound like I was being all girly-girly by being afraid to travel to a foreign country."

"Idiots."

Wren shrugged. She actually liked her coworkers, but she had to agree that going into a situation when you didn't have all the information you could wasn't exactly smart.

"Fine. We'll tell you everything you need to know, and if shit goes south, you can tell them what to do."

"Seriously?" she asked.

"Yeah. They'll be looking to you because you'll have the tools and knowledge to get them out of whatever shitstorm comes your way."

"Um...no, they won't. They already dismiss a lot of things I say, and if something happens, they're *definitely* not going to suddenly look to me for answers or help."

Bo sighed. "Okay. Then my team and I will focus on your safety. If you can help the others, if they *let* you help them, great. If not, at least you'll know how to take care of yourself."

"Thank you."

Bo looked over at her. "Don't thank me. I'm being selfish. I want you to come back home safe and sound. Besides, if you think you're taking one step out of this country *without* me grilling you about what to do and what not to do, you're as crazy as your boss."

For some reason, Wren laughed.

"I'm being serious," he warned.

"I know. And I appreciate it. More than you'll know. I promise to listen to everything you have to say."

"Not just me. The entire team."

"What?"

"We're all going to have a sit-down. Tell you what we know. Talk about different scenarios. It's how we plan for our own missions. We discuss the good, bad, and ugly, and the different ways we might react to any given situation. We're going to do the same with you."

"I don't want to be a bother," Wren said softly.

"You could never be a bother. Oh, and I should probably tell you that there might be one or two of our former SEAL friends there too. Not sure who can make it. It depends on when we set it up. And Tex will probably want to patch in via video or phone as well."

"I...Bo, I don't think all this is necessary for just me."

"You're wrong. I'd call in whoever it took to satisfy myself that you have all the knowledge and tools you need to keep yourself safe. I told you before that I liked you, and being apart from you for the last eight hours hasn't suddenly changed how I feel. I want to see where things between us can go, and that can't happen if you disappear into the wilds of Africa."

"Disappear?" she choked out.

"Yeah."

Wren swallowed hard. She knew what he meant. Kidnappings of foreigners was on the rise in South Sudan. The last thing she wanted was to be one of the unfortunate on that list. "Okay. Since you were brave enough to say it, I can admit that I feel the same. I like you too, Bo."

"Good. I'll set the meeting up with the guys. You hungry?"

Wren's mind spun. How had they gone from talking about the possibility of her being kidnapped, to them liking each other, to food? "Yeah."

"Do you like Mexican?"

"Um...who *doesn't* like Mexican?" she retorted.

His lips twitched. "Right. So we'll stop at My Sister's Closet and pick up the things Julie put aside for you to try, then we'll go eat. Okay?"

"What things?"

"No clue. I talked to her this morning and told her a little about your situation and gave her your sizes. She said she'd see what she could put together. Got a text from her before I picked you up, saying she was ready for us to come by."

"Julie is who again?" Wren asked.

"She's the former commander's wife. I'd invite her to come to our meeting to talk about your trip, but honestly, she didn't fare well when she was kidnapped in Mexico. So she's probably not the best person to talk to. But, before you get all worried, she's okay now."

"Wait, *what*? She was kidnapped?"

"A long story for another time. But I promise to tell you all about her and Fiona's experience at the hands of sex traffickers, and how they were rescued by Cookie and his team. Along with Caroline, Summer, Cheyenne, and Jessyka's stories. Come to think of it, hearing about Tex's wife, and her experience with a stalker, might be good too."

"You're kidding, right?"

"Unfortunately, no. But they're all great now. Happy. Married. With families."

"Holy crap."

Bo just smiled as he drove.

My Sister's Closet turned out to be a cute little storefront tucked into the heart of the old-fashioned downtown area of Riverton. Bo found a parking spot on the street and took Wren's hand as they walked to the front door of the store.

It felt natural and right to hold his hand. Wren had held hands with men before, but with Bo, it felt like something they'd done every day for the last ten years. She'd just met the man. How she could feel so at ease with him after everything that had happened was a mystery. But for once, she refused to question it. Her life felt a little out of control at the moment, and she'd learned long ago when to just go with the flow and do what she could to keep her head above water.

A bell tinkled as Bo pushed open the door and Wren stepped into an adorable little shop. There were racks of clothes everywhere, and the store was bright and cheery. Nothing like any secondhand thrift store she'd ever been in. She expected it to smell musty and have items haphazardly stacked on shelves or jumbled on racks. But My Sister's Closet looked like any other high-end women's clothing shop. Not that she'd seen too many in person, but still.

"Safe!" a woman exclaimed as she came out from a room in the back.

"It's good to see you, Julie," Bo said. He stepped away from Wren and greeted the woman with a kiss on the cheek before he came back to Wren's side and took her hand once more.

Julie was shorter than Wren, and slight. She was a tiny thing, actually, but she seemed to have a huge personality.

"And you must be Wren!" she exclaimed.

"I am," Wren agreed.

"You're just as pretty as Safe said you were. He also said you and I had about the same build, except you were taller, which isn't surprising as almost *everyone* is taller than me. I hope you don't mind, but he also told me you were a PR rep, so you needed classy clothes that would look good not only on your frame, but on TV and in pictures too. So I went through what we had, and I think I found some good stuff. It's in the back. I'll have Safe grab it for you. Take it home, see what works and what doesn't. You can bring back anything you don't want or that doesn't fit."

"Oh, thank you," Wren said in surprise. "I can just look through it here..."

"No, no, no. Take it all with you. Take your time. Sometimes things look and feel different in a store than when you're at home. It's not a big deal, really."

It *was* a big deal, and Wren wasn't sure what to say. She was shocked by the woman's kindness.

"Did you put in some casual stuff as well as work clothes?" Bo asked, preventing Wren from having to say anything. Not that she could in her sudden emotional state.

"Yup. Jeans are harder to size without trying them on, but I put in a few pairs. Along with T-shirts, and some pants and shorts to lounge in. Oh! And I probably overstepped, but after Safe told me what happened to your apartment, I figured you probably needed some underthings too? On my lunch break, I went to the lingerie store down the street and picked up some underwear and a few bras. I got two sports bras, because they're easier to size, but I did get you a T-shirt bra too...I think that's what they're called? I have a few and they're *super* comfortable."

"Thanks, Julie," Bo said.

"Of course! If you want to go and start grabbing the bags from the back, I'll wait here with Wren. They're the ones just to the right of the door."

"Will do," Bo said. He squeezed Wren's hand, then he was striding toward the door Julie had appeared from.

Wren wasn't sure what to say. This woman had gone above and beyond for a stranger. She hadn't been the recipient of such generosity very often in her life. "Thank you so much for everything," she managed to say.

"Of course," Julie repeated. "Anything for a friend of Safe's. He's amazing. As are all his friends. Patrick, my husband, talks about them all the time. He's retired now, but I know he sometimes misses it. The camaraderie. Once a SEAL, always a SEAL. And Wolf and his team saved my life, even though I was a complete bitch to them. I'm grateful they gave me a chance to apologize for my behavior. I've made it my mission in life to give back ever since. Not only to them, but to anyone who's down on their luck. I mean, I would've helped you even if you hadn't had your apartment broken into, but...shoot. I'm saying this all wrong," Julie said, suddenly sounding miserable.

"No, you aren't," Wren said quickly. "I understand." Looking around, she scrambled for something else to say to put Julie at ease. She spotted a poster on the wall. "Oh, you donate dresses to high schoolers who don't have anything to wear to their formal dances?"

"Yes! It's awesome. You wouldn't believe how the girls light up when they see themselves in a dress they wouldn't otherwise be able to afford."

"Actually, I would. I could've used a program like that when I was in high school," Wren admitted.

"Yeah?"

"I was in the foster program, and the family I was living with during high school couldn't afford dresses for their foster kids to attend big events like that."

"Did you get to go to a formal dance?" Julie asked.

Wren shrugged. She hadn't thought through to the end of

the story when she'd brought up the topic. "I went to one. In the badly fitting hand-me-down dress of one of the daughters who'd graduated five years before."

Julie winced. "Ouch."

"Yeah. It wasn't great." That was an understatement, but Julie didn't need to hear the story about how her date had ditched her at the dance to go drinking with his buddies because he was embarrassed to be seen with her.

"Well, that's one of the original reasons why I started my store. To help out the kids. But it's become much more than that. I only accept gently used designer clothes and useful household items. Not the junk that people want to get rid of when they're moving and wonder why they bought it in the first place."

Both women laughed just as Bo stepped back into the store. His arms were full of at least half a dozen shopping bags.

"Oh crap," Wren breathed at seeing all the clothes overflowing in the bags.

"I know it's not as much as you need, but when I get more donations in your size, I can let you have first dibs," Julie said, misinterpreting Wren's exclamation.

"I'll come back and grab the others when I get these in the Jeep," Bo told her.

"There's more?" Wren gasped.

"Just a few bags," Julie said. "I wanted to make sure you had plenty to choose from and you didn't have to settle for something you didn't love."

Wren was literally speechless. She figured Julie might have found a few outfits, but by the looks of the overflowing bags, she'd included enough to completely replace Wren's entire closet, plus some.

"I'll be right back," Bo told them as he backed out the front door.

"You want a snack?" Julie asked. "I have some stuff in the back I can get. I keep finger foods on hand for people who might be hungry while they shop."

"Bo and I are going out to eat when we leave here," Wren said.

"Oh, cool."

Wren wasn't sure what else to say. She wasn't good at small talk. But luckily she didn't have much time to stress about it because Bo returned quickly. He smiled at her, then headed to the back room. He returned much quicker this time, and only had one arm loaded with a handful of bags. He walked toward Wren and took her hand in his free one. "Thanks again, Julie. You're a lifesaver."

"If you need anything else, just let me know. I'll see what I can do."

"I appreciate it," Wren told her before Bo could.

Julie smiled. "I hope to see you again. Maybe at one of the SEAL beach barbeques. They're awesome."

"Maybe," Wren hedged.

"I'll be sure to bring her to the next one," Bo told her. Then he pulled Wren toward the door. "Gotta go. I'm starving," he called out to Julie.

The other woman laughed. The last thing Wren saw when she turned back right before the door closed was Julie smiling as she typed something on her phone.

"She's texting Caroline and the others," Bo told her.

"Why?"

"To gloat that she got to meet you first."

"Um...not sure that's gloat-worthy."

"Sure it is," Bo said with a smile. "She knows you're special to me. And she wants to spread the gossip that I've got a girl."

"You have a girl?" Wren repeated, feeling as if she was in the twilight zone.

"Yeah. You think I hold hands with *every* woman I meet in a bar, take home, infiltrate her apartment via covert means, and invite to live with me for the indefinite future?"

Wren couldn't help but smile at that. "Um, I'd hope so?"

Bo chuckled. "Yeah, okay, when I say it out loud, I'd hope so too. But trust me when I say I don't usually do any of those things. So you're special, and Julie knows it. And soon, all the others will know it too. Come on, I really am hungry. Kevlar kicked our butts today on the beach, and then I did some research into things you could bring with you on your trip."

Wren couldn't keep the small smile off her face as Bo towed her toward his Jeep. Her life had taken the weirdest turn, but it certainly didn't suck.

CHAPTER NINE

"I'm so stuffed," Wren complained as she sat on Safe's couch.

He grinned. He was just as full as she was, but it was worth it. They'd talked for hours as they ate chips and salsa and devoured tacos. He'd learned a little more about the woman sitting next to him, but he still wanted to know more. She'd mostly talked about her past jobs and how she'd ended up taking the position here in California.

The only bad part of the night was when her phone had rung. He'd expected her to answer, but when she looked at the screen, she'd stiffened slightly...and frowned. She shrugged it off, saying it was just another unknown number, probably a telemarketer, but for some reason her reaction seemed too concerned for a simple sales call. But then she'd asked how he'd become interested in the Navy and being a SEAL, and he'd put the call to the back of his mind.

Now they were at his house, lounging on his couch, trying to recover from eating too much food.

"I love Mexican food, but I don't eat it a lot because I simply can't control myself," Safe said.

Wren chuckled. "Right? Only a heathen can leave chips in the bowl and salsa uneaten."

Silence fell between them, but it was a comfortable silence. Safe hadn't felt this at ease with another person, other than his SEAL team, in a long time.

"Bo?"

"Yeah?"

"Thank you."

"For what?"

"Everything. For helping me in Aces. For making me feel as safe as possible when I woke up in a strange place. For taking me to my apartment to get my stuff. For not making it weird when I freaked out about getting under the bed. Talking to the police with me. Taking me to work and picking me up. Getting me clothes. Offering to teach me stuff about being safe. *Everything.*"

Safe wanted to tell her that everything she'd just listed off were things any normal, decent person would do, but even he knew that wasn't true. So instead, he simply said, "You're welcome."

"Will you tell me more about your sister?"

"Susie?" Safe asked in surprise.

"Unless you have another one?"

He chuckled and settled deeper into the couch, his head resting on the cushion behind him, his legs stretched out, his hands resting on his belly. "No, Suz is the only sister I have. Thank goodness. She's a pain in the butt."

"She is?" Wren asked, sounding surprised.

"No, not really. But I think all siblings are supposed to think that. It's a rule or something."

"I always wanted a brother or sister," Wren said wistfully.

Safe wanted to know more. But he didn't push. "She's four years younger than me. Twenty-eight."

"And she has two kids?" Wren asked.

"Uh-huh. She was assaulted her freshman year. Went to a party and that's where her drink was spiked. The guy who did it took her upstairs to his room, and two of his friends followed. As I told you before, they were caught because one of them filmed it all." Safe took a deep breath. Even thinking about what his sister went through enraged him all over again.

"She was determined to follow through with pressing charges. It was extremely difficult on her. She dropped out of school and got a job close to home. For a while, we weren't sure if she would be able to pull through. But we underestimated her. Yes, she still has some issues today. I told you about being afraid of the dark and having issues when she meets new people. But she's funny, the greatest mom ever, and somehow she still has that sweet, innocent quality she always had."

"I want to ask something, but I don't want to be offensive," Wren said quietly.

"Ask," Safe encouraged.

She nodded but didn't say anything for the longest time. Safe took the opportunity to study her. She was curled up at the other end of the couch, leaning against the armrest. She had a pillow clutched in her lap and was staring into space. Her short black hair was a bit mussed, and her brown eyes held a wealth of emotion that Safe couldn't begin to interpret.

"Her oldest is five, right?" Wren finally asked.

"Yeah. Anders. Inez, her daughter, is three."

"So that means she had him when she was twenty-three. Conceived him when she was twenty-two. You said she was attacked when she was a freshman. So she was probably what, eighteen? Nineteen?"

"Yeah."

Wren looked at him. "So...she got over what happened in like, three years?"

Safe wasn't offended by her question. If he didn't know his sister, and Tomas, his brother-in-law, he'd be curious as well. "She didn't get over it. Not like you might be thinking. What happened will always be a part of her. It changed her in a way that makes me incredibly sad. But she was determined not to let those men rob her of living her life.

"She met Tomas when she was working in the grocery store in our hometown. She stocked shelves, and Tomas was a manager there. They clicked. Almost immediately. He was patient with her. Didn't push her for anything she wasn't ready to give. It took a while for Susie to agree to go out with him, and to Tomas's credit, he didn't blink an eye when their first date was at my parents' house, with not only our mom and dad there, but me too."

"You?" Wren asked.

"Yeah. I was stationed in Virginia, but there was no way I was going to miss being there for Susie. She asked if there was any way I could get leave to come meet the man she thought she might want to date. Of course I was there."

Wren was looking at him in a way Safe didn't understand.

"What're you thinking?" he asked her.

"I just...honestly? I don't understand that. At all. I mean, your parents were there. Why would you spend the money and take the time off just to go home for a dinner?"

"Because Susie asked me to," Safe said. "And because I knew what a big step that was for her, and that she was terrified. First, she had to have the meeting in a safe place for her, and that was the home where she grew up. Tomas couldn't do anything, like spike her drink, with her family around. And I think she wanted reassurance from her family that he was as good a guy as she hoped he was."

"Hmmm."

Safe didn't know what that low sound meant, but he went on. "Bless Tomas, he didn't blink an eye at the odd arrangement. He was a perfect gentleman, and their next four dates were also with my parents in attendance. My brother-in-law is perfect for Susie. They complement each other. She's a terrible cook, and he loves spending hours getting a meal just right. He doesn't like to drive, and she enjoys the freedom of it. They're both pretty low-key and low-maintenance, and when she has bad days—and yes, of course she has them—he does what he needs to do to help her get through them. Anders was a surprise for them both, but a much-loved surprise. They didn't get married until after he was born."

"I'm glad she found him."

"Me too," Safe agreed.

He could tell something else was on Wren's mind. But he didn't push. The woman next to him was strong and stoic on the outside, but he had a feeling just under the surface, she had a lot of churning emotions.

What she said next made Safe realize he was right. And

the sort of deep anger he experienced at his sister's trial came back all over again.

"Her home, *your* home, being a safe place isn't something I understand either. Mine was a house of horrors, and I can only hope it's long been destroyed. Burned down, bulldozed. Something."

Safe sat up. This was a heavy conversation for two people who recently met, but the longer he knew Wren, the less odd their connection felt. "If you want to talk about it, I'm willing to listen," he told her.

"It's not a pretty story," she warned. "I mean, it's probably not something two people who like each other and who just met should be talking about so soon."

"Screw that," Safe said urgently. "I think our meeting has been anything but normal anyway."

"True."

When she didn't speak after a moment, Safe got up. He went to the kitchen and put a cup of water in the microwave. As it was heating, he got a mug down from the cabinet and filled it with hot chocolate. When the water was boiling, he removed it from the microwave and poured it over the powdered chocolate. After stirring the drink, he turned off the overhead light and returned to the couch. The room felt softer with the light off. Less intimidating, maybe? All Safe knew was that he wanted to make Wren feel comfortable.

"What's this for?" she asked softly after taking a small sip of the drink he'd made for her.

"One thing I've learned from my sister and my mom is that chocolate helps almost any situation."

Wren's lips curled in a small smile. "I think they aren't wrong," she told him.

"I'm not going to judge you, Wren. I might have had a good childhood, amazing parents, but that doesn't mean I'm not aware of the shit that happens to people. I've seen my share of horrible situations while on missions. Children begging on the streets. Women being abused. Suffering. Starvation. I help when I can, but each and every time I see something like that, it hurts my heart."

After a moment, Wren spoke. She looked into her mug of hot chocolate instead of at him, and there was nothing Safe wanted more than to take her into his arms, but he'd give her all the space she needed to say what she needed to say.

"I don't know who my father was. I think I was around four or five when my mom told me that he was a random guy she met in a bar. She screwed him, then stole his wallet when she left him sleeping in the motel they'd gone to. She told me he was no good, had done time in prison for murder, and that I was lucky she'd realized she was pregnant too late to abort me."

"Fuck, Wren."

"There were times I wished she had. Gotten rid of me, that is. She didn't love me. Not even a little. I was always a burden. She told me that all the time. Told me I was stupid when I didn't understand my homework, resented having to spend money to feed me. And *especially* hated that having me around was sometimes a deterrent to her getting laid. She'd go out and find some random man, bring him home, fuck him all night. If he was a good fuck, she'd keep him around for as long as possible. Playing the part of the poor single mother.

She'd parade me out when it was convenient, but most of the time she made me stay in my room."

Screw not touching her. Safe moved closer and reached for one of her hands. Thankful when she didn't pull away, Safe held her hand tightly as she continued.

"I recognized the feeling of being drugged when I was in Aces because my mom used to do that to me all the time. She'd put stuff in my drink or my food. She wanted me out of the way, quiet and unable to tell anyone what she was doing. I'd go to my room and lie on my bed and feel the room spinning. For the longest time, I didn't understand where those feelings came from. But when I finally figured out that I only felt that way after my mom cooked, I stopped eating the things she made for me. I'd make my own dinner, making sure to only use foods that were sealed."

Safe felt sick. And outraged on Wren's behalf. "How old were you?"

Wren shrugged. "Six? Seven, maybe?"

The Mexican food he'd eaten earlier threatened to come back up. "And the hiding-under-the-bed thing?"

"When I was around eight, some of the men she brought home started expressing...interest in me. They'd sit next to me on the couch and put their hand on my thigh, or play with my hair. My mom thought it was *funny*. She sat me down one night and told me that men were only interested in one thing—and they'd pay good money to get it. She explained what sex was, and informed me that the time was coming when she'd expect me to contribute to the household. She said I could start out with blowjobs. She seemed almost giddy at the idea of how much money she could make by prostituting her own kid out for sex."

"Are you fucking kidding me?" Safe asked. The question was harsh, but he managed to keep his tone mostly level and even.

"No. She wanted her eight-year-old to have sex with the men she brought home because she knew the perverts would pay. I, of course, didn't want to do that. The guys who hung around our house were gross. Overweight or missing teeth or smelly. I started spending as much time as I could at school. Joined after-school programs, forged my mom's signature. Did everything I could...but I still had to go home eventually. That's when I started hiding under my bed. Trying to stay away from whomever Mom was screwing each night."

Safe scooted closer to Wren. "Did they..." His voice trailed off. He couldn't even think about what she might have suffered.

"No. I went to my teacher first, told her what was going on, but I think she thought I was making it up. I mean, who would ever believe any mom would do that to their daughter? Then I called the child abuse line one day. The police came out to talk to Mom. She turned on the charm, and they believed her. Made up a story about how I was constantly lying to get attention. Showed them around the house. It was clean enough, my room looked like a normal girl's room to them, I guess.

"The police sat me down and warned me about lying, how I could go to jail for telling fibs. Then they left. That night... Mom was extra pissed. She put something in a glass of water and forced me to drink it. Literally sat on me and poured it down my throat. I knew that was it for me. If I stayed there, she'd let some man do whatever he wanted. So I ran away."

"How old were you?" Safe asked.

"Ten. And I didn't get very far at first. I passed out under a bush in a park, about a mile from our house. I woke up the next day, disoriented and dizzy. I was still under that bush. There was a bird staring at me when I looked up into the branches. I decided then and there that I was done. I wasn't ever going back to that house. I knew what would happen if I did. So I walked for miles. I didn't know where I was going or what I was going to do, I just wanted to get away. It was scary, but I was more afraid of my mom finding me than I was the people on the streets.

"I stayed for a few nights with a mentally ill woman, who was actually really nice. She shared the little food she had, and I stayed in her tent. But then she disappeared, and I was on my own again. Eventually, a couple of the homeless people I was hanging around with decided I was just too young to be on the streets, and they took me to a police station.

"I told them my name was Wren Defranco—that was the surname of the woman I stayed with for those first few nights. And I have no idea if the bird in that bush I woke up under was a wren or not, but I couldn't tell them my real name, because then they'd call my mom to come get me. When they found no record of me, and no missing children's reports, I was put into the foster care system...and that was that."

Safe was honestly stunned. This woman...she...*fuck*, he couldn't even think.

"Honestly? My life in the foster system was much better

than what it had been. I always had a roof over my head. I didn't have to worry about being drugged. And most places were decent. The reason I asked that question about your sister earlier is because it took a long time for me to have any desire to be with a guy. Years and years, way later than most teen girls start thinking about boys. The things my mom told me about sex were scary, and they stuck in my head. I was a weird teenager, and I kept to myself. I certainly didn't date. I can't image Susie going through what she did and then getting into a relationship so soon after...you know."

Safe wasn't sure what to say. He was grappling with some pretty extreme emotions at the moment. Fury at her mom. Disbelief that a ten-year-old was living on the streets. Awe at Wren's unbelievable strength and resilience.

"I didn't tell you all that for you to feel sorry for me. I'm fine. I got through it. I'm *nothing* like my mother. I got jobs to support myself, took classes at a community college, and worked my ass off to get where I am today."

Safe squeezed her hand. "I'm in awe of you. You're amazing."

But Wren shook her head. "No, I was in survival mode for so long, I was doing whatever I needed to do to keep putting one foot in front of the other."

"Right—which makes you amazing. You ever hear from her again?"

Wren knew who he was talking about. "No. And I don't want to. I don't care where she is or what she's doing."

Thoughts swirled through Safe's head. About getting her mom's name. Having Tex find her. About going to wherever the bitch was now and making sure she knew she was a piece of shit, and how amazing her daughter was, despite her upbringing.

But he quickly dismissed those thoughts. If Wren didn't want to have anything to do with her mom again, he'd respect that.

"Wren?"

"Yeah?"

"I'd like to hug you. If that's okay."

She looked up at him through her lashes, then turned and put the now empty mug on the table next to where she was sitting. Then she leaned toward him.

Safe closed his eyes as her arms wound around him. He hugged her back, lowering his head and burying it into the crook between her neck and shoulder. He took a deep breath. Then another.

His life had changed the moment this woman had fallen into his arms in that hallway in Aces Bar and Grill. And tonight, it had changed again. So much about the little things she'd said made sense now. Wren had been to hell and back, and amazingly, she'd come out the other side dented and banged up, but whole. He made a mental vow to be the kind of man, friend, she could depend on.

Wren pulled away slightly, and Safe immediately loosened his grip. "Thank you for listening. For not judging me."

"Our experiences make us who we are," Safe said. "Take Blink, for example. He doesn't talk much, but when he does, his words have purpose. And Susie. She has scars from what happened, but she didn't let it keep her from opening her heart. My parents are now overprotective, even though Susie was an adult when she was assaulted. And you, Wren

Defranco, are a beautiful example of resiliency. I respect the hell out of you."

She blushed and looked down.

"Look at me? Please?"

Her gaze lifted to his.

"I'm sorry for being overbearing this morning. About your job and your upcoming trip."

But Wren shook her head. "Don't be. You saying what you did validated the concerns I already had. I mean, people at work are acting like it's not a big deal, and I was starting to question my own worries about the trip. You going all macho protective made me realize I wasn't crazy."

"You aren't crazy. But it wasn't my place to insist you not go. As you said, it's your job. And there are plenty of places I go that I don't want to, but have to because it's what I'm ordered to do. My team and I are going to do everything in our power to make sure you have the knowledge to get through it. Okay?"

She quickly nodded. "I appreciate it. Even if my coworkers think it's silly and overkill, I want to know everything you have to tell me."

"It might mean some long nights, for both of us. Between you with your work and me with mine. We're gearing up to head out again, like I mentioned at dinner. So I'm not sure what our schedule will be like. And I'm not going to forget about this psycho Matt either. I'll get you a key to my place tomorrow and we'll figure out transportation for you. We can get a new key for your car, but will you let me arrange for my friends to pick you up from work? I can take you most mornings, but how late I work will be a crapshoot while we're preparing for a mission."

"You don't have to—"

"I know. But I want to. Please let me make sure you get home safe. You'll never have to be solely responsible for your safety again, not if I can help it."

Her eyes filled with tears.

"No! Don't cry! I can't stand it when women cry. It tears me up inside."

Wren chuckled. "Sorry."

Safe gently wiped her cheek with his thumb when a tear fell. Then he slowly leaned forward, giving her time to object, and kissed her forehead. "Your life changed when you asked me for help, Wren. For the better. I know that sounds conceited as hell, but I'm going to do everything in my power to make up for the first years of your life by giving you anything you need."

"I don't need you to give me anything," she told him. "I just need someone I can trust. Who won't let me down."

"I wish I could promise to always be that person, but I'm not perfect. I'll eventually do something boneheaded that will probably disappoint you. But I *can* promise that you can trust me. If I screw up, you need to tell me, although I'll probably already know. Give me a chance to prove to you that not everyone is like those fuckerheads you knew growing up."

Wren smiled at the word. "They *were* fuckerheads for sure."

"And I'm not. Now...it's late. You're tired. I put the bags Julie packed for you in the guest room. You can go through them in the morning to find something to wear. If that's all right."

"It is. There's no way I can try anything on tonight with all the chips and salsa that are in my belly."

Safe smiled, happy the conversation had eased up on the intensity. But he couldn't resist saying one more thing. "My parents and sister are going to love you. And Anders and Inez will have you wrapped around their finger in no time."

"You want me to meet your family?" Wren asked, sounding shocked.

"Of course I do. You'll meet my other family, my SEAL team, soon. And the retired SEALs and their wives. I'm a package deal, hon. If you're with me, you get them too. And trust me, it might sound like a good deal, but you'll see soon enough that my family can be a pain in the ass too."

In response, Wren leaned forward again and hugged him hard.

Safe returned the embrace. It felt like a promise. A new beginning. It felt good that Wren had opened up to him. He'd been impressed with her before, but knowing what he did about her childhood, he was even more so now.

"I haven't had the best luck with families, but I want yours to like me."

"They will," Safe reassured her.

He wanted this woman. Wanted her in his bed, in his arms, in his life. But things had been very intense for them both in the few days they'd known each other. He needed to go slow. Prove that he was someone she could trust. Tonight had been a good start. She'd opened up to him. Told him about her childhood. He wouldn't disrespect her by making a pass at her. No matter how much he wanted to.

"Come on," he said, disengaging and standing up. He held a hand out to her. "I could sit here and talk to you all night, but Kevlar would kick my butt if I was late in the morning, and your boss probably wouldn't be happy either."

She placed her hand in his and stood. Safe couldn't make himself let go, so he walked down the hall toward her room with her hand still in his.

"I should put my mug in the sink," she protested.

"I'll get it later," Safe said. When he reached the guest room door, he took her face in his hands. "You're safe here," he told her, wanting to make sure she truly understood that. "My door will be open if you need anything. If you want to get up and get a snack, feel free. My house is your house. I realize you still need a lot of stuff to replace everything that asshole destroyed, and we'll deal with that. In the meantime, do what you want, when you want. I'm not the boss of you, Wren. You're your own boss."

She smiled up at him. "Thanks."

"Get some sleep. I'll see you in the morning. Cereal again?"

"Of course."

Safe grinned, then couldn't stop himself from leaning down and kissing her forehead once more. "Good night."

"Night."

Safe dropped his hands and did his best to look nonchalant as he walked away from her. He wanted to turn around, see if she was watching him. To get one more glimpse of her, but he resisted the urge.

Baby steps. He wanted what his sister had. What his parents had. What Kevlar had. And he wanted it with this woman.

CHAPTER TEN

The next few days felt both normal and surreal to Wren. Her time at work was normal. Plans continued for their trip to Africa. Lots of meetings, lots of papers to review, lots of names to memorize as she'd need to be able to recognize and converse with both important media representatives as well as government officials.

The surreal part was her time away from work. Matt still hadn't been found. The unknown phone calls continued, and with each one, Wren's concern heightened. She was aware she should probably tell the police or Bo about them, but he was neck-deep in preparations for his mission and really didn't need any more stress piled on top of that. He'd already done so much for her, more than anyone ever had, and annoying phone calls were the last thing she wanted him to have to deal with on top of everything else.

Besides, he'd already arranged for someone to pick her up from work every day, so she was able to push concerns about

Matt to the back of her mind. One day it was a woman named Alabama. She was soft spoken but funny. The next it was Jessyka, the owner of Aces Bar and Grill. She apologized profusely for what happened to Wren, and reassured her that she was doing everything in her power to keep it from happening to someone else.

Today, it was a woman named Caroline and a large, intimidating man she introduced as her husband, Wolf. They'd taken her to an early dinner on the Navy base.

Wren had been intimidated at first, both by the security to get onto the base and by Wolf. But by the time they'd finished eating, she'd relaxed. Caroline was down-to-earth and so darn open. She'd talked a lot about the SEALs in general, and had explained that her husband was retired, but he and his former teammates now consulted and helped the newer SEAL teams that rotated through the area.

Wolf had joined in the conversation now and then, but mostly seemed content to let his wife do the talking.

When they were waiting for the check, Wolf leaned his elbows on the table and said, "You couldn't do better than Safe."

For some reason, Wren blushed.

"I'm trying not to be a nosey gossip, but when he called, asking if I'd be willing to pick you up today, I was surprised. Not because of the request, but because he's never gone out of his way to help a woman like he has you."

"Oh, is that bad?" Wren blurted.

"Not at all. It's good. Very good. But I wanted to make sure you knew that men like Safe...a lot is expected of them. They're asked to go into dangerous situations that most people are running *away* from. They see a lot of bad things, follow orders, and aren't allowed to talk about what they do and see. Relationships with special forces operatives are hard. A lot of times, men in those positions have trouble maintaining connections with people other than their teammates."

"Okaaaaay," Wren said, not liking where the conversation was headed.

"You're freaking her out," Caroline scolded. "What my husband is so badly trying to say is that Safe hasn't seemed interested in *anyone* the way he's interested in you. And that means you're different. Important. We know this thing with you guys is new, and you have some serious stuff going on with that asshole who tried to hurt you, but don't think for a second that Safe isn't completely invested in you."

"He'd probably help anyone who was in my situation," Wren said.

"Yes and no," Wolf told her. "He'd want to help anyone who asked him for assistance, but he wouldn't invite them to live in his house, and he wouldn't be involving his friends like he has with you either."

"Oh."

"Yeah, *oh*," Caroline agreed with a smile. "He's a good man. One of the best. You honestly couldn't do better."

"Really?" Wolf asked with a raised brow.

Caroline laughed. "Present company excluded, of course," she told him with a wink.

"You ready to go?" Wolf asked.

"As soon as the waitress brings the dinner I ordered for Bo," Wren said.

"He needs someone like you," Wolf said. "He's so used to

taking care of others, he needs someone like you to return the favor. I hear his team's meeting with you soon about your upcoming trip."

"Yeah, Bo's been stressing about it. I think because he's afraid he'll have to go on his mission before we can meet."

"If he does, my team and I will step up."

Wren was starting to understand that's how things worked between Bo and his friends. It was such a foreign concept to her, but she found that she liked it. A lot. Liked knowing Bo had the kind of people in his life who would be there for him no matter what. And since she was getting that kind of consideration simply by being with him, she was doubly thankful.

"Thank you," she told Wolf.

He shrugged off her thanks, which wasn't a surprise anymore, as everyone who'd helped her out recently had done the same thing.

After the waitress placed the takeout bag on the table, Caroline stood. "We need to get going."

"Are we in a hurry?" Wren asked.

"Kind of. We're supposed to meet someone at Safe's house," she said.

Wren frowned. "We are?"

"Well, *you* are, yes."

"Who?"

"Remi."

She frowned in confusion. "Why?"

"From what she told me, she's chomping at the bit to meet you. She's heard a ton about you from Kevlar, and she said she was done waiting for her turn to pick you up from work. So she told Safe that she'd come over and keep you company while the guys were in their meetings. She also said something about helping you with all the clothes Julie gave you?"

"Oh."

"I heard she went overboard and you haven't had time to go through everything yet."

Wren should've felt embarrassed that so many people seemed to know her business. But instead it felt surprisingly nice. "I haven't," she admitted. "I'm usually tired when I get home, and after Bo gets home, I want to spend my time talking to him."

Caroline beamed at Wren as they walked to Wolf's large black SUV. She even saw him grinning.

While Wren was looking forward to meeting Remi, she was also a little stressed over the idea. Bo had talked about the other woman often, and the fact that she was a famous cartoonist made her even more nervous. She wasn't the best in social situations as it was, and she really wanted to make a good impression on one of Bo's best friends.

"Don't worry. You'll love Remi, and she'll love you," Caroline said, as if she could read Wren's mind.

The drive back to Bo's house went by quickly, and when they pulled into the driveway, and a light blue Honda Civic immediately pulled in next to them, Wren's nervousness increased. "Are you coming in?" she asked Caroline and Wolf.

"No, we need to get home. Jessyka's bringing her kids over so she and Benny can go out to dinner. You'll be fine, Wren, promise."

Wren nodded. "Thank you for the ride home."

"You're welcome. And don't worry, this crap with that asshole will be over soon. I know it," Caroline told her firmly.

"I hope so. See you later."

"Bye!" Caroline said with a wave before Wren shut the door.

Taking a deep breath, Wren turned toward the woman getting out of the Civic. She was taller than Wren by a few inches, and her reddish-brown hair was pulled back in a messy bun at the back of her head. She had wisps of hair around her head, as if it simply refused to be constrained by the scrunchie.

"Hi! I'm Remi," the woman said, but she didn't move away from her car. "Is it weird that I'm here? If it is, I can go. I just really wanted to meet you because I've heard so many great things about you from Vincent. That's Kevlar's real name. I know it can be confusing, the whole two-names thing. I just finished up a few cartoons that I was under deadline to get done and before I started on a new project, I thought maybe I could come over and we could hang out. But if you don't want to, or you're too tired, I understand."

She blurted everything out fast, and the other woman's nervousness somehow calmed Wren's. "It's okay. I've heard a lot about you too, and I'm glad to meet you. And I have to say, I love your cartoon. Pecky the Traveling Taco is awesome."

"Thanks."

"I mean, who doesn't love a talking taco?" Wren said with a small grin.

"Right? That's what I thought when I started drawing," Remi told her.

"I should probably get this in the fridge for Bo," Wren said, gesturing to the takeout bag in her hand.

"Bo? Oh, sorry. Safe. Yeah, right. I figured I could maybe help you go through the things you got at My Sister's Closet. Julie told me that she probably went overboard in finding things for you to try on."

Wren smiled as she walked up the front walkway to the door. "She did. But I appreciate it all so much."

"Well, I'm not a fashionista. I mean, I usually sit at home in my sweatpants and T-shirts drawing, but I can maybe help organize the things as you go through them."

"Any help I can get would be appreciated. And sitting at home in sweats sounds like heaven," Wren said as she unlocked the door and walked inside.

"It is and it isn't. I mean, there was the time I met the mailman at the door to sign for a package and hadn't showered in a couple of days because, you know...deadline...and my hair probably looked like medusa—it gets super frizzy, especially when it's humid—and I had a coffee stain on my top from that morning, and I hadn't bothered to change because I was in the zone with my drawing, and I had two different colored socks on. I probably looked like something the cat dragged in."

"But I bet you were comfortable. Try wearing uncomfortable heels to make yourself taller than you really are because tall somehow equals having authority, an equally uncomfortable suit, and," Wren paused and shuddered exaggeratedly, "panty hose."

"Oh, the horrors!" Remi cried, placing the back of her hand to her forehead in a mock swoon.

They both giggled. And Wren knew at that moment that things between her and Remi were going to be just fine. She hurried to the kitchen to put the food in the fridge and paused to send Bo a quick text, letting him know she had dinner waiting for him, and that Remi was visiting and they'd be going through the clothes Julie had picked out.

She got an immediate text back, saying that he should be home within the hour and thanking her for the food.

Smiling, Wren turned back to Remi, who was looking around the small living area with curiosity. "I haven't been here before," she told Wren, when she noticed she was done texting. "It's nice."

Wren thought it was more than nice. It wasn't big, but it was cozy. Homey. Both things Wren had rarely experienced before. "It is," she agreed. "Want me to get the bags and bring them out here? Or we can go to my room?"

"Oh, don't go out of your way to drag everything out. Let's go to your room. Maybe we can lay everything on the bed and you can decide what you definitely don't want right off the bat. Then you can try on the things you need to try on and I'll give you my two cents...but beware, that's about all they'll be worth."

Wren laughed. "Oh, I doubt that. If I could live in fat pants, I would, but unfortunately, I need professional clothes for my job. And I think another woman's opinion would be invaluable. Most of the time I'm winging it when I go to the thrift stores to pick out work clothes."

"You shop at thrift stores? I love them too! Maybe we can go together sometime?"

Wren felt as if she was having an out-of-body experience.

She never expected to find someone who might actually want to shop at a secondhand store. Especially in California. Okay, that was terribly judgmental of her to think that before she'd even met anyone from the state, but she cut herself some slack. "Yes, I'd like that," Wren said.

Before she knew it, they were knee deep in material as they tried to sort everything out that Julie had picked. Wren had never seen so many designer clothes in one place before. She had no idea how much the clothes would cost at regular price, but knew it had to be thousands.

"I can probably make do with just a few of the suit sets," she mused, feeling overwhelmed. "I can mix and match them with different shirts under the jackets."

"I don't know. If your job is to speak to the media, you don't want to be seen wearing the same thing too often," Remi mused.

She was right. Wren knew it, but she couldn't fathom how much all the clothes on her bed and floor would cost to purchase.

The next hour went by quickly, and Wren realized she was actually having fun. Remi had gone out to the living area to sit, and Wren tried on each outfit, strolling out to the other room as if strutting a catwalk at a fashion show. Remi oohed and ahhed, then they decided together if they liked the outfit or not.

Some of the clothes didn't fit right. Others were uncomfortable. But Wren actually liked way more items than she thought she would. Julie had done an amazing job figuring out what might look good...all from a few sizes and Bo's description of her. And the underthings she'd gone out of her way to pick up were also some of the most comfortable Wren had ever worn.

She'd just put on the last item in the final bag—a little black dress. It would be inappropriate for anything work-related, as it was a little too short and a little too low cut.

And the second Wren put it on, she wanted it.

She'd spent most of her life trying to keep her head above water, keeping men at arm's length. But when she slipped the dress on and zipped it up, she felt *sexy*.

Still...

"I don't know about this one," Wren called down the hall, reluctant to go out and show Remi.

"Get out here!" her new friend insisted with a laugh. "I want to see!"

Wren didn't have any shoes that went with the dress, so she padded down the hallway in her bare feet.

The second she appeared in the doorway, Remi's eyes widened. "Holy crap, Wren...that's...you look *amazing*!"

Wren bit her lip. "You think?"

"Oh yeah. Absolutely. Turn," Remi ordered.

Wren did a slow spin, then faced the other woman once more.

"I don't care what you do with the rest of the stuff, but you *have* to keep that one!"

"It's not very practical. I have no idea when or where I'd even wear this thing. It's not as if I get invited to any formal occasions. And it's a little much for going out to dinner."

"No, it's not. Besides, the Navy has formal balls now and then. It'd be perfect!" Remi gushed.

"I agree."

Wren spun around and saw Bo standing in the front foyer. She and Remi had been so engrossed in their little fashion show that neither had heard him enter the house.

For some reason, Wren was embarrassed.

Bo walked toward her slowly, and it felt as if they were the only two people in the universe at that moment. His gaze ran from the cleavage displayed in the dress, down her torso, to her legs.

Wren ran her suddenly damp palms down the sides of the dress, realizing once more how short it was. The material came down to mid-thigh and had spaghetti straps holding it up on her shoulders.

"You're beautiful," Bo said softly.

Looking down, Wren said, "It would look better with the right shoes."

She felt Bo's finger under her chin, and she lifted her head to look at him at his urging. "It's perfect," he told her, echoing Remi. His hand moved from her face to her arm, then his large warm palm slid down to rest on her waist. He leaned in until his lips brushed her ear, and she shivered at the contact.

"Beautiful," he whispered. His hand tightened at her waist for a moment, before he took a deep breath and took a step back.

Wren felt almost bereft at the loss of his touch. Something happened between them just then, and she wasn't sure what.

No, that was a lie. She knew. The two of them had intense chemistry, and it was all she could do not to throw herself at him and beg him to take her into his room and peel the beautiful dress off and have his wicked way with her.

"I told you, Wren. *Perfect.*"

Remi's words snapped Wren back to the present. She'd forgotten all about the other woman's presence.

Doing her best to pretend she hadn't been about to melt into a puddle at Bo's feet, Wren turned toward the couch. "I'm not sure which one of the other outfits I should put in the take-back pile if I choose this one."

"Wait, why would you need to do that?" Bo asked.

"Because. There's no way I can afford all the things Julie sent with me."

"No," Bo said. He didn't elaborate.

Wren frowned. "No...what?"

"If something she sent fits, and you like it, keep it."

Wren stared at him for a moment, then said, "It's not that easy, Bo."

"Sure it is."

"Sorry, did I miss a money tree growing in your backyard? Because that's the only way I'd be able to afford everything she picked out. Bo, everything I tried on is designer. Like, one outfit costs hundreds if not thousands of dollars. Even at a secondhand rate, there's no way I can afford more than a couple. The jeans and casual clothes, sure. But not the designer stuff."

In response, he reached into his back pocket and pulled out his phone.

"Bo?"

He didn't respond, simply clicked a button on his cell. He'd obviously put it on speaker, because Wren could hear it ringing.

"Bo!" she hissed.

But she was too late.

"Hi, Safe. What's up?"

"Hey, Julie. I was calling about the clothes you sent home with Wren."

"Yeah? Did they fit? If not, I got some more stuff in today that I can go through and see if they'll work better."

"No, what you sent was good, I think. I'm looking at Wren wearing a black dress. Excellent choice, by the way."

"Oh! I hoped that one would work!" Julie exclaimed.

"It works," Bo said gruffly.

Wren could feel the blush on her cheeks with the way his gaze was practically burning into her.

"So, what's up?" Julie asked.

"Wren's concerned about the cost of the things she picked out," he said bluntly.

Wren wanted to sink into the floor and die.

"Tell her she's getting the friends and family discount," Julie said.

"You're on speaker, she can hear you," Bo informed her.

"Good. Wren?"

"I'm here," she managed to choke out.

"Safe is trying to be sweet, but his execution is definitely flawed. Ignoring that for a moment...I don't know what you decided would work and what wouldn't, but how does four hundred sound?"

Wren swallowed hard. Four hundred was more than she could afford to spend on an outfit. She ran through the items she'd tried on and loved and mentally discarded about three fourths of the outfits she'd hoped to keep. "That sounds fair. I could probably swing two of the pantsuits."

"No," Julie said with a little laugh. "Four hundred for everything you want to keep."

Wren's mouth fell open. "What?"

"Is that too much? I can do three hundred."

"Julie, what...*no*. Each of the outfits in those bags has to cost at least double that."

"True. But I didn't pay that much for them. I didn't pay *anything* for those clothes. They were donated."

Wren's head was spinning. She looked down at the dress she was wearing and longing hit—hard. She wanted it. Wanted all the things she'd tried on. But she didn't want to take advantage of anyone. "But you have bills to pay. You can't go around giving away the clothes in your shop for basically free."

"Why not? That's exactly what I do. Wren, you wouldn't know this, but I don't need the money. And I didn't start my shop to *make* money. I did it to give back. As my way of apologizing for being a bitch in my former life. And from what I understand, you *need* those outfits. I'd give them to you for free if I thought you'd let me get away with—"

"No," Wren said firmly.

"That's what I thought. So four hundred for whatever you want. Just send Safe back with the stuff that doesn't work for you. Please, let me help you. Us women have to stick together. That asshole who broke into your apartment and ruined your things shouldn't win."

Wren's throat closed up. How was this her life? She'd struggled for so long, and somehow she'd managed to find not only a man as generous and kind as Bo, but people like Remi,

Julie, and Caroline in the process? "Okay," she managed to squeak out. "Thank you."

"You're welcome. And please take a picture of yourself in that black dress. I want to see!"

"Will do." It was Bo who answered. "And if you and Hurt go to the Navy Ball, you'll see it in person...if she'll go with me."

Remi squealed from the couch, but Wren couldn't look away from Bo.

"Oh! That's awesome!"

"What's the Navy Ball?" Wren asked.

"It's a once-a-year thing where everyone dresses up and parties," Julie told her. "It's wicked fun."

Bo laughed.

"Great, so I'm thrilled the clothes worked out. If there's anything else you need, just let me know," Julie told her.

"Thank you again."

"Of course. Safe?"

"Yeah?"

"Don't be such a stranger. Before Wren, I hadn't seen you in way too long."

"Hazard of the job," Bo told her.

"Yeah. Well, maybe I'll have Patrick talk to your commander and tell him to send you and your team on fewer missions."

"I'm okay with that!" Remi called out.

"Right. Tell Hurt I said hey," Bo told Julie. "Gotta go."

"Stay safe out there. Talk to you later, Wren and Remi!"

"Bye!" Wren called out at the same time as Remi.

Bo clicked off his phone and put it in his pocket. He

stepped closer to Wren but glanced at Remi. "Thanks for coming over and helping Wren."

"Of course. And that's my cue to go," she said as she stood with a big smile on her face.

"Oh no! Don't feel like you have to leave just because Bo's home."

"It's not that," she said, but Wren had a feeling it was *exactly* that. "If Safe's home, that means Vincent probably is too. And with the team heading out soon, I want to spend as much time with him as I can."

Wren nodded. She didn't want to think about Bo leaving.

As if on cue, she heard her phone vibrating on the kitchen counter, where she'd left it while she was trying on the clothes. Before she could maneuver around Bo, he'd already taken a step forward and picked it up. He looked at the screen and frowned.

"Unknown," he told her as he handed her the phone.

Wren took it, silenced the ringer, and turned to Remi. She gave her a hug, thanked her for helping her decide which of the outfits to keep, and walked her to the door. She felt, more than saw, Bo at their backs. They stood at the doorway until Remi had gotten in her car and pulled away from the house.

Then Bo closed the door and turned to Wren. "Who was that on the phone?"

"I don't know," she said as casually as she could. "It said unknown."

"Why did you tense up when I said it was an unknown number?"

"Is this an interrogation?" she asked defensively.

In response, Bo stepped toward her, and Wren took a step

back. They kept that up until her back was against the wall in the small foyer. Bo leaned in, putting his hands on the wall on either side of her shoulders. "What's wrong?" he asked.

"Nothing," Wren said without hesitation.

"Bullshit. You tensed when you heard your phone vibrate, and when I picked it up, you got even more tense. Talk to me, Wren."

She had a decision to make here. She could continue to lie, to say nothing was wrong. To deny the unknown calls were freaking her out. Or she could fess up. Bo would do what he could to help her, Wren knew that as well as she knew her name. But it was extremely difficult for her to ask for help.

But she wasn't eight anymore. And this was Bo. He'd stepped up for her more in the last week than anyone ever had in her entire life.

Which was *another* problem. He'd already done so much.

"I don't know who it is," she blurted, looking up at him. She realized she'd reached for him and was grasping the material of his Navy camouflage uniform shirt with both hands. "But I've been getting two or three calls a day, sometimes more, since my date with Matt."

To her relief, Bo didn't flip out. He simply nodded. "Okay."

"Okay? What does that mean?" Wren asked.

"It means that I'll talk to Tex. Tell him about the calls. He'll trace them. Figure out who's been calling."

"It's probably just telemarketers. They got my number from somewhere and are being stubborn about getting someone to answer."

"That's possible," Bo said reasonably. "Have there been any messages?"

Wren shook her head.

"Which doesn't really mean anything. Have you answered any of the calls at all?"

"No," Wren admitted, feeling stupid all of a sudden.

"All right. If you get another call, would you let me answer it? Maybe before I call Tex and take him away from something else he's working on, I should see if I can get whoever's calling to back the hell off."

That small slip of anger actually made Wren feel better. Less like she was overreacting. And the last thing she wanted was for Bo to call this Tex guy, who she'd heard was extremely busy and apparently a genius when it came to tech stuff, if there was nothing untoward going on with the calls.

"Has he been able to find out anything about Matt?" Wren asked.

"Nothing useful. Found his deleted profile on the dating site, but no surprise, all the info on there was bogus and he used a public library's computer to set it up, so he couldn't track where he lives that way. And the address he used to set up the account led back to a gas station. So there's been nothing concrete yet, but Tex isn't giving up. If you get another call, will you let me deal with it?" Bo asked, repeating his original question.

"Yes. I'm happy to have you answer it. To see if it's Matt or simply a telemarketer."

"Thank you. Can we change the subject now?"

Wren nodded.

He smiled down at her and said, "You really do look amazing in this dress."

Wren looked down at herself reflexively—and realized if *she* could clearly see her cleavage, he'd have an even better view, seeing as he was taller than her.

He leaned down and nuzzled her neck and shoulder, near the strap of the dress.

"Bo?" she whispered, as her hands clenched the material of his shirt even tighter.

"Hmmm?" he replied, the response vibrating against her skin.

Wren felt her nipples tighten, and she swallowed hard. She forgot what she was going to say. All she could do was stand against the wall and...feel.

"I have dinner for you in the fridge." It wasn't what she wanted to say, but then again, she couldn't really think right now.

Bo lifted his head and smiled again. "Yeah?"

"Uh-huh. Caroline and Wolf took me to dinner, and I thought that you might be hungry when you got home. So I ordered a sandwich and salad for you to go. But if you already ate..." Her voice drifted off.

"I haven't eaten. I'm starving. A sandwich and salad sounds awesome. Thank you."

"You're welcome."

Bo hadn't backed away, and Wren hadn't let go of his shirt. She licked her lips, and she saw Bo's gaze follow the movement. Then drop down to her chest.

Her nipples tingled, and Wren had a feeling Bo was

getting a pretty good idea of how much she liked being this close to him.

Then his gaze moved back up to hers, and he leaned down. Slowly. So damn slowly, Wren thought she was going to die if he didn't hurry the hell up. She lifted her chin and waited.

To her frustration, he stopped with his lips hovering over hers. "Wren?" he whispered.

"Yes?" she breathed.

Then he closed the distance between them. His lips brushed over hers. Once. Twice.

On the third pass, he stepped closer and pressed his chest to hers. Wren's arms went around him, pulling him harder against her.

This was the second time they'd kissed, and somehow it was better than the first. Wren felt safe in Bo's embrace. Valued. Protected. As if they were the only two people in the world, and they might as well have been for all the attention they paid to their surroundings.

When he finally lifted his head, they were both breathing hard.

"Hi," she blurted.

He grinned. "Hi," he echoed. "Have I told you that I *really* like this dress yet?"

It was Wren's turn to smile. "Yeah, you said that a time or two."

"Good. But I think I should say, as much as I like this dress, because I can see your gorgeous long legs and your tits—"

Wren couldn't stop the snort of laughter that left her lips.

"Not that I have much in the way of boobs," she said with a little shrug.

"What you have is perfect," Bo told her firmly. One hand was at her waist, and he stroked her with his thumb, the feeling, even through the material of the dress, going straight between her legs. "But what I was going to say was that while I do love you in this dress, I like you just as much in sweats and my T-shirts. I like seeing you comfortable with your guard down, curled up in the corner of my couch or in my recliner. Knowing you're sleeping in the room next to mine, safe, once again in my shirt...and not much else."

Unlike his touch, his words shot straight to Wren's heart. Who didn't want to know the guy they had a crush on liked her just as much in lounging clothes as he did in a fancy dress? "Bo," she whispered, overwhelmed.

"I just wanted to make sure you know I'm not kissing you because of what you're wearing. It's because of who you are. What you've overcome. Because even though life has dealt you a shit hand, you're still a kind person, and you work so hard, and a part of me dies every time you're surprised when others do something nice for you. I want to prove to you that not everyone is out to get you, and that there are people out there, like me and my friends, who don't have an agenda when we hang out with you."

Wren closed her eyes and rested her forehead against Bo's shoulder. She felt his hand caressing her hair. It felt good to be held by him, but she needed to hear those words. Somehow he'd gotten under her shields. And the more time she spent around him and his friends, the more those shields were cracking.

"Don't hurt me," she whispered against him. "If you're playing me, or just want to get in my pants, it would kill me."

"I'll prove to you that you can trust me if it's the last thing I do," Bo said.

Wren took a deep breath. Things were pretty intense and she needed a break. "Right, so...it seems as if I have a bunch of new clothes I need to hang up and others I need to package to bring back to Julie's store. And you need to change and eat."

"You'll sit with me while I eat?" Bo asked.

"If you want me to," Wren said with a shrug.

"I want you to," he reassured her.

"All right. I'll change and meet you in the kitchen."

"Deal. Wren?"

"Yeah?"

"I like coming home to you. Just thought you should know."

A memory flashed through Wren's brain. She wasn't sure how old she was, but she was young. She'd arrived home from school to an empty house, relieved her mom wasn't there. She'd quickly gotten something to eat because she wasn't sure if she'd be eating later or not; sometimes her mom fixed dinner, and other times she told Wren to go to her room and not come out.

That particular night, when her mother had walked in the door, she'd taken one look at Wren, curled her lip in disgust, and told her to get the fuck out of her sight. That the last thing she wanted to look at when she got home was Wren's ugly face.

Bo's words couldn't take away the bad memories, but they went a long way toward making them fade a little more.

Going up on her tiptoes, Wren kissed Bo. It was a short kiss, but no less heartfelt. Meant to convey how much his words meant to her.

They headed toward the hallway to their bedrooms together, Bo's hand warm on her back as they walked. She stopped at her room, and Bo slid past her to go to his. He turned back at his doorway and smiled at her before disappearing inside.

Wren closed the door to her room and leaned against it for a moment with a small smile on her face. Then she pushed off it as she reached for the zipper at her back. The beautiful clothes she'd been trying on were strewn over her bed, and she couldn't wait to hang them in her closet. But she was more excited to spend the evening with Bo, talking about his day, continuing to get to know him, than putting away the most amazing clothes she'd ever owned.

CHAPTER ELEVEN

The next morning, over bowls of cereal, Safe couldn't take his eyes off Wren. She had on one of her new outfits, and it fit her perfectly. The black slacks made her legs look longer than usual, and the matching jacket over a pale pink blouse was both feminine and professional at the same time.

"I set up the safety meeting for this evening," Safe told her.

"You did?"

"Yeah, is five-thirty okay? I figure we'd be able to get from your office building to the base by then with no problem. I can pick you up."

"Oh, okay."

"You don't sound so sure," Safe said, trying to read the emotions on her face.

"No, I am. I just...I know you don't want me to go to Africa, and I'm nervous about the trip myself. I'm afraid hearing about all the things that could go wrong will make my nervousness worse."

Safe felt bad for her. And she wasn't wrong. Talking about the fact that she could get kidnapped or caught in a literal crossfire between warring political parties wasn't high on anyone's list of fun things to discuss. But it had to be done. "Any chance some of your coworkers will change their mind and come too?"

Wren shrugged. "I doubt it. But I'll try talking to them again today. I think a couple of them, like maybe Luke and Oliver, are interested, but they're too scared to look weak in the eyes of the others if they agree."

"Idiots," Safe couldn't help but mutter.

Just then, Wren's phone vibrated on the table next to her.

They both stared at it for a beat, before Wren looked at Safe. "Unknown," she whispered, as if whoever was on the other end of the line could somehow hear.

"May I?" he asked, his hand hovering over the phone.

Wren nodded.

Safe's heart rate spiked. If this was Matt, he had some definite words to say to the asshole. "Hello?" he barked into the phone. "Who is this?"

"Um...is Wren Defranco there?" a deep male voice asked.

"I asked, who this was," Safe retorted.

"My name is Easton Farris. I'm looking for Wren Defranco. Is this her number?"

"Why do you want to speak to her?" Safe asked.

"It's a private matter."

"And I'm telling you that if you don't tell me what the hell you want with her in the next two seconds, she's blocking this number, and you won't ever get to speak to her, period," Safe growled.

He felt Wren's hand on his arm and looked up at her. She was biting her lip as she stared at him. Taking a deep breath, Safe tried to relax his muscles.

"I'm her half-brother."

"What?" Safe asked, shocked. That wasn't what he'd expected to hear at all. "Wait a minute..." He put the phone on speaker. "Say that again," he ordered.

"I'm Wren's half-brother. We share a father."

"But...that's impossible," Wren whispered.

Easton clearly heard her.

"Wren? Holy crap, I can't believe I found you! It's possible. My dad met your mom at a bar when he was twenty. He went to a motel with her and they slept together. When he woke up, she was gone. He never saw her again." Easton was talking quickly, as if he expected to be hung up on at any second. "I've taken it upon myself to look into my genealogy and did one of those DNA tests. I was shocked to be matched as a close relative of a Wren Defranco. And even more surprised when it said we shared a father."

"I did one of those tests on a lark a few years ago," Wren said. It was Safe's turn to put his hand on *her* arm now, to support her. Her eyes were huge in her face, as if she wasn't sure what was happening. "I was told my father was a felon. That he'd done time in prison for murder."

Easton gasped. "That's a lie. When he woke up in that motel, he realized his wallet was gone, the bitch he slept with—oh...er...sorry. Your mom had taken it. So if anyone was a criminal, it wasn't my dad."

"She *is* a bitch," Wren confirmed.

"Look. I know this is a huge shock. But when I brought the information I'd found to my...*our*...dad, he was adamant that he wanted to meet you."

"Why?" Wren asked.

"Why? Because you're his *daughter*. He didn't even know you existed before, but now that he does, he wants to connect. Look, we don't want anything from you other than your time. Our dad's a great guy. He lives in Mission Viejo, just south of Los Angeles. I don't know where you live, specifically, but he's willing to travel to wherever you'd like to meet you. Or fly you here. No strings attached."

"Mission Viejo?" Wren asked, sounding dazed.

"Yeah."

"She's going to have to think about it," Safe told Easton firmly. "You can't expect her to just fly off to LA to meet someone she has no proof she's actually related to."

"You're right. Of course. I can send you all the info I have from the website I found her on. Also, my dad isn't just some random dude. He's Tyler Farris. One of the founders of Farris Morgan, the energy transportation company."

"Holy shit, really?"

"Yeah."

"I applied for a job there," Wren said.

"You did? Wow! Okay then. Small world. Well, my dad's been married for twenty-six years, and my mom is excited and nervous to meet you too. You have two other half-brothers besides me, and two nieces and a nephew. Not to mention aunts and uncles and cousins. We're a big group, and we'd love to at least introduce you to your family."

Family, Wren mouthed softly, looking at Safe with tears in her eyes.

"Send the information you have to me. I'll text you my email address," Safe said. "After I have people I know look into you and Tyler, to make sure what you're saying is on the up and up, we'll reach out."

"I'm not lying, and you can look into us all you want. All we want, all my dad wants, is to meet the daughter he never knew he had. He had three sons, and I think he always wanted a girl. Wren?"

"Yeah?"

"What you said about your mom...did you...was your life growing up...okay?"

Safe's nostrils flared in agitation as he looked at Wren.

"No," she said simply.

"Shit. Okay, well...I'm sorry. My dad didn't know about you. If he had, he would've done what he could to take care of you."

Wren nodded, but Easton of course couldn't see her. Couldn't know how emotional his words were making her.

"Send the information," Safe said. "We'll be in touch."

"All right. Thank you. On behalf of my dad and the rest of our family, we really do hope you'll consider at least talking to us."

"Later," Safe said, before hanging up. He put the phone down, then immediately stood and pulled Wren to her feet. He hugged her hard, knowing she was stressed out just by how tightly she gripped him in return.

A minute or two went by before Safe pulled back so he could see Wren's eyes. "That was intense. Are you all right?"

She looked up at him, her eyes swimming in tears. "I have a family," she whispered.

"Looks that way. But before you get too excited, you have to let me check things out. Make sure he's legit."

"He knew about the wallet my mom stole. How would he know that if his dad wasn't there?"

She had a point.

"I applied to work at Farris Morgan."

"You said that."

"It was my first choice for jobs, but I'd already accepted the job here at BT Energy before Farris even started their interviewing process. So I withdrew my application. Wouldn't that have been a weird coincidence if I'd met my father and neither of us knew?"

"I, for one, am glad you're here and not up in LA," Safe told her.

She gave him a watery smile. "And he's not even that far from here. This is so crazy!"

"At least it took your mind off the meeting this afternoon."

Wren chuckled. "Very true."

"You okay with this?" Safe asked in a serious tone.

"I don't know. One part of me is thrilled. The other part is cautious. I mean, I've found that if something seems too good to be true, it usually is. But then again, what would these people have to gain from lying about who they are? It's not as if I'm worth anything, money-wise. They have more to lose if they claim me than I do."

"They could be using you to get info on BT Energy that they can steal," Safe suggested.

"True. You're really going to look into them for me?"

"Of course."

"And if I do decide to meet them, will you go with me?"

"Try and keep me away," Safe practically growled.

Wren looked up at him in a way he couldn't interpret.

"What?" he asked gruffly, feeling off-kilter himself with what they'd just learned.

"I just...*you*. Everything. I feel as if I'm in a dream. A good one," she said quickly with a small smile.

"Things have been pretty crazy, between that Matt guy, your apartment, us, your upcoming trip, my upcoming mission, and now this...But I'll tell you one thing. I wouldn't change a damn minute. We're gonna get through this. Maybe years from now we'll look back and laugh. Maybe write a book about how everything went down."

Safe was taking a chance saying that. But he realized it was what he truly wanted. This woman at his side. Years and years from now. Looking back on how they met and everything that happened. With any luck, they'd have exactly that —decades together.

"Yeah," Wren said wistfully.

"One good thing is that hopefully the mystery of the unknown caller is now solved," he said. "And we've got the locks on your apartment changed. Alabama and Fiona have almost finished cleaning things up over there and—"

"Wait, *what*? They have? Why?"

"Because I talked to their husbands, and they spoke with their wives, and they wanted to help. So the four of them— because no way would Abe and Cookie let their wives be there without backup, considering we haven't found this Matt asshole—have spent the last couple days repairing what they could and trashing anything that's not salvageable. Also, I probably should tell you that Summer and Cheyenne went shopping, and they've replaced all your plates, cups, and glasses, and the silverware that was bent beyond repair. I'm told that nothing matches, but that it's 'eclectic and funky and cool as hell.' Their words, not mine."

"Bo..."

"I know. It's a lot. And I know you just said that you have a family now. But sweetheart...you already had one. *Here*. With me and my friends, and now *your* friends. We take care of our own, and since you're with me, you're one of us."

"I can't wrap my mind around all this," Wren said with a small shake of her head.

"Well, you don't have to right this moment. We both need to get to work. I'll pick you up at five, and we'll grab something quick to eat before we head to the base. My team has been researching what they think will work for you, and what they can teach you in the time limits we have."

"Oh crap! I haven't even met the rest of your team yet," Wren said.

"No, don't stress about that. They already love you. You don't need to worry about it," Safe told her.

"Right," Wren mumbled.

"You don't," Safe insisted. "They've heard all about you from me. Wren this, Wren that. They've been bugging me about finally getting to meet you in person. All you have to do is be yourself. They'll adore you."

"I don't think I can take much more stress today," Wren told him.

Safe kissed her. Just leaned in and covered her lips with his. It wasn't passionate, but he was no less moved by the experience. He loved being able to touch her and kiss her whenever he wanted. New relationships were always exciting, but this was more. Better. He was as comfortable with her as if they'd been together for years, rather than the short time he'd actually known her.

"You're the epitome of the saying that you never know how strong you can be until you have no choice. You've got this, Wren. No matter what life has thrown at you, you've persevered. And now you have me. You no longer have to deal with shit on your own. You can lean on me. And our friends. Okay?"

"I'm starting to believe it," Wren said.

"Good. Come on. Kevlar will kick my ass if I'm late. Let's go."

"Bossy," Wren teased.

"You have no idea," Safe told her, his mind going to the things he wanted to do with her in the bedroom. It was definitely too soon for that, but he wouldn't be a guy if he didn't at least think about it.

"Promises, promises," she sassed.

Safe's cock twitched in his pants. Lord, this woman was going to be the death of him. But at least he'd die a happy man.

CHAPTER TWELVE

Wren's day had gone by lightning fast. She had a lot of things to think about—her father, half-brother, meeting Bo's team, and hearing things she wasn't sure she was ready to hear about her trip to South Sudan.

She'd tried to talk her coworkers into coming with her to the meeting, but as expected, they weren't receptive. So Wren decided she'd take as many notes as she could, then send them to everyone. If they chose to read them, fine. If not, that was their problem. Why they wouldn't want as much information about how to be as safe as possible was beyond her, but she didn't have time to dwell on it, as Bo was pulling up in front of her building.

She went outside to meet him and climbed into his Jeep. He leaned over and kissed her, as if they'd done it every day for years. It felt normal and comfortable and exciting, all at the same time. She loved how their relationship was progressing. Bo never pressed her for more than she was willing to give, which she appreciated. She might be living with him, and he might be taking over her every thought, but she wasn't ready to sleep with him. That was a huge step, and she wanted to be sure he was exactly who he was portraying himself to be before she went there.

Because she was falling in love with him. And if she went to bed with him, and he turned out to be using her for sex, Wren wasn't sure she'd survive the betrayal. Maybe that line of thinking wasn't fair to Bo, but he didn't seem eager to turn their budding relationship physical yet, either. So maybe he was still unsure of her, as well.

"Hi," he said once she was settled with her seat belt on. "How was your day? Any luck getting the others to come tonight?"

"It was fine. And no."

Bo grimaced, but shrugged. "Their loss. We're going to give you all the information necessary so if the need arises, you can save *all* their asses. Okay?"

Wren laughed. "All right. Do I get a cape too?"

"You can have anything you want," Bo told her with a wink. "Burritos to go sound all right for dinner?"

"Did you seriously ask me if Mexican was all right?" Wren asked.

"Well, it's not sit-down Mexican. It's just from one of those fast-food type places."

"A burrito is a burrito. And the answer is yes, it's more than fine."

"Perfect."

It took about fifteen minutes for them to drive to the takeout place, get their meals, then reach the base. Bo took her hand as soon as they were out of the car, then they were heading into a nondescript-looking building.

"Is this where you work?"

"Yes and no. We sometimes use the meeting rooms here, but we have conference rooms all over the base that we use, depending on the sensitivity of the information we're talking about and receiving from outside sources."

That made sense.

He walked them up to the second floor and down a hallway. All the doors looked the same, and he opened one about halfway down the hall. Wren swallowed hard when she saw all the men already gathered around the large circular table inside.

She knew Kevlar, but not the others. And as she mentally counted in her head, she realized there were a couple more people here than just Bo's team.

Standing awkwardly next to Bo, she wondered what they were thinking. If they were disappointed that their friend was with her. Deep-seated insecurities from her past swam through Wren. She desperately wanted Bo's teammates to like her. Or to at least not hate that she was with him.

There was silence for a beat—which felt like eons to Wren, but was probably only a couple of seconds—and then a man stepped forward.

"I'm Preacher. You must be Wren. Have to say, we're all a little upset that Safe didn't call us to help you get your stuff the other night."

"And *I* have to say, it probably would've been a good thing if some of you were there. Maybe Matt wouldn't have gotten away," Wren replied with a small shrug.

"See? Even your girlfriend knows you were a bonehead that night," one of the other men told Bo.

Wren couldn't stop the small smile from forming on her face.

"Uh-huh. I'm gonna do introductions so we can eat and start this meeting," Bo said. "Everyone, this is Wren Defranco. Wren, you know Kevlar, of course. That's Blink, MacGyver, Flash, and Smiley. And those two," he said, nodding toward two men standing together, "are Dude and Mozart. They're on Wolf's SEAL team. Retired now, but still hanging around like bad pennies."

"Hi," Wren said, giving everyone a small wave, which immediately felt like a dorky thing to do.

But to her relief, no one called her on it, and everyone began to take seats around the table. Bo led her to a chair, and to her surprise, Blink tapped MacGyver on the shoulder and motioned with his head for him to move down, obviously wanting to sit next to her for some reason.

She didn't have time to think about it, because Mozart began to dig through a cardboard box on the table and call out names as he tossed what looked like sub sandwiches to the other men. Wren was thankful that she didn't have to eat her burrito in front of everyone else if they weren't eating, because that would've felt awkward as hell.

Everyone dug into their dinners, and Wren did the same. She was starving. It had been a long day at work and the burrito really hit the spot.

"You doing okay?"

Turning to Blink, she studied the redhead as she chewed then swallowed the bite of food she'd just taken. She recalled what Bo had told her about him. How everyone on his team had been injured or killed on a mission. How he'd had a hard time coping. How he'd stepped in and saved Remi from being killed by one of Bo's previous teammates. "Yeah. Why wouldn't I be?" she asked.

"You've had a hard time lately," Blink said.

Wren huffed out a breath. "I admit that being drugged was awful. As did finding out my apartment was ransacked, and knowing the asshole is still out there, probably watching and waiting to try to get his hands on me again. But honestly, living with Bo hasn't been a hardship. Being chauffeured to and from my job...again, that doesn't suck. All in all, my life is actually pretty good right now."

Blink stared at her for a moment, no expression on his face.

Just when Wren thought she'd said something wrong, Blink's lips twitched upward a fraction. "You remind me of Remi. Resilient, practical, strong."

Wren felt warm and fuzzy inside. She liked Remi. Was impressed by her. Especially after hearing everything she'd been through from Bo, after she'd left his house last night. Blink's compliment felt amazing. "Thanks," she said softly.

He nodded, then turned his attention back to his sandwich.

"Wren?"

She turned to look at Bo.

"I need you to remember to breathe tonight, okay?"

"Huh?"

"We're going to be talking about a lot of stuff that might freak you out. But this is what we do. We talk about all the worst-case scenarios. Pick them apart. Discuss what we'd do if the worst happens. If you know ahead of time what can happen, it makes it easier to deal with if any of those things occur. You said you've done some research on South Sudan, so you know some of what we're going to talk about, but we'll probably be bringing up things you might not have thought of. I just need you to not panic. Okay?"

Wren nodded. "I'm not naïve. I mean, I probably am about some stuff, but my life hasn't been sunshine and roses. I'm aware of a lot of crap that can happen. And yes, I've researched, but honestly? Despite how nervous I was this morning, I've still been looking forward to talking to you and your friends. You're the experts. I'll take any advice I can get. I have no choice but to go on this trip, but I can damn well be sure to go completely prepared for anything."

"You're gonna be fine," Bo said firmly. "No matter what happens, you've got the inner strength and smarts to make it through."

The second amazing compliment in as many minutes was enough to make Wren feel almost weepy. "I hope so," she said softly.

"I know so," Bo said without any doubt in his tone.

Talk around the table was general and relaxed until Kevlar stood up and cleared his throat.

Wren couldn't help but tense. This wasn't simply a meeting to get to know Bo's friends. There was a very serious reason they were all here.

"Okay. I figured we'd get started. Remi's waiting for me at home, as I'm sure Cheyenne and Summer and their kids are waiting for Dude and Mozart. We're here to discuss Wren's safety as she travels to South Sudan in a couple of weeks. We've all been to that region, and we know what a shitshow she's walking into...sorry, Wren, but it's true."

"It's okay," she reassured him. "I know."

"The *best* thing would be for you to get out of going. Break a leg? Get a virus? Find a new job?" Preacher suggested, looking at her hopefully.

"None of those things are on my immediate agenda," Wren told him.

"Figured. But I had to at least try," he said with a shrug.

Wren wasn't upset, she respected him for saying what everyone else had to be thinking.

She jerked a little in surprise when Bo took her hand under the table. He didn't look at her, just rested their intertwined hands on her thigh. It felt good to have his support, especially when she knew she was about to hear some uncomfortable things.

"We all know that South Sudan has a level-four do-not-travel advisory right now," Kevlar continued. "There's armed conflict between various political and ethnic groups. Crime and violence is an everyday occurrence. Foreign nationals have experienced armed robberies, sexual and other assault, carjackings, shootings, kidnapping, and other violent crimes."

Wren had read the same thing about the country she was voluntarily about to enter, but hearing Kevlar list off the various tragedies that could happen while she was there made her situation all the more real.

"You aren't a journalist in the strictest sense of the word, but since you'll still be working closely with the media, you have to have the proper documentation from the South

Sudanese Media Authority. Do you know if you've gotten that?" Kevlar asked.

Wren sat up straighter. "We have. My boss, Colby Johnson, has a liaison over there who's been helping us with our itinerary and making sure we have all the proper documents."

"Good. The other thing you need to be aware of is that our government has limited ability to provide emergency consular services to US citizens in the country. I'm assuming you'll be under a strict curfew, same as the few US government personnel who are in the country. They have to use armored vehicles for all their movements, and they aren't allowed to travel outside Juba. Do you know what your plans are while there?"

Wren nodded. "We won't be leaving Juba either. The pipeline is scheduled to run north and south of the city, but we aren't there to actually visit the proposed sites. We're there to explain the positive results of South Sudan having the pipeline placed in their country. I don't know about the armored vehicles, but I'm hoping Colby's contact has that under control."

"All right. So...with the potential for violence, it's a no-brainer for me to say that you should never go off on your own. Do not *walk* anywhere, even in groups. If someone suggests going down the street to a restaurant they saw, don't do it. Stay in the hotel. If you can, make sure the rooms you're meeting in don't have windows. Under no circumstances should you go to any kind of public demonstrations or gatherings. Do not take pictures or video, even from inside your vehicle. Photography, even in public places, is strictly controlled."

Wren's gaze was glued on Kevlar's. With every word out of his mouth, she got more tense. Bo had warned her, and while she already knew most of what the other man was saying, it was still difficult to believe BT Energy thought this trip was a good idea.

"Do you have a will, power of attorney, and your insurance beneficiaries all set?" Smiley asked solemnly.

Wren nodded. "Yes."

"Good. Can you tell us what your schedule is?" Kevlar asked.

"It's a four-day trip. Day one is basically a wash, since we'll be traveling most of the day. Day two, there's a meeting with the government officials who approved the trip. There's also a question-and-answer session with some bigwigs who were integral in getting the pipeline approved. After, I'll be giving a short interview to their state-run media program about the project.

"Day three, some of the different ethnic groups are coming in to ask questions, and so we can explain exactly where the pipeline is going and the benefits to the South Sudanese people. I'll be leading that session, acting as moderator for Colby and the other guys, who will have a panel-like presentation. We have some free time that afternoon, before we'll be going to a dinner at the president's home. I don't know if he'll be there or not, but apparently it's a huge deal.

"The last day is another travel day. We'll head to the airport in the morning and head home."

The room was quiet for a moment, before Dude said "fuck" under his breath.

Wren wasn't sure what part of the schedule concerned him the most. But she didn't have to wait long to find out.

"Jesus, that schedule is a shitshow," Dude said, running a hand through his hair. "Who the hell thought it would be a good idea to get representatives from different ethnic groups together in the same room? That's not going to turn out well. And going to the president's house will just make you targets."

"Right, so...this is probably a good time to talk about specifics," Kevlar said. "First off, if violence breaks out during any of the interviews, your first job is to drop to the floor. Get flat."

"And belly crawl toward the exit," Flash continued.

"If you can't get to a door, get behind a piece of furniture. An overturned chair, a table, something. Keep your head down and cover it with your arms," Mozart added.

"Don't bring any attention to yourself," Bo told her. "And this goes for whatever you're doing and wherever you're going. From the moment you step into the country to the moment you leave. No screaming, no laughing too loud. Don't dress flashy. Leave all your jewelry at home, even though I haven't seen you wear much. You even need to leave your watch in your bag. Do *not* pull out your phone in public. Keep your head down, stay quiet."

Wren couldn't take her gaze from Bo's. She licked her lips nervously and nodded.

"Now's probably a good time to talk about clothes," Smiley said.

"Yeah," Kevlar agreed. "I don't know what you usually

wear at this kind of thing..." His voice trailed off, waiting for her to answer his unasked question.

"Professional. Skirts that hit below the knee, jackets, blouses."

Kevlar was already shaking his head. "No. No skirts. Don't pack even one. If your boss doesn't like it, tough shit. It'll be too late for him to complain once you're over there. Pants at all times. Preferably cargo pants. Not the slick, useless pantsuits that will be way too hot in Africa anyway."

"And boots," Dude added. "The hiking kind, not the high-heeled designer kind."

"It's going to be hot, so while I'd suggest long-sleeve wicking shirts for the protection, you could probably get away with a short-sleeve one," Preacher said.

Wren must've made some sort of face, because Dude stood up and placed his hands on the table, leaning toward her. "You and your coworkers are already going to stand out like monkeys in Antarctica. You're going to have targets on your foreheads the second you arrive in that country. The likelihood of one or all of you becoming the victim of some sort of violence to either make a point, or to try to extort money from the rich Americans, is basically one hundred percent. Would you rather try to get to safety in a skirt and high heels, or while wearing pants and shoes you can run in?"

"The latter," Wren said quietly. "It's just that...I'm expected to have a certain image at all times. Think of a weather forecaster, or someone on the six o'clock news."

"But they don't do their jobs in the middle of a country in the throes of a civil war," Preacher countered.

"Look, if your boss was here, we'd tell him the same thing.

No suits and ties. No useless leather shoes. You have to assume the worst and be relieved if the best happens. If you're dragged off into the jungles south of the city, you need to be prepared. Cotton clothes are not fun in a hot climate like Africa's," Flash told her.

It was finally sinking in that the four days she'd be in South Sudan were going to be four of the most stressful of her life.

"In the hotel, you shouldn't be in a room by yourself," MacGyver continued. "Do you trust any of your coworkers enough to room with them?"

Wren thought about it for a moment, then said, "Probably Luke. He's close to my age, and I think he would've come tonight if he didn't think he'd be made fun of by the others."

Just about all the men around her rolled their eyes. It was obvious they didn't think much of someone who couldn't do the right thing, even if it wasn't what his peers thought he should do.

"Do what you need to do, but do *not* be alone at night. It's way too easy for someone who works at the hotel to pass on intel that you're alone, what room you're in, and even give out a key to someone," MacGyver told her.

"And bring one of those alarm things. The ones that look like a door stop. You put them under your door and it'll make a horrible noise if someone tries to open the door. It'll at least ruin their ability to catch you unaware."

"We need to discuss the possibility of kidnapping," Blink said quietly.

"Right," Kevlar said with a sigh. "Having seven Americans

from a successful energy company there will be like dangling a carrot in front of a starving donkey."

The analogy was funny, but Wren wasn't in the mood to laugh. Not at all.

"They could strike at any time. When you're leaving the airport, when you're traveling to the hotel, while you're in your meetings, heading to the president's compound...literally at any time, so you'll need to be ready," Dude said.

"Be alert. If something does start going down, remember what we said earlier. Don't bring attention to yourself. Be compliant. Do what they tell you to do," Smiley said.

"I shouldn't try to run?" Wren asked.

"No!" at least three of the guys said at the same time.

"If you do, it's likely they'll shoot at you," Kevlar explained.

"Your best bet is to go along quietly. I know that sounds scary and counterintuitive," Mozart said. "But we'll set up a proof-of-life plan. Since Safe and his team will be deployed, you can email one of us every couple of hours. Let us know you're good. If you miss a check-in, we can use our connections to immediately find out what's happening."

Wren glanced over at Bo. He was staring at his friend with a small frown on his face.

"If you do get kidnapped, we have the ability to get people working on it," Dude agreed.

"Can I say something?" Wren interjected.

"Of course," Kevlar told her.

"What will you be able to do? You wouldn't even know where I am. And it's not like you guys are still SEALs. I mean, you are, that sounded rude...but you're not active duty. You can't just hop on a plane and come get me."

"First, you're right. We can't. But that doesn't mean we don't know other people who can," Dude told her. "And we *will* know where you are."

Wren frowned in confusion.

"I think it's time to get to the other part of tonight's meeting," Kevlar said.

MacGyver stood up and walked over to a narrow table against one of the walls. He picked up a small cardboard box that Wren hadn't noticed before and placed it on the conference table. "Wren? Can you come over here, please?"

Wren looked at Bo, but his attention was on MacGyver and whatever was in the box. She stood up, feeling kind of off-kilter when she had to let go of Bo's hand, and walked over to where MacGyver was standing.

"We put together some things for you. Remember, these are all worst-case-scenario survival items, not things we even want you to have to use. Okay?"

For some reason, Wren was kind of excited to see what these men considered "survival items." She nodded.

The first thing MacGyver pulled out of the box was a small plastic envelope with something white inside.

"This is just some cotton wool that's covered in Vaseline. We were thinking it could either go in your boot, or it can go inside the hidden pocket in this," MacGyver told her, as he pulled a belt out of the bag.

Wren took the belt from him and noticed the concealed zipper along the inside. Feeling a little like she was Inspector Gadget or something, she unzipped it. Taking the small plastic bag from MacGyver, she tucked it into the little pocket of the belt. "Wouldn't it be more practical to have some money or an ID in here, rather than this?" she asked.

"If you're in the middle of the jungle, would you rather have money and an ID, or a way to start a fire?" Kevlar asked.

"Oh, is that what the cotton is for?" Wren asked, feeling stupid.

"Yeah. The combo of the Vaseline and the cotton wool is an excellent fire-starter."

Wren frowned in confusion. "But how would I start it? Are you going to teach me to rub two sticks together to get sparks?"

The men kind of chuckled. "No. I mean, we *could* teach you, but using that method is difficult. And would take too long. Look at the buckle of the belt you're holding," Preacher told her.

Wren brought the buckle closer to inspect it. "I don't understand."

"May I?" MacGyver asked, holding out his hand.

Wren put the belt into his hand without hesitation. He turned the buckle and pointed. "See this little bar here?"

She nodded.

"That's the ferro rod."

Wren looked at MacGyver in confusion. "The what?"

She saw the look of surprise—or maybe dismay?—on his face.

"I'm sorry. I don't know anything about camping or being outdoors."

"It's okay, Wren," Bo said, getting up and coming to stand beside her. He took the belt from MacGyver. "We can practice when we get home. But basically, a ferro rod is covered with stuff that can make sparks when you rub it off. This one is tiny, which makes it harder to use, but since we're going for stealth, it's imperative that someone who searches you doesn't find it or realize what it's for."

His words made Wren swallow hard. The thought of someone "searching" her didn't sound fun. Not at all.

"This belt buckle has the fire-starting rod, or ferro rod, and the prong that goes into the holes of the belt is what you'll use to rub along it to create sparks. If you pile up some small twigs and any kind of grass, and the cotton wool covered in the Vaseline, then strike the rod like this," Bo unclipped the little prong and ran it along the ferro rod thing, and sparks shot off the end onto the table, "you get fire."

"Oh!" Wren exclaimed. "That's cool."

Bo smiled. "It is."

"Okay. So then you can put the belt back together?"

Bo nodded and showed her how to reassemble it.

"What else?" Wren asked, excited to see what other super-secret Navy SEAL stuff they had for her.

"Lipstick," MacGyver told her, holding up a tube.

Wren's brow wrinkled. "I don't usually wear it," she informed him.

"You don't have to. This brand is petroleum-based. Again, if you cut off a chunk—or better, shave it off—it can help you start a fire."

"Right. And kidnappers probably wouldn't care too much if I was carrying a tube of lipstick."

"Exactly," Smiley said from across the table.

Wren shot him a small nod, then turned back to

MacGyver. Bo hadn't gone back to his seat. He stayed beside her, which Wren appreciated.

"Safe said he'd take you to find a pair of boots. You'll need to make sure you break them in before you leave, which means you probably need to start wearing them to work. He'll switch out the shoelaces that come with them with this...550 paracord."

"I've seen bracelets made out of this stuff," Wren said as she took the cord from him and ran her hands over it. "What would I use this for?"

"You can use it to make a shelter, to tie sticks together, improvised fishing line, a tourniquet, traps, tie up any stray material you find to make a backpack, fire-starter—it'll burn really fast—or cut through zip-ties."

"Okay, most of that stuff is going to be a no-go for me. I have no idea how to make a shelter, and I'm sure I'd be hopeless at fishing or making traps. But...you've got to be kidding me about cutting through zip-ties."

"He's not," Flash told her. He wasn't smiling, he was completely serious. "If you find that your hands are secured with zip-ties, you can get the cord out of your shoes and use it like a saw to weaken the plastic until it breaks. Make a loop with the cord, thread it around the zip-ties and your feet. Then move your feet back and forth, like you're riding a bike, and eventually the friction will heat up the plastic and you can break it."

"Wow, seriously?"

"Another thing we'll practice," Bo promised. He put his hand on the small of her back.

"Right, okay. What else?" Wren asked.

MacGyver pulled out a small black metal object, and Wren leaned in for a better look.

"It's a barrette," Mozart told her. "We have a friend who was in the Delta Force, and his wife used one of these to get out of a bad situation in Egypt one time. I know you have short hair, but you could use it as a decorative accessory. At least we can hope that's what anyone would think."

Wren picked it up out of MacGyver's palm. It was indeed a simple snap barrette. But even to her untrained eye, she could tell it was so much more.

"It can be a screwdriver, a ruler, a wrench, but the serrated edge can cut through all sorts of things. Canvas, zip-ties...or anything, really. The edge can also be used with the ferro rod if needed."

Bo reached for the barrette and unsnapped it. Then he gently pushed it into her hair at the side of her head and clipped it shut. "It matches your hair, so it's not super obvious."

For some reason, Wren blushed. Feeling his hands in her hair felt really nice. It wasn't the time or place for her to be thinking about how his touch would feel on other parts of her body, but she couldn't stop her wayward thoughts.

"And then there's this," MacGyver said, bringing her attention back to him. He held out something that looked tiny in his big fingers. It was a knife. A very small folding knife. He flicked his wrist and the tip was exposed, looking sharp and deadly.

"We figured this could also go inside your boot," Dude said. "Or maybe in the hidden pocket in your belt. But it's harder to hide than the other things we found for you. Maybe

Safe can come up with some other way to conceal it, somewhere that won't be obvious for anyone looking for hidden weapons."

"It's not big enough to really use as a weapon, and the last thing you want to do is go one-on-one with a kidnapper," Blink told her.

"Right. If the worst-case happens and you get taken, as we've said, be compliant. Don't speak unless you have to. Don't yell at them, try not to cry. Be as stoic as you can. Eat what they give you, because you never know when you might get food again," Flash said seriously.

"And drink water. It's a crap shoot, because you don't know if it's clean, but without water you'll weaken, and any chance for escape that arises, you might not be strong enough to take it," Smiley added.

"Speaking of escape, you have to be smart about it. You'll probably either be taken to a safe house in the city where the kidnappers have holed up, or they'll take you into the jungle. Most likely the latter, because it's easier to defend and there will be fewer people to see their captives," Preacher told her.

"The city would be better, easier to escape, but not necessarily safer. Because an American woman wandering alone isn't safe. Not at all," Kevlar mused. "But the jungle isn't exactly good either. You'd have to figure out which way to go to get to safety—and I use the term safety loosely, since anyone you'd run across could potentially cause you harm. Then find water, food, and shelter."

"Jungle is definitely better," Bo said firmly. "She can find a place to hole up and wait for help to arrive."

Wren's mind spun. While it might've been fun to see all

the stuff the guys had brought for her, thinking about being on her own in the middle of a jungle in Africa wasn't appealing at all. No one had mentioned animals and insects, but she assumed pretty much anything in the trees could kill her with one bite.

She pushed the thought to the back of her mind and blurted, "What help will arrive? I mean, the State Department already said Americans were on their own if they went to the country, and you've pointed out more than once that anyone I run across probably wouldn't want to take me to their house for tea and cookies."

She wasn't trying to be funny, but she saw a few lip twitches on the men around the table.

"I think that's my cue to bring in Tex," Mozart said. He reached for a phone that was sitting in the middle of the table and pushed some buttons.

Within seconds, Wren could hear ringing coming from the speaker.

"It's about time," a man on the other end of the line complained in a slightly southern drawl.

CHAPTER THIRTEEN

Safe was not having a good time, but this meeting needed to happen. It would've been better if all of Wren's coworkers could've been there to hear it too, but they were being macho boneheads and wouldn't admit there might be something they could learn from a bunch of Navy SEALs.

As much as he enjoyed Wren's obvious delight in some of the things his friends had brought for her, the reasons why she might need them were a heavy burden on Safe's heart. The thought of her being in any situation where she might actually need to use any of the survival gear they were outfitting her with made him want to puke.

But he was also very proud of the way she was handling the huge amounts of info being thrown at her. He'd sit down with her in the next few days and answer any other questions she had, and make sure she knew how to use all the equipment she'd been given. He'd help her shop for appropriate clothes and shoes. Safe would do *anything* to help make this asinine trip she was going on a little safer. With a little luck, she wouldn't need anything she was given tonight and it would all be overkill.

The only reason he hadn't pressed her harder to get out of the trip—he really did understand that if she insisted on not going, she had a possibility of losing her job—was because of the man on the other end of the phone at the moment.

"Tex! Thanks for agreeing to join us tonight," Mozart said.

"Don't have anything else going on right this moment," he drawled.

Everyone chuckled at that. Tex always had something going on. Someone he was tracking.

"Wren? You there?"

"Um...yeah, I'm here," she said, giving Safe a sideways glance.

Wanting to reassure her, Safe stepped closer and put his hand on the small of her back.

"First things first. You don't have to worry about Matt Smith anymore. I found him."

"What?"

"You did?"

"Where was he?"

The questions came from Safe's teammates, and he was happy to let them ask the questions he was dying to know the answers to. Wren gasped, muscles tightening under his hand, and he stepped closer, wanting to reassure her.

"His real name is actually Barry Simpson and he's wanted in two states. He has a warrant out of Wyoming for terrorist threats and another out of Washington for sexual assault and stalking. On a hunch, I looked up all the Matt Smiths on other dating apps and cross referenced the info on all of them. Idiot used the exact same info in his profiles. He messed up and used the Wi-Fi in the motel he was staying in, up in Chula Vista, to set up one of them. The sheriff department's warrant squad was headed out to apprehend him before your meeting started."

"Seriously?" Wren whispered.

"Yes."

"Wow."

Safe was equally as shocked, but pleased at the same time.

"Moving on. You get all the stuff the guys brought for you?" Tex asked.

"Uh-huh."

"And the toe ring?"

"We saved that for last," Dude told him. "Haven't told her about it yet."

"Got it. So...if you get taken, the kidnappers, if they're not complete idiots, will take all your jewelry. Watches, earrings, necklaces, bracelets. All of it. I'm a big fan of putting tracking devices in earrings. But since I'd advise against you bringing any kind of jewelry with you, not even a damn watch, and because I don't want my tech being thrown into some African jungle river, I went with a new thing. A toe ring."

Safe saw Wren frown in confusion.

"Tex is a master at making tracking devices," he explained. "When we go on missions, we all have one."

"There was one in my wetsuit when I was left in the ocean in Hawaii," Kevlar explained. "That's how Remi and I were rescued so quickly. Tex realized I'd been in the water too long for a normal dive excursion, and he contacted a former SEAL who lives out in Hawaii to come check on me. Thank goodness."

"You asked what help would arrive if shit hits the fan in South Sudan?" Preacher said. "*We* will. Well, maybe not us specifically, but Tex knows basically everyone. He'll figure out who's closest, and who can get in and out without completely pissing off the government—ours and theirs—and they'll come get you."

Wren stared at the tiny, almost delicate ring MacGyver was now holding out to her.

"We figured kidnappers will take obvious jewelry...rings, necklaces, and the like. But they'd have to not only remove your shoes, but your socks, too, in order to find the toe ring. And since it looks plain and not worth any kind of money, the chances of them leaving it alone are high," Kevlar said.

"I do have some trackables that can be swallowed, but the reception isn't as good as it is with a wearable one. And if you're gone too long...well, not to get too graphic, but your body would expel it at some point and that would defeat the purpose of being able to lead a team straight to you," Tex said.

"If something happens, do *not* give up," Blink said in a low voice. "No matter what. Tex will be watching. If you end up anywhere other than at the hotel or the president's compound, Tex will sound the alarm and someone will be coming for you and your coworkers. Understand?"

Wren pressed her lips together and nodded. Safe saw that she'd closed her fingers around the ring and was holding it tightly in her fist.

"I...I don't know what to say," she said quietly.

"Whatever it is, it better not be thank you," Tex bitched from the other end of the phone.

Safe chuckled, along with his friends.

"Tex hates to be thanked," Dude explained, seeing Wren's confusion.

"Oh, well, okay. Then if something happens and this little toe ring comes into play, I'll simply have to name my firstborn after you," Wren told him.

"Another one?" Tex asked.

No one held back their laughter at that.

"Trust me, no one wants to be named Tex," Mozart said.

"You don't need to thank me or name any of your children after me," Tex said after everyone stopped laughing. "I don't do what I do because I want anyone to be in my debt or because I want the gratitude. I do it because I hate to see evil win. It pisses me off. And the more I can thwart the bad shit in the world, the more chance kindness has to prevail. And from where I'm sitting, we need more of that for sure."

"I agree," Wren said quietly.

"Uh-huh...so, while you're feeling all warm and fuzzy about me, now's a good time to let you know that I looked into your father. Tyler Farris is the real deal. Forty-nine, three kids, married once. Lives in Mission Viejo and is co-CEO of Farris Morgan. His company is above board and doesn't accept shady contracts."

Safe tensed. Yes, he'd contacted Tex about Wren's father and asked if he would look into the man, but he hadn't expected him to act so quickly. He should've known better.

"I asked him to see what he could find out," he told Wren.

"I wanted to make sure he was on the up and up. That you wouldn't be hurt further if you decided to talk to him, or to meet him or your half-brothers."

Wren looked at him, but Safe couldn't read what she was thinking. He was nervous, wondering if she was pissed or pleased.

Then, as he watched, tears formed in her eyes, and she turned and leaned against him, her head resting on his shoulder as she stood motionless, her arms at her sides.

Safe immediately wrapped her in his embrace.

"Wren?" Tex asked. "Did you hear me?"

Wren nodded.

"She heard you," Safe told him.

"Good. Far as I can tell, Tyler's a good man. Safe told me what your mother said about him, and it seems that was a lie. He hasn't even had a speeding ticket in over twenty years. And trust me, I *tried* to find dirt on him. Now, your *mother*—"

Wren came alive in Safe's arms. She spun toward the table and yelled, "No!" interrupting Tex. "I don't want to know. I don't want to hear her name ever again. She's out of my life, and that's where I want her to stay."

"All right." Tex's voice was gentle now.

Wren took a deep breath, then sagged against Safe's side. He wrapped an arm around her waist, holding her tight.

"So...anything else you think Wren needs to know before she leaves on her trip next week?" Kevlar asked Tex.

"Just to stay smart. Alert. And just because Safe and the others are advising you to stay compliant, doesn't mean you shouldn't do what you can to keep yourself safe. And, Wren?

If the opportunity arises, get the hell away from them. Don't be a martyr and stay because all of you can't escape at the same time. When help comes, it'll come for all of you, even if you aren't together. Understand?"

Wren sniffed once, took a deep breath and said, "Yes."

"Good. I've got to get going. My wife just let me know that dinner's ready, and I don't miss sitting down with my family at night if I can help it. Have a good trip. I'll be watching."

And just like that, Tex disconnected the call.

Dude snorted. "Have a good trip. Whatever," he muttered.

"Wren?" Kevlar asked.

She looked over at him. "Yeah?"

"You've never met your father?"

Safe wanted to stop this conversation right there. Didn't want Wren to talk about something that was obviously difficult for her, but she spoke before he could shut down his team leader's questions.

"No. My mom always told me he was a piece of shit. A felon. A murderer. I was conceived after a one-night stand. Recently, my half-brother started calling out of the blue. Scared me, actually, because I thought it was Matt. Said they didn't know anything about me, and that they all—him, his two brothers, my dad, and my...I guess stepmother—would love to meet someday."

"And they're in Mission Viejo?" Kevlar asked.

Wren nodded.

"Well, say the word, and once you're back from your trip,

and we're back from our mission, we'll go up there with you, if you want. Have your back."

Wren stared at Kevlar with eyes as big as saucers. "Why?"

"Why what? Why would we go with you? Because you're one of us now," Kevlar said simply.

"I...I...This is so confusing," Wren whispered.

"What is?" Smiley asked.

"All of it. You guys meeting with me about safety. Bringing me all this stuff. Tex and the tracker..." She opened her fist and looked down at the small ring on her palm. "Julie and the clothes, Remi helping me pick out what to keep, Matt being found, Caroline and Wolf buying me lunch. I don't know what to do with it all."

"My suggestion?" Blink said with a small, introspective smile. "Just go with it."

"Right. Go with it," Wren echoed. Then she looked up at Safe and said, "It's over."

"Not until we hear that he's actually in custody," Kevlar warned.

"You think there's a chance he can escape?" Wren asked with a frown.

"Honestly? Not really. Tex wouldn't have sounded so sure of himself, wouldn't even have told you if he didn't think it was a done deal."

Wren relaxed against Safe.

He was relieved that Simpson had been found, of course he was...but he was also struck by a sense of disappointment that there was no longer any reason for her to stay at his house.

"Of course, I'd suggest since your things were destroyed that you don't immediately go back to your apartment yet. At least until you get furniture and stuff." Kevlar winked at Safe.

"Yeah. Since we've been busy with our mission planning, and you've been just as busy at work getting ready for this trip, it doesn't make sense to go back to your place yet, considering how much stuff you still need to go over with Safe," Preacher agreed.

"Exactly. How will you learn how to use the ferro rod if you're living all the way across town?" Flash added.

Safe couldn't help but roll his eyes at his friends. They weren't being very subtle. He appreciated them acting as his wingmen, but they were being a bit heavy-handed.

"You guys can discuss that later. I want to get home to Remi," Kevlar said.

"And I just want to get home," Smiley said with a yawn.

"Same time in the morning?" MacGyver asked Kevlar.

Their team leader stood and nodded solemnly. "It's looking like we'll be headed out in about four days."

"Shit, thought we had another week?" Preacher asked.

"So did I," Kevlar said with a shrug.

Such was life as a Navy SEAL. They all were well aware they could be deployed at a moment's notice. The fact that they'd had significant notice for this mission was somewhat unusual. But since they were going back to Chad, where they'd just been a couple weeks ago, they'd needed the extra time to make sure their plans were extremely solid—to be certain they wouldn't have to go back for a third mission.

There'd be no unexpected loose ends this time around.

"All right. Drive safe going home. I'll see you all in the morning," Kevlar said, effectively dismissing them.

Safe stepped back from Wren as each of his friends approached and told her that if she needed anything, had any questions, or simply wanted to talk, they were available.

Mozart and Dude were the last to say good night.

"I trust Tex with my life. More importantly, I trust him with my wife's life," Dude said.

"He's had a hand in saving all our women at one time or another," Mozart added. "If the worst happens, trust that he'll come through for you."

"What if they take the toe ring?" Wren asked nervously.

"He's reassured us that he imbedded some sort of technology that can track the temperature of the person wearing it. If it's removed, it'll be obvious and he'll know the worst happened. He'll send help," Dude said succinctly.

Mozart nodded.

Wren took a deep breath. "Okay."

"Okay," Mozart echoed.

"Need to get you together with our women," Dude said. "They all met Remi and loved her. It's your turn." He looked at Safe. "See if you can make that happen when she gets back. Bring her to Aces."

"I'm not sure—"

"When you fall off a horse, you get back on," Dude said gently, interrupting Wren. "I know bad shit happened there, but Jessyka feels horrible about that and has made some changes. If you're willing to give it another chance, I promise you'll have a different experience."

She took a deep breath and nodded. "All right."

"Good. Safe'll set it up. We'll be in touch," Dude said. He gave her a chin lift and headed for the door, with Mozart at his side.

Then it was only Safe and Wren left in the room.

"Wow," she said. "My head is spinning."

"Yeah, that was a lot. What's the main thing you're thinking about?" Safe asked, turning her toward him and loosely putting his arms around her waist. He thought she'd mention the tracker. Or one of the other gadgets she'd been given. Or maybe even the info she'd learned about her father. But she surprised him.

"I don't want to go back to my apartment yet. I know Kevlar said Matt, or Barry, whatever his name is, has probably been arrested by now, but...I'd like to stay. At least until you leave."

"You can stay as long as you want. Even after I head out on my mission," Safe told her without hesitation. In the past, the thought of someone being in his space while he was gone made him cringe. But knowing this woman was there, amongst his belongings, eating his food, sitting at his table, sleeping under his roof...it felt right.

"Okay. I can get your mail and stuff," she told him.

"Don't give a shit about that. I can put a hold on it. Don't get anything important anyway, it's all junk. I *want* you there. Want you safe and comfortable. You aren't on your own anymore," Safe reminded her. "You have me, my team, Remi, and Wolf's team and their wives. You have a SEAL family, Wren."

"We just met," she whispered.

"When you know, you know," Safe countered. "You think I've done this before? Met a woman and within a few days, moved her in and introduced her to the most important people in my life? The answer is *hell* no. There's something about you that's so special. I know it, and I'm not stupid enough to turn my back on that. To let it, let *you*, slip out of my hands without a hell of a fight. Things between us might not work out...but what if they do? Stay at my house, Wren. Please."

"Okay."

"Okay," he echoed. "You ready to head home?"

"Yeah."

"Tomorrow when I pick you up, we'll go shopping. See what we can find that will not only look professional, but be functional. We'll go through all the survival stuff the guys brought you again and make sure you can use it. All right?"

"Sounds good."

"Tonight, we'll decompress. Think about nothing. Watch some trash TV. Relax."

She smiled. "That sounds *perfect*. To be honest, my head hurts a little. Bo?"

"Yeah, hon?"

"I'm worried about myself and this trip, but I'm also worried about you. And now all the other guys too. You're leaving soon, and I know you can't tell me anything about your mission, but I'm still worried."

"I wish I could take that worry away, but honestly? It feels good to have someone concerned about my well-being. It's a new feeling for me." Safe wished he could reassure her that he'd be fine. That their mission would be successful, and he'd be home maybe even before she left for South Sudan. But he couldn't and wouldn't do that to her.

Blink was a good reminder that not all missions went the way they were supposed to. He could be hurt—or worse, killed. He hated that, but it was a fact of life for him as a Navy SEAL. Yes, he and his teammates were well-trained... but that hadn't helped Blink's team.

So he'd reassure Wren however he could and hope everything turned out well. He wanted a chance to get to know this woman better. He wanted to make her his in every way that counted. But first, they both had to get through their upcoming trips. When they got back, he'd work on deepening their relationship.

"Well, I do care. I do worry. Don't forget that while you're out saving the world from bad guys."

Safe grinned. "Trust me, I won't forget."

"Good."

Safe turned and helped her pack all the things back into the box, then he picked it up, took her hand with his free one, and headed for the door.

It wasn't lost on Safe that if things *did* go bad for Wren and her coworkers, he and his team would be on the same continent. They'd be the closest available help. Safe knew it. Kevlar knew it. Dude and Mozart knew it. And so did Tex.

No one had said anything out loud, but it was in the back of his mind. Kevlar and the others were probably already thinking about the ramifications. Of getting their mission done as quickly as possible so they'd be able to cross the border into South Sudan from Chad if necessary.

As Wren smiled up at him from his side, Safe sent a prayer

upward that she'd be fine. She'd go to Africa, do her thing, and come home a couple days later. That all their planning and precautions would be for naught.

But if being a SEAL had taught him anything, it was that nothing ever went according to plan. Safe just hoped that if something did happen to Wren, she'd be able to keep her head and stay safe until help arrived.

CHAPTER FOURTEEN

Wren was panicking. It was ten o'clock at night, and Bo would be leaving in four hours to head to the Naval base for his mission departure. She wasn't ready.

For the last few days, she'd been living in denial. Denial that he'd be leaving. That *she'd* be leaving. The closer it got to the date she and the others from BT Energy would be going to South Sudan, the more scared she became. And that was saying something, because Wren didn't scare easily.

She'd lived through a lot of terrifying things. But this?

It hadn't been so bad when Bo and his Navy SEAL friends had given her all those survival items. She'd felt good that they cared enough to try to help her.

But when Bo made her practice using the ferro rod, when he took out some zip-ties to see if she could use the paracord in her shoelaces to get out of them...it sank in more and more just how concerned he really was that she was traveling to South Sudan.

And if Bo was freaked, Wren knew she should be too. So the dread built up. With each day that passed, the closer the time came for her to leave, the more she wished her boss would cancel.

And now the time was here for Bo to head out on his own mission. And she was worried about him too. She didn't know the specifics of his trip, he couldn't say, but she'd gotten enough of a gist to know that whatever it was he and his teammates were going to do in Africa, it was dangerous. Beyond dangerous. And the thought of this man possibly not coming back, of never seeing him again, wasn't something she wanted to contemplate.

The last few weeks had been life-changing for Wren. Bo was...well, he was amazing. Considerate, playful, affectionate, respectful. And she wanted more.

But with both their lives about to get very dangerous, she wasn't sure she'd have the opportunity for more. And that sucked.

"What are you thinking about so hard?" Bo asked.

They were sitting on his couch, both reluctant to go to bed because that meant they'd have to say goodbye. Bo already told her that he wasn't going to wake her up when he left, so when they said good night, that would be the last time they saw each other until they both returned. *If* they both returned.

Wren shivered.

"Are you cold? Here," Bo said, pulling a blanket off the back of the couch and holding it out to her.

Making an impulsive decision, Wren sat up, then scooted over to where he was sitting. She brought her knees up and leaned into him, snuggling into his side. "Is this okay?" she whispered.

"Oh yeah," Bo said in a tone that had Wren thinking that maybe, just maybe, he needed this as much as she did.

His arm went around her shoulders, and he held her against him as he relaxed against the cushions. He stretched his legs out in front of him and sighed as they both got comfortable against one another.

Several moments went by before he asked, "You hear from the detective today?"

Wren nodded. "Matt...sorry, *Barry*, was extradited back to Wyoming for the terrorist threats. Since those are federal charges, they're more serious. Then he'll have to go to Washington to face the charges there."

"Will they need you to testify about anything?"

Wren shrugged. "If he goes to court for the assault and stalking charges, maybe."

"I was serious about you staying here for the next week before you leave," Bo said. "You don't need to go back to your apartment."

"I know. And I appreciate it. I like this place. It's cozy."

"Small and a little run down," Bo corrected with a laugh.

But Wren didn't join him in his laughter. Picking up her head, she met his gaze. "It's small, yes, but it's clean. There aren't cigarette butts lying on the tables and floors. There's food in the fridge and pantry. It smells like laundry detergent and lemon from whatever you use to clean the floors. The doors lock securely, and I don't have to worry about mold in the walls and cockroaches crawling into my ears at night."

"Wren," Bo said in a sad tone.

But she shook her head. "No, don't feel sorry for me. Growing up the way I did gave me a better appreciation for the things I have. The things I earned. It sucks that Barry destroyed all my possessions, but it was just stuff. He didn't hurt me, thanks to you and Kevlar. And you've all done way more than your fair share in helping me get set up again. But being here with you made me realize something important."

"What's that?" Bo asked, tightening his arm around her.

Wren rested her head back on his shoulder. "That I've been living a very solitary existence. I tricked myself into thinking I was trying to be more social, just because I joined a dating site. But in reality, I've always pushed people away because I was afraid of getting hurt. Of being in a relationship like the ones my mom had when I was little. I was so worried about protecting myself from being hurt, I isolated myself instead. I changed jobs so often because it was easier than opening up, than making true friendships.

"And now, I've gone and done what I'd always resisted doing in the past. Made friends. I don't know how it happened, but I finally realize what I've been missing out on in my life. *Connection.* I guess I was afraid once someone got to know me, the real me, they'd judge me and find me lacking. And that would hurt way more than not having friends in the first place.

"But you and your friends accepted me. Without reservation. You've gone above and beyond to help me prepare for my trip, even though you don't agree with my choice to go to South Sudan. Caroline, Julie, Remi, and other women I haven't even met yet, they've helped me without wanting anything in return. That's so rare."

Taking a deep breath, she looked up at Bo again. "I'll stay here until I leave. Why would I want to go back to my apartment when some of the best memories of my life so far, I've had in this house? Laughing with you while we watch TV, making dinner together, eating sugary kid cereal in the mornings at your table. Waking up in the middle of the night to use the bathroom and having you stick your head out of your room because you heard me, asking me in your sleepy voice if I'm okay. You might have a hard time getting me to leave when we both get back."

Wren hadn't meant to blurt out that last part, but she didn't regret saying it. She wasn't brave enough to tell this man how much he was coming to mean to her, but that didn't mean she couldn't tell him in covert ways.

His hand moved to cup her face and his gaze was intense as he stared at her. He didn't speak, just leaned toward her. Wren eagerly tilted her chin to receive the kiss she knew was coming. When his lips touched hers, tingles ran from the top of her head down to her toes.

A little moan escaped from deep in her throat, which made Bo ease his hand to the nape of her neck as he deepened the kiss. His thumb caressed the sensitive skin there as he devoured her mouth.

Bo shifted on the couch until he was lying back, pulling her down on top of him. His hand was still locked on her nape and the other was pressed against the small of her back. She could feel his erection against her belly, but he didn't rock his hips or do anything that might make her feel uncomfortable in his embrace.

When she moved a hand down his side and shifted up so

she could reach the buckle of his belt, Bo gently grabbed her wrist and moved her hand back up to his chest.

"Don't you...I mean...we can..." Wren wanted to roll her eyes at her inability to say what she wanted.

"I want you," Bo said bluntly. "But when I make love to you for the first time, I don't want to be rushed. I want to be able to take my time. Memorize the feel of you under me, over me, and how you feel when I'm deep inside your body."

Wren's womanly parts clenched at that.

"What I *don't* want is some sort of desperation fuck that's rushed because I'm leaving. We're both coming back, Wren. We'll be able to explore this chemistry and connection we have in depth when we get home. I'm glad you like my house, because if it was up to me, you'd never leave. I'm that serious about you."

She didn't like that first part, about the desperation fuck, but...he was right. She *was* feeling a little desperate. "You can't know what will happen. You're the one who's warned me about all the horrible things that can happen to me while I'm on this trip."

"You *will* come home," Bo said with so much conviction, Wren had no choice but to believe him. "And I will too. I've done hundreds of missions. This will *not* be the one that finishes me off, especially not when I have you to come home to."

"Bo," Wren whispered, feeling overwhelmed.

"Life is hard," he said. "When you're at your lowest, life has a way of trying to kick you down even further. It's the people who can lift their middle finger and say 'no way will you get the better of me' who come out on top. I'm counting on you to do just that. I hope and pray that your trip is boring as hell and goes exactly as planned. But if it doesn't, remember everything we've told you, stay calm, and know that you aren't alone. You have a group of former and current Navy SEALs who will do whatever it takes to get to you."

"I'm thinking it's not quite that easy," Wren said. "I mean, you have to have permission to come into the country, right? By our government and your bosses and the South Sudanese people."

"If you're in danger, no one will be able to keep me away."

His words made tears well up in her eyes.

"Don't cry," he ordered gruffly.

"I can't help it. You're being sweet."

"You want me to be a dick?" he asked.

Wren laughed. "No."

"That's better," he said gently, wiping her cheek with his thumb.

"Can we sleep here?" she blurted.

Instead of saying how uncomfortable the couch was compared to a bed, or arguing that he needed his sleep before leaving for his mission, Bo simply nodded. He shifted her until she was snuggled against his side, her back to the cushions, one of her legs draped over his thighs and her arm over his chest. Then he grabbed the blanket and covered them both.

"You'd probably sleep better in your bed," she felt obligated to mumble.

"Wouldn't sleep," he told her. "I'd be thinking about you."

"I'm gonna miss you," Wren admitted.

"Not as much as I'll miss you," Bo countered.

A couple minutes went by without either of them speaking, then Wren said softly, "I thought being drugged was the worst thing that could happen to me. It gave me so many flashbacks of growing up, of being scared of my mom and her boyfriends. But...it turned out to be one of the best things that ever happened to me."

"No," Bo said sternly. "You being drugged against your will is *not* one of the best things to happen to you."

"But it led me to you," Wren protested, lifting her head to try to see him better.

"I would've found you regardless," Bo told her.

"How?"

"I don't know. But there's no way with the connection we share, we wouldn't have found our way to each other eventually."

Oh man, that was one of the sweetest things anyone had ever said to her.

"I'd already noticed you," he went on. "In Aces that night. I saw you with that asshole and wondered what you were doing with him. I would've found a way to talk to you. I don't know how, but I felt drawn to you even before we'd said one word to each other. So you being drugged *wasn't* a good thing. It wasn't the catalyst to us meeting."

Wren liked that. A lot. "Okay, Bo."

"Close your eyes, Wren."

She didn't want to. She wanted to savor the feeling of being in his arms. Neither of them knew what the future would bring, and if she was being honest, she wanted to beg him not to go. To help her figure a way out of going to South Sudan. But that wasn't the kind of woman she was.

Laying her head back on his chest, Wren closed her eyes as Bo ordered. She'd planned to stay awake until it was time for him to leave, but with the warmth of his body along hers, the sound of his heartbeat under her ear, the feel of his chest rising and falling, it all conspired to make her succumb to sleep within minutes.

* * *

Safe didn't sleep. Not one wink. He could sleep on the plane on the way to Chad. For now, he was too busy memorizing every second of holding Wren in his arms.

One of the hardest things he'd ever done was pull her hand away from his cock. He wanted to feel her hands on him. Her mouth. Wanted to strip her naked and lose himself inside her.

But he hadn't lied, there wasn't enough time to do everything he wanted to do the first time they were intimate. He needed at least an entire night.

So instead, he held Wren as she slept. The more he learned about her childhood and her life, the more impressed he was with this woman. Many people wouldn't be able to survive what she had. They would've turned to drugs or alcohol to cope. Would've made the wrong kinds of friends. Something.

But his Wren had a core of steel.

He had no doubt she had triggers. Had moments when she'd wanted to give up. But she hadn't. She kept putting one foot in front of the other and finding ways to succeed.

He *hated* that she was going to South Sudan. He had a very

bad feeling about that trip, but he hadn't lied. If something *did* happen while she was there, he wouldn't let anyone keep him from going after her. Safe had already talked about it with Kevlar, who'd discussed the entire situation with their commander. They were going to be in Chad, a country bordering South Sudan. According to their very detailed plans, their own mission should take a week, tops. That meant by the time Wren reached Africa, they could be in South Sudan in hours, if need be.

Safe prayed they wouldn't need to. But if anyone dared hurt her, he'd be ready—and they'd be dead. Period.

He had no problem killing bad guys. He'd done it time and time again without remorse. Men and women who'd chosen to hurt others. Who'd planned to murder hundreds of innocent people. But the thought of just one particular person being hurt, *his* person, made his usually even-keeled emotions swirl out of control.

He turned his head and inhaled deeply, smelling Wren's shampoo and her own unique scent.

He needed her.

Pressing his lips together, Safe was more determined than ever to get through this deployment and come home to further his relationship with Wren. Nothing and no one would keep him from making sure she knew how it felt to be treasured. To be put first in a relationship. To be loved.

There it was.

Did Safe love her?

Probably...?

He'd never felt this way about a woman. Never wanted to spend every waking—and sleeping—moment with anyone.

Had never had as much in common with someone else as he did Wren. Safe couldn't wait to see what their future held. Knew they could make it through anything, as long as they worked together.

Two a.m. came way too soon. Even before his watch vibrated on his wrist, Safe knew it was time to go. He slipped out from under Wren, and she barely moved. She was exhausted, not only from working long hours but the stress of the last couple weeks. Stress over her work situation, Barry, trying to decide what to do about her long-lost father, and worrying about his mission.

Safe took a fast shower, brushed his teeth, and dressed. Then he went back to the couch and leaned over a still-sleeping Wren. He'd told her he wouldn't wake her up when he left, but he was feeling selfish. He needed to talk to her one more time.

He kissed her forehead and shook her gently. "Wren?"

"Hmmm?"

"I'm headed out."

That woke her up. Wren's eyes opened and she studied him with her dark brown gaze. "Be careful. I'm gonna hold you to that whole all-night lovemaking session when we get back."

Safe grinned. "Deal. *You* be safe," he retorted.

"I will."

They stared at each other for a beat before Safe leaned down and kissed her lips gently. He wanted more, much more, but this was already killing him.

He stood, then turned and headed for the door without looking back. If he did, he might not leave.

Taking a deep breath, he opened the front door and walked out, locking the door behind him. He stood on his front step for a moment, his eyes closed, praying that Wren would be safe. That his mission would go as planned with no surprises. Then he walked briskly toward his Jeep, trying to turn his mind to SEAL mode. He had a job to do.

Afterward he'd get his reward. Wren.

CHAPTER FIFTEEN

Wren had never been so stressed in all her life. Maybe if she was still in the dark about just how dangerous this trip could be, she might be enjoying it a little more. But all she could think about were the stories she'd read online and that she'd heard from Bo and his friends.

The week after Bo left was...hard. While she'd been relieved the threat from Matt/Barry was over, she'd still felt the urge to look over her shoulder at all times. Wolf had been a huge help in getting a new key for her car, and the locks on her apartment had long-since been changed. Remi had gone with her to the apartment one evening and helped her put away everything her new friends had bought for her, and to start looking online for some of the bigger things she needed, like furniture.

But Wren had felt lonely since the moment Bo walked out the door.

Which was crazy. She'd been surrounded by people all day

at work. Communicating with Remi and Caroline via text on and off each day. She'd also heard from Mozart, who began checking in with her as soon as Bo left. It was a part of his "proof of life" plan he and Dude had put together. She was supposed to text or email one of them at least twice a day. Wren supposed some women would resent having to check in so often, but she wasn't "some women."

She'd spent most of her life alone, so knowing there were so many people out there who cared what was going on with her was comforting.

But even with all the communication with Bo's friends—now *her* friends—Wren still couldn't stop wondering where Bo was, what he was doing, whether or not he was okay. She supposed the latter had to be true, otherwise Wolf or someone would have told her. But that didn't make her worry any less.

Being in his house without him was weird. She missed him. A lot. Coming home to an empty space had felt much more difficult, now that she'd met Bo. She'd missed cooking dinner with him. Laughing together. Asking about his day. Watching TV. Talking.

The night before she left for South Sudan, Wren sat down and wrote a letter to Bo that she left at his house. If something happened to her, she'd wanted him to know how much she cared about him. How much he'd changed her life. It was mushy, and probably way too much information, but she consoled herself with the fact that he'd never see it if there were no problems on her trip.

And so far, there hadn't been. The flights were uneventful—Wren had been sure not to accept ice in her drinks on the planes, after hearing what had happened to Caroline, Wolf, and his friends on a flight long ago—and they were now all at the hotel in the heart of Juba.

Colby was acting like he was king of the world, wanting all the attention on himself, which was fine with Wren. She remembered Bo's warnings about staying under the radar. Not being noticeable. The two men Colby had brought along as his security, Bob and Tom—which made Wren chuckle to herself, as that was the name of a very popular morning radio talk show she sometimes listened to—stood out like sore thumbs. They wore all black, spoke to each other through little radios attached to harnesses they wore around their chests, and insisted on "clearing" each room before they entered it.

In Wren's opinion, they were acting more like movie versions of bodyguards than real ones. Not that she'd had all that much experience with real bodyguards, but she would've hoped they didn't act like these men.

The other five coworkers who'd traveled to South Sudan—Aaron, Luke, Dallas, Archie, and Oliver—had so far been pretty quiet. Archie and Dallas hung around with Colby, going where he went, doing whatever he told them to. The other three set up laptops in the room BT Energy had rented in the hotel for their briefings and meetings, to communicate with the team back in California, and to continue to do research and paperwork for the pipeline. Installation was slated to start in three months, if everything went according to schedule.

But of course, it wasn't. The fighting south of the capital was intensifying, making it difficult to recruit workers, and the exact placement of the pipeline was still under intense negotiations. There were disagreements because the government wanted it in a particular spot, and locals were protesting it being on "their" territory.

Colby hadn't been pleased when Wren had arrived at the airport back in California. Instead of the feminine skirts and pantsuits he'd gotten used to seeing her wearing at the office, she'd donned a pair of the cargo pants Bo had helped her find, a long-sleeve shirt made of lightweight wicking material, and her new boots. She'd been wearing them everywhere—except at work—for the last week to help break them in.

But it had been too late to change, and now that Wren was in Africa, she was doubly grateful for the suggestions from Bo's team. If she'd worn a skirt, she knew she would have gotten a lot more stares.

"Are you ready for this afternoon's press conference?" Colby asked.

They were all currently sitting around a table in the rented room, discussing the afternoon's schedule.

"Yes," Wren told him.

"You can't stray from the agenda," Colby warned.

Wren did her best to tamp down her irritation. "I know."

"I'm serious. If you say anything off script, you could get arrested. And we won't be able to do anything about it."

"I *know*," Wren said again, impatience clear in her tone.

"I'm just saying," he said as he sat back in his chair. "And I'm not sure your outfit is appropriate. We want to portray a gentle, safe presence to the people of this country. Convince them that having this gas pipeline is a good thing, not a militaristic takeover. And seeing you in those boots and pants, not to mention that manly shirt and your short hair, will project anything but gentle vibes. I hired you to bring a feminine face to BT Energy, and I'm not sure you're doing that right now."

Wren stiffened but did her best to not let her irritation show on her face. She needed this job. But she also needed to be safe. If Colby had let Bo come talk to the group, he'd understand why she was dressed as she was. And maybe he and the others wouldn't be wearing the expensive suits and ties they currently had on. They definitely stuck out in a glaring way. Even in the luxury hotel, they didn't fit in.

"I'm sorry, but according to the experts I consulted, South Sudan isn't a safe place to be a foreigner, especially a woman. What I'm wearing is for my safety. And I doubt anyone will be thinking about my clothes when I speak. They'll be more interested in what I'm saying. How BT Energy can help them," she said as calmly as she could.

"You're being naïve," Colby told her. "You were hired *because* you're a woman. Because we want people to be more interested in what they're looking at than what they're hearing. I'm going to have to insist on approving your wardrobe for future trips."

Oh *hell* no. That was on the tip of Wren's tongue, but she kept her mouth shut.

She'd had no idea her boss was such a misogynistic person when she'd accepted the job. If he thought she was going to let him paw through her clothes, he was very mistaken.

Flashbacks of her mom telling her over and over that she had to have long hair, because that was how girls attracted boys, almost overwhelmed Wren. She would've taken a pair of scissors to her long black hair as a child if she wasn't so scared of what her mom might've done to her. The first thing she'd done while on the streets was cut it. And she'd never looked back. She loved her short hair. It was easy to take care of, to style, and she didn't feel any less feminine because it wasn't long. Hell, the little clips she had in her hair might be practical survival tools, but in all honesty, they made her feel cute.

And now Colby was threatening to take away even that little sense of confidence in how she looked. What a fuckerhead.

Wanting to smile at the juvenile slur, Wren made sure to keep all emotion off her face.

"I kind of agree with Wren, I'm not sure it matters what she's wearing," Luke said. "I wish *I* was in cargo pants and a more comfortable shirt like hers. These suits make us stand out in a way that's not very comfortable."

"I don't give a shit what's comfortable and what's not," Colby said with a scowl. "When you're representing BT Energy, you will look professional at all times."

"Right," Luke said in a subdued tone.

Colby began lecturing them all about the details of the pipeline that they already knew. About how important this trip was and how much money they'd make as a result.

Wren looked over at Luke and mouthed *thank you*. He nodded at her, then turned his attention back to their boss.

Thankful that she was rooming with the youngest member of their team, and not Archie or Dallas, Wren sighed. Colby had leered at her suggestively when she'd requested that sleeping arrangement, but to her relief, Bob and Tom both agreed that it would be safer if she wasn't in a room alone.

The minutes crawled by as Colby went over every aspect of the pipeline. Even though they were all very well-versed on the ins and outs of the project, he still felt the need to hear himself speak.

Wren supposed he was nervous about the question-and-answer session they were hosting. Some major government officials were coming to talk to them. Well, mostly to talk to Colby, who would be giving an update on costs and where they were in regard to starting construction.

Dallas and Aaron were assisting Colby with the government officials during the session, and before it began, the others were dismissed. Wren was relieved to have a bit of free time away from Colby, who she was seeing as if for the first time. When she was hired, she'd been excited about the opportunity and had respected Colby as the CEO. Now? She just wanted to get through this quickly and go home. Get away from his overbearing countenance and disparaging looks.

The Q&A session lasted about an hour and a half, and Wren returned to the room to find the hotel workers setting up for the press conference she'd be presiding over.

The large table was cleared out and replaced by rows of chairs. A podium was placed at the front of the room for Wren and microphones set up. She didn't have a problem speaking in public, but for some reason this press conference felt different. Probably because of all the warnings from Bo and his team rattling around in her head. That, and Colby's critical remarks about her clothes and looks.

When it was finally time for her to speak, Wren was surprised at how few people had come. There were five people in the roughly thirty seats in the room. They were all men, and they looked bored beyond belief.

Clearing her throat, Wren launched into her presentation.

It went flawlessly. She detailed all the pros about the pipeline and what it would mean for the country of South Sudan. She explained how it would work and where the gas would come from and where it would flow. She thought she'd done a good job, but when she was finished, the men still had the same bored expressions on their faces.

It finally occurred to her that the government had probably handpicked who would be allowed to hear the information she was sharing. While there had been a video camera running, from one of the state-run television stations, Wren wondered if the footage would ever see the light of day.

She asked if anyone had any questions, and she wasn't surprised when no one did. Her first international press conference was kind of a letdown. The five spectators filed out and silence filled the room.

Colby pushed off the wall at the back of the room and left without a word, Bob and Tom at his heels. Archie and Dallas quickly followed.

"You did good, Wren," Oliver said when they were gone.

"Thanks."

"Did anyone else think that was...well...weird?" Luke asked.

"Extremely," Aaron agreed.

Wren was relieved to know she wasn't the only one who'd gotten weird vibes from the supposed press conference. "How was the meeting with the bigwigs?" she asked Aaron.

"Fine, I guess. Colby did most of the talking. We just sat there nodding our heads."

"Did it feel as if they were pleased with the project?" Luke asked.

"Yes? I mean, it all seemed pretty robotic to me. As if those attending didn't have any say in approving it or something," Aaron explained.

"It feels as if being here is just part of a big dog and pony show," Oliver said. "Like, it doesn't matter what we do or say, the government is going to do what they want regardless."

"Let's just hope what they want is to get this pipeline put in," Aaron grumbled. "Otherwise, we've done a hell of a lot of hard work for nothing."

"What do you think the dinner at the president's compound tomorrow night is going to be like?" Luke asked.

"There's no telling," Oliver said. "It'll either be like today, where it'll be us and a few handpicked people who wouldn't dare say anything that might be considered controversial, or it'll be a mob scene."

Wren had to agree with him. She had no idea what to expect, even with all the research she'd done and what she'd learned from Bo about the country.

"We need to stay vigilant," she blurted. The men in the room with her hadn't bothered to talk to the SEALs, but that didn't mean she didn't want them to be safe. "When we go outside of the hotel, we're vulnerable. A bunch of Americans who work for an energy company would be a very nice target for a group that wants some quick cash."

"We aren't going to get kidnapped," Oliver said with a roll of his eyes.

"I'm not saying we are," Wren snapped back. "But we also aren't in Riverton anymore. We have to be careful."

"We will be," Aaron told her.

"We're going out for a beer tonight," Oliver told her. "You want to come?"

Wren's eyes widened. "What? Outside the hotel? No!"

All three men laughed.

"You sound so scandalized," Aaron said. "It'll be fine. Bob and Tom are coming too."

"It's not a good idea," Wren told them. "Why not stay here and go to the small bar downstairs?"

"Because. We want to experience some of the culture in this country. Are you going to be the scared American who stays holed up here?" Oliver taunted.

Wren refused to rise to his bait. "Yes."

"Your loss," he said with a shrug. Then he turned to Aaron and Luke. "Meet you guys in the lobby in an hour?"

"Sounds good."

"Okay."

Wren could only shake her head at how stupid her coworkers were being. They hadn't heard all the things Bo and his team had to say, but still. They'd gotten the same info she had from the State Department about the dangers of the country. Why they felt as if they were in some sort of safety bubble was beyond her.

She walked up to her room with Luke and the second they were inside, she turned to him. "Please don't go, Luke. It's not safe."

"It'll be fine. Colby actually suggested it. He said it'll be a way to show some goodwill toward the people who live here. You know, spend some money, talk with the locals. Let them see that we're more than untouchable businessmen. It's our only free night."

"It's *dumb*," Wren told him. "You read the same warnings I did. About not walking around, especially after dark."

But Luke shrugged. "There will be eight of us. No one's gonna mess with eight guys. It's probably better you aren't going though. As a woman and all."

For the first time, Wren didn't feel the urge to punch someone when they made a comment about how women were weaker than men.

"Seriously, we'll be cool. We have Bob and Tom with us. We'll have a beer or two, then come back. Tomorrow, we'll have that meeting with the leaders of the various ethnic groups, then go to the president's place to hobnob."

Thinking about having to moderate tomorrow's discussion made Wren nervous as hell. One wrong word and the men could be at each other's throats. The tension between all the different groups in the country was extremely high. She would be partly responsible for keeping everyone calm. It was a lot of pressure.

"I really don't think it's a good idea," she told Luke, not willing to let it drop.

"Noted," he said. "I'm going to get out of this monkey suit and put on some jeans. You're welcome to watch," he said with a lifted eyebrow.

Wren rolled her eyes and headed for the bathroom. She was aware that Luke was teasing, but she didn't want to give him any kind of encouragement that the two of them would ever have a fling.

Luke called out that he was done changing, and Wren went back into the room. They didn't talk much after that. He was checking his email on his laptop as Wren scrolled through the channels on the TV, looking for something to watch.

"Gotta go meet the guys. I'll be back in a couple hours. If not, we've been kidnapped, call the authorities." Luke was grinning as he said it.

"That's not funny," Wren scolded.

"Come on, it was a *little* funny," Luke countered. "Loosen up, Wren. If you want to fit in at BT Energy, you need to relax." Then he waved and headed for the door.

After it shut behind him, Wren got up and threw the dead bolt. She was nervous to be left alone in the hotel, but not nervous enough to risk going with the rest of the group.

Sitting down on the bed, she pulled out her phone and pulled up her email. She typed out a quick note to Mozart, checking in as he'd requested.

Her phone dinged with a reply email five minutes later.

You made the right decision not to go out. Safe and his team weren't kidding about the dangers. One more day, then you'll be on your way home. I'll look for your email in the morning.

Wren was exhausted. The travel, plus the stress of the meetings was catching up with her. But she knew she wouldn't be able to fall asleep until Luke and the others were back safe and sound. She wasn't a big fan of her coworkers, but that didn't mean she wanted anything to happen to them.

Four hours later, Wren heard a quiet knock at the door. She leaped out of bed and looked through the peephole. Relief almost made her dizzy at seeing Luke standing there. She undid the dead bolt and opened the door.

"Sorry for waking you," he said a little sheepishly as he entered the room. He smelled like cheap beer and body odor. But Wren was still very glad to see him in one piece.

"How was it?" she asked.

"Okay," Luke said with a shrug. "We spent lots of money, drank lots of disgusting, warm beer, and now we're back. You should've gone. It was fine."

Wren went back to her bed and climbed under the covers as Luke went into the bathroom. He came out and stripped out of his shirt and jeans, leaving them in a pile on the floor. Then he lay down on his own bed, and Wren swore within seconds he was snoring.

She assumed he'd probably passed out, but she was too relieved to have him back at the hotel to care.

* * *

"She's fine," Preacher told Safe.

Safe took a deep breath and nodded. They were still in Chad, and they'd done what they'd come to do. The high-value target they'd been sent to eliminate after he'd taken over for his brother was no more. It was his twin who they'd eliminated last time. The twin no one knew about. The *real* terrorist leader had tasked his brother with making public appearances for him, for safety reasons. The man wasn't an idiot.

And when his twin was taken out by Safe and his team, the leader had no choice but to come out of hiding to reassure his followers that the US hadn't succeeded in assassinating him, after all. Which had been his one and only mistake.

Intelligence had quickly gotten back to the States, and the SEAL team was sent to Chad to complete the original mission.

They should've been on their way back home to California as of yesterday...but their commander had pulled some strings. Since learning about BT Energy's trip to South Sudan, he'd been just as concerned about it as Safe and the rest of the team. So they were holing up for an additional forty-eight hours. Just in case.

It was that "just in case" that was nearly making Safe go out of his mind with worry. "I know," he belatedly told Preacher.

"We would've gotten word if something had already happened," Flash agreed.

"One more day," MacGyver threw in.

Safe nodded. He wanted to talk to Wren. To hear for himself how things were going. To make sure she was all right. But he couldn't. He had to trust the intel that she was safe.

"One more day," he said under his breath. It would be the longest twenty-four hours of his life. Until he got word from their commander that the employees from BT Energy were on a plane and headed home, he wouldn't be able to relax.

CHAPTER SIXTEEN

Wren wanted nothing more than to sleep the rest of the day away, but she couldn't. She was obligated to go to the presidential thing, which was unfortunate, because after this morning's session, her nerves were shot.

The meeting with the different ethnic groups had been unbelievably tense. There was a lot of arguing and accusations of corruption flung back and forth. It was all Wren could do to keep everyone calm enough not to start fighting right there in the conference room. She did her best to explain how the pipeline would benefit everyone, but the men in attendance were more concerned with how much money their communities would get.

It had been exhausting, and combined with the very little rest Wren had gotten the night before, all she wanted to do was sleep. But Colby had told them all in no uncertain terms that they'd be going to the presidential compound, and ordered them to meet in the lobby at six o'clock sharp.

All Wren could think about was making it to tomorrow morning, when they would get on a plane and fly back to California. She had no idea if this trip had accomplished anything. If they'd managed to convince the people of South Sudan and the men in power that the pipeline was a good idea. The project had already been approved, but this trip was supposed to finalize the details and be a shiny, glossy PR campaign to convince the citizens that the partnership with BT Energy and the government would be beneficial for everyone.

She had no idea who would be at the dinner tonight. Didn't even know what to expect. She supposed there would be food. Maybe drinks. More schmoozing with mucketymucks. More putting on a happy smile to convince everyone in attendance that all was well with the project and BT Energy.

But the shine was gone for Wren. She simply wanted to be home.

Wanted to see Bo. Wanted to joke with Remi. Wanted to set up a meeting with her father.

She'd thought about Tyler Farris a lot over the last few days. All her life, she'd assumed he wasn't a good guy. That he'd left her mom high and dry. That he'd even *killed* someone. And to learn that none of that was true, and in fact he was a very successful, prominent, well-liked businessman, had been a shock.

Though in hindsight, it shouldn't have been. Her mom was a horrible human being. The fact that she'd lied about her father shouldn't have been a surprise at all.

Regardless, now that the shock of his existence had faded, Wren was curious. Did she look like him at all? Did they share any traits? And she had three half-brothers. Not to mention two nieces and a nephew!

Knowing her dad wanted to meet her was both scary and exciting at the same time. She wanted to meet him as well. At least once. Maybe they wouldn't get along. Maybe he wouldn't like her. But she'd gotten to the point where she at least wanted to meet him face-to-face. See for herself what kind of man he was.

And Wren had no doubt that Bo would go with her. He'd stay by her side, protecting her from anyone saying or doing anything hurtful, while she faced a part of her past she didn't think she'd ever get to experience. Hadn't *wanted* to experience.

Then there was her relationship with Bo himself. She wanted so much more with him. Sleeping together on the couch the night before he left had been so new and unfamiliar. She'd had sex, of course, but had never spent the night with a man. Had never trusted anyone enough to completely let down her guard that way.

She'd slept hard in Bo's arms. She wanted to do it again. She also wanted more of his kisses. His touches. Wanted to be intimate with him. To take him deep inside her body and watch him lose himself in her. Just as she wanted to lose herself with him.

"You gonna get ready or what?" Luke asked as he walked out of the bathroom.

Wren sighed. She was just losing herself in the fantasy of what it would be like to be with Bo, and Luke had to go and ruin in. "Yeah," she told him.

"We're leaving in fifteen minutes. Better get your ass in

gear. I'm headed down to grab a beer before we leave. I'm hoping if there's beer at this thing tonight, it'll be better than the crap we drank last night." Luke shivered. "Warm piss, that's what it tasted like."

"Maybe it was," Wren said with a small smirk.

"Mean," Luke told her with a shake of his head. "I had no idea you were so mean when I agreed to room with you."

Wren laughed, and was glad to see the smile on Luke's face. Teasing felt good. Released some of the tension in her tight muscles.

"All right, I'm headed down. See you soon. Don't be late. You know how tense Colby has been. And Bob and Tom haven't been much better."

"I'll be there," Wren said.

Luke left the room, and Wren headed into the bathroom. She put a clip in her hair, made sure her toe ring was still snug around the second toe on her right foot. Then she went into the bedroom and put on a clean pair of cargo pants, then the belt with the ferro rod. She made sure the secret pocket still held the cotton wool slathered with Vaseline. She grabbed the tube of lipstick and put it into one of the many pockets of her pants. Then she sat on the bed and grabbed her boots. She made sure the tiny knife was still under the insert in the arch of the left boot. Thankfully, she couldn't feel it when she walked.

Finally, content she had all the super-secret things the SEALs had given her in place, Wren took a deep breath and checked herself out in the mirror over the dresser. She bit her lip. She didn't look like a commando. She looked like a woman who needed a good night's sleep and was ready to go camping or something.

She supposed Colby did have a small point about her clothes. She looked nothing like the put-together professional woman she'd been when she'd interviewed with BT Energy. But then, this wasn't sunny California, and she'd sacrifice looking pretty for being safe.

Turning her back on her image, Wren grabbed her phone and sent a quick email to Mozart. Letting him know she was about to leave for the thing at the president's compound. She reassured him that she'd email again when she was back at the hotel, and thanked him for being her point of contact.

Shoving the phone in her back pocket, Wren left the room and headed to the lobby. One more social requirement, then she was home free. In twelve hours, they'd be on their way to the airport. She couldn't wait.

* * *

Everyone piled into two small minivans. Bob, Tom, Colby, Luke, and Aaron got into one van, and Wren, Dallas, Archie, and Oliver got into the other. Both had native drivers and another man, each introduced as members of the president's security team. There was also a man who wore what looked like a police uniform and was driving a motorcycle with flashing lights, leading their group.

They drove away from the hotel down a very busy street. There were people everywhere, going about their business, which actually made Wren feel better. Women with packages, men talking on street corners, shop owners selling their wares. It all seemed so...normal.

They'd only been driving for about ten minutes when Wren sensed something was wrong. They were no longer in the city proper, but instead driving at a high rate of speed down what seemed like a pretty rural road.

"Where are we going? Is this the way to the president's house?" she whispered to Dallas, who was sitting next to her.

"No," the older man said succinctly.

"Stay calm," the supposed presidential security guard said from the front seat. He turned around and pointed the rifle he'd been holding—one like all the military and police officers in the country carried—at the occupants of the minivan. "Don't do anything stupid."

Wren froze.

This wasn't happening. Of course, Bo and the others had warned that it might. But it still felt totally unreal.

"Where are we going? Where are you taking us?" Archie demanded harshly.

"No questions!" the man barked.

"Screw that!" Archie said. "You can't just take us away from our hotel without telling us where we're going!"

"I can't?" the man said with an evil-looking grin. "Looks like we did just that. Now shut up. Do what we tell you and you'll be fine."

"Right, sure we will," Oliver muttered.

"This is bullshit!" Dallas exclaimed. "Do you know who we are?"

"Of course. Why do you think we're taking you? Your company will pay money to get you back. Well, at least the man in charge. You? I'm not so sure." The man holding the weapon on them laughed.

"Is this happening?" Oliver asked no one in particular. "Are we seriously being kidnapped?"

Wren wanted to smack him. Of *course* it was happening. They'd been warned. Time and time again, and yet no one took the possibility seriously. Except her and Bo.

She wanted to reach into her pocket and grab her phone, but it wouldn't work anyway. It only worked when she had Wi-Fi, and there was definitely no Wi-Fi out here in the middle of nowhere.

She wondered what was going on in the other van. Was Colby freaking out? Had Bob and Tom attempted to do something to stop this kidnapping? She wasn't sure what they could do in a van with a rifle pointed at them.

They drove for what seemed like forever, but was probably only around thirty minutes. Enough time to leave the city of Juba far behind. The road had turned to hard-packed dirt, and everyone in the van was bouncing around like pieces of popcorn in a microwave. The flat, dry land was replaced by more and more trees, until the dirt road they were driving on was completely surrounded by lush jungle.

Finally, the van came to a halt.

"Don't do anything stupid," their captor reminded them. Then ordered, "Get out."

Oliver reached for the door handle, and suddenly the van was surrounded by armed men. They appeared as if out of nowhere. The door was wrenched open and Oliver was pulled out by a hand on the front of his shirt. He sprawled onto the ground on his hands and knees. Someone kicked him in the stomach, and he fell to the dirt with a moan.

Wren braced as the rest of them were yanked out of the vehicle without fanfare. She managed to stay on her feet and did her best not to look anyone in the eyes. They were all hustled over to where the rest of her coworkers were standing.

"I demand you take us back to the hotel!" Colby shouted.

No one listened. Looking around furtively, Wren couldn't count all the men, but there were over a dozen, more than enough to subdue their group. Every man was holding a rifle or gun of some sort. They wore tattered and torn clothes and their skin was filthy. It looked as if they'd been living in the jungle for quite a while.

"Search them," ordered the man who'd been on the motorcycle, leading their small motorcade.

Within seconds, Wren was grabbed from behind and another man was in front of her, running his hands up and down her legs. She held still, hating his touch but knowing if she protested—or kicked him in the face, like she really wanted to—things would become much worse for her in a hurry.

He reached into her pocket and pulled out her phone with a grin, throwing it onto a cloth that had been spread on the ground nearby. Then he shoved his hand into the pocket along her thigh and held up the lipstick she'd put in there earlier.

He smirked and said something in a language she didn't understand. The man holding her elbows responded—and to her surprise, the lipstick was put back into her pocket. The man resumed his search, either not noticing or not caring about the small clip in her hair. Pulling up her shirt and pulling down the cups of her bra, he checked for anything she might have hidden there. Wren was humiliated, but still she didn't fight. She stood stock still and let him do what he'd been ordered to do.

Eventually, he shook his head with a look of disgust and reached into his pants.

Wren froze, thinking this was it. This was when she'd be violated.

But instead, he pulled out a pair of plastic zip-ties. The man behind her shoved her arms forward, presenting her wrists. The cuffs were attached, pulled extremely tight. Wincing at the discomfort, she held her tongue. The last thing she wanted to do was piss these men off. She was at their mercy. They knew it, she knew it. And as the only woman in a group of men, she was in deep trouble.

Keeping all the advice from the SEALs in mind, she did her best to be compliant. To not bring any attention to herself.

The same couldn't be said for the rest of her coworkers. Colby was trying to fight off the men who were searching him. Swearing and outraged when they took his expensive watch, his phone, his gold bracelet, and everything else he had on his person.

The others were also being stripped of anything and everything worth money. The literature they'd all received before the trip had warned them not to wear anything expensive or flashy, but most of the men had obviously ignored that advice.

The pile of their belongings on the cloth had grown quite large, and when their captors were sure they'd gotten everything they could find, one of them tied the corners of the cloth together, making a bag of sorts, and got back into one of the minivans and drove back the way they'd come.

"Walk," the guy in charge ordered.

Everyone else also had their hands cuffed in front of them. Her coworkers looked a little disheveled and a lot scared. Wren figured she had the same expression on her face as well.

To her surprise, Bob suddenly yelled, "Now!"

Bob, Tom, Luke, and Aaron broke away from the group and started running into the jungle.

Without hesitation, shots rang out from all around them. Wren dropped to a crouch, trying to protect herself as best she could with no cover and without the use of her hands.

The men were yelling as they fired off shots, the sound deafening, and when all was quiet again, Wren opened her eyes and looked around.

She gasped when she saw four bodies lying motionless on the ground about ten or fifteen feet into the trees. Luke, Aaron, Bob, and Tom were all dead. Whatever strategy they'd hatched in the van on the way here, obviously hadn't gone the way they'd planned.

Wren wondered what they'd hoped to accomplish. Where were they going? How did they think they could get away from more than a dozen armed kidnappers? It was stupid and such a damn waste!

Thinking about Luke, how young he was, how excited he'd been when he was chosen to come on the trip, made Wren want to burst into tears. She struggled to hold them back. Knowing if she made a scene, she could be the next one lying in a puddle of blood.

"Anyone else want to try to escape?" the man in charge yelled.

No one said a word.

The leader stalked toward Colby and shoved the barrel of his rifle under his chin. Colby flinched and tried to take a step back, but was stopped by another kidnapper standing right behind him.

"It's hot!" he complained, obviously talking about the metal from the barrel against his bare skin.

"That's because I just shot your friends," the leader sneered. "Stay quiet, do what we say, and maybe we'll let you live. You better hope your people are willing to pay to get you back. Otherwise..." He shot off a round into the dirt at his feet.

Colby, and everyone else, jerked in surprise and fright.

"They'll pay," Colby babbled. "I'm the CEO. They'll pay for me!"

Wren frowned as the implication of his words sank in. Was he saying that they'd pay for him...but not the rest of them?

She didn't have time to reflect on it before they were all being marched into the jungle.

Trying to stay calm, Wren carefully and stealthily used any opportunity to look around until she'd counted the men holding them hostage. Twenty. There were four captors for each of the remaining five members of her group. There was absolutely no chance of escaping at the moment. But just as

Tex had predicted, the toe ring wasn't found in the search of her body. The man hadn't even bothered to take her boots off.

She had to hope that wherever this Tex person was, he'd know that a jaunt into the jungle wasn't exactly on the official itinerary. And he'd call someone to help.

Wren hated that their kidnapping would ultimately put others in danger. It sucked that Colby hadn't listened to all the warnings about coming here, and now his bodyguards and Luke and Aaron were dead.

"Do as we say, and you'll not be hurt," one of their captors said as he jerked Archie by the arm when he stumbled.

That was the key. Do what they said. Stay compliant. Lay low. Don't bring any attention to herself.

It would be one of the hardest things she'd ever done, but Wren hadn't lived through her shitty childhood, hadn't found a man she felt she could finally trust with her true self, hadn't found out her father wasn't a deadbeat asshole, only to die now. In the jungles of South Sudan, her body left to rot. No, she'd do whatever it took to survive.

Tex would know something was wrong. Mozart would also know when he didn't get her proof-of-life email. They'd send help. She had to believe that. Otherwise, she'd fall apart.

CHAPTER SEVENTEEN

"Uh-huh. Roger. Any intel coming through yet? Right. Send coordinates and keep me updated. We're moving out now."

Safe stared at Kevlar as he spoke to someone on the phone. He knew down to his bones that whatever information was being shared wasn't good. And he also had no doubt who it was about.

He'd been waiting for this moment ever since the day Wren arrived in South Sudan.

"Wren?" he asked as soon as Kevlar hung up.

The team leader nodded once.

"Sit rep?" Preacher asked in an urgent tone.

"The group was taken when they were on their way to the president's compound. They were driven southeast, just as we expected they would be—toward the jungle, where there are more places to hide," Kevlar said.

"What's the plan?" Flash asked.

Safe was glad his friends were asking the questions. He couldn't get the ball of dread out of his throat to speak.

"Tex is working on getting coordinates. We'll fly to Lototuru, Uganda, secure a safe house and go north, cross South Sudan's southernmost border heading into the East African Montane Forest, toward Mount Kinyeti. Intel says they have a rebel camp in the jungle near the base of the mountain. It's doubtful we'll be able to intercept them, which would be ideal. We'll have to figure out a way to get them out of the camp once we're there."

"Shit," Smiley swore.

"Any casualties?" Blink asked.

Safe held his breath as he waited for Kevlar's response.

"Unknown."

That wasn't exactly what he wanted to hear, but he supposed it was better than the alternative.

Leaning over, Safe picked up his pack. It was ready to go, had been since they'd completed their own mission. He hated that their worst-case scenario had come to fruition, but he had faith in Wren. She was tough and smart. She'd hold on until they could get to her.

Anything else was unthinkable.

* * *

Wren was miserable. She was hot, tired, and despite breaking in her boots, she had at least two blisters on each foot. It was one thing to wear her boots and socks on a seventy-two degree day back in Riverton. It was another thing altogether to slosh through a jungle, through streams, in what had to be at least mid-nineties temperatures. Her shirt was covered in sweat, as were her pants. Not to mention her hands felt numb from the zip-ties around her wrists.

All-in-all, being kidnapped and force-marched through the jungle sucked. The ride to where they were forced to get out of the vans had been mostly through savannah, flat land with tall grasses blowing in the breeze. But now they were well and truly in the jungle. And while the shade was nice, it was so humid, Wren felt as if she was trying to breathe while underwater.

"When are we stopping?" Dallas asked for what seemed like the hundredth time.

Just like the last ninety-nine times he'd asked the question, none of their captors answered.

"It's so hot," Archie whined as he tried to wipe his brow with his shoulder.

As bad as she felt for herself, Wren felt worse for her coworkers. They were woefully unprepared for this hike. She wasn't exactly enjoying it, but thank goodness she was wearing boots and her shirt was made out of wicking material. It was still stuck to her with sweat, but it was obvious the others were *really* suffering.

Their cotton long-sleeve shirts and suit jackets had to be absolute torture. They hadn't been able to take the jackets off because of the way their hands were zip-tied in front of them, but they'd done their best to shrug the material off their shoulders. The loafers on their feet were completely inappropriate in this environment.

But worse than being uncomfortable and scared, if they

didn't shut their mouths, they were all gonna be killed before they could be rescued.

As she had the thought, Wren wiggled her toes on her right foot, feeling the ring nestled safely in her boot. She didn't feel quite so alone or helpless, knowing that Tex guy would eventually see where she was and send help.

"I need some water," Colby ordered.

No one made any move to get him what he wanted.

"Did you hear me?" he asked the man closest to him. "If you don't want us dropping dead here on the forest floor, we need water. If you think you'll get any money for a dead man, you're wrong."

To her surprise, the man who seemed to be in charge, walking at the front of their little procession, stopped. He turned and stalked back toward Colby.

Wren braced—because the man did not look happy.

Without a word, he lifted his weapon and swung it at Colby.

The butt of the rifle hit her boss in the face and he went down like a sack of potatoes. Moaning, he got to his knees but stayed hunched over on the ground, his hands holding his now bleeding face.

The rebel gestured toward the rest of them with the rifle. "Anyone else thirsty?" he asked.

Everyone quickly shook their heads.

"Fucking weak Americans," he muttered before walking toward the front of the group once more. "Move out!" he yelled.

Colby was still moaning on the jungle floor.

"Get up," Wren whispered, more to herself than anyone else.

"Get up, man," Oliver urged Colby.

"I can't," he groaned.

"If you don't, they'll hurt you more," Archie added.

Oliver reached down and awkwardly grabbed Colby's upper arm. "I'll help you, come on."

Somehow, Oliver got Colby to his feet. Wren suppressed the gasp that threatened to escape when she saw his face. The butt of the rifle had opened a gash in his cheek at least two inches long. She wasn't an expert, but even she knew it probably needed stitches. And having an open wound like that in an environment like this was just asking for trouble.

The group started moving again, and Wren did her best to swallow. She was just as thirsty as the others, but it was more than obvious the men who'd captured them had no intention of letting them have any of the water in the canteens they all carried around their chests.

What had to have been at least another hour passed when the leader finally came to a halt next to a small stream. "Five minutes!" he called out. "Then we head out again."

"Water!" Archie exclaimed and immediately fell to his knees next to the stream.

"Wait! It's probably contaminated," Oliver said.

"If we get diarrhea, we're fucked," Dallas added.

"We're already fucked," Colby muttered, then fell to his knees next to Archie.

For once, Wren agreed with her boss. She remembered what Smiley had told her...

...without water you'll weaken, and any chance for escape that arises, you might not be strong enough to take it.

She understood those words much better now. She felt as weak as a kitten. Almost dizzy with dehydration. With how much she was sweating, she needed the liquid.

Archie and Colby were trying to use their cuffed hands to scoop out water and bring it to their lips, but Wren was too impatient to do it that way. She lay on her belly, arms tucked uncomfortably under her, and leaned down and drank from the stream directly.

Seeing that her way was much more efficient, the others copied her, and soon all five of them were slurping noisily and greedily.

Wren heard their captors laughing all around them, but she didn't care. She concentrated on drinking the water—which tasted freaking amazing—not on the men who were making fun of them for lying in the dirt.

She could practically feel her cells soaking up the much-needed liquid. Every muscle in her body hurt, she wasn't used to this much physical activity, but she refused to think about it too much. If she did, she wouldn't be able to get up and start walking again.

"I don't think I can walk another step," Archie complained.

"My feet hurt so damn bad," Oliver agreed.

"It's so hot," Dallas added.

Wren kept her mouth shut. She agreed with all three of them, but bitching about their problems wouldn't help. She'd learned that the hard way growing up. And especially in this situation, it was better to keep her lips sealed, her head down, and survive from one minute to the next. That's all she had to do. Bo was coming. Or one of his special forces friends. Tex knew she was out here, she just had to be patient.

She thought about telling the others that help was on the way. That she had a tracker on her...but this wasn't the time or place. They were surrounded by rebels who could overhear, and the last thing she wanted was someone opening their big mouths at some point and ruining any surprise advantage whoever came for them might have.

But Wren was scared out of her mind. She didn't like being the only woman in a group of men this large. If one decided he wanted to sexually assault her, she had a feeling everyone would want a turn. She'd seen the way some of the men had leered at her already. Didn't like the way the man who'd searched her had stared at her bare breasts.

"I want to make a call," Colby told one of the men standing guard over them.

She winced. That wasn't the way to stay unnoticed, for sure. Hadn't he already learned his lesson?

"Do you?" the man asked.

"Yes," Colby said, sounding more sure of himself, now that one of their captors was talking to him. "If you're holding us for ransom, the trustees of BT Energy need to be notified. I can do that."

"Oh, they will be notified," the man said. Then he and his rebel buddies laughed.

The man in charge walked toward them.

"Oh shit," Dallas said under his breath.

Wren agreed with his assessment wholeheartedly.

"Hold him," the leader ordered his men, nodding at Oliver.

"What? No! Stop!" Oliver screeched in a high-pitched tone when he was grabbed by three men and hauled to his feet.

"We're going to notify your people," the leader said with a smirk. "They'll know in no uncertain terms that we're serious about wanting money. And wanting it soon." Then he nodded at the men holding Oliver, and they forced him to his knees and wrenched his arms over his head. Then they pushed him forward until his face was in the dirt. One of the men sat on his shoulders, holding him down. Another grabbed his wrists and held them to the ground, splaying one hand open.

The third took out a huge machete.

"Oh God, no! Don't!" Archie begged.

Wren couldn't move. She was frozen in terror as the rebel brought the machete to Oliver's hands—and calmly and methodically cut off his pointer finger and his thumb.

Her coworker screamed, and Wren knew she'd hear the sounds that came out of his mouth in her nightmares for years to come.

Blood immediately spurted from Oliver's hand. The water Wren just drank threatened to come back up, but she forced herself to swallow hard. Breathing through her nose, she watched as the rebels laughed and played with Oliver's fingers. Throwing them back and forth as if they were some sort of ball.

Oliver was still bent over, and Wren could hear him moaning and gagging against the ground.

The leader came over to where Colby was still sitting next to the stream. "Any other demands?" he sneered.

Colby merely shook his head, his gaze locked on Oliver.

"Didn't think so. Get up. We have a long way still to go."

In shock, Wren stood, along with Archie and Dallas. Colby continued to sit and stare at poor Oliver.

"Get up," the leader ordered.

But Colby seemed to be in some sort of trance. Shock, probably.

"Get up," Wren whispered.

Still, he didn't.

The leader moved quickly. His foot flying out and connecting with Colby's shoulder. He fell over, and when he was on his side, more rebels came over and began to kick him.

Wren wanted to shout at them to stop, but self-preservation kept her quiet. She simply backed away from the melee, along with the other two men.

A minute later, the rebels stood back, smirking down at the bleeding and bruised man on the ground. His fancy pressed suit was dirty and ripped. Stained with sweat and now blood. The gash in his face was still oozing, and now he had wounds all over his torso from where their captors' steel-toe boots had broken his skin. She could see new injuries through his filthy white dress shirt.

"Get him up," the leader ordered Archie and Dallas. They moved without hesitation toward their boss, helping him to his feet.

"If he stops walking, he's dead," the leader told his men, then turned and headed into the jungle.

"I can't," Colby muttered.

"You have to," Archie told him.

As the two men were helping Colby, Wren slowly walked over to where Oliver had been hauled to his feet by the men who'd held him down. He was white as a sheet, and she could see a pool of bile where he'd lain.

"Hold your hands against your belly and wrap your shirt as tightly as you can around your hand," she told him quietly. When he stood there staring at his bleeding hand, where his fingers had been, Wren moved quickly.

She grabbed his hands and pressed them into his stomach. He hissed in pain, but Wren forced herself to ignore him. She did her best to wrap the bottom of his shirt around his hand, using it as a bandage. It wasn't great, but it was better than nothing. "Hold your hands there as we walk," she said as calmly as she could.

"It hurts," Oliver whispered raggedly.

"I know," she said. "But you can do this. You *have* to do this. Understand?"

"They're going to rape you," he said flatly, as if he was talking about the weather.

Wren wanted to lash out. Ask him why the hell he'd say something like that. But she knew. He was in shock. They all were.

Instead, she simply hurried to follow the rebels as they filed back into the jungle.

Looking back to make sure the others were coming—not that she'd be able to do anything if they weren't—Wren saw Oliver's fingers lying on the ground. It was one more sign that their kidnappers had no intention of doing a damn thing to help them survive. They hurt them because it was fun.

Because they'd grown up surrounded by violence and knew nothing different.

She was well aware that at any moment the group could turn on her. They were having fun torturing Colby and the other men, but eventually they wouldn't be able to resist their baser urges. They had a woman at their mercy. Wren had no doubt when their attention turned to her, it wouldn't be to cut off a finger or two.

Shivering, even though she was sweating profusely, she regretted not asking Bo and the others how long it would take for someone to get to them if they were kidnapped. Because she could feel the clock ticking. Her time was coming, time for her to be in the captors' crosshairs.

Taking a deep breath, Wren's resolve hardened.

No. Just *no*. She'd do whatever it took to prevent that from becoming her fate. She'd bide her time. Be smart, just like the SEALs told her to do. She had the tools they'd given her. She'd use them. She just had to wait until the right time.

* * *

By the time they stumbled into the camp, Wren could barely stay on her feet. Her coworkers weren't doing any better. Especially Colby and Oliver. They had absolutely no color in their faces and hadn't said much in the last few hours.

They were brought over to a large tree and shoved to the ground. The pressure off her feet was welcome. Wren scooted closer to the tree, away from their captors and behind Archie and Colby.

"Water?" Dallas asked quietly and hopefully. But the men

who'd brought them to the tree either didn't hear the request or ignored it. They walked toward a large fire, where all the other men were gathering.

Looking around, Wren noted that there weren't that many more additional men at the camp when they'd arrived. It seemed as if the majority of the group had escorted them through the jungle. It was the first positive thing she could think of that had happened since they'd been kidnapped. The fewer men, the easier it would be to overcome them when help arrived.

Or...maybe the easier it would be for Wren to escape unnoticed.

A niggling of guilt went through her. If she got away and left her coworkers behind, the captors would probably take their anger out on them. But the guilt wasn't enough to make her want to stay.

She watched as the men started drinking something out of bottles. She assumed it was liquor of some sort. If they got drunk, their inhibitions would be lowered, and any meager morals they might have would be gone. If one person got it in their head to rape her, they'd all follow suit.

No, she had to get out of there. As soon as she could.

It had gotten dark a while ago, and while some people might be scared of being alone in the jungles of Africa, in the middle of the night, Wren wasn't one of them. She'd take the animals in the forest over a group of drunk men any day.

The leader strode over to where Wren and her coworkers were huddled against the tree. "Tomorrow we contact your people. See how much your lives are worth to them."

He laughed, then took a giant swig from the bottle he was holding.

"Until then...be good. There's no escape from here. You have no idea which way to go and the animals in Africa are far worse than anything that might happen to you here. If you think a few lost fingers and bruises are bad...wait until you're eaten by a cheetah. You won't see him coming. He'll stalk you and pounce before you're aware he's even there. Lions, leopards, rhinoceros, they can all outrun you. And don't get me started on the poisonous snakes and insects...Sleep well. We'll talk in the morning."

He laughed again, then turned his back on them and headed back to the others gathered around the fire.

"I'm hungry," Dallas mumbled.

"Shut up," Archie scolded.

"They have to keep us alive if they want any ransom," Colby argued weakly.

Wren wasn't so sure about that. Yes, the trustees at BT Energy should be smart enough not to send any money unless they had proof of life, but the second even one cent had been received, their captors would probably kill them.

"If you'd have kept your mouth shut, I'd still have my fingers!" Oliver hissed at their boss.

"That wasn't my fault," he protested.

"The hell it wasn't!" Oliver practically yelled.

Wren winced when a few of their captors looked toward them.

"All I did was tell them that I could get a hold of the trustees."

"And they cut off my fingers in response!" Oliver screamed.

The men around the fire laughed.

"Shut up!" Archie told Oliver.

"Why? He's the one who decided this trip was a great idea. And look what happened! We shouldn't have come. He's too fucking greedy!"

Wren agreed with Oliver, but it was way too late for any of them to be second-guessing the trip now.

"Seriously, shut the hell up!" Dallas hissed. "You want them to come over here and cut off something else?"

Yet again, Wren agreed with one of her coworkers.

Oliver and Colby fell silent. Neither looked happy, but none of them wanted any more attention from their captors. Eventually the rebels' attention went back to the food they were eating—and not sharing with their captives.

"We're going to die," Oliver said in a low, hollow tone a minute later.

"No, we aren't," Colby countered just as quietly.

"We're in the middle of the African jungle. You've been beat to hell for no reason whatsoever, my fingers are food for whatever fucking animals are in this hellhole, and Wren's gonna be gang-raped. I'd rather die than find out what other tortures they have in store for us."

Wren really wished he would stop talking about her being raped. She was barely keeping the images out of her head as it was.

"No one knows where we are. You read the literature; the State Department isn't sending anyone to rescue us. We were *warned*. We're dead. I'd rather be shot in the head than starve to death," Oliver continued. "I think your bodyguards and the others were lucky to have been shot. At least they died quickly."

Wren tried to block out his ramblings. The worst thing they could do was fall into despair. Another thing she'd learned from Bo and his team. Stay positive. Hang on no matter what. Do not give up. It sounded as if Oliver had already done just that.

"I'm hungry," Dallas repeated, as if they hadn't heard him the first time.

"Shut up. We all are," Archie said testily.

Her coworkers fell silent. Wren took the opportunity to study their surroundings. They'd been placed against a huge tree on the edge of a small encampment. There were tarps stretched over smaller trees near the fire, which gave the rebels shelter from the weather. Other than the fire, the area was pitch dark. Out here in the jungle, without any kind of light pollution, once away from the fire, Wren wouldn't be able to see a foot in front of her.

But if *she* couldn't see, neither could anyone else. Of course, their captors had flashlights, but the dark should help her...if she was able to get away.

The good thing was, the rebels were confident in the fact that their captives were cuffed and terrified and out of their element. And if they kept them hungry and thirsty, they'd be less likely to try to escape.

Screw that. Wren was getting the hell out of here. She had no desire to see what the rebels had in store for them in the morning.

Just as she had the thought, it started raining. And not a

gentle pitter-patter of raindrops either. One second it was clear, and the next they were soaked to the bone.

The men around the fire didn't bitch about the sudden rainstorm, they were probably used to it, they simply dispersed to their respective lean-tos and settled in with their bottles of alcohol.

"Fucking hell!" Colby exclaimed.

"I'm going to get crotch rot," Archie bitched.

"I hate the rain," Oliver said almost sadly.

"This sucks," Dallas added.

But Wren was thrilled. She hoped it kept raining. The sound would hopefully conceal her escape. She just needed to be patient. The rebels had to sleep at some point. Maybe they'd even pass out from all the alcohol they were guzzling.

Meanwhile, she was exhausted but not tired. That made no sense, but there was no way she was letting down her guard to go to sleep. She'd stay awake for as long as it took for the opportunity to get the hell out of there to present itself.

The advice Bo and his team had given her about escaping into the jungle came back. As if Bo was right there with her, whispering in her ear, she heard him say, *Find a place to hole up and wait for help to arrive.*

That was just what she planned to do. She'd get as far away from this damn camp as she could, then wait. She had the tracker. Whoever Tex sent to South Sudan would come straight to her. He'd know where the encampment was because by now, he had to have tracked her. Would see that she was no longer moving. Would assume this was a rebel camp.

She was making a lot of assumptions, but Tex wasn't

stupid. She didn't know him personally, but he was obviously respected by Bo and the others. He'd figure out this shitstorm. He had to.

Just as she had to get away. She knew without a doubt the longer she stayed, the more danger she was in. She had her survival gear. She'd fend for herself until she was rescued and brought back to the States. Then she was never leaving again. Never.

CHAPTER EIGHTEEN

Safe wanted everything to move faster. Kevlar had received a link from Tex with information from the tracker in Wren's toe ring. She was moving deep into the jungle. Their team was moving as fast as they could, but it wasn't fast enough.

He couldn't stop imagining all the horrible things Wren was going through. He'd taught her as much as he could in the limited time they'd had, but he hadn't gone into detail about what the rebels might do to a group of captives. He'd seen firsthand how brutal they could be. And he hated to think of Wren being at their mercy.

They'd arrived in Uganda without incident. Soon they'd slip over the border into South Sudan, where Kevlar was currently making plans for them to fast-rope out of a helicopter into the jungles around Mount Kinyeti. But everything was still moving too slow for Safe.

He stared down at the hand-held GPS that showed Wren's location. The dot on the screen hadn't moved in a couple of hours. Which could mean one of several things. They'd reached the rebels' camp; she was dead and her body was left behind in the jungle; or the toe ring had malfunctioned or been found.

None of the choices were good, but if he had to choose, Safe would pick the first option.

"She's going to be okay," Blink said quietly from next to him.

Safe glanced at the newest member of their group. "You don't know that."

"Yes, I do. She's tough. Tougher than anyone thinks."

She was, but Safe wasn't sure he was in the mood for meaningless assurances.

"Most women would've freaked out when we started talking about the possibility of being kidnapped. But Wren took it all in carefully. She heard our advice. Took it to heart. She's going to be okay."

Safe took a deep breath and closed his eyes. Worst-case scenarios kept flashing through his brain. Each one scarier than the last, but he forced himself to clear his mind.

Blink was right. Wren *was* tough. She wouldn't have made it through her horrible childhood if she wasn't. "Okay," he said on an exhalation as he opened his eyes.

"Okay," Blink echoed. He clasped his hand on Safe's shoulder before walking over to where Smiley and Flash were going through their gear.

Two minutes later, Kevlar said, "We're headed out in five minutes. Make sure you've got all the necessary gear in your packs. We're going fast and light, so only bring the essentials. Let's do this."

Safe didn't need to check his pack. He knew down to the tiniest detail what was in there. First-aid gear, two MREs, water purification tablets, bug repellent, a multitool, compass, LED squeeze light, fire-starting kit, collapsible water bottle—currently full—electrolyte tablets, signal mirror, thermal blanket, paracord, safety pins, can opener, duct tape, razor blade, and a handcuff key. The items in the safety kit every SEAL carried was something they'd memorized back in school. He was ready for anything and everything and simply wanted to get moving.

Ten minutes later, the seven men climbed out of the back of an old pickup that dropped them in a dark field less than a mile from the South Sudanese border, where a chopper waited. They climbed onboard and immediately began to don the harnesses they'd use to lower themselves into the jungle. There was a chance the chopper would be heard by the rebels, but using it was much faster than traversing the mountain to get to where Wren's tracker was pinging. As it was, they'd be dropped a few miles from the ping so they could hopefully have the element of surprise.

The plan had been discussed and agreed on during their flight to Uganda. Safe would keep the GPS with Wren's location and his only responsibility was getting her to safety. The others on the team would go after the eight men. Of course, no one knew who'd been kidnapped, other than Wren herself. They had to assume, based on limited intel, that the entire group had been taken. It would remain to be seen how they could extract the group, based on what kind of shape everyone was in when they found them.

As for the rebels...as far as Safe was concerned, they'd

made their choice when they'd kidnapped the Americans. They would be eliminated without a second thought.

No word had come through about any kind of ransom demand, but it was still early yet. Not even a day had gone by since they'd been taken. Safe and his team assumed that would happen in the morning, if ransom was the kidnappers' intent.

Safe shifted in his seat as the chopper rose off the ground. He was calm. Focused. He'd made a promise to Wren that she'd be rescued if anything happened. He wasn't about to go back on that promise now. She was a part of his family, and no one fucked with one of their own.

* * *

Wren swallowed hard. She was terrified, but it was time. It was now or never. It was still raining. She was soaked to the bone, but she barely even noticed. She and the others had been able to rig up a rain cache system with the largest leaves around them, so they could drink a little bit. It wasn't enough, not nearly enough, but it was something. It would have to do for now.

The men around her were all sleeping. They were lying on their backs or sides. Wren had curled up on her side against the base of the tree, trying to stay hidden behind the men.

What was the saying? Out of sight, out of mind. She'd hoped that would be the case as the rebels continued to drink for a few hours after they arrived. To her relief, most of them had passed out or fallen asleep under their lean-tos. The fire had also died down enough that the light didn't reach their little corner of the camp.

It was time.

Guilt once again rose within Wren. Guilt that she didn't tell the others what she had planned. Guilt over what the ramifications of her being gone would mean for her coworkers. She had no doubt their captors wouldn't be happy to find her missing.

Very slowly, not making a sound, Wren rolled onto her back. Then she sat up and looked around. No one glanced her way. Everyone was sleeping. She scooted on her butt until she cleared the large tree, circling around it.

She got to her knees, then balanced on her feet, staying low. Taking one last look at her sleeping coworkers—she was startled to see Oliver's eyes open and staring right at her. He was lying a little away from the others, closer to the tree she was now hiding behind.

Wren froze. She had no idea what he would do if he thought she was escaping. He'd been hurt because of Colby. Would he call out a warning and blow her escape, simply to protect himself?

She was surprised when he whispered, "Go."

"I'm sorry," she whispered.

But Oliver shook his head. "Don't be. We should've listened to you. Should've gone to that training—or better yet, said no to this trip. Get out, Wren."

"They're coming," she surprised herself by saying. "For all of us. I have a tracker. They're coming, Oliver. You just have to hang on until they get here."

She didn't explain who "they" were, and Oliver didn't ask.

She could barely see him in the dark of the early morning, but she saw him nod.

"I'll tell them you went to pee and I heard scuffling, and you never came back."

Swallowing hard, and wishing she could save all the guys, she simply nodded. "I'll scuff up the ground a bit. Make it look like I was attacked by something."

"Good luck," Oliver told her.

"You too." Then, before she could change her mind, Wren turned, staying low until she was deeper into the trees, then she quickly walked into the darkness.

When she was far enough away from the camp that she thought she could make a little bit of noise, she found a tree branch on the ground and made gouges in the jungle floor and tore up the vegetation in the area. It probably wasn't good enough to fool anyone for long, especially someone who lived in the jungle like the rebels did, but hopefully they'd be too busy trying to contact someone for a ransom to worry about a stupid American woman who'd wandered off in the middle of the night to pee.

Walking quickly with her cuffed hands in front of her, Wren zigzagged through the jungle. She had no idea where she was going, other than away from the rebel camp. She needed to get the cuffs off her wrists, but more importantly, she needed to put space between her and the danger.

It was way harder than she thought it would be to make her way through the trees. First, it was dark as hell. Second, the route they'd taken to get to the camp had obviously been traversed back and forth often. It was only a trail, like a deer trail, but still walkable.

What she was doing now...wasn't easy. Not at all. The undergrowth kept tripping her. She fell to her knees over and over. Branches smacked against her face. And every minute or so she swore she heard someone coming after her, making her drop to a crouch and get as small as she could to try to hide.

She wasn't moving fast enough, Wren knew that, but she literally couldn't go any faster. "One foot in front of the other," she whispered, hoping that just hearing her own voice would give her the energy and fortitude to keep going.

But it wasn't until she noticed she could actually see where she was walking that fear struck. Hard.

They'd know she was gone by now. Would probably be coming after her. She was most likely leaving an easy trail for one of the rebels to follow. They could move a lot faster than her because they weren't cuffed, had machetes, and were used to the jungle.

She suddenly felt dizzy, and Wren realized she was hyperventilating.

Leaning over, bracing her cuffed hands on her thighs, she tried to slow her breathing. "You can do this. You're okay," she told herself softly.

Making a decision, Wren plopped down onto her ass. She didn't worry about the dirt or the wet ground. She was already soaked.

Fumbling with the laces of her shoes, she fought to get the wet paracord untied. She thought about using the tiny blade in her shoe to try to cut off the zip-ties, but dismissed the idea because she'd never be able to reach the plastic without seriously hurting herself.

Praying wet paracord would work just as well as the dry

stuff she'd used when she and Bo had practiced, she managed to get the cord tied in a loop through the plastic the way he'd taught her. She put her feet in the loop and began to scissor them back and forth.

When nothing happened, tears sprang to her eyes.

She blinked them away angrily. She couldn't cry. She didn't have enough liquid in her body to waste what she *did* have on tears. And this had to work. It had to! She could continue walking with her hands cuffed, but it would be difficult to defend herself against anything, man or animal.

Stubbornly, she continued to move the paracord back and forth over the plastic. She tired way faster than she had when she'd done this back in California, but determination took over and she refused to quit.

Just when she was about to admit defeat, she felt her wrists shift.

Looking down, she saw the plastic was breaking! Just as it was supposed to.

Renewing her efforts, Wren smiled huge when the plastic snapped completely. Her wrists were bruised all to hell, but she was free.

Hearing the scream of some animal behind her, Wren's elation disappeared. She quickly re-laced her boot and tucked the plastic pieces of the cuffs into one of the pockets of her pants. She didn't want to leave anything behind that might give someone an idea that she'd been there. Wren pulled the tiny knife out of her boot as well, and palmed it. It wouldn't be much of a weapon against a rebel with a rifle or machete, but it was better than nothing.

Feeling better now that her hands were free, Wren started

walking again, needing to put as much space as she could between the rebels and herself.

* * *

Wren was reaching a point where she physically couldn't go on any longer. She was exhausted, hungry, thirsty, and had started tripping over her feet more than she was walking. She needed to find a place to hide, but nothing around her looked safe. There were no caves, no trees with holes she could crawl into. She couldn't even climb a tree and hide like one of the heroines in a book she'd read once had done.

A sound reached her then, and Wren immediately froze in terror. It took a minute before she was able to move again. And by then, she recognized what she'd heard.

Water.

Walking as fast as her feet would carry her, which wasn't very fast, Wren moved toward it. She almost fell into the stream when she finally found it, and stopped herself from tumbling right into it at the last moment. It looked deeper than the one the rebels had stopped at, allowing her and the guys to drink. It would be more difficult to get to, as well, as there were steep banks on both sides.

A noise to her left caught her attention, and staying in the shelter of the trees, Wren peeked around to look. What she saw left her in awe. A crash of rhinoceroses. She knew that was what a group of the animals was called because the detail had been included in some of the material she'd received from BT Energy before the trip.

There were about ten of them standing together in the

water, thankfully downstream from her location. They seemed relaxed but alert. Wren knew their eyesight wasn't great, so she edged out of her hiding spot. She slid down the bank to the water, keeping her eyes on them as she leaned over to drink. She was sure the water probably wasn't the cleanest, but she needed to rehydrate.

She stopped way before she was satiated, not wanting to push her luck, and stayed crouched in the shallower water near the bank, watching the animals.

She'd seen a rhino before...at a zoo. This was very different. These were wild animals, enjoying a drink, cooling off, hanging out before they went off and did whatever it was a rhino did. They were beautiful, ugly, and scary, but Wren was in awe.

Before long, they began to amble off, across the stream and heading into the trees.

It was seeing them disappear so quickly that had Wren's nerves surfacing once more. It was entirely possible she could run into some wild animal as she was slinking around as well. Hopefully they'd hear her before they saw her, and run away.

Shivering even though it wasn't cold, Wren clambered up the bank and back into the trees, on the opposite side of the stream from where the rhinos had gone.

Looking around, she had no idea which way to go. Or what to do.

Water, food, shelter.

The words echoed in her head. She'd found water, had no idea what to do about food—but honestly, sleep sounded better than food right now—and she needed to find a place to hide. With that thought in mind, she started to hike.

* * *

Just when she didn't think she'd be able to go another step, Wren saw something out of the corner of her eye, to her right. She'd been walking long enough for the sun to be high in the sky now. It shone brightly between the thick branches of the trees, not directly over her head, but close.

Blinking, trying to be sure she was seeing what she thought she saw, Wren walked in a zombie state toward the large group of bushes on the forest floor. She'd passed bushes before, but for some reason, she'd stumbled upon around fifteen or twenty of them, all right next to each other in a massive group.

Picking up a heavy stick, she threw it on top of the vegetation and braced herself for anything that might come charging out of the safety of the bushes.

But nothing happened.

"Please be empty," she mumbled before getting down on her hands and knees and pushing into the tangle of leaves and branches. It wasn't easy, the branches were tightly interwoven together, but Wren pressed on. If she had a hard time getting to the middle of these plants, so would someone else. And she'd hear them coming.

Unfortunately, there was no open space welcoming her to make a little den when she got as far as she felt she could go without coming out the other side. But Wren didn't care. For the first time in days, she felt safe. Which was crazy, considering she was alone in the middle of an African jungle, possibly with a group of pissed-off rebels on her tail, who wanted to rape and kill her.

She wiggled and contorted her body until she had a few branches at her back and others poking into her front. There was a stick pressing painfully into her belly and another that scraped her head, but Wren didn't care.

Ignoring what creepy-crawlies there could be lurking with her in the bushes, she closed her eyes. Her muscles went lax, and sleep overcame her almost immediately.

CHAPTER NINETEEN

Safe heard the rebel camp before he saw it.

The men didn't even seem to consider the thought that they should keep their voices down, that they might not be alone in the jungle. But why would they? They'd chosen their hideout well. It was miles from any kind of road and no one would dare venture into this part of the jungle if they knew what was good for them.

But Safe had no fear of the rifles the men carried. No fear of the men themselves. *They* were the ones to be feared, not the assholes who kidnapped innocent men and women.

Moving forward, Safe got into position. He and his fellow SEALS had surrounded the camp and were scoping out the situation before acting. At his request, Wren had shown him pictures on the BT Energy website of the men she'd be traveling with. He could see Dallas, Archie, Oliver, and Colby... but that was it.

Wren wasn't with them. But then again, he knew that already from looking at the GPS tracker. She was about three miles away, and until about half an hour ago had been moving at a steady pace.

Safe wanted to immediately head in her direction, but he needed to make sure his teammates had the current situation under control first.

"Anyone got eyes on the others? The bodyguards and the other two men?" Kevlar asked through their earpieces.

"Negative."

"No."

"No sign of them."

"Shit. There's a possibility they split them up," Preacher said.

Seconds after his teammate spoke, Safe could hear what looked like the leader of the ragtag group taunting his captives, as if he'd somehow heard Preacher's suggestion loud and clear.

"You want to make a run for it too? Do it! I'll shoot you in the back just like I did your friends. But I might let you get a little ways away. Make you think you can make it before BOOM!"

"Fuck," Kevlar said through the radio. "Guess that answers that. Safe, you got our girl on radar?"

"Ten-four," Safe said as he slowly eased backward, away from the clearing.

"We'll meet you at the extraction point at twenty-two hundred. If you aren't there, we'll intercept where we can."

Safe acknowledged his team leader's words before turning

to go the long way around the camp and in the direction the tracker showed Wren had gone. He was also wearing a tracker, so Kevlar would know where he was at all times. So if something kept him and Wren from meeting up with his team—God forbid—they'd come to *him*. He had absolutely no doubt of that whatsoever.

His only mission right now was finding Wren. He hoped she'd been able to sneak away, but he wasn't willing to hang around to find out what the rebels knew. Ultimately, it didn't matter. He'd find her one way or another. And if someone had taken her away from camp for his own nefarious purposes, he'd regret it.

Completely focused, Safe concentrated on making his way through the thick jungle. His respect for Wren increased with every step. He'd expected this. Was prepared for it. He had a machete to help hack through the strongest branches in his way. Wren had nothing but her wits and determination.

Thankful all over again for all the precautions they'd made for this trip—for the tracker, the boots, the hiking clothes—Safe split his concentration between where he was walking and the GPS screen with the blinking dot. He sidestepped a forest vine snake, thankful he'd seen it. There was no antivenom for a bite from the snake, and its venom killed by preventing clotting and causing the internal organs of its prey to bleed profusely.

He also saw a leopard sleeping lazily in a tree, but it seemed to have no interest in Safe as he slipped through the jungle.

When Safe got within a quarter mile from where Wren's

dot was blinking, he slowed. Walked more carefully. Silently. If someone was with her, holding her hostage, hurting her, he needed to approach cautiously. The last thing he wanted was Wren getting hurt because of his rash actions.

Every molecule within Safe urged him to rush forward. To call out Wren's name. But he moved stealthily, as he'd been trained. Not sure what he would find when he got to the target coordinates, but hoping against hope it would be Wren, alive. Probably scared, but relieved to see him.

* * *

Wren had no idea how long she'd been asleep, but it couldn't have been too long as it was still bright out. She felt like shit; short naps always did that to her. Made her feel worse than when she'd shut her eyes in the first place. That, along with the branches trying to slice her in half where she was awkwardly lying in the middle of the bushes, made further sleep impossible.

Exhaustion filled every cell of her being, but she couldn't afford to stay in one place for too long. The consequences could literally be deadly.

She started to wiggle, trying to get out of the cocoon of branches, when she thought she heard something nearby.

Freezing, Wren tilted her head, trying to figure out what she'd heard.

Then panic swiftly set in.

Someone was out there. Or *something*.

Moving slowly, she reached into her pocket for the knife. It wouldn't do a damn thing against one of the rebels, but she felt better having some kind of weapon in her hands. The only good thing about this situation was that it would be almost impossible to drag her out of the mess of branches currently surrounding her.

"Wren?"

The sound of her name didn't compute for a second.

"Wren? Are you there?"

Holy shit! That was Bo! She'd recognize his voice anywhere! Wren's entire body shook as she tried to extricate herself from the bushes. The more she struggled, the more stuck she seemed to get.

"Wren? Tell me that's you in there and that you're okay."

Bo's voice was firmer now. Bossy.

"Bo!" she croaked.

"Easy, sweetheart. I'm here."

Even in the middle of freaking Africa, after she'd been kidnapped by rebels, Bo sounded calm.

Wren fought to get out of the bushes, and the second she crawled into view, she wanted to cry. Looking up, she saw Bo standing there, looking larger than life. He had on a pair of green camouflage pants and a shirt, a pack on his back, the scruff on his face was much longer than when she'd seen him over a week ago, almost a full beard.

He was *not* smiling. Not even a little.

But that didn't bother Wren. He was here! He came!

One second she was on her hands and knees, and the next she was in his embrace. Wren shoved her face into the space between his neck and shoulder and held onto him as if her life depended on it. And honestly, it kind of did.

"Shhhh, I've got you," he murmured as he held her so tight, it almost hurt.

"Bo..." she said against his sweaty skin.

"I'm here," he told her. "I'm here."

She had no idea how long they stood like that, Bo's arms wrapped around her and Wren clinging to him like a baby monkey does its mother. Eventually she took a deep breath and lifted her head, but she didn't let go.

"How? I don't think it's even been twenty-four hours since we were taken," she stuttered.

"Eighteen and a half," he told her.

"How are you even here?"

"We were in the area. Finished our mission and didn't have anything else to do."

That Wren could find anything to laugh about right now was a freaking miracle. But chuckle she did. "Right."

"But seriously, we were killing time in Chad, waiting for your flight to leave South Sudan. Once that happened, we would've headed home ourselves."

"Wait," Wren said with a frown. "You were done, but were waiting for me to be finished with my trip before you left?"

"Just said that, I think. But yes."

It was that moment when Wren fell completely in love with this man. She was already mostly gone, but knowing he'd gone out of his way to make sure she was heading home safely before getting on a plane himself made it clear in a way no words ever could how much he cared about her. That whatever was happening between them wasn't casual.

"Bo," she whispered, almost speechless.

"Breathe, Wren. I know this is...a lot. But I need you to

stay strong. We need to get going. Can you walk? Are you hurt? Are you hungry?"

Pushing the awe she felt that this man and his team had purposely not left the country because she was still there, Wren took a deep breath and said, "Yes, no, and more thirsty than anything. I found some water early this morning, but didn't drink a lot because I was worried about creepy-crawlies."

At her response, Bo dropped his arms from around her and shrugged off his backpack. Wren watched as he rifled through it for a moment before pulling out a bottle of water, twisting off the cap, then handing it to her.

She took it without a word and brought it to her mouth. The water inside was warm, but so damn good. She guzzled down a few swallows then forced herself to stop. "You want some?" she asked.

Wren couldn't read the look in his eyes as he shook his head. "No, you need it."

She did. Wren could feel her body soaking up the life-saving liquid as fast as she could drink it. It didn't take long for her to finish the entire bottle. Her belly hurt a little, but being full also felt amazingly good.

Bo collapsed the bottle and put it back in his pack, then pulled out what Wren knew was an MRE and opened it. She was about to tell him she wasn't hungry when he pulled out something in a small green plastic container, putting the rest of the MRE back into his pack. Then he zipped it shut and put it back on his shoulders. He opened whatever he'd taken out of the MRE and held it out to her. "Eat this."

"I'm not hungry," Wren told him.

"I know, but you need the calories. You've been walking all night, stressed, your body needs it."

Knowing he was right, Wren took the small square. "What is it?" she asked.

"Lemon poppy seed pound cake."

Wren took a small bite then looked up at him in surprise. "It's good."

His lips twitched. "Yeah. Some desserts are better than others, but I've always been partial to that one. You'll be thirsty when you're done, and I have some more water for you." He patted one of the pockets of his pants.

Every muscle in Wren's body protested the fact that she was upright and walking. She was sure she'd walked more in the last day than she had in her entire life. And now that she'd had some water, she'd begun to sweat as well. She was scared, miserable, and exhausted, but not one word of complaint would leave her mouth, because Bo was here.

"I'm assuming the toe ring worked," she stated as he led them through the jungle. She had no idea where they were going, but she had no problem giving control over to Bo as to their destination and what would happen next.

"It worked," he told her. Then after a moment of hesitation, he said, "Can you tell me what happened?"

Wren sighed. "We were on our way to the thing at the president's house but instead of being driven there, we were taken out of the city to this jungle."

"Ransom?" Bo asked.

She nodded. "Yeah."

"I know this is hard, but I have to ask. Where are the others? Were you separated?"

Wren swallowed hard, the poppy seed cake settling like a rock in her belly. "No. I guess they came up with some plan to run when we got out of the vans. They're dead."

Bo stopped so abruptly, Wren almost ran into him. He turned and once more hugged her. Hard. "I'm sorry."

"Me too," Wren mumbled into his neck.

Then Bo took her by the shoulders and stooped so he could look her in the eye. "I'm getting you out of here."

She nodded. What else could she do?

"You did good, sweetheart. You kept your head, got the cuffs off." His gaze went down to her bruised wrists. Her hands were resting on his chest and the marks were clearly visible. "And you hid until I could get to you. I'm so proud of you."

Wren blinked. How many times had anyone told her that they were proud of her in her life? Zero. She couldn't remember anyone ever telling her that before. She soaked his words in, reveled in them. Before reality set in.

"The others? I was afraid our kidnappers would take my escape out on them."

"They're okay. The rest of my team is extricating them."

Wren had a lot of questions. What would happen to the rebels? What about their stuff back at the hotel? What would happen to the bodies of the other guys? How would they get out of the country without their passports? Would the pipeline project even go forward now? Were her coworkers mad that she'd left them back in that clearing?

But she swallowed them all down. Now wasn't the time to ask anything. "Okay."

Bo studied her. As if he could tell she was bursting with

questions, he said, "We're going to meet up with the team now. We'll fly out of here into Uganda. Tex has already arranged for replacement passports to be delivered for all of you."

Of course the mysterious Tex had access to passports. The man had probably already delivered them to the US Embassy in Uganda before they'd even left the US. But Wren couldn't be upset about that. If only Colby had used some common sense and canceled this trip.

Wren realized Bo was still watching her carefully, as if waiting for her to say something.

"Okay," she repeated belatedly.

"If you need to stop and take a break, let me know. We have some time before we have to meet my team."

Wren nodded. The truth was, she wanted to lie down in the middle of this damn jungle and sleep for days. But since that wasn't a feasible option right now, she'd do whatever Bo told her to do or die trying.

"Tough as nails," he told her, before leaning forward slowly. His lips on hers were welcome. Grounding Wren. Making her believe that maybe, just maybe, they'd get the hell out of here.

Without another word, Bo took the hand that wasn't holding the pound cake and started walking once again.

* * *

Safe had never been so relieved to see anyone in his entire life. He truly hadn't known what kind of shape Wren was going to be in when he found her. He'd imagined so many awful scenarios that even though she was bruised, scratched, dirty, and had dark circles under her eyes, seeing her alive and upright made his knees weak.

He'd been terrified that she'd be hurt...or violated. He had no doubt that had probably been on the rebels' minds, but thankfully Wren had taken her well-being into her own hands and gotten the hell out of that camp before they could do anything.

Of course, he didn't know with certainty that she hadn't been raped, but he'd seen the aftermath of enough sexual assaults to be able to recognize the signs. Wren hadn't hesitated to let him touch her, didn't have the vacant look in her eyes that he'd seen in the gazes of too many other victims. They needed to have a long, in-depth discussion about exactly what she'd been through, what she'd survived, but first he needed to get them to the rendezvous point. He had no problem being in this jungle on his own, but in this particular case, he'd feel better when he had his teammates on his six—and Wren's.

Because they weren't out of danger yet. All sorts of threats lurked in these trees. The two- and four-legged variety alike. They had about three klicks, or a little less than two miles to go for the rendezvous point. Safe wasn't too worried about the large animals in the jungle, it was the smaller ones, like the snakes and poisonous insects that worried him. But he also had no doubt there were other groups of rebels camped out in the area as well.

The men who'd taken Wren and her coworkers weren't the only ones who used this forest as a hideout. If they ran across anyone else, things could get ugly fast.

Safe didn't want to let go of Wren's hand, but he needed both of his free just in case he needed to protect them. "Hold on to my pack," he told her. "Stay close."

"If you think I'm getting more than two feet from you, you're crazy," she retorted.

Safe's lips twitched, but then he sobered. Getting through the jungle to the meet-up point wasn't going to be easy. He wished Wren didn't have to make this trek, but as he'd told her, she was tough. She could do it.

He wanted to talk to her, hear her voice, reassure himself that she really was all right, but he needed to listen to the jungle around them. Be alert for any kind of danger. Safe wasn't too surprised that she seemed to understand that and didn't attempt to make small talk. Then again, it was possible she was simply too tired to speak.

They'd been walking for thirty minutes, and had probably only gone about half a mile in Safe's estimation. Walking in the jungle was very different from taking a walk in a neighborhood or on an established trail. It took longer to make a path, and since they couldn't walk in a straight line they were adding steps and mileage as they went.

A noise to their left made Safe stop in his tracks. Wren actually ran into him, but he steadied her by reaching a hand back.

"What?" Wren whispered.

Safe heard the subtle sounds of someone's approach—and already knew they didn't have time to hide before they were surrounded by half a dozen men. All holding rifles.

Fuck.

Wren whimpered behind him.

"Hands up," one of the men ordered.

"Bo?" Wren whispered.

"Do it," he told her. He was good. But not good enough to take out half a dozen armed men. They'd be shot before he could mitigate the threat. Their best bet was to do what was asked of them. Wren still wore her toe ring, and he had a GPS tracker on him as well.

Wren cried out when she was wrenched away from him, and it took everything in Safe not to lash out at the man who'd grabbed her. He held her still while Safe was relieved of his backpack, rifle, earpiece, and had all his pockets emptied.

"Who are you? Why are you in our jungle?" asked the man who'd told them to put their hands up.

"We were on our way out," Safe said, meeting the man's gaze, ignoring the weapons pointed at him and Wren.

"And why were you here in the first place? This isn't exactly a destination for tourists...and you look like anything *but* tourists."

Safe ran over possible scenarios in his head. He could tell Wren to run, but with the way the man was holding her, she wouldn't get far. He could lie and insist they were tourists, but the man questioning them was obviously too smart for that.

Safe decided the truth was the best bet in this situation.

"She was in your country with her coworkers. They've been working with the government to put in a gas pipeline. They were kidnapped last night. Brought here. My team and I came in to rescue them."

Silence greeted his words...and for a second, Safe was afraid he'd made the wrong decision.

Then the man let out a disgusted grunt and spat on the

ground. "Let me guess. The government says the money will be good for South Sudan. For our economy."

For the first time, Safe took his eyes off the leader of this small group and looked over at Wren. Her face was white as a sheet and she was shaking. Her captor stood behind her, holding her biceps and forcing her arms behind her back. She looked uncomfortable and scared, but not hurt. Thank God.

"That's right," she said in a voice that only trembled slightly.

"Liars! They're all *liars*! They take money away from the citizens. We're starving, we don't have enough water or food to live off of. While they live as kings! Who took them?" the man asked Safe.

"I don't know," he replied.

"There were around twenty of them. We thought we were going to the president's compound for a dinner, but instead we were driven here, to the jungle. There was a man leading us, on a motorcycle," Wren said.

The leader spat on the ground again. "They're as corrupt as the government," he said bitterly. "Receiving inside intel. And money to buy guns."

Safe wasn't sure if this group's hatred for the other one was a good or bad thing. "She got away from them during the night. I found her, and I'm taking her back to where my team is waiting to leave the country."

The leader stared at Safe for a long, uncomfortable moment. He looked at Wren, then back at Safe. "She must be important for the US to send someone for her."

"She's important to *me*," Safe said firmly.

"She yours?"

"Yes." There was no hesitation in his response. Because Wren *was* his. His to cherish. To protect. To love. Not in the way this man meant his question, but his all the same.

"I need to consult with my men. You come with us. We will kill you if you try anything," the leader said.

It wasn't what Safe wanted to hear, but it wasn't as bad as the alternative...getting shot where they stood.

The man holding Wren let go of her with a shove and she stumbled forward. Safe grabbed her before she could fall and held her against his side.

The leader started walking in the opposite direction they needed to go to meet his team.

Internally sighing, Safe didn't let any of his irritation and worry show on his face. The different ethnic groups in the country didn't get along. And if these men were pissed at the other group, the ones who took Wren and her coworkers, that might work in their favor. He wasn't going to make the mistake of thinking they were the good guys, but since they hadn't simply shot them on sight, he was taking that as a win.

No one spoke as they trudged through the jungle toward what Safe could only assume was another rebel camp. When he and Wren didn't show up on time at the rendezvous spot, Kevlar would come up with a plan B. Most likely sending the civilians away on the chopper as he and the rest of the SEAL team came after them.

They just had to be patient. Calm. It was the same advice Safe had given Wren in case something happened.

They walked for quite a while, and with every step Safe could feel Wren sagging against him a little more. She was completely done in, and he hated that he couldn't do anything for her right now.

Eventually they walked alongside a small stream and came upon what looked like a giant cave. It was almost hidden in a hillside and, more importantly for the rebels, completely defensible. No one could sneak up behind them and they could be sheltered from the daily rainstorms in this part of the country.

They joined about a dozen other men, and to Safe's surprise, there were even a few women with the group. They were led inside the cave toward the back, and the leader pointed to a spot next to a wall. "You. Stay. I'll talk with the others."

Safe nodded. He could plead their case, remind the man they weren't there to hurt anyone, that they just wanted to leave, but he needed to take care of Wren first.

He lowered her to the ground and squatted in front of her on the balls of his feet. "How are you holding up?" He knew the answer to his question—not well—but he asked anyway.

"I'm good."

Safe snorted. She wasn't good. Not even close. But he shouldn't have been surprised that she downplayed how she was feeling.

"I'm going to get you some food. And water," Safe told her.

"But he said for us to stay here," Wren protested.

"I'm not going to sit here while you suffer. I'll be right back." Safe then stood and turned toward the large space. The leader was at the mouth of the cave, talking with several others. A man had been left behind to guard them.

He raised the rifle he was holding when Safe took a step toward him.

Immediately holding his hands out to his sides, showing that he was unarmed, Safe said, "Please. I need my pack. My woman is exhausted. She needs water and food. I have both in my pack."

"No," the man said sternly.

Safe wasn't about to take no for an answer. "Look. I don't care if you take everything I own. I've got things with me that will be useful for you all. But please, she was kidnapped, tied up, scared out of her mind, then she escaped and walked through the jungle for hours. Now she's had to walk even longer. She's not used to this heat, hasn't eaten in who knows how long. Please let me take care of her."

It wasn't the man who responded to his pleas, but one of the women. She walked over to the man holding the rifle and scowled. "Put it down. Let him feed his woman."

"He probably has weapons in his bag," the man argued.

Safe didn't move an inch. The fact of the matter was, he *did* have weapons in his bag. A few knives. A handgun.

"Fine," the woman said as she went over to Safe's backpack that was left in the middle of the cave.

"Thank you," Safe told her. "There are two MREs, meals ready to eat, we only need one. You can have the other. I'll also need some of the water purification tablets. They're in a small baggie in that outer pocket. Yes, that one. And if it wouldn't be too much trouble for you to fill that collapsible water bottle for us, it would help a lot."

He was pushing his luck, Safe knew that, but the woman seemed willing enough to help, so he figured it couldn't hurt to ask. To his great surprise and relief, the woman walked toward him and handed him the MRE and the tablets. He nodded his thanks before the woman left the cave, hopefully to get some water out of the stream.

When he turned toward Wren, the sight that greeted him had Safe both relieved and frustrated. She'd lain down in the dirt and fallen asleep. He was glad she was finally getting some rest, but frustrated that it wasn't in a chopper as they headed out of the country to safety.

He hated to wake her up, but he needed to get some calories into her. And more water. Then he'd let her sleep again and watch over her while she did so.

Sitting next to her, Safe put a hand on her shoulder and shook her gently. "Wren. I need you to wake up."

"No," she moaned.

"Just for a little bit. I have some food for you."

"Not hungry," she mumbled.

"I know, but again, you need to eat. Come on, sit up. This one isn't bad. Chili and macaroni. You already ate the best part, the poppy seed pound cake, but the jalapeno cheese spread on the crackers isn't awful. Although I suggest not eating the beef sticks, they taste like dog food."

That earned him a small smile. Wren sighed then pushed herself upright. Safe moved her so she was sitting in front of him, her back against his chest, his legs on either side of her. He wrapped his arms around her while he opened the MRE.

The woman returned with the water he'd asked for. Safe thanked her, as did Wren.

Using some of the water to heat up the chili and macaroni, Safe then put a purification tablet into the bottle, along with the orange beverage powder that came with the MRE. It would be a strange-tasting drink, but the powder had carb-electrolytes, and Wren's body needed all the boosting it could get. Their situation was much better than he could've hoped after being surrounded by another group of rebels in the jungle, but they weren't out of danger yet.

While they were waiting for the noodles to heat up, Safe spread some of the cheese on a cracker and handed it to Wren. She ate it without a word, moving almost robotically, as if spaced out. Safe supposed she was still half asleep, at the end of her rope. But that was okay. As long as he could get some calories and water into her, he'd let her sleep as long as she could before whatever was going to happen next.

The three women he'd seen outside entered the cave and sat across from him and Wren, watching them silently. Safe ignored them. His only concern at the moment was the woman wilting in his arms.

Resting his chin on her shoulder, he scooped up a spoonful of the macaroni dish and blew on it, making sure it wouldn't burn Wren's mouth, then held the spoon to her lips. She opened without a word, and Safe couldn't help but feel satisfaction deep inside him that he was able to provide for her.

They shared the macaroni, taking turns eating small bites. He made sure she drank plenty of the orange-flavored water between spoonfuls of the meal. When they'd almost finished the pouch of rehydrated food, she sighed and turned onto her side in the circle of his embrace. Her head rested on his chest, right above his heart.

"Can I sleep now?" she slurred.

"Sleep, Wren. I've got you," Safe reassured her. He kissed her forehead as she snuggled into him. She was asleep in seconds, her deep breaths making her chest rise and fall under the arms he'd wrapped around her.

"She okay?" the leader asked as he walked toward them.

Safe didn't move. The remnants of their meal were strewn around him, but all his attention was on the man who held their fate in his hands. "Exhausted," he told him.

The man nodded. Then asked, "How much is she worth? To her company. How much would they pay to get her back?"

Safe tensed. This conversation wasn't starting out how he'd hoped. "How much is she worth? She's priceless," he said. "As for how much BT Energy would pay to get her back? I don't know. She was just hired a little over a month ago. She's not one of their executives." He was doing his best to make it sound as if Wren was simply another employee. No one important.

"Why was she here then?"

"She's their PR person. Public relations. She talks to the media. Explains the project, highlights the benefits."

The leader's lip curled. "So she's a liar just like all the press."

Safe shook his head. "No. She might concentrate more on the pros of a project than the cons, but she doesn't lie."

The leader stared at him for a long moment. Sweat dripped down the back of Safe's neck. He felt as if this moment was a turning point. Things for them could go either way right now.

"What about you? How much would the US government pay to get back one of their soldiers?"

It was a good thing the man didn't know he was a SEAL right about now. Safe shrugged. "Considering my team and I aren't supposed to be here in the first place, I'm not sure they'll pay *anything* to get me back." That wasn't exactly true. The commander had pulled some strings to get them permission to be able to bop across the border, save their countrymen and woman, and get the hell out, but as far as the president and other muckety-mucks went? Yeah, they didn't know and wouldn't approve of this rescue mission.

"Huh," the leader said with a disappointed grunt. "How many more of you are there? Will they come for you?"

"Six. And yes, they'll come."

"They know where you are?"

Safe didn't bother lying. "Yes."

"How?"

"I have a tracker on me. As does she," Safe said, nodding toward Wren.

"So even if we kill you now, they'll still come."

Safe nodded, holding his breath.

This was it. Decision time.

"When?"

"When what?" he asked in confusion.

"When will they get here?"

Doing some quick calculations in his head, Safe replied, "I'd say within three hours."

"Then you better be on your way. Maybe you can meet them along their way here," the leader said, turning away abruptly.

"Wait!" Safe blurted.

"What?"

He couldn't believe he was about to ask this, but he could see and hear the rain falling outside. "Can we stay for a couple of hours? She literally can't walk anymore right now. She's too tired."

"And your team? Will they shoot first and ask questions after?"

It was a valid question. "No. They'll observe first. Make contact with me before they do anything."

The leader's head tilted. "You aren't a regular soldier, are you?"

"No."

They stared at each other for a beat before the leader said, "Don't make me regret this."

"On the contrary, I'll do what I can to compensate you for helping us." To be fair, the man hadn't really helped them. He'd simply intercepted them. If it wasn't for being detained, Safe and Wren could've been in a chopper and out of South Sudan right this moment. But the man hadn't hurt them. For Safe, that was enough.

The leader nodded and turned away. The man who'd been guarding them with the rifle followed behind.

Feeling his muscles relax for the first time since he'd learned Wren and her coworkers had been kidnapped, Safe rested his head on the wall behind him. Wren lay curled in his arms, sound asleep. She was as vulnerable as she'd ever been, but Safe wouldn't let anything happen to her. He wouldn't sleep, no matter how tired he was. He didn't even have the urge to close his eyes. He'd stay vigilant and watch over her until his team arrived.

And he had no doubt they would. He just prayed he hadn't lied to the leader of this ragtag group of rebels.

If Kevlar and the others shot first before figuring out the situation, they were as good as dead. But his team was good at what they did. Very good. They'd scope out the area, get all the intel they could before making a move. Safe just had to wait for their signal and send the all-clear in return. Things would work out. There was no other alternative.

CHAPTER TWENTY

Wren woke with a start. She wasn't sure what had startled her, but when Bo whispered into her ear, "Easy, sweetheart. We're okay," she calmed immediately.

Looking around, Wren saw they were in the cave she vaguely remembered being led to by the newest group of kidnappers. She recalled Bo feeding her, but the memories were fuzzy. As if they were a dream instead of real life.

But right now, there were around a dozen very tense-looking rebels holding rifles, standing near the entrance of the cave.

"What's happening?" she whispered.

"The guys are here," Bo said calmly.

"What? What guys?" Wren asked, turning to look at the man holding her. Her muscles were stiff and it hurt to twist around, but she had to get ready to move. To run. To do *something*.

But Bo looked relaxed. Well, as relaxed as he could be, considering their current situation.

"*Our* guys. Kevlar, Preacher, and the others."

Spinning around to look at the mouth of the cave, Wren couldn't see anything beyond the line of rebels.

"Where?"

"They're out there. I heard Flash's bird call. Responded. And now they're waiting for me to make the first move."

"Then why are we still sitting here if you need to do something?" Wren asked.

"Because you were sleeping."

She stared at Bo as if he had two heads. "Wait, your team is here to rescue us, and you aren't doing anything because *I was sleeping?*"

"Yup," Bo said. "You were exhausted. Couldn't keep your head up. Could barely eat. You needed the sleep."

"I'm not asleep now," she told him slowly, as if he'd somehow gone crazy while she'd been napping.

He grinned. "Nope."

"Bo?" she asked.

"Yeah?"

"I'm confused."

"Right, sorry. Had a talk with their leader while you were getting some much-needed rest. He agreed to let us stay here while you recuperated. Told him my team would compensate him and his friends. Now the guys are here, and we'll be heading back out into the jungle and hopefully onto a helicopter before anyone else can decide to entertain us."

Just then, all the men in the cave raised their rifles and pointed them toward the jungle.

Bo said, still in a casual tone, "Can you get up, sweetheart?"

Scrambling, Wren scooted away from Bo so he could stand. She did the same, noting that Bo made sure to keep himself between her and the others.

"It's my men!" Bo said loudly and firmly. "They won't hurt you. We're fine, Kevlar!"

"You have ten seconds to put down your weapons before we start taking you out!" a deep, menacing voice shouted from the direction of the trees.

No one said a word, but one of the rebels turned around and pointed his rifle at Bo.

Maybe it was because she was still half asleep, or maybe it was pure insanity, but Wren found herself reaching into the pocket of her cargo pants and pulling out the miniscule knife she'd put there earlier...yesterday? This morning? She had no idea what time it was, all she knew was that she wasn't going to let anything happen to Bo. Not because of her.

She leaped around him and pointed the knife at the man. "Stay back!" she yelled almost hysterically.

It was ridiculous. She was holding a blade no longer than half her pinky finger, pointing it at a man with a rifle, while a dozen of his friends—all with their own weapons—stood behind him. What she thought she was going to do with that tiny little knife, she had no idea, but she was tired of feeling helpless. Of having people point guns at the heads of her friends.

"Easy, Wren," Bo said from behind her.

"No!" she exclaimed, not taking her gaze from the man in front of her. "All I want is to go home! I've met some awesome people here in South Sudan but I'm tired, scared, and hungry, and I just want a giant cheeseburger and a soft mattress that isn't soaking wet!"

"And you'll get them," Bo reassured her. Then she felt him press against her back. He didn't reach for her little knife. Didn't do anything except put his hands on her hips and lean into her. His warm breath tickled her ear. "It's all right, Wren. It's okay."

It *wasn't* okay. Her hand shook, but she couldn't stand down.

The man pointing the rifle lowered the weapon. His lips twitched as he stared at her.

That was the last straw for Wren. To be *laughed* at. She tried to take a step forward, to show the man smiling at her that she wouldn't hesitate to stab him. Granted, her tiny blade would probably hardly even be able to penetrate his skin, but she'd do what damage she could.

Except Bo tightened his grip, and one arm went around her chest, holding her tightly against him.

She wriggled, but Bo held firm. "It's over, Wren."

"Hey."

Surprised by the familiar voice, Wren looked up and saw Kevlar standing at the entrance of the cave. He wasn't exactly smiling, but he didn't look like was on the verge of slaughtering everyone in sight either. The other five men on Bo's team were fanned out behind him. They all looked cautious and on guard, but no one was shooting anyone else, so she took that as a win.

"Hey," Bo responded.

"You guys good?" Preacher asked.

"Yeah."

"Time for you to go," the leader of the latest group of hostage-takers said. To be fair, they hadn't been restrained. Had been given water, and now that everyone had lowered their weapons, they didn't seem ready to start shooting anytime soon.

"Thank you for your hospitality," Bo told him.

Wren wanted to snort, but she managed to hold it back.

The man eyed Bo for a heart-stoppingly long moment, then nodded.

"Can I speak to my friend for a moment...alone?" Bo asked.

Wren thought for sure he'd gone too far, so she was surprised when the leader nodded. Then he said, "She stays where she is."

The last thing Wren wanted was to be separated from Bo, but she locked her knees when he nodded and his arm dropped from around her.

"I'll be right back. Try not to shank anyone while I'm gone."

Wren glared at him. "This isn't funny."

"No, it's not," Bo told her with a solemn look on his face. "But give me three minutes and we'll be out of here."

"If you or anyone else gets shot, I'm never forgiving you," she warned.

Then, right there in front of his team, the dozen rebels, and the women, Bo kissed her. It wasn't passionate. It wasn't long. But he didn't hesitate to lean in and cover her lips with his own.

"Noted," he said when he lifted his head. His hand came

up and he caressed her cheek with a whisper-soft touch, then he turned and walked toward Kevlar.

Wren could still feel his fingers on her face as she watched him talk to his team leader. Within seconds, Kevlar turned to say something to the other men, and all six of them unshouldered their packs and began unloading them.

MREs, bandages, ferro rods, fishing line, paracord, duct tape, and more were thrown into a pile near the entrance to the cave.

While they were doing that, Bo walked back to where Wren was standing. "Ready to go?" he asked.

"Why are they giving them their stuff?" she asked.

"Because I promised to compensate them if they helped us. Don't worry, we aren't going to need the MREs or the other stuff, because we're getting out of this jungle in less than an hour."

"We are? How do you know?"

"Because. I do."

That wasn't an answer, but Wren figured now wasn't the time to go into details. She wanted out. Of this cave, this jungle, this country. "Okay."

"Okay," he agreed with a nod. Then he went over to his backpack, left where they'd been sitting, and shrugged it on.

"Were you followed?" the leader asked Kevlar, as Wren and Bo walked toward the mouth of the cave.

In response, Kevlar snorted. "No. And I'm assuming you know where the other camp was located. If you hurry, you can probably go and gather up anything you might deem useful for your own cause."

The leader's brows rose. "Yeah?"

"Yeah," Kevlar told him. "They won't be needing their supplies anymore."

The words seemed to change the leader's attitude toward Kevlar and his team. "There were twenty men at that camp."

"Yes. There were," Kevlar agreed.

The leader nodded without another word.

"You ready?" Bo asked Wren.

She nodded eagerly.

With a hand on the small of her back, he urged her toward the exit. The jungle was just as hot and humid as she remembered, but suddenly she was glad to be back amongst the trees. She and Bo hadn't been threatened, not really. And yet she had a feeling the men they were leaving behind were just as deadly as the ones who'd kidnapped her yesterday.

"The others? Colby? Dallas, Archie, and Oliver?"

"Safe," Flash told her.

Wren nodded, then frowned. "Are they waiting for us somewhere in the jungle?"

She heard someone snort, but the question had been genuine.

"No, Wren. We got them on a chopper. They're in Uganda, waiting for us."

"Wait, you guys didn't go with them? Why not?" Wren asked.

"SEALs don't leave SEALs behind. Period," Blink told her.

She turned toward the man who never seemed to say much. He wasn't looking at her, was concentrating on getting through the jungle toward wherever their destination lie. She swallowed hard, the understanding of just what these men had done hitting her hard. They'd come into a country they'd told her time and time again wasn't safe, that she shouldn't enter, and not only rescued her coworkers, but they'd come after her and Bo, simply because they didn't want to leave one of their own behind.

She thought she understood loyalty. Bravery. But she'd had no clue.

"Were you really going to stab that guy with that tiny blade?" MacGyver asked with a small grin.

Wren felt herself blush. Thinking about what she'd done, she realized now how stupid it was. She could've easily escalated the already tense situation to a point where the rebels and the SEALs felt they had no choice but to start shooting. Thankfully no one had taken her threat seriously.

"He threatened Bo," she mumbled.

"She's meant for you," Smiley told his teammate.

"She is," Bo agreed. "You still have it? The knife?"

Wren nodded.

"Good. Keep it."

"You think I'll need to use it again?" Wren asked in alarm.

"No. But the thought of you having it, and being willing to use it to protect me, makes me feel warm and fuzzy inside."

Wren couldn't believe she was smiling. She smelled horrible, had blisters on her feet, was walking through a jungle in Africa with a team of Navy SEALs, had no passport, no change of clothing, and her belly was rumbling with either hunger or the threat of explosive diarrhea, and yet she felt amazingly calm.

"Whatever," she told him.

Bo reached for her hand, and Wren gladly gave it. Their palms were sweaty and dirty, but nothing had felt so comforting as holding onto Bo. He'd come for her, just like he said he would. Bad things had happened, some of her poor coworkers had been killed. Yet somehow, she was still alive.

Wren had always done her best to stay strong, to keep going just to spite others, like her mother, but she was beginning to realize that she really was tougher than she'd ever thought.

Of course, the longer they walked, the hotter it got, the more Wren's muscles hurt, the less tough she decided she was. All she could think of was getting into a hot bath and then sleeping for three days straight. She decided she was never leaving Riverton again. She'd gladly become a stay-at-home cat lady if it meant she never had to go through anything remotely like what she was doing at the moment.

Just when she didn't think she could take another step, Kevlar stopped walking. "We're here."

Wren looked around in confusion. "Here, where?" she asked.

"Where we catch our ride."

All Wren could see was trees. There was no landing pad, no road a car could get down.

Then she heard an unmistakable sound. A helicopter.

"Do you trust me?"

Turning toward Bo, she answered without thought. "Yes."

Smiley chuckled. "She said that without hesitation. But we'll see how she feels when she sees how we're getting *into* our ride."

She looked at Bo uneasily as he stepped into her personal space and palmed the side of her neck. Internally, she cringed, because she was slick with perspiration, and the last thing Bo should want to do was touch her nasty, sweaty neck. But he didn't even seem to notice. His gaze was locked on hers.

"We're going up. The guys in the chopper will drop a rope and we'll be hoisted. Five minutes and we'll be out of here."

None of that sounded fun. She felt obligated to point out, "The last time I tried to climb a rope ladder was in middle school, and trust me, it didn't go well. Like, at all." She heard laughter from more than one person around her, but she kept her eyes on Bo.

"I've got you."

She wanted to protest more. But the truth of the matter was, she *did* trust this man. With her life. How could she not? He'd come to freaking South Sudan to rescue her from kidnappers. If he told her they were going to jump off the side of a huge cliff and land safely at the bottom, she'd believe him.

"The Night Stalkers know what they're doing," Blink said from beside them.

Tearing her gaze from Bo, she glanced at the other man. "The what?"

"Night Stalkers. They're Army, but they're all right."

The SEALs all chuckled.

"My brother's one," Blink told her.

"A Stalker?" Wren asked.

"A Night Stalker, yes. They're the best of the best when it comes to helicopter pilots."

"You have a brother?" MacGyver asked, a brow raised.

"Yeah. My twin," Blink said.

"No shit?" Flash exclaimed.

"No shit."

"Wow. Bet the Army-Navy football game is pretty stressful in your house," Smiley joked.

"Nah, we know the Navy's superior," Blink said with a shrug.

"What the hell? Was that a joke?" Smiley asked. "From *Blink*?"

But Wren was too worried about what she was about to be asked to do, and failing, to joke about football scores. She put a hand on Blink's arm. "Is he up there?"

"My brother?" Blink shook his head. "No. Last I heard, he was on a ship in the Middle East, shuttling special forces in and out of places they aren't officially supposed to be. But I guarantee whoever *is* up there knows what they're doing. They'll get us all out of here in a jiffy."

"Holy shit, now the man just said *jiffy*. We're all dead and this is an alternate universe, isn't it?" Smiley joked.

Kevlar smacked his friend on the back of the head. "Shut it, Smiley. Seriously."

But their joking around made Wren relax a little more. If they were truly worried about this extraction, they wouldn't be making fun of each other.

"He's right," Bo said, bringing her attention back to him. "Those pilots are the best of the best. They'll come down as low as they can before they lower the rope. As soon as you're secure, they'll haul you up and into the cab."

Wren nodded. What else could she do? She literally had no choice but to go along with this crazy plan. It was either be hauled up into a helicopter hovering over the jungle, or hike back to the city, which wasn't something she wanted to do anytime soon.

The sound of the helicopter got louder and louder, and soon the trees above them began to blow in the downdraft. She squinted her eyes as she looked up into the sky. She wasn't able to see the chopper clearly, only get glimpses of it through the blowing trees.

Jumping in fright when a long rope appeared as if out of nowhere, she fell against Bo.

"Easy," he said, even as he was urging her forward toward the rope.

Wren didn't want to go first. Didn't want to get tied to the end of a rope and yanked into the abyss. But she also didn't want to be a baby.

To her surprise, Blink began to secure himself to the rope. Then Bo did the same, leaving about four feet of rope between him and Blink. He turned to her and held out his hand. "Come here, Wren."

She stepped forward as if in a trance. Kevlar approached and began to wind the end of the rope around both her and Bo. He made a loop and told her to step onto it.

"This'll give you leverage, a way to support your body weight as you're hoisted up. Just hold onto Safe. You'll be fine."

Wren didn't feel fine. Yes, the rope had been wound around Bo and his arms were holding her tightly against him, but still, all that was between her and certain death by splatting to the ground was a measly piece of rope!

"Look at me," Bo ordered as she felt movement in the rope.

Swallowing hard, she did just that. His golden-brown eyes were fixated on her. "I'm proud of you."

Wren gasped as the rope tightened around her waist. Her knee buckled before she locked it, holding her own weight on the little loop around her foot. They rose above the ground, slowly at first, then with increasing speed. Bo had told her that he was proud of her before, but each time he said it, it felt better and better.

"I'm serious," he said in her ear as they were being lifted up toward the helicopter. "You have no idea what kind of hysterics we've had to deal with in regard to hostage rescues."

"You're just saying that," Wren retorted, trying desperately to take her mind off what was happening.

"No, I'm not," Bo insisted. "We once had to extricate a government official from the rooftop of a building, and he not only pissed his pants—which honestly, I don't hold against him, we were dodging sniper fire—but he grabbed me around the neck and almost strangled me by the time we got to the chopper. Kevlar had to punch him and knock him out cold in order to loosen his grip, just so I could breathe."

"Holy crap!" Wren gasped.

"Yeah. So believe me when I tell you that you're doing great, sweetheart."

She glanced down—and stiffened when she realized she couldn't see the ground anymore. Then she looked up, which was almost worse. All she could see was the underside and skids of the helicopter. She had no idea how the hell they were going to get inside the thing, not dangling as they were on this tiny rope.

"When we get home, I'm going to lock us in my room—no more sleeping in the guest room for you—and make love to you for hours. I meant what I told that rebel in the cave.

You're mine...and I'm going to prove it over and over, until you pass out from orgasm fatigue."

That got her attention, as Wren supposed Bo meant it to. "That's not a thing," she protested, but deep down she couldn't help but hope it was.

"Sure it is. And I'm going to prove that too. I love you, Wren Defranco. You're the woman I want to spend the rest of my life with. You've proven over and over that you're tough as nails. Being with a SEAL isn't easy, but I have no doubt whatsoever that you can hack it."

"Bo," she whispered.

"I need to introduce you to my family. Susie, her husband, kids. My parents. We need to set up a meeting with your father so you can meet him and your brothers. We have to discuss how you feel about having kids of our own. I want them, but I want time with you all to myself before we even think about that. And if kids aren't something you want, I'll deal."

Wren's mind was spinning. "I want kids," she blurted.

He smiled at her. "Good. Now, hold on and let them do all the work."

For a second, Wren was confused. Let their unborn kids do all the work? But she was brought back to reality when she felt someone tugging at the rope around her waist. She panicked for a millisecond, until she felt herself held in a firm grip around both upper arms and being pulled upward. It was only moments later when Bo was there as well, holding her as he urged her to scoot backward, away from the open helicopter door.

Blink gave her a thumbs up from where he was crouched

near the door. The rope was being lowered again, and Wren knew it was only a matter of time before the rest of Bo's team was in the helicopter with them and they were on their way.

He'd successfully distracted her from what was happening...but almost immediately she began to worry that was all his words were. A distraction.

Until he leaned in and put his lips against her ear. It was loud inside the chopper, and any kind of true conversation was almost impossible. But she heard him when he spoke directly into her ear.

"Proud of you. Love you."

There was no better combination of words that Wren could imagine hearing from the man she loved. And while she hadn't said the words to Bo, she felt deep in her heart that this man was hers. How could she *not* love him?

The rest of Bo's team was quickly hoisted into the helicopter, then they were turning and flying away.

Closing her eyes, Wren allowed herself to fully relax for the first time probably since she'd landed in the country. She had no idea what her future held, what the future held for BT Energy and the pipeline project they'd all worked on so hard. But whatever it was, she had no doubt that she'd have Bo at her side.

CHAPTER TWENTY-ONE

The trip across the border was uneventful, which Safe was thankful for. Not every extraction went as smoothly as this one had. He hadn't lied when he'd told Wren that story about almost being choked to death by someone he was rescuing. But they still had a very long way to go before they were back in California.

Wren was once more unsteady on her feet as she walked next to him toward the truck that would take the team to where Dallas, Archie, Oliver, and Colby were hopefully still holed up. Kevlar had word from a contact on the ground in Uganda that they'd arrived and were safe, but until they all saw them, no one would relax. Hell, they wouldn't let down their guard until they were in the air on the way back to Riverton.

They were spending the night in Uganda before heading to the airstrip to catch a flight to Germany, where everyone would be checked out at a military hospital. Then they'd finally be on their way back to the States.

He could feel how tense Wren was as they walked, but he didn't interrupt her thoughts. He'd sprung a lot on her as they were hoisted up to the chopper, but every single word was from his heart. He wanted a future with Wren, but they had a lot to get through before either of them could see if it was even possible.

Kevlar led them as they climbed into the back of the pickup truck and headed into the nearest town to meet up with Wren's coworkers. She was tense as she sat in the middle of his team, but it was the safest place for her as they traveled to their destination. Everyone was on alert. Even though they were out of South Sudan, Uganda wasn't exactly the safest place for American soldiers and civilians either.

They reached the house where Wren's coworkers were supposed to be, and Safe breathed a sigh of relief when the door opened and Archie and Oliver stepped outside. He and his team jumped out of the bed of the truck, and Safe helped Wren climb out as well. As the truck drove off, Wren finally noticed the two men. She practically ran to them and gave first Archie, then Oliver a hard hug.

"Are you guys okay?"

"Yeah. You?" Oliver asked.

"I'm good. I'm so sorry I left you guys. Did they...were they mad?" Wren stumbled over the question.

"They were pissed," Archie told her. "But you did the right thing. They were going to...you know...hurt you. So it's good that you got away."

"Thanks, Archie. I know that I annoy you most of the time, and you were tired of me going on and on about safety. I'm just glad they didn't take my escaping out on you guys," Wren told him.

"That's only because of your friends," Oliver said. "They were totally planning on killing us. They just didn't get a chance. When they realized you were gone, they sent six guys into the jungle to find you and bring you back. Then they argued about what to do with us. The leader guy took out a video camera. An honest-to-God camera from like the eighties, and ordered Colby to say some stuff. He refused, so a bunch of guys started beating him again. They were so busy doing that, they didn't even see your friends slip into camp. Before anyone knew what was happening, it was over. They were all dead."

Wren's eyes were huge in her face. She glanced at Safe before turning back to her friends. "Holy crap!"

"Yeah. And I guess the six guys they sent after you met the same fate because they didn't come back, and they didn't find you either, I take it."

"No," Wren agreed.

"We intercepted them," Smiley said without any emotion.

"Right," Oliver said. "Anyway, they gave us water, wrapped my hand, helped Colby as much as they could, then we headed into the jungle to the extraction point."

"When you didn't show up, they sent us on while they went back for you...and here we are," Archie finished the story.

"Where's Colby and Dallas? Are they okay?" Wren asked.

"Colby's hurting, they really beat him up bad. His face where he had that cut is also infected. He's lying down inside. And Dallas is with him. He's been watching over him," Archie told her.

"Sucking up to him, you mean," Oliver mumbled.

"And your hand?" Wren asked.

"Still missing two fingers, hurts like hell. But I'm alive," Oliver said.

"Well...I'm just glad you're okay," Wren told them both.

"Yeah. We all should've taken your concerns more seriously," Oliver said quietly.

Wren simply shrugged.

"Can we take this inside?" Safe asked.

"Are we still in danger?" Archie asked.

"No," Safe told him. "But I'm sure Wren would like to eat and drink something. And shower."

"Shower?" she asked breathlessly, looking up at him.

He chuckled. "Yeah, with water and everything."

Archie and Oliver stood back as Wren practically ran them over trying to get into the house, and presumably to a shower.

"Never get between a girl and her shower," Oliver joked.

It wasn't until they were inside that Safe saw Wren hesitate.

"What? What's wrong?" he asked, pulling her aside. The rest of his team was already looking in cabinets and pulling out items, he assumed to make a meal for everyone.

"I don't have anything clean to put on."

Safe relaxed. He took her by the hand and pulled her toward one of the four small bedrooms, where his team had stashed their things. When they'd come to Uganda from Chad, they'd stayed here while anxiously waiting for an available chopper to take them over the border into South Sudan. Safe went over to his duffle against the wall.

Unzipping the bag, he pulled out a clean T-shirt, a pair of boxers, and some sweatpants. Holding them out to her, he said, "They'll be big, but they're clean. There's no washing machine here, but there's a basin out back that the others used to wash their things. I'll get started on yours while you're in the shower."

Wren stared at him without saying anything and without reaching for the clothes.

"Wren?"

"You're going to wash my clothes?"

"Yeah," Safe said, not sure what was wrong.

Wren closed her eyes, her brow furrowing, and she swayed slightly.

Alarmed, Safe threw the clothes onto the nearest mattress and pulled Wren into his arms. "What? Talk to me, Wren."

Her eyes opened, and she looked up at him. "For as long as I can remember, I've done my own laundry. When I was five, I remember having to climb up on a chair to reach the buttons on our ancient washing machine. Even in foster care, I was responsible for my own clothes. No one has ever offered to wash my clothes before. And you're going to do it by hand?"

"I love you," Safe told her. "Anything you need, I'll do my best to provide for you. Food, water, shelter, clean clothes... you name it."

She stared up at him for the longest time. Safe could see a

riot of emotions swirling in her eyes. Then she broke his heart when she whispered, "Is this what it feels like to be loved?"

He ran his hand over her head, smiling a little when his palm snagged on the snap clip in her hair. "Yeah. I guess it is."

"It's overwhelming," she retorted with a small frown.

"Well, get used to it," he told her, pulling her close and resting his cheek on the side of her head.

She held on tightly, seeming to need this moment as much as he did. Then she mumbled into his neck, "You stink."

Safe chuckled. "You aren't exactly a fresh, clean daisy yourself, sweetheart."

To his relief, she pulled back with a smile on her face. "You want to shower first?"

"No. Take your time. There's not a lot of hot water, so I'm guessing you won't be in there long, but you always come first from now on. Hot water, the last glass of wine, the best space on the couch. It's yours."

"Bo?"

"Yeah, sweetheart?"

"Thanks for not saying 'I told you so.'"

"I'd *never* say that," he said firmly. "Should you have traveled to South Sudan? No. Did you have a choice? Not really."

"I could've said no," she said sadly.

"We've been over this. And all the arguments you had for not saying no before still stand."

"I don't know if I can go back to work there," she whispered, as if scared that saying the words out loud would somehow make him think less of her.

"Then don't," Safe told her.

"It's not that easy," she protested.

"It is and it isn't," Safe said with a shrug. "You're right, California is expensive. But I make a decent salary. And have decent benefits. We'll be all right until you figure out something else. Find another job."

She stilled in his arms and gaped at him.

"What?" he asked.

"We?"

He nodded. "Was I not clear back when we were hanging on that rope? I want you in my house. My bed. My life. I love you. You're mine, and I take care of what's mine. You want to quit your job and stay home and collect acorns and make art with them and sell them on the Internet, fine. Great. I'll support you. You want to continue to work for BT Energy. That's fine too. You want to find another PR job? No problem. I know it'll take some time for this to sink in, but you aren't on your own anymore, Wren. You aren't that little girl hiding under your bed from your evil mother. You've got me. My team. Remi. Caroline and her friends. Wolf and his team. Things won't always be smooth sailing, because we've both lived alone for quite a while, but we'll figure it out. Together."

"I'm scared."

"I know." And he did. Leaning on someone else wasn't something she'd done much of, if at all, in her life. But that was changing. Now.

"I don't deserve you," she told him.

"You're right," Safe said without hesitation. "You deserve someone better than me. Someone who can give you all the finer things in life. Someone with a safer job. Someone you can come home to every day, without fail. I'm not that man. But I *am* a man who will bend over backward to make you happy. And when I'm not able to be there for you, I'll arrange to have others at your back until I get home to you."

Wren swallowed hard. "I love you," she whispered.

Safe felt as if his heart was going to explode. "And I love you. Now...please go shower before you have moss growing in your hair and your stinkiness sinks into the very essence of this room."

Wren smiled and smacked his shoulder. Then she sighed. "I have no idea how this happened."

"Because I'm irresistible," Safe joked.

"True."

Then Wren went up on her toes and kissed him. Safe wanted to deepen the kiss. Wanted to throw her on the mattress behind them and strip off all her clothes and bury himself deep inside her body. But now wasn't the time or the place. He'd wait until he had her in his house, and his bed, where they wouldn't be interrupted, before showing her with and without words how serious he was about loving her.

He pulled back, picked up the clothes he'd grabbed for her, and held them out once more. "Put your stuff outside the door and I'll wash it while you're showering."

Wren nodded then took his clothes. Safe led her back out into the hallway and into the bathroom. It had a toilet, a sink, and a shower. There was no stall, just a pipe coming out of the wall and a drain in the middle of the tiled floor.

Safe put his hand on her cheek, and she leaned into him. "Thank you for being smart, tough, and staying calm. I don't know what I would've done if you'd been hurt," he said quietly. Then he kissed her forehead and left the room, closing the door firmly behind him.

He went into the main room and announced, "Wren's in the bathroom. If anyone disturbs her, you'll answer to me." He was feeling growly and protective. Just being out of her sight, even though he knew exactly where she was, made him feel off-kilter.

"No one's gonna bother her," MacGyver said. "Come eat something. It'll make you less grouchy."

Everyone laughed, but Safe wasn't in the mood to eat. He felt itchy, unsettled. He heard the bathroom door open and shut, and turned, seeing a mound of clothes sitting in the hallway. Knowing Wren was naked on the other side of the door made his skin heat. He wanted her. But he could wait. As long as it took.

He walked back and picked up her shirt and pants, noticing her underthings weren't with her clothes. Then he went through the main room and out onto the small back patio without a word.

"Hey, want to do mine too?" Flash called out.

Safe lifted a hand and gave his friend his middle finger. Laughter rang out in the room behind him, and for the first time in days, Safe relaxed a fraction. He was safe, Wren was safe, his friends were safe. It was only a matter of time before they were back in Riverton. He couldn't wait.

* * *

Hours later, Wren looked around the room and had to pinch herself. Not too long ago, she was sitting on the jungle floor, her hands bound together, wondering if she and her coworkers would live through another day.

And here she was, her belly full, her body clean—well, as clean as she could be with the barely functional shower and cold water—snuggled with Bo as her coworkers and Bo's teammates sat around talking about their favorite TV shows. It felt a little like a dream.

She hadn't changed back into her clothes—truthfully, she was going to burn the shirt and pants the second she had a chance when she got home—because they were still damp and drying. She'd washed her bra and underwear in the shower herself, feeling too awkward to have Bo clean those for her. She was sitting on his lap, using his chest as a backrest, and his arms were holding her against him.

She was comfortable and relaxed...and feeling guilty as hell. "How's Colby doing?" she asked Dallas during a lull in the conversation.

"Hurting, but okay," the other man said. "And feeling like shit. It wasn't his plan for Bob, Tom, Luke, and Aaron to run, but he said he also didn't discourage them. He honestly thought that we'd be okay. That nothing would happen to any of us. So for them to have been..." Dallas cleared his throat before continuing. "...killed. It was a shock."

Wren nodded and felt Bo's arms tighten around her.

"I wonder where the project stands now," Archie mused.

"Who the fuck cares," Oliver said heatedly. "People died. It's not safe for anyone to work on any kind of pipeline until things work themselves out here. If they ever do."

Everyone was silent, lost in their own thoughts.

Then Wren said, "For what it's worth, I still think the pipeline can do good things for South Sudan. But until the corruption in the government is stopped, any money that's earned will go into the pockets of the people in control, and not to the citizens who need it the most. I will never think that kidnapping and extortion is the right thing to do, but...I can understand why they did it. Desperation makes people do desperate things. None of us know hunger, not like the people here do. We don't know thirst."

"Agreed," Dallas said quietly.

"Same," Oliver said with a nod.

"Yeah," Archie added after a moment.

"I'm going to go check on Colby. When are we leaving?" Dallas asked.

Kevlar looked at his watch. "Five hours, give or take."

That seemed to be the sign everyone needed to get up and head off to get some sleep. It was going to be a long trip to Germany, then back to California.

Wren found herself in the room where Bo's duffle bag had been stored. He motioned for her to climb onto a twin-size mattress on the floor, against one wall, and he immediately joined her. Wren turned onto her side, and Bo spooned her from behind.

Blink stretched out on the other mattress in the room, and Kevlar lay down near the door. She didn't feel the least bit weird about sleeping next to Bo with his friends in the room. In fact, it was what she needed. To be surrounded by not only the man she loved, but two others he considered his brothers. No one would get to her here.

Safe. It was the name of the man whose arms held her tight, but it was also how she felt when she was anywhere near him. She'd never experienced true safety in her life until she'd run into him in that hallway at Aces Bar and Grill. Somehow, deep in her gut, she'd known even then that this man would protect her. Keep her safe.

CHAPTER TWENTY-TWO

Wren was done.

Done with flying. Done with being poked and prodded by the military doctors in Germany. Done with people asking her the same questions over and over. Done with the uneasy looks from her coworkers. Done with being ignored by her boss. Done with Bo's concern and attentiveness.

Done with it all.

She wanted to be home. Alone. In a hot-as-hell bath or shower. Out of these damn clothes, which still seemed to be damp even after the hours of travel.

She was irritated, tired, sore, and so damn sad about Luke and Aaron. Bob and Tom too, even if she still wanted to smile at hearing their names said together because it reminded her of the talk show with the same name.

She was even irritated with herself for being irritated. She should be grateful. Thankful. Relieved to be back on US soil.

But instead she wanted to scream. To get the hell away from all these...*men.*

And that wasn't fair. They'd been nothing but kind and gentle with her. The SEALs had saved her life. She and her coworkers had a deeper bond that could only be caused by shared trauma.

And yet, she still wanted to scream at them all to leave her the hell alone.

They'd landed at the base in Riverton after nightfall, and thankfully, her coworkers had all left immediately to go to their respective homes. The bodies of Aaron, Luke, Tom, and Bob couldn't be recovered, but the families would certainly want to honor their loved ones. She guessed services for the men would be held in the upcoming weeks, and Wren was dreading the thought.

Now, she was standing off to the side in the hangar as Bo and his team met with their commander. She understood what they had to do, but the longer she stood there, the more she wanted to run.

A door opened at the end of the massive space, and Wren turned to see who had entered out of habit. To her surprise, she saw Caroline walk in with her husband, Wolf.

Her friend walked straight for her, as Wolf headed toward the group of SEALs.

"Come on," Caroline said as she approached Wren. "I'm taking you home."

As irritated as Wren had been seconds earlier, she suddenly wasn't sure she wanted to be separated from Bo.

"Wolf is telling him now that we're taking you to his

house. To get you settled. Trust me, I've been where you are now. Exhausted and hurting, both physical and mentally. And as much as I loved Wolf and his team, I just needed some time to myself. To process everything that had happened to me."

"Oh." Wren remembered the story about what happened to Caroline, and her heart went out to her.

"Yeah, oh. Now, come on. I'm going to take you home, get you settled in the bathtub with a huge glass of wine, where you can decompress. Safe will be here for a while, debriefing. Wolf and I will stay at the house with you until he gets home. We'll stay out of your hair, let you do your thing, but you won't be alone. I don't think Safe would even agree to that anyway. And as much as you're wanting some space, I'm guessing you don't really want to be alone either. Demons rising and all that."

Looking back at Bo, she saw Wolf standing next to him with his hand on his arm, holding him back. Bo looked worried and stressed, and for the first time, Wren realized how hard this entire thing had been on him too. She'd simply overlooked it because he was a big bad SEAL. "I'm okay," she mouthed.

"You sure?" he mouthed back.

Wren nodded. She saw his shoulders relax, and he nodded at Wolf and said something to him. Wolf gave him a chin lift, then headed in her and Caroline's direction.

"See? It's all good. Let's go."

Wren couldn't help but smile a little at the thought she was being kidnapped once again. But this time, she wanted to go with her captors.

Before she knew it, Wolf was pulling his huge SUV up to Bo's house.

"I'll be back," Wolf said, leaning over and kissing Caroline before she got out.

"Where's he going?" Wren asked as they watched him pull out of the driveway and head off down the street.

"Picking up Mexican."

"Seriously?" Wren asked, unable to keep the excitement out of her voice.

"Yup. Safe mentioned it was your favorite food, and since this is your homecoming, that's what you're getting," Caroline told her.

Wren smiled at her friend. "Awesome."

"Yup. Now come on, that bathtub is calling your name."

Two hours later, Wren's fingers were wrinkled beyond recognition and she finally felt clean, now that she'd been able to scrub her body, shave, and brush her teeth five times. She had on a pair of fleece fat pants, a long-sleeve oversize Navy shirt that she'd stolen from Bo's drawer, and a pair of fluffy socks on her feet. She'd stuffed herself with chips and salsa and a burrito as big as her head, and she finally felt more like herself.

She was as tired as she'd been back in that jungle in Africa, but she knew she'd never be able to fall asleep. Not until Bo was home. Caroline and Wolf had fallen asleep on the couch, both snoring slightly in each other's arms. Wren appreciated them not pressuring her to talk about her ordeal. They made a little small talk as they ate, but then turned on the TV and gave her some space.

As much as Wren was grateful they were there, and that they'd brought her home, she was ready for Bo to be back.

Just as she had the thought, Wren heard a key in the lock. Wolf obviously heard it too, because he was sitting up and setting Caroline gently to the side, as if he'd known exactly when Bo would arrive home.

He was standing between her and the front door when Bo entered. The two men nodded at each other and, without a word, Wolf leaned down and picked Caroline up off the couch.

"What? Is Safe home?" she asked sleepily.

"He's home. We're leaving," Wolf told her succinctly.

"Okay. Talk to you later, Wren. Glad you're home and all right," Caroline said, before putting her head back down on her husband's shoulder, trusting him to get her to the car and home safely.

Bo closed and locked the door behind them, then turned to Wren. He looked exhausted.

"Are you hungry? We saved you some enchiladas," she said gently.

But he shook his head. "We ate. I need a shower."

Wren nodded, feeling awkward for some reason.

"Come here," Bo ordered, holding out his arms.

Rushing forward, Wren threw her arms around him and held on tightly, feeling as if everything in her world was all right, now that she was in his embrace.

"I'm sorry I was a bitch! I guess I'm just not used to that much peopleing. It just got overwhelming."

"Shhhh, you weren't a bitch. You were fine."

She wasn't, but Wren loved Bo all the more for not calling her out on her testy behavior.

"You smell amazing."

She couldn't help but laugh at that. "That's because I don't smell like eau de jungle anymore."

"True. But I probably do."

"No, you don't." She was only slightly lying.

Bo chuckled, and Wren could feel it along every nerve ending of her body, especially because she was still plastered against him.

"I would kill for a shower and some sleep," Bo said after a moment.

Wren reluctantly pulled away from him. "Then go."

"You'll be there? In our bed, waiting for me?"

His words sent goose bumps racing down the back of her neck. "Yes."

"Good." Then he turned almost like a zombie and headed down the hall.

Wren made sure the door was locked, then followed in Bo's footsteps. He was already in the bathroom with the water in the shower running when she got there. Slipping the sweats down her legs, Wren changed into a short-sleeve T-shirt—another one of Bo's—and took off her socks before getting under the covers.

Five minutes later, Bo appeared in the doorway of the bathroom. He had on a pair of boxers...and that was it.

Her heart was in her throat as he walked toward her, detouring to the wall to turn off the light before joining her under the sheet and blanket. She immediately cuddled into him when he lay on his back. Her arm went over his chest and she rested her head on his shoulder.

"This," he said.

When he didn't say anything else, Wren whispered, "This, what?"

"This is what I've been dreaming about. You, in my arms, in my bed. Safe. Healthy. Alive."

Wren closed her eyes. She'd had some of the same dreams. "Me too," she admitted.

But Bo was already asleep.

She smiled at how fast he was able to nod off, but quickly sobered. He had to be utterly exhausted to have been able to fall asleep that fast. He also had to feel completely safe here. Otherwise, he wouldn't have been so quick to let his guard down.

He'd watched over her from the time he found her in the jungle until this second.

Swallowing her tears down, Wren snuggled into his side. And was rewarded by his arm tightening around her and his lips on the side of her head.

"Love you," he murmured sleepily.

"Love you too," she responded, before falling into a deep sleep herself.

* * *

Safe opened his eyes and knew exactly where he was and who he was with.

Wren.

She was really here.

In his bed.

He was moving before his brain could advise him that what he was doing probably wasn't the best idea.

He slipped down her body and settled himself between her legs. The shirt she was wearing, *his* shirt, had rucked up around her waist as they'd slept, and all she had on was a tiny pair of cotton underwear.

His mouth watered, and he wanted nothing more than to pull them to the side and bury his mouth in her pussy. But he'd never do anything without her consent. And at the moment, she still seemed to be sleeping soundly.

Safe nuzzled her lower belly, gently pressing her legs apart. His thumbs caressed her inner thighs as he waited for Wren to wake up. She did so gradually, stretching in his grasp and arching her back, pushing her pussy up toward him in the process.

"Morning," Safe said quietly.

Wren froze, then looked down at him. "Bo?"

"Yeah?"

"What are you doing?"

"Nothing...yet. But there's lots I *want* to do."

"Oh. Um...now?"

"You got anything better to do?"

"No."

Safe stared up at her as he continued to caress her sensitive inner thighs. When she didn't say anything else or try to move away from him, he said, "We can get up and have some cereal and get on with our day. Or, I can show you how much I adore you by eating you to orgasm, then making slow, sweet love to you until you're begging me to come."

A choked sound escaped Wren's mouth before she said, "Door number two. Please."

Safe smiled and immediately reached for the waistband of her underwear. He slowly peeled it down her legs before settling himself right back where he was. "This isn't going to be fast," he warned. "I've been thinking about being here for way too long. I'm going to take my time, find out what you like, what turns you on the most. It's going to take at least two orgasms before I'm satisfied."

"Bo," she whispered.

But Safe was done talking. He lowered his head and licked between her lips, stroking up to her clit. Then he did it again. And again. Glancing up, he saw Wren had lain back down and was staring at the ceiling. "Look at me," he ordered.

She immediately picked her head up and looked down.

"Watch me love you. Watch how perfect we are together." Without breaking eye contact, he covered her clit with his mouth as he used one of his hands to tease her soaking-wet entrance.

He saw Wren's chest rising and falling as she trembled in his arms. She still had his shirt on, but somehow that was more exciting than if she was naked. He could see her nipples pressing against the cotton. Truthfully, the shirt looked better on her than it ever had on him.

He pressed on her thigh, opening her further to him as he continued to use his tongue to stimulate her clit, while using the suction of his mouth to torment the little bud.

It wasn't long before she was writhing, rocking her hips. Seeing her lose some of the control she carried on her shoulders like a shroud made Safe feel ten feet tall. He lifted his mouth off her long enough to say, "That's it. Show me what you want," before lowering his head once again.

As he brought her closer and closer to the edge, she began to pump her hips harder and faster, essentially trying to fuck his mouth. Safe's cock was throbbing against the mattress. He wanted this woman. Loved how uninhibited she was. Tightening his hold on her thigh, he plunged his index finger deep into her body. That earned him a long moan.

The sound went straight to his dick, and Safe knew he wouldn't be able to hold out much longer. The taste of her, the smell, the feel of her reaching for the orgasm that was just out of reach. He loved this woman so damn much.

Desperately wanting to see her come, Safe tongued her clit like a man possessed. She stiffened against him and widened her legs as she pushed up, trying to get even closer. Then she began to shake uncontrollably, and her inner muscles clenched around his finger. She flew over the edge almost violently.

It was all Safe could do to keep his mouth on her clit. Her cream was all over his face, running down his finger, soaking the sheets beneath her...and he wanted more.

Lifting his head, Safe added another finger inside her. Feeling her muscles fluttering around them made it almost impossible to wait to get inside her. But he'd promised her at least two orgasms before making love to her...and he wasn't a man to go back on a promise.

This time he wanted to watch. Scooting up on his knees, Safe wrapped her legs around him as he settled himself between her thighs. Her pelvis was tilted upward, and he had an upfront and personal view of her pussy. She'd obviously trimmed her pubic hair and shaved her nether lips, and he'd never seen anything sexier than her juices all over her inner thighs, dripping down to her ass.

Unable to resist, Safe pulled his fingers out and brought them to his lips, licking them clean. "So damn good," he told her.

Wren blushed as she stared up at him. Suddenly, he needed to see her naked on his sheets. "Take off the shirt," he said as he brought his hand back down between her legs.

Wren had a difficult time removing her shirt, since she was lying on her back, but watching her wiggle and shift as she tried to get it off was an erotic show in itself. He could feel her inner muscles clenching around his fingers as he lazily pumped them in and out of her body while she moved under him.

"It's not fair that you can see me and you're still wearing underwear," she said on a little pout.

Looking down, Safe could see the outline of his cock in his boxers. Smirking, he reached down and shifted the material until the head was sticking out of the slit. It was almost purple with need and glistening with precome. "Happy?" he asked with a grin.

Wren tried to touch him but couldn't quite reach with the way he had her draped over his lap. "No," she grumbled.

"It's for the best. If you touched me right now, I'd blow my load prematurely. Now lie back and let me make you come again like I promised."

Wren settled back on the bed, jamming another pillow under her head so she could see what he was doing without having to strain her neck.

"You are so beautiful," he told her, as he stared between her legs. "So wet. So hot. So responsive."

"I'm too skinny," she murmured.

"No, you aren't. You're who you are, and who you are is perfect."

He saw her eyes close at his words, and Safe vowed to compliment her more often. Society was an evil bitch. If you carried too much weight, you weren't considered pretty. If you didn't wear makeup, the same. If you were too skinny, too tall, too short, had hair that was too short or too long or too frizzy, or any other deviations from the exact likenesses of the models on TV and in magazines, you weren't deemed an "ideal" woman.

It was bullshit. All of it. Women came in all shapes and sizes, and while Safe couldn't deny he'd been with his fair share of the opposite sex, and he recognized the unique beauty of each, he'd never slept with anyone just because of their looks. He was attracted to what was between their ears. Their intelligence and personalities.

And Wren was everything he wanted in a woman. He hadn't ever wanted her to be in the kind of situation she'd found herself in while visiting Africa, but he couldn't deny he was so fucking proud of how she'd dealt with it all.

Safe leaned over her, putting a thumb on her clit and pushing two fingers of his other hand between her slick folds. Then he began to rub. Hard and fast. He was done with foreplay. He needed to be inside her. Now.

"Bo!" she exclaimed, reaching up and grabbing hold of his arms.

"That's it. Hold onto me as you come apart." Safe loved

the feel of her fingernails digging into his skin. Loved the way she writhed against him. She tried to close her legs but couldn't because his body prevented it. She was at his mercy, and he'd give her exactly what she needed.

It didn't take long. He'd primed her with the earlier orgasm. Licking his lips, Safe watched with barely concealed lust as her belly contracted and once again she began to shake beneath him.

Her mouth opened as her back arched and she exploded. The way her body was squeezing his fingers was erotic as hell, and the only thing Safe could think about was how it would feel to be inside her when she came the next time.

Safe sat up and wrenched his boxers off. He probably looked hilarious as he ungracefully flopped around on the bed to kick them off, but he didn't care. Leaning over to the nightstand next to his bed, he wrenched open the drawer and pulled out the box of condoms he'd bought before leaving for his mission.

He felt as if this was the first time in his life that he'd ever had to open a condom wrapper as he fumbled with the foil and swore.

Then he heard a giggle. Looking down, he saw Wren wore a smile on her face, her upper chest flushed from her orgasms. Her nipples were hard on her small, perky tits, and she looked more than satisfied.

He'd done that. Made her look that way. The sight of her calmed his lust a notch.

They hadn't discussed birth control, but he wasn't about to disrespect his woman by asking to go bare their first time.

There would be time to come inside her; now was for pleasure. For both of them.

Safe donned the condom without any other issues then leaned over Wren, caging her in as he studied her. His cock pulsed against her belly, but he didn't rush to push inside her. He needed her to want this as much as he did.

* * *

Wren had never felt so...turned inside out after sex as she did right this moment. Wait, but she hadn't even had sex yet. Bo was fairly easygoing in everyday life, but here in his bed? He seemed to know exactly what he wanted from her, and how to get it. She'd never come so hard in her life. Yes, Wren had masturbated plenty, but *nothing* had felt the way it had when Bo pushed her over the edge.

Having his fingers inside her while she'd come had felt amazing. But she wanted more. She'd only gotten a glimpse of his cock, but what she saw had her licking her lips in anticipation. He was long. Not overly thick, but that was okay with her.

She waited for him to enter her, but when all he did was hover, staring at her, Wren frowned.

"What?" she asked.

"I'm just memorizing this moment. You. In my bed...*our* bed. Flushed pink from the orgasms I gave you. The smell of your cream on the sheets, my face, my fingers. This is a dream come true, and I can't believe you're here."

"Should I not be?" Wren couldn't help but ask.

"Probably not," he said with a shrug.

Wren tensed. What didn't she know about him? Was she making a mistake?

"No, don't freak. I just mean, I'm a SEAL. I'm gone a lot. Being with a military guy isn't easy, and being with a SEAL is even harder. Your life has already been difficult. I don't want to make it even more so."

Wren relaxed. "I can handle your job, Bo. And I'd never ask you to stop doing what you're obviously so good at. You forget that I saw firsthand what it is you do. I'm proud to be yours. To be here with you."

He closed his eyes and inhaled deeply.

Wren took the time to study him. His hair was mussed and sticking up all over his head, probably because he hadn't brushed it after getting out of the shower. His own cheeks were flushed, as if seeing her get off was just as exciting as if he'd orgasmed himself. His biceps bulged as he held himself over her. He was an amazing-looking man, and he was *hers*.

Seeing him on the edge like he was gave her the courage to reach down between them and stroke his cock.

He jerked in her grip and his eyes flew open. "Don't. I'm close," he warned.

But Wren ignored him. She widened her legs and scooted up a little, so she could get him where she wanted him. All the while, he stayed motionless over her, staring at her with an intensity that was a little scary but a lot exciting.

She ran the tip of his cock over her clit and twitched a little. She was still very sensitive from her earlier orgasms. Then she notched the mushroom head between her very wet pussy lips. She ran it up and down, lubricating him with her cream.

"Put me in, sweetheart. Take me in."

She did just that. Lifting her hips, Wren welcomed Bo into her body. He sank down as she pushed up, and they both moaned at the feel of each other.

Bo's arms collapsed, and he buried his face in her neck.

"Holy shit...Give me a second," he murmured.

Grinning, Wren tightened her Kegel muscles, squeezing him as hard as she could with her body.

"Fuck! Do that again," Bo ordered as he shivered against her.

Loving the control she had, she did it again. And again. Caressing his cock from the inside.

Bo lifted to his elbows and stared at her. "You have no idea how amazing that feels."

Wren smiled as she ran her hands up and down his torso. "And you have no idea how good you feel inside me."

"How about we make each other feel even better?" he asked as he moved his hips.

The pleasure took Wren by surprise. "Harder," she ordered, digging her nails into his sides.

He obliged. Holding himself up, Bo began to move in and out of her with hard, measured thrusts. It felt good...but it wasn't enough for Wren.

"Bo, *more*," she whined.

"I want this to last," he told her.

"Why? If you come, you can just do it again. And isn't the whole point to orgasm?" she argued.

He chuckled, and Wren felt it all the way from her pussy to her toes. "Well, yeah, but I want to make you feel good in the process."

"I feel good," she told him. "Reeeeeally good. More. *Please.*"

Thankfully, he began to move faster.

"Oh yeah, that's it! I can feel you so deep," she gasped.

"I'm gonna ruin you for anyone else," Bo promised.

"You already have," Wren whispered.

The serious look in Bo's eyes intensified. He shifted onto his toes, his strong body hovering over Wren's. "Watch me take you for the first time," he ordered, staring between their bodies.

He'd left enough space that he wasn't touching her pretty much anywhere except where his cock was gliding in and out of her pussy. Looking down, Wren was startled by how erotic and insanely hot it was to watch him take her.

She couldn't help but lift her hips to meet his next thrust.

"That's right. Take your man the same time he's taking you. We're claiming each other, Wren. There's no going back."

"I don't want to go back," she said between pants. There was nowhere to go back *to*. It felt as if the second she saw this man, she was done. *His*. It was right. Meant to be.

Bo balanced himself on one hand, demonstrating his strength and agility while he continued to fuck her hard. He reached between them and flattened his other hand on her belly. He used his thumb to rub her clit as he moved in and out of her body.

Wren gasped and began to writhe. So many feelings bombarded her at once. Bo was so long, it felt as if he was hitting her cervix with every plunge. The small pinch, combined with the pleasure from his thrusts and his thumb on her still very sensitive bundle of nerves, was enough to make her feel as if she was going to explode into tiny pieces.

She closed her eyes, on the verge of coming.

"No!" Bo barked in a hoarse voice. "Watch us. Watch yourself come all over my cock."

She was helpless to deny him. Wren's eyes opened and she looked down, panting. His cock was shiny with her juices, and he pulled out to the tip on every pass, then thrust inside her again and again. Seeing how long he was, how much of him she was taking, only served to turn her on even more.

"I'm going to come," she warned him on a gasp.

"Good. I'm there too. I wanna feel you squeezing the come out of my cock. Take me, Wren. All of me."

And just like that, she toppled over the edge. Her vision went dark at the edges, but Wren didn't take her gaze from the sight of Bo loving her.

His hand slammed back to the mattress next to her head, his knees widened her legs, and he began to fuck her faster. Her whole body shook with his thrusts, and Wren grabbed his ass, loving it. Wanting all he had to give. He grunted once, twice, then pushed inside her so hard and so far, Wren came again.

Bo shook above her, his ass clenching as he released his load deep inside her body.

"Your body, it's...*fuck*, Wren...feeling you around my cock is...it's...." His voice trailed off, and Wren could only smile.

She felt as if she were floating. That had seriously been the best sex she'd ever had in her life. And she wanted more. Maybe not right this second, but she wanted to experience everything there was to experience in the bedroom with this man. Wanted to be on top, wanted him to take her from behind, wanted to suck him off, wanted to feel him come on her tits...she wanted it all. But only with Bo. Only ever with Bo.

"What are you thinking?" he murmured into her neck. He'd collapsed on top of her, but even in the throes of his own pleasure made sure not to crush her.

"Just that I'm happy," Wren sighed.

That made Bo lift his head. He was still deep inside her, and Wren could feel how wet she was between her legs. Her thighs were covered in her own cream, but she wasn't embarrassed, didn't feel the least bit weirded out by anything she and Bo had done.

"Yeah?" he asked.

Wren nodded. "When I was little, hiding under my bed, scared of my mom's boyfriends, and even my mom, I never thought I'd ever get to a point when I was this happy. I was too scarred. Too afraid of everyone. And yet...here I am."

Bo's brows had furrowed at her words, but then he relaxed and leaned down to kiss her forehead. "Here you are," he confirmed. "I love you."

"I love you too," she returned. The words weren't easy to say. They gave the other person power. But for once in her life, Wren felt as if the person she'd given them to wouldn't use that power against her. He'd keep her safe. Literally.

"I need to get up and take care of the condom," he told her after a moment.

Wren wrinkled her nose and sighed. "Okay. But...I have an implant. Got it when I was a teenager, kept it up. And I haven't been with anyone in years."

He looked surprised. "But you were dating."

"*Trying* to date," Wren corrected. "Matt...or Barry, was the first attempt in a long while. As you know, that didn't work out so well."

"Are you saying I can come inside you?" Bo asked.

Wren blushed. She shouldn't be embarrassed. This conversation was a part of being an adult and dating. "Have you been tested?"

Bo didn't seem offended by the question. "Every three months by the Navy. And I haven't been with a woman in well over a year."

Taking a deep breath, Wren said, "Then yes. You can come inside me."

Without a word, he pulled out of her, and they both winced. He practically leaped from the bed and ran into the bathroom. Wren shifted on the bed and made a little face when she felt exactly how wet she was, now that Bo wasn't inside her anymore.

Then her attention went back to Bo, who was striding across the room toward her. His cock was bobbing in front of him—as hard as it'd been when she'd taken him in hand to guide him inside her.

He practically jumped back into bed, climbing on top of her. "Now?" he asked.

"Now what?" Wren asked, confused.

"Can I come inside you now?"

She laughed a little. "I thought men needed some time to recover."

"The woman I love just told me I can come inside her. I'm recovered," he said with a small grin.

In response, Wren smiled and pressed on his chest. Rolled them until she was on top...though really, Bo did all the rolling. “Only if I can be on top.”

“Sweetheart, you can be on top, behind, under, across, or any other place you want to be, as long as my cock can be inside your hot, wet pussy.”

“Oh, so romantic,” she said with a laugh.

But when Bo lifted her hips and brought her down hard and fast on his dick, her laugh turned to a little gasping sound.

“Okay?” he asked, sounding concerned, his fingers digging into her hips.

He felt just as deep, if not deeper, than he'd been minutes earlier, but it didn't hurt. In response, Wren lifted her hips—then came down just as hard, taking him to the hilt.

“Fuck!” Bo exclaimed.

“It's more than okay,” Wren told him.

The rest of the day was spent in and out of bed. Laughing, bonding, eating, making love...and Wren couldn't remember a time she was ever happier than she was now. Being with Bo was everything she'd ever wanted in her life and never expected to have. He was, quite simply, meant for her.

Real life would intrude before either of them were ready, but for the moment, they were reveling in the love they'd found in each other.

CHAPTER TWENTY-THREE

Wren frowned as she sat in Bo's Jeep two days later. They'd holed up for a full forty-eight hours, loving each other. And in between all the bonding, Bo had held Wren's hand as she'd called her half-brother and told him she wanted to meet not only him and his brothers, but her father as well. Easton was overjoyed and said he'd be in touch soon to discuss details.

Bo had enjoyed his days off from work, but today they both had to face reality. Wren by going back to the office to see what kind of damage control had to be done because of the disastrous trip to South Sudan, and Bo had to go back to being a Navy SEAL.

As much as they wanted to stay in his house and make love all day and night for the foreseeable future, that wasn't exactly practical.

"Call me at any time," Bo told her as he squeezed her hand. "Seeing your coworkers again is bound to bring up some bad memories."

"I'll be okay," Wren assured him. But deep down, she wasn't sure. She felt nauseous, the cereal she'd had for breakfast sat like a lump in her belly, and she was afraid she was going to barf any second.

"Look at me," Bo ordered.

Turning her head, Wren met his gaze.

"Sometimes shit hits you days, weeks, or even months later. You can be fine in the moment, but then later, when you're safe, it just sneaks up on you. What you went through. If that happens, you call me. I can either come get you or talk you through it. All right?"

"But you have stuff you have to do today."

"*Nothing* is more important than you. Kevlar and the others will understand. We've all been through it."

"You have?"

"Yes, Wren. We aren't machines. What we see and do affects us. Sometimes immediately and sometimes months later. The flashbacks are tough, and nightmares are kind of a given in our line of work."

Wren felt bad. She hadn't even thought about how Bo might suffer after some of the stuff he'd seen and done in his line of work. She squeezed his hand. "Like Blink. How he had to work through losing part of his team."

"Yeah."

Wren had heard all about the other members of Bo's team over the last two days. He'd told her how close they all were, details about their lives, and a little more about what had happened to Blink on the last mission before he'd joined their SEAL team—and how much he'd suffered afterward. Her heart hurt for Bo and his friends.

"So call me if you need to, okay?"

Wren nodded.

"I love you. Cut yourself some slack, Wren. You went through something traumatic. You're allowed to feel upset about it and take as much time as you need to heal."

She wished that she'd had someone like Bo on her side back when she was growing up. It would've made the feelings she'd suffered through so much easier to deal with.

"Thanks."

"If I don't hear from you, I'll be here at the usual time to pick you up. Thought we'd go out for Mexican tonight before heading home."

"That sounds perfect."

Bo leaned over and kissed her. It was long and passionate and by the time he pulled back, Wren was hot and bothered. He smiled as if he could read her mind, then he reached down and adjusted his cock in his pants.

Smirking, Wren climbed out of the Jeep and shut the door. She waved and turned toward her office building.

The second she opened the door to the lobby, butterflies started swimming in her gut. She went up the elevator to her floor, and the moment she saw Dallas, goose bumps broke out on her arms and bile rose in her throat. She nodded at him and walked to her cubicle. Sitting down, she took a couple of deep breaths in through her nose.

That was all the respite she got before one of the interns came over and told her that Colby wanted to see her in the conference room.

Dread churned in her belly once more. She had no idea what he wanted to talk about, but just the thought of seeing the man who'd casually dismissed all her concerns and warnings about the trip made her want to puke.

Metaphorically pulling up her big girl panties, Wren grabbed a pad of paper and a pen and headed down the hall.

She froze in place when she opened the door.

Inside was Dallas, Archie, Oliver, and two other men she'd seen around the office but didn't know. Colby was sitting at the head of the table. He had a bandage over the stitches in his cheek, still had bruises on his face, and was wearing a brace on his wrist, but otherwise looked impeccably dressed in his suit and tie.

"Good, Wren is here. We can get started now," he said a little impatiently.

Wren sat in the nearest chair and perched on the edge of the seat tensely.

"Things didn't go as planned in South Sudan, but the good news is that the deal is still on. We had some good press and the investors are still interested in going full steam ahead. So with that said, we—"

Wren was already done. She abruptly stood, and her chair made an ear-splitting screeching sound as it slid along the tile floor.

"Wren? Where are you going?"

She heard Colby's question but didn't acknowledge it. She walked out the door, straight to her cubicle, packed the personal belongings at her desk—which weren't many—and headed for the elevator. She was starting to hyperventilate slightly, but she couldn't get herself to stop.

Colby wasn't even going to acknowledge what had happened. Wasn't going to admit that he'd made a huge mistake. Wasn't going to talk about the freaking *two fingers* Oliver had lost because of that clusterfuck of a trip. Was actually going forward with the project.

Luke and Aaron were *dead*—and he didn't even seem to care! Not to mention the men who had been tasked with protecting him had also died. And all Colby cared about was the stupid deal.

Maybe she wasn't being fair. There was a lot of money tied up with the pipeline project, but Wren couldn't go to work every day and pretend that nothing happened. That they hadn't been kidnapped. That people hadn't died. How many more had to die before Colby realized any amount of money that could be made wasn't worth it?

She wanted no part of it. Couldn't do it.

When she got to the lobby, Wren's hands were shaking so badly she could barely hit the right button to call Bo.

He answered after one ring.

"Wren? What's wrong?"

She couldn't speak. She couldn't get any air into her lungs.

"Breathe, Wren. In through your nose, out through your mouth. Slow it down. In...out...in...out...good. Just like that."

When she felt as if she could finally speak, Wren asked, "Will you come get me?"

"Already on my way, sweetheart. Hang on for just a little longer. I'm coming."

He was coming. Of course he was. Wren closed her eyes and leaned against the side of the building. She didn't even remember coming outside, but here she was.

It didn't take long before she saw Bo's Jeep careening around a corner. He double parked and was coming toward her before she could even step away from the building. Bo took her by the shoulders and crouched slightly, staring into her eyes.

"Are you okay?"

Wren managed a weak nod. "I couldn't do it," she whispered. "He immediately started talking about continuing the project, has even brought in two people to replace Luke and Aaron. I couldn't stay!"

"It's okay," Bo soothed. "Come on, I've got you."

Wren let herself be led to the Jeep and got in without another word. After a moment, she asked, "Where are we going?"

"To the base."

"Oh, but you have work. You can take me home."

"Nope. I don't want to leave you alone. You can come with me, hang out with us."

Wren had no idea what Bo did all day, but she wasn't sure having a civilian "hanging out" with a bunch of Navy SEALs fresh off a mission was something that was actually allowed. Regardless, she couldn't deny that being around Bo made her feel less shaky.

"All right."

Bo kept looking over at her, probably to make sure she wasn't losing it, but now that she was away from the office, and with him, she was feeling better and better. She had a lot to figure out. Probably had to officially quit, needed to find a new job, should call her landlord and tell him she'd have to move out.

But for now, she didn't need to do anything. Bo would take care of her.

* * *

Safe was worried about Wren. When she'd called so soon after he'd dropped her off, he'd immediately turned around to go get her. She seemed to be all right now, but he knew better than most how traumatic events could affect someone for days, weeks, even years after they happened.

He'd brought her to base and got her settled into an office while he had some mandatory meetings with his commander and team. Every time he'd checked on her, she seemed okay. At lunch, she'd asked if he'd take her back to her place so she could hang with Remi. He had, and when he'd picked her up that evening, he was relieved to see that she seemed a bit more relaxed. As if leaving her job was just what she needed in order to move on from what had happened.

She told him she'd emailed Colby her official resignation and how good she felt about it. They'd gone out to eat—Mexican, as they'd planned—and now they were at his house, where she'd been quieter than usual.

They were sitting on the couch when she turned to him with a small frown on her face.

"I don't have a job anymore."

"I know, sweetheart."

"I'm just saying that I won't have any money coming in for a while. I never wanted to be that person. The kind of girlfriend who mooched off her man. But I can't—"

Safe held up his hand, stopping her. "No," he told her with a shake of his head.

"No, what?" she asked, frowning harder.

"You aren't allowed to feel bad about being here with me.

And you aren't mooching. You can take a moment or two to collect yourself. To breathe. What happened to you was *bad.* You saw some horrible things. And having you here isn't a hardship. Not in the least. Take your time. Get your bearings. Then you can decide what you want to do. It's not as if I was going to let you pay any part of my mortgage, or for food, or anything else."

"Wait—why not? If I'm living here, I should pay my way."

Safe shook his head again. "I'm *that* guy, Wren. The man who doesn't want his woman paying for shit. You want to buy snacks? Stuff to make cookies? Pictures for our walls or pillows for the couch? Go for it. But I've got the utilities, the mortgage, and all the other things associated with owning a house."

She glared at him, and it made Safe want to throw her on the floor and fuck her hard. She was adorable when she was mad, but he refrained, knowing that telling her how cute he found her right now wouldn't exactly get him where he wanted her—under him in their bed.

"I'll have you know, Bo Cyders, I've never made cookies in my life, and I'm not about to start now. Not when there's a perfectly good store down the street that sells them ready-to-eat."

He couldn't help it; Safe burst out laughing. When he had himself under control, he said, "Noted."

"But seriously, Bo. I want to pay my way."

"And you will. By being exactly who you are. Being here when I get home from work. Talking with me, telling me about your day. Making me laugh, making me look forward to going home when I leave the Naval base. I love you, Wren.

There's nothing I wouldn't do for you. Name it and I'll do it... except say that you want to pay half the mortgage, because that isn't happening." He added that last part quickly, because he had a feeling Wren would exploit every loophole she could to get what she wanted.

She smiled at him, then sobered. "Will you come with me when I go up to Mission Viejo to meet my father?"

Safe stared at her in confusion. "You actually thought you were going by yourself?"

"Well...maybe? You have work, and now that I don't, I thought I'd go up during the day for lunch or something. So if it's awkward, I could end it and not feel weird about leaving early."

"Hon, I'm not only going with you, but Remi and Kevlar already said they'd go too."

She frowned. "They did?"

"Of course. And that was after the team drew straws to see who'd get to go with us. They all wanted to go, and I said that was overkill. Preacher was pissed. He *really* wanted to come, but Kevlar won, and he proclaimed that Remi was coming too because it would be less awkward for you to have a woman with you. You know, like if you needed to go to the bathroom, the two of you could go together and decide whether or not you needed us to get you out of there or something."

Tears formed in Wren's eyes.

"No! Don't cry," Safe told her, brushing his thumbs over her cheeks, banishing the tears that had fallen. "I can't stand it when you cry."

"These aren't sad tears," she told him. "They're...I don't know what they are."

"I told you before and I'll keep telling you, you aren't alone anymore, Wren. You have family. And speaking of which, I should tell you that my mom and dad are already bugging me about meeting you. And Susie is on my case too. So we're going to have to plan a trip to Ohio to see them."

"I love you," Wren said as she threw herself into his arms.

Safe caught her and held her tightly. "I love you too."

Then she pulled back. "How full are you from dinner?"

"About to burst," he admitted.

"Okay, then you can just lie there while I do all the work," she told him with a twinkle in her eye.

Safe was up and moving before she'd finished speaking. The thought of Wren sucking him off while he ran his hands through her silky hair was enough for him to be hard as a spike within seconds.

She giggled as he towed her toward their bedroom. It was safe to say that he was head over heels for this woman. And it wasn't because of the sex. He was a goner before they'd even thought about going to bed together. She was his match in every way, and he'd do whatever it took to make sure she knew every day of her life how much he appreciated and loved her.

CHAPTER TWENTY-FOUR

Wren was nervous. Today was the day. She was going to meet her biological father. After so many years of thinking he was a deadbeat and a horrible person, finding out he was a normal, respected member of his Mission Viejo community was still a surprise.

The first time she'd spoken to him over the phone, with Bo at her side, holding her hand even though she was leaving marks in his skin with her fingernails because she was squeezing him so tight, had been awkward for several tense minutes, but the more they talked, the more she relaxed.

He seemed...nice. And heartbroken that he hadn't known about her, and that she'd had such a horrible childhood.

The plan was for Bo to work a half day, then they'd drive up to southern LA with Remi and Kevlar and have a late lunch/early dinner with her father and her half-brother. If that went well, they'd discuss having another get-together with her other brothers, her nieces and nephew, and her stepmother.

Wren's head was spinning. It was so hard to believe that she'd gone from being completely alone in the world to not only having a large family, but having Bo's relatives and teammates in her corner. It would've been overwhelming if it wasn't so awesome.

After quitting her job with BT Energy, she'd not heard a word from her ex-boss. Not from any of the men she'd been through hell with either. No one reached out to make sure she was all right. They'd all just presumably gone back to work as if nothing had happened in South Sudan.

She'd gone to the memorial services for Luke and Aaron but felt awkward and out of place. No one said anything rude to her, but she'd gotten a lot of side-eyes from her former coworkers.

Now she was trying to move on, and with Bo's help, she felt as if each day was getting better.

But Wren was very nervous about today. Even though the few phone calls with her father had gone well, she still had worries that he'd reject her. That he'd somehow see whatever it was her mother had seen in her and walk away without a backward glance. Bo reassured her over and over that her mother was a bitch, and that everything she'd done had nothing to do with Wren as a person, but it was hard to shake the feeling that the way she'd been treated had somehow been her fault.

She was lost in her spiraling thoughts and panicking about the upcoming trip north, so when a loud knock sounded on the front door, Wren jumped in fright.

She frowned. Who would be knocking so forcefully? It wasn't as if Bo got a lot of visitors, and he certainly didn't get any solicitors.

Wren had been so surprised by the knock, she didn't immediately go to the door to answer it. She was in the middle of reorganizing their pantry—because who *didn't* do that when they were stressed?—so she was still standing in the kitchen when the first loud thump sounded.

Jerking again, Wren was confused for a moment. But when the sound happened again, she realized what was happening.

Whoever was out there was trying to kick the door in.

Wren lunged for the counter where her phone was sitting. Her first thought was to get help. She didn't know who was outside, trying so desperately to get in, but nothing good could come out of someone kicking in a door.

She managed to hit the button that would call 9-1-1 just as the door burst open.

Wren let out a small scream of fright and backed farther into the kitchen.

The last person she expected to ever see again was standing in the foyer.

Matt.

No. His name was Barry. He was wearing a dirty pair of jeans and a long-sleeve T-shirt. His brown hair was greasy and slicked back, and his eyes narrowed when he spotted her.

"You *bitch*!" he exclaimed as he stalked toward her.

"Help!" Wren said into the phone, praying someone was on the other end. She knew from watching crime TV that even before the operator answered, the call was recorded, so she hoped that someone would hear what she was saying.

"Barry Simpson broke into my house! I have a restraining order! I'm at 432 West Oak—"

Before she could finish what she was saying, Barry smacked the phone out of her hand. It flew against the wall before clattering to the floor. The screen was cracked and dark, the fall obviously breaking it.

Before she could do or say anything else, Barry grabbed her arms and threw her against the counter. The granite bit into her side, but Wren didn't feel any pain. Adrenaline was coursing through her veins and she knew if she didn't get away from this man, she'd be as good as dead.

She tried to duck and run around him, to get out of the house through the front door he'd stupidly left open, but he grabbed her before she could manage more than a few steps.

Wren fought like hell. She kicked and punched him where she could, but he was too strong. He towered over her five-foot-five frame by almost a foot. And he was big, muscular. Once upon a time, Wren had been impressed by his physique. But that was before he'd drugged her so he could try to violate her, and before she'd learned about his violent past.

"You had me arrested!" he hissed as he wrapped his hands around her throat and pressed her back against the counter.

Wren frantically tried to push him off her, to pry his hands off her neck, but it was no use. He was too strong and too tall for her to get any leverage. Her feet slipped on the tile as she struggled to keep them under her, but he just bent her backward farther over the counter.

Looking up into his black eyes—Wren realized this was it.

She wasn't going to be able to meet her father and half-brothers. She'd miss out on getting to know Bo's family. Seeing him with his mom and sister. Miss out on an entire lifetime with Bo.

Visions of their unborn kids flashed in her brain...

And anger replaced fear deep inside her.

No. This was *not* how she went out. She'd lived through too much shit for this asshole to kill her this way.

Throwing her hand out for something, anything, to use to try to get Barry off her, she knocked over something heavy on the counter. Desperately grasping for one of the knives in the block she felt under her fingers, Wren felt blackness creeping in at the sides of her vision. She was going to pass out in seconds, and if she did, this murderer wouldn't hesitate to continue until he'd choked the life out of her. She knew that as well as she knew her name.

The same time she wrapped her hand around the hilt of one of the fancy, way-too-expensive knives Bo took such pride in using when he cooked, Wren heard what sounded like the roar of a lion.

Her mind wasn't working right, probably because of lack of oxygen. There was no way a lion would be in her kitchen. But she had the brief vision of the big jungle cat biting Barry's head off, right before she plunged the knife she was gripping as if her life depended on it—and it did—into the side of her attacker's unprotected neck.

He screamed into her face, making Wren's ears ring, but he instantly let go of her and brought both hands to his neck in shock.

Wren had no strength to hold herself up. She fell to a heap

on the kitchen floor. Her last thought before she went unconscious was that she needed to stab him again. Make sure he couldn't strangle her a second time.

* * *

Safe frowned as Kevlar pulled into his driveway. He'd offered to drive up to Mission Viejo, and Safe had gladly agreed, as he wanted to be able to give his full attention to Wren. To keep her calm on the way there and to discuss in detail how the meeting went on the way home.

But seeing his front door standing wide open made all that fly out of his head. He wasn't sure what was happening, but his senses immediately told him something wasn't right.

He vaguely heard his friend telling Remi to stay in the car, but Safe was out of the back seat and moving even before Kevlar had put the vehicle in park.

Racing to the door, Safe heard sirens in the distance but he ignored them, focused on getting inside and making sure Wren was all right.

The sound that escaped his mouth when he saw a man with his hands around Wren's neck was a mixture of rage and despair. He felt Kevlar at his back as he charged toward the kitchen. His only goal to get the guy's hands off Wren.

To his surprise, before he reached the man, he screamed and dropped Wren, who fell like a stone to the floor. Blood was spurting out of the man's neck, all over the floor and counter as Safe grabbed him and threw him as hard as he could away from his woman.

The attacker landed hard on the floor. Before he could

even try to move, Kevlar had him on his stomach with a knee between his shoulder blades and his hands secured at the small of his back.

"Wren!" Safe exclaimed, ignoring the blood spatter on the floor and all over the front of the woman he loved.

His life flashed before his eyes as he frantically tried to find a pulse in her neck. For a moment, he felt nothing, and he would swear his soul literally shriveled up and died. But after shifting his fingers, he felt it. A weak and thready *thump thump thump*.

"That's it, breathe, honey. *Breathe*," Safe begged as he shifted Wren so she was lying flat on her back on the floor. He hovered over her, his gaze watching as her chest slowly rose and fell. Tears fell from his eyes onto her shirt as he kept his fingers on her throat, making sure her heart continued to beat.

"It's Simpson," Kevlar told him.

That got Safe's attention. "What the *fuck*? I thought he was extradited to Wyoming?"

Kevlar shook his head and shrugged.

"Yes, we're at 432 West Oak Street. Someone broke into my friend's house and tried to kill her. It looks like she managed to stab him, and her boyfriend got him away from her. Yes, my boyfriend subdued him. But there's a lot of blood. I think she's okay...unconscious. Yes, she's breathing. But the guy...he's not doing so well."

Safe heard Remi's voice as if from the end of a long tunnel. The sirens got louder until it was obvious they were right outside his house.

Remi ran out of the house, yelling about what happened and telling the police to get inside and help.

The next few minutes were nothing but chaos. The police came in with their weapons drawn, forcing both Safe and Kevlar up and out of the kitchen. Barry Simpson was lying motionless on the tile floor, way too close to Wren for Safe's comfort. The only thing that kept him from losing his shit, and probably getting arrested, was that he could still see Wren's chest moving up and down from where he was standing in his living room.

The paramedics arrived, and after a quick examination of Barry, they wrapped the knife still sticking out of his neck and loaded him onto a stretcher and carried him out of the house, a police officer at their heels.

A paramedic and EMTs were kneeling around Wren when she regained consciousness. She instantly began to flail on the floor, kicking and fighting against the men and women trying to help her.

Without thought, Safe charged into the now very crowded kitchen. "You're okay, Wren! It's me, Bo! You're all right!"

Safe felt two cops trying to drag him away, but he fought them, needing to be at Wren's side. To calm her.

"Bo?" she asked, stilling.

"Let him stay," the paramedic told the officers sternly. Then, turning to Safe, ordered, "Get up by her head and stay out of our way."

Safe wasn't about to protest. He moved to where he was instructed and leaned over Wren so she could see him. He put his hands on her cheeks as he hovered over her. "It's me. You're good, Wren. Understand?"

"It was Barry!" she croaked. Her voice was raspy and the sight of the already bruising skin around her throat made Safe want to hunt down the asshole who'd hurt her and twist the knife sticking out of his neck to make sure the fucker bled out.

"Shhhh, I know. You were so smart by calling 9-1-1. They got here just about the same time I did."

"Did I get him?" she asked. Her brown gaze bored into his own.

Safe wasn't sure if he should lie and tell her that she missed, or admit that she had most likely struck a fatal blow with the knife.

Her next words made the decision easy.

"Please tell me I got him!"

"You got him," Safe told her. "He dropped like a stone. You did good, sweetheart. I just wish I could've gotten here a minute earlier. When I came in, and he had you bent backward over the counter, I—" He couldn't continue. It was a sight that would haunt him for the rest of his days.

"I heard a lion...was that you?" Wren asked with a tiny smile.

Safe closed his eyes for a moment. This woman...she was so fucking strong, it was humbling. He opened his eyes again and looked down at Wren. "That was me. I was so furious. I wanted to yell at him to let you go, to stop, *something*, but all that came out was this sort of yell-scream."

"It was hot," she told him unashamedly.

"Sir, if you can stand back, we're ready to go," one of the EMTs told him.

"Can I come?"

"Can he come too?"

Safe's words came out at the same time as Wren's.

"Sorry, it's company policy not to allow family members inside the ambulance unless the victim is under the age of five," the paramedic said as they transferred Wren to a stretcher.

Safe wanted to protest, but Kevlar touched his shoulder. "We'll get you there. We'll be right on their bumper the entire way."

Safe nodded, then looked down at Wren. She was pale, her hair was sticking up all over her head, she had blood on her hands—thankfully not her own—and every time she swallowed, she winced. But she was alive. He was so damn thankful for that.

"I'll meet you at the hospital," Safe told her.

She nodded, then winced again and whispered, "Okay."

Not able to stop himself, Safe leaned down and kissed her forehead. "Love you," he whispered.

"Love you too," she responded.

As she was being wheeled toward the door, Safe heard her tell the EMTs to stop. He rushed over to her. "What? What's wrong?" he asked frantically.

"Nothing," Wren said. "But my father's going to wonder where we are. If we stood him up."

"I'll call him. Don't worry. I'll take care of it."

"Thanks."

"No need to thank me for that. Warning, Wren—you're going to be *very* tired of me waiting on you hand and foot and not letting you out of my sight for the foreseeable future."

She let out a small huff of laughter. "Yeah, right. Okay, you go on believing that."

Safe couldn't believe he was smiling as Wren was wheeled out the door. He watched until she was safely inside the ambulance. After a few minutes, it slowly pulled away from the curb.

"Come on, we need to roll if we're going to beat them to the hospital," Kevlar said. "I've called Wolf and Dude. They're going to come over and hang out until the cops are done with their investigation here. Preacher and the rest of the team, along with detectives who need to get our side of what happened, will meet us at the hospital."

Safe nodded. Now that Wren was safe and he knew she'd be all right, the adrenaline that had shot through his system at seeing that asshole's hands around her neck quickly waned. He was glad for the arm that Kevlar threw around his shoulders. He felt as weak as a newborn. That had been the scariest moment of his life, hands down.

"She's okay," Kevlar told him, as if he could read his mind. "When I found out Remi was missing, I felt the same way. I've got you."

It was comforting to realize his friend knew exactly how he was feeling. Taking a deep breath, then another, Safe climbed back into Kevlar's Subaru. He pulled out his phone the moment he sat down. He needed to call Tyler Farris and let him know what happened to his daughter.

CHAPTER TWENTY-FIVE

Wren's mind was spinning, but strangely, even though she had a headache from hell, her throat felt like a thousand bees had stung it from the inside, and she was crazy hungry—though couldn't imagine actually swallowing anything—she was happy.

The doctor in the emergency room had said she would be fine, but recommended she stay at least one night for observation. She protested but was outvoted by Bo.

He'd stayed true to his promise and when she'd been wheeled into the ER, he'd already been waiting for her. She wasn't sure how he did it, but somehow he'd been allowed to stay by her side the entire time she was there. Thank goodness.

When she'd first woken up on the kitchen floor, she was confused and disoriented, but as soon as she heard Bo's voice, she'd remembered what happened. She'd met with a detective and told him everything. She'd admitted to stabbing Barry, but she didn't feel a lick of remorse. The memory of the blackness slowly taking over her vision was still as vivid as it had been when it was happening. It was either stab him and make Barry let go of her neck, or die. And she sure as hell hadn't wanted to die. She had too much to live for.

Looking around her small hospital room, Wren smiled. This. *This* was why she'd fought so desperately to live. Bo's teammates were lounging around the room looking like a bunch of *GQ* models, and every nurse who came in to check on her did a double take, clearly surprised there were this many good-looking men in one place.

Not only that, but the meeting she'd been both anticipating and dreading with her biological father hadn't been postponed, after all.

When Bo had called Tyler to let him know what happened, he drove down to Riverton to see for himself that she was all right. And if she'd thought the meeting would be awkward, she was wrong. So very wrong.

Tyler Farris had walked into the room, and Wren knew *exactly* who he was the moment she'd spotted him. They looked so much alike, it was almost scary. He had black hair, just like hers. Of course, his was lightly peppered with gray, but he in no way looked old. She remembered from their conversations that he wasn't yet fifty. Nor was he overly tall, which explained why she was only five-five.

But more than the height and hair, it was his features that had Wren instantly tearing up. He had the same nose, the same lips, the same eyes that she saw in the mirror every morning. There was no denying this man was her father.

They'd both cried. Lying in a hospital bed wasn't how

she'd planned on meeting her father, but honestly, in the end, she was simply grateful that he wasn't the deadbeat her mother had always insinuated, and that he seemed genuinely grateful to have found her.

Her half-brother Easton had driven down with his father, and even meeting him seemed almost natural.

The hospital room was crowded with people, all there to make sure she was all right. It wasn't something Wren could have imagined even a few months ago. Having friends like these. Bad things happened to good people all the time. For years, Wren struggled with why it seemed that more bad things had happened to her than others. But she finally figured it out. It was so she could properly appreciate what she now had in her life.

"Okay, everyone, Wren needs some sleep. Time to go!" Bo announced.

Wren smiled at the grumbles that went through the room, but she was grateful for him looking out for her. She was exhausted, could barely keep her eyes open. As much as she loved having all her friends and her real dad and brother there, she wouldn't mind if they left so she could close her eyes and not feel as if she was being rude.

It took some time for everyone to vacate the room, because they all had to come over to her and say goodbye one by one.

Her dad and brother were two of the last people to leave. Tyler approached the bed and looked down at her with what Wren could only imagine was fatherly pride. "Your young man told us what happened in South Sudan. Everything you went through. This probably isn't the time or the place...but I wanted you to know I looked up the resume you submitted to Farris Morgan. I was really angry we didn't get to the interviews before BT Energy did, because I would've hired you in a heartbeat. And that has *nothing* to do with you being my daughter.

"And forgive an old man for being nosey, but I'm also aware that you submitted your resignation to BT. If you want or need a job, you'll always have one with Farris Morgan."

Wren blinked in surprise. "Oh." She looked over at Bo, who was standing off to the side, letting her have a semblance of privacy to say goodbye to everyone while obviously having no intention of actually leaving her side—for which she was grateful. "I don't know what to say," she finally stuttered out.

"You don't have to say anything right now. And we wouldn't expect you to move away from Riverton. Obviously, this is where Safe is stationed. We'll figure out the details if it's something you're interested in."

The offer was extremely generous, and Wren knew she'd be an idiot to turn it down. Even without knowing the exact details about what she'd be doing, or how it would work logistically if she wasn't living in Mission Viejo, the truth was, Farris Morgan had been her choice in companies to work for. The interview and offer from BT Energy had just come first.

"Thank you. Seriously."

Tyler nodded. Then he looked uncertain for a moment before asking, "Can I hug you?"

Wren nodded and held up her arms. Her father leaned down and gave her a very careful hug.

"I won't break," she whispered.

His arms tightened, and Wren closed her eyes. It was hard

to believe this moment was happening. That she was here with her dad, and he wasn't a jerk, or killer, or any of the other things her mother had claimed over and over.

When Tyler stepped back, Easton also gave her a hug. "Good to meet you...sis. Dad's always wanted a daughter. Us boys were such a disappointment."

"Shut up," Tyler said, smacking his son's shoulder.

"At least family holidays will be prettier with Wren in attendance now," Easton said with a smile.

Wren swallowed hard, on the verge of tears. She'd never dreamed she'd have a family to sit around a large table with at Thanksgiving. Or to laugh and celebrate with at Christmas. Or to hide easter eggs and watch together as the youngsters went on the hunt.

As soon as her dad and brother left, Wren took a deep breath.

"Too much?" Bo asked as he sat in the chair next to her bed.

Wren shook her head. "No. It's just...unbelievable. Did you see, Bo? How much he looks like me?"

Bo smiled at her as he ran his thumb over the back of her hand. "I did."

"I know it sounds stupid, but I finally feel like I belong somewhere. That I'm not just out in the world on my own. And I realize I have you and everyone else now, but it just feels different to have a father. And brothers. A biological family."

"Speaking of which...my mom and dad are on their way. They'll be here tomorrow. I told them to meet us at the house, since you'll be discharged in the morning."

"What?" Wren asked.

"I called and updated them about what happened. They weren't happy. Actually, that's a lie. They were pissed way the hell off that someone would dare hurt you. They're in the air right now. They'll get a hotel tonight near the airport, and Flash is picking them up in the morning to bring them over to the house."

"But they don't even know me," Wren protested.

Bo chuckled. "Honey, they know you. Every time I've talked to them since the day we've met, all I talk about is you. How amazing you are. How smart. How beautiful. They know all about your job, your trip to Africa, hell, even how awesome you were over there, how you escaped your kidnappers. And now they want to see for themselves that you're all right. Susie was upset she couldn't come out as well, but it's a little harder for her to travel with her kids being so young."

Wren was overwhelmed. She'd not only gained a biological father, stepmother, brothers, two nieces and a nephew, she'd somehow also gained a second mother and father as well. And a sister-in-law, niece and nephew.

"I love you."

Bo shook his head. "You have no clue how much I love *you*, sweetheart. Seeing you like that...I've never been more scared in my entire life."

"When he was...when I realized I was dying, I was so damn sad," Wren admitted. "I was going to miss out on a life with you. Then I got pissed. That's when I managed to find that knife block."

"I'm going to get the damn thing bronzed," Bo said. Then he sighed. "Sorry. That's fucked up. Bad memories and all."

But Wren shook her head slightly. It still hurt to move more than that. "No. I have no regrets. I'm *glad* he's dead. He tried to kill me. They're sure he's dead, right?" she couldn't help but ask.

She'd been informed by the detective that Barry Simpson had died from the injury he'd received in the altercation with her in the kitchen. But because of the obvious strangulation marks around her neck, the 9-1-1 call she'd made, and what Bo had seen when he'd entered the house, backed up by both Kevlar and Remi, no charges were going to be filed against her.

"He's dead," Bo said firmly.

"How did he even get here? To California, I mean?" Wren asked.

"Apparently he climbed through an air duct in the jail in Wyoming and got onto the roof. He shimmied down a drain pipe and stole a truck. Ditched it once he was away from the city and stole a car. Came straight to Riverton."

Wren pressed her lips together and sighed. "Well...it's over now."

"It is," Bo agreed. "Now, what can I do for you? Another pillow? More blankets? Water?"

"I'm so tired," she told him. "But I'm hungry too. Do you think you can find me a milkshake? It's cold, so it should numb my throat, but also filling so my belly won't feel so empty, then maybe I can sleep."

"Of course. Vanilla?"

"Sounds perfect."

"I'll be back as soon as possible. Sleep if you can," he told her.

"Bo?"

"Yeah, sweetheart."

"Will you stay? Tonight, I mean."

"Nothing could tear me away."

"I'm sure the cots they have aren't very comfortable."

Bo simply laughed. "Hon, if you knew some of the places I've slept, you wouldn't even worry about that. Trust me, it'll be fine. Besides, I won't be sleeping much tonight anyway, if at all."

"Why?"

"Because I'll be up watching you breathe."

"Bo," Wren whispered in an anguished tone.

He simply shook his head. "When I got to you...the best sight I've ever seen in my life was your chest moving up and down. I can't lose you. Not when I just found you."

Wren reached for him then. Pulled on his shirt until he was leaning over her. She scooted and made room for him on the tiny mattress.

"Wren, I'm not supposed to—"

"Don't care," she mumbled into his chest.

"But your milkshake..."

"Don't care about that either. I just need you. To feel you against me. Hear your heart beating under my cheek. I almost died today, Bo. I know that. You know that. Hell, Barry knew what he was doing. No one is going to dare say a damn word about me holding you like this."

A small chuckle rumbled under Wren's cheek. "You're probably right," Bo said as he made himself as comfortable as he could in the hospital bed with her.

"I *am* right," Wren said firmly. She settled into Bo's arms and finally, *finally* felt safe. Her lips twitched with the thought. "I finally understand why your nickname is Safe."

"I already told you why," he said.

But Wren shook her head. "No. I mean, yes, you did, but that's not it. It's not because of a softball game, it's because around you, people feel safe. Protected. Your friends back in SEAL school, or whatever it's called. Your teammates. Me."

"You *are* safe with me," Bo vowed. "I'll do whatever it takes to make sure you always feel that way when you're around me. Mentally and physically."

"I do," Wren said with a sigh. "I'm going to sleep now," she murmured, her words slurring.

She felt Bo's hand palm the back of her head as he held her against his chest. "Sleep, sweetheart. I'll watch over you and keep the mean nurses away as long as I can."

Wren chuckled. "Thanks. My knight in shining armor." That was the last thing she remembered saying as she fell into a deep, healing slumber.

* * *

"Knight in shining armor, my ass," Wren said under her breath as she paced back and forth across the bedroom.

The first thing she'd done when she got home from the hospital had been to grab the letter she'd left for Bo. It wasn't that she was ashamed for him to read it, she just thought maybe she'd tuck it away and hold onto it for some time in the future. To show him how much she cared about him before that trip to Africa.

Since she'd been home, she'd reveled in Bo's attention and

affection. Meeting his parents had been scary as hell, but also amazing, as they were just as kind and welcoming as he said they would be.

The relationship with her father and half-brothers was progressing as well, and she'd agreed to take the job with Farris Morgan.

She'd been officially cleared of any wrongdoing in the death of Barry Simpson and the case had been closed. Somehow, Bo had ended her lease agreement with her former landlord, and he and his team had fixed up all the holes in the walls and other damage Barry had done when he'd gotten inside and wrecked the place, so she even got her security deposit back.

All in all, the last three weeks of her life had been very good...except Bo was being *way* too over-protective. He didn't want her to go anywhere, didn't want her to drive, didn't think it was a good idea for her to stay up too late.

And worst of all, he refused to do anything other than hold her close at night.

She was healed. The bruises around her neck were finally gone. She wasn't sore anymore, could eat whatever she wanted. And yet, Bo still refused to make love to her because he didn't want to hurt her.

The hell with that. Wren was *fine*. And it was time her boyfriend got the memo.

He'd gone to base today after making her promise not to leave the house. Wren loved their little house, but she was tired of seeing nothing but four walls.

Next week, she was scheduled to go up to Mission Viejo for her orientation with Farris Morgan. It was about an hour and a half trip, and she was looking forward to getting to know a new group of people and to start working for her father's company. She would still be working in PR, but not in front of any cameras. Her job would be to write press releases, help design and plan PR campaigns, be the go-to person for phone and Zoom interviews, and to help develop crisis management approaches.

Wren knew Bo was nervous about the planned trip north. Even though Remi and Caroline had said they'd go with her—they were looking forward to shopping while she was in her meetings—Bo was still leery of letting her out of his sight.

Nope. She was done.

Tonight, she decided. Tonight was the night he'd get over his need to keep her in a protective bubble...otherwise known as their house.

Smirking to herself, she quickly undressed and moved toward the bed, her blood already pumping through her veins faster as she opened the bedside drawer. She wanted this. Had missed the sexual connection she and Bo shared. He wouldn't be able to resist her...she hoped.

Hearing Bo's Jeep pull up outside the house, right on time, she hurried to get into position.

The front door opened, and Bo called out, "Wren? I'm home!"

"I'm in our room!" she yelled.

She held her breath as she waited for Bo to appear in the doorway.

His reaction when he saw her was all she'd dreamed of and more.

She was completely naked on their bed, her back propped

against the headboard, her legs spread wide...and the vibrator she'd ordered online deep inside her body.

Without a word, Bo began to strip off his camouflage uniform. Seeing him in it always made Wren hot, but seeing him out of it was even better.

Before she knew it, he was completely nude and climbing onto the mattress. His cock was hard and she could see it dripping from where she was sitting. He needed this as much as she did, maybe more. She understood that he'd been through his own kind of hell when he'd seen her being strangled.

Still without speaking, he pushed her hand away from the toy between her legs and began to manipulate it himself, even as he leaned down and latched his mouth to her clit. She was already on the verge of an orgasm before he'd entered the room, so the second he sucked her bundle of nerves into his mouth, she exploded. Endorphins flooded her bloodstream.

"More!" she begged as she took his head in her hands.

He didn't hesitate. Within minutes, she was once more quaking under his masterful tongue and hands.

Then he pulled the vibrator out of her body, not even bothering to turn it off, and scooted up the mattress. He notched his cock between her folds—and hesitated.

"Are you sure?"

"I'm more than sure. I love you, Bo. I'm *fine*. All healed. I need you. More than you know."

"Oh, I know," he said, then he sank balls deep inside her with one fast thrust.

They both gasped—and just like that, Wren was coming again.

Apparently, he was as much on edge as she'd been, because his face contorted as he thrust just twice more, then his ass flexed as he emptied his load deep inside her body.

Wren couldn't help but chuckle. "So...that was faster than I thought it would be."

"I'm just getting started," Bo reassured her.

And amazingly, as he began to thrust lazily in and out of her now thoroughly lubricated body, she realized he was still hard.

Thirty minutes later, they were both sweaty, exhausted, and limp on the mattress. Wren had no idea how many times she'd orgasmed, but she felt as if she'd run a freaking marathon or something. And Bo seemed just as wiped out.

He was on top of her, his cock still deep inside her body. Flaccid now, but because of his length, he was able to stay buried inside her even after he came. He braced himself over her on his elbows and studied her face.

Wren loved this. Loved being surrounded by him. Pressed into the mattress. Having him inside her body.

"I went too far, didn't I?" he asked.

"A little," Wren said with a small smile.

"It's just...you scared me, sweetheart. For a split-second, I saw what my life would be without you...and I didn't like it."

"I know. But I'm okay now. All healed, as I think I just proved. Besides, you can't keep me holed up here forever."

Bo nodded. "But you're safe here."

Wren shook her head. They both knew that wasn't true. Hell, all it had taken was a few kicks and Barry was inside. Of course, Bo had replaced his front door with a solid steel one with reinforced locks and hinges. No one would ever be kicking that door open again. Not unless they had a hell of a battering ram.

"Oven fire, electrical fire, I could slip and fall and crack my head open. I could—"

Bo put his hand over her mouth. "Okay. I get it. I've been overprotective and crazy. I'll tone it down."

Wren reached up and took his hand off her mouth. "I love you. I love that you're protective. That you want to keep me safe. But I still have to live, Bo. And...the next time you withhold sex for what you think is my own good, I won't be as nice about things."

He smiled down at her. "Okay."

"Okay," she echoed. "Now, I'm hungry. I think we should go out for Mexican."

"Or we could order it in..." Bo suggested with a little thrust of his hips.

Wren could feel his cock hardening inside her already.

"Again?" she asked incredulously.

"Hey, it's been a long three weeks," he protested.

"And whose fault was that?" she huffed.

"Totally mine," Bo said without hesitation.

"You think you can order our dinner and make love to me at the same time?" Wren teased. "Because I'm not moving, but I *am* hungry."

"We'll see," Bo said with a laugh as he reached for her phone sitting on the table next to the bed.

They ended up eating a tub of refried beans, queso, and eight à la carte tacos for dinner because Bo totally got distracted while trying to order, but Wren didn't complain. Not in the least.

EPILOGUE

Blink stared off into space.

Kevlar and the others weren't going to be happy. Not at all.

Hell, Blink wasn't all that happy himself. Not to be traveling to the Middle East without his new SEAL team, and not to be going back to the place where he'd watched his previous team members get killed and injured.

But when his commander called him in the middle of the night and told him to pack his bags, that's what he'd done.

Since he'd been in the exact place where the new team was going, and since their mission now was exactly the same as *his* had been on that fateful day what seemed like a lifetime ago, Blink was going along.

Visions of his friends and teammates being blown to pieces threatened to overwhelm him, but Blink forced himself to do the calming breathing exercises he'd learned from his therapist. This time, things would be different. They were more prepared. Smarter. Less likely to underestimate the people they were dealing with.

But none of that really mattered. Blink wished Kevlar was here. Hell, all of them. Safe, Preacher, MacGyver, Flash, Smiley. He'd bonded with them already and trusted them to have his back without reservations.

While the men he was traveling with now were fellow SEALs, they weren't *his* team. But he'd do his duty, then go home and hopefully not have anyone too mad at him. Although it wasn't as if he was being given a choice.

Blink's mind wandered to Remi, wondering how her newest cartoon was coming along. He hadn't understood the allure of the talking taco character, but he'd started reading her older stuff and found himself laughing out loud at times. Thinking of the woman he'd saved from certain death made him feel good deep down inside. He couldn't save his former teammates, but he'd done what needed to be done to save Remi.

And Wren...she was one tough cookie. Safe had told them all some of what she'd gone through when she was a child, about being drugged by her own mother to keep her quiet and out of the way while men were at the house. It was unbelievable and sickening.

He was happy for his teammates that they'd found strong women.

That's what he wanted. Someone he could let down his guard with. Who could be comfortable with his quirks...the fact that he didn't like to talk all the time. Someone he could trust with his innermost demons. But he wasn't sure he could ever trust *anyone* like that. Not even his teammates. He would give his life for them, but talk to them about the shit swirling around in his head?

No.

"Touchdown in thirty!" one of the SEALs called out.

Blink wasn't even sure of all their names yet. He'd been sent on this mission with no new information and had spent most of the flight being given as much intel as possible by the other SEALs. Now he was returning to the one place he wasn't sure he was ready to face again.

But again, as an employee of the United States Government, he didn't have a choice. It was decided he was going, so here he was.

Gritting his teeth, Blink did his best to push any and all emotions as far down inside him as he could. It would be the only way he was going to get through the next several days.

* * *

Josie England had pushed any feelings and thoughts she had so far down inside her brain, she was simply going through the motions of living. Hell, what she was doing wasn't actually living at all. She wasn't even sure why she was still fighting to stay alive in this hellhole.

She'd tried to keep track of how long she'd been there, but it became almost impossible, so she'd long-since given up.

When Ayden had begged her to come visit him while he was on R&R in Kuwait City, she'd said no. But he'd asked again, then again. He wouldn't stop.

Their relationship was over, and not because Ayden had been deployed. He was younger than her by five years, and she knew for a fact that he was sleeping with one of the women in his platoon. Why he'd wanted her to fly halfway across the world to see him when he was already getting plenty of pussy was beyond her.

But she'd allowed herself to be convinced. Telling herself that it would be an adventure. When else would she ever visit Kuwait? Never.

So she'd gone. Intending to have a heart to heart with Ayden. He didn't love her and she didn't love him, but for some reason they were both holding onto the relationship.

And as a result of her weakness, here she was. In some dim, dilapidated cell, deep in the heart of Iran. Time had no meaning here. She'd been thrown in here and basically forgotten. She couldn't remember the last time anyone had brought her any food or water. The only reason she was still alive was because of the slow-dripping water along one wall of her cell. It took three days to fill the metal cup one of her captors had thrown at her when she'd first arrived. It had bounced off her head, and Josie was sure she'd probably needed stitches to close up the small laceration the sharp rim had caused. But of course, that wasn't happening here.

So she had water, a hole in the floor to use as a bathroom, and that was it. She was still wearing the bikini and coverup she'd had on when she and Ayden had been taken captive.

Looking down at herself, Josie scowled. Skin and bones. That's all she was. At four foot nine, she'd been a petite person to start with. But now? She was literally wasting away.

Her new life was a mixture of boredom with doses of extreme terror. Anytime anyone opened the door to her hellhole, she expected she was about to die. She felt more animal now than human. Growling at anyone who dared show their face, literally baring her teeth. Doing her best to seem more dangerous than she was.

Because the truth? She had no defenses. She was completely at her captors' mercy. No one was coming for her. Josie wasn't sure anyone even knew she was here...or cared. She wasn't a soldier, wasn't an actress, wasn't in politics. She was a normal person who'd found herself in the most fucked-up situation possible.

Curling into herself, Josie huddled against the wall at her back. The *drip drip drip* of the water into her cup used to annoy the crap out of her, now it was her only companion. The only thing keeping her even slightly sane.

Staring at her dirt-encrusted toes, she prayed for something to happen to end her torment. An earthquake, World War III, someone remembering she was there and coming in to kill her. She didn't care at this point. All she knew was that she couldn't continue to do this. To waste away in this cell. Forgotten and discarded. She'd rather die than stay here another minute, day, second.

Just as she had the thought, the door at the end of the hall was flung open. It scared her so badly, she jerked hard enough to hit her head on the concrete behind her. The light streaming down the hall hurt her eyes.

Blinking to try to clear her vision, Josie braced. This was it. Someone was coming. They were either going to kill her, torture her, bring her food...or maybe, just maybe, release her.

To her surprise, no one even looked at her in the small cell. She was still huddled in a ball in the corner, so maybe they didn't see her? They certainly acted as if they didn't know she was there. They were talking excitedly amongst themselves in Persian as they entered the cell next to hers, dropped someone on the ground with a loud thud, then proceeded to kick the shit out of whoever it was.

They only stopped because someone from outside the hallway door called out. A man spat on the person, then they left as quickly as they'd appeared. Leaving Josie once more.

She huffed out a breath. Okay, she was glad they didn't notice her. Because the last thing she wanted was to be treated like whoever it was they'd put in that other cell. But... she would've done practically anything for even the smallest crust of bread.

The darkness seemed more complete now. Being plunged back into the shadows after seeing light for the first time in... days?...made Josie want to cry. It felt more oppressive now. More dangerous.

Then she heard something from the cell next to hers.

A quiet groan.

Scrambling up to her knees, ignoring the pain from the random pebbles on the concrete floor, she strained her eyes to stare into the cell. Wondering if whoever had been brought in was a man or woman, military or civilian, or some poor local who'd been in the wrong place at the wrong time.

"*Fuck*."

Josie froze. That answered her question. It was a man. And surprisingly, he'd spoken English.

Life as she knew it had suddenly been turned on its head. Again. Someone else was finally here with her. Another prisoner. The thought both terrified her and gave her hope. But hope was a dangerous thing for someone in her situation. A forgotten, nobody-important American.

Only time would tell what this new addition to her living hell would mean.

* * *

Can you believe I'm not making you wait until the last book in the series to get Blink's story? But hold on...it's going to be a doozy! Blink has to find a way to get them both out of that prison...which will be easier said that done! Find out how it plays out in the next book in the series, Protecting Josie

Scan the QR code below for signed books, swag, T-shirts and more!

Also by Susan Stoker

SEAL of Protection: Alliance Series

Protecting Remi

Protecting Wren

Protecting Josie (Mar 4, 2025)

Protecting Maggie (Apr 1, 2025)

Protecting Addison (May 6, 2025)

Protecting Kelli (TBA)

Protecting Bree (TBA)

SEAL Team Hawaii Series

Finding Elodie

Finding Lexie

Finding Kenna

Finding Monica

Finding Carly

Finding Ashlyn

Finding Jodelle

The Refuge Series

Deserving Alaska

Deserving Henley

Deserving Reese

Deserving Cora

Deserving Lara

Deserving Maisy

Deserving Ryleigh (Jan 2025)

Eagle Point Search & Rescue

Searching for Lilly

Searching for Elsie

Searching for Bristol

Searching for Caryn

Searching for Finley

Searching for Heather

Searching for Khloe

Game of Chance Series

The Protector

The Royal

The Hero

The Lumberjack

SEAL of Protection: Legacy Series

Securing Caite

Securing Brenae (novella)

Securing Sidney

Securing Piper

Securing Zoey

Securing Avery

Securing Kalee

Securing Jane

Delta Force Heroes Series

Rescuing Rayne

Rescuing Aimee (novella)

Rescuing Emily

Rescuing Harley
Marrying Emily (novella)
Rescuing Kassie
Rescuing Bryn
Rescuing Casey
Rescuing Sadie (novella)
Rescuing Wendy
Rescuing Mary
Rescuing Macie (novella)
Rescuing Annie

SEAL of Protection Series

Protecting Caroline
Protecting Alabama
Protecting Fiona
Marrying Caroline (novella)
Protecting Summer
Protecting Cheyenne
Protecting Jessyka
Protecting Julie (novella)
Protecting Melody
Protecting the Future
Protecting Kiera (novella)
Protecting Alabama's Kids (novella)
Protecting Dakota

Delta Team Two Series

Shielding Gillian
Shielding Kinley

Shielding Aspen
Shielding Jayme (novella)
Shielding Riley
Shielding Devyn
Shielding Ember
Shielding Sierra

Badge of Honor: Texas Heroes Series

Justice for Mackenzie
Justice for Mickie
Justice for Corrie
Justice for Laine (novella)
Shelter for Elizabeth
Justice for Boone
Shelter for Adeline
Shelter for Sophie
Justice for Erin
Justice for Milena
Shelter for Blythe
Justice for Hope
Shelter for Quinn
Shelter for Koren
Shelter for Penelope

Ace Security Series

Claiming Grace
Claiming Alexis
Claiming Bailey
Claiming Felicity
Claiming Sarah

ALSO BY SUSAN STOKER

Mountain Mercenaries Series

Defending Allye

Defending Chloe

Defending Morgan

Defending Harlow

Defending Everly

Defending Zara

Defending Raven

Silverstone Series

Trusting Skylar

Trusting Taylor

Trusting Molly

Trusting Cassidy

Stand Alone

Falling for the Delta

The Guardian Mist

Nature's Rift

A Princess for Cale

A Moment in Time- A Collection of Short Stories

Another Moment in Time- A Collection of Short Stories

A Third Moment in Time- A Collection of Short Stories

Lambert's Lady

Special Operations Fan Fiction

http://www.AcesPress.com

Beyond Reality Series

Outback Hearts

Flaming Hearts

Frozen Hearts

Writing as Annie George:

Stepbrother Virgin (erotic novella)

ABOUT THE AUTHOR

New York Times, *USA Today*, #1 Amazon Bestseller, and #1 *Wall Street Journal* Bestselling Author, Susan Stoker has spent the last twenty-three years living in Missouri, California, Colorado, Indiana, Texas, and Tennessee and is currently living in the wilds of Maine. She's married to a retired Army man (and current firefighter/EMT) who now gets to follow *her* around the country.

She debuted her first series in 2014 and quickly followed that up with the SEAL of Protection Series, which solidified her love of writing and creating stories readers can get lost in.

If you enjoyed this book, or any book, please consider leaving a review. It's appreciated by authors more than you'll know.

www.stokeraces.com
www.AcesPress.com
susan@stokeraces.com

facebook.com/authorsusanstoker
x.com/Susan_Stoker
instagram.com/authorsusanstoker
goodreads.com/SusanStoker
bookbub.com/authors/susan-stoker
amazon.com/author/susanstoker
tiktok.com/@susanstokerauthor

Printed in the USA
CPSIA information can be obtained
at www.ICGtesting.com
CBHW011004051124
16934CB00016B/48

9 781644 994139